SWEET AS CINNAMON

"Can I tell you a secret?" he asked.

Fern turned to him eagerly.

"I've been addicted to your cinnamon buns for years. Every morning, I sent Caroline to buy them."

"Those were for you?"

"*Jah.* I didn't want you to know it, so I asked my sister to get them."

"But you haven't had any since I started working here. Except for one that very first day."

"I know, and I've been craving them."

"Why didn't you ask?" She reached into the case with bakery tissue and handed him a cinnamon bun.

Gideon took a bite and closed his eyes. "Mmm." He finished chewing. "Delicious. I missed these."

"I'll give you a roll every morning from now on, but you didn't answer my question."

"I didn't ask because I was too busy fighting my attraction to you . . ."

An
UNEXPECTED
AMISH
PROPOSAL

RACHEL J. GOOD

ZEBRA BOOKS
KENSINGTON PUBLISHING CORP.
www.kensingtonbooks.com

Chapter One

Fern Blauch hummed as she arranged cinnamon rolls in her glass case at the Valley Green Farmer's Market. She'd baked extra today because they always sold so fast. Most Saturdays, she sold out within an hour or two.

The warm, yeasty smell of sticky buns perfumed the air as she filled the next shelf. With their syrupy coating dotted with nuts, they were her second-best seller. She arranged bear claws and pastries beside them. As she opened a container of cupcakes, Russell Evans, the new owner of the market, strode toward her.

"Here," he said gruffly, holding out a paper. "The new rental agreement for your stand."

Fern missed Russell's father, who'd retired two months ago. He'd been jolly and kind, unlike Russell, who was a hard-edged businessman.

She took the paper he held out. Before she had time to glance at it, he scuttled off toward the next stand. No hellos, goodbyes, or pleasantries. His dad always took time to chat with everyone.

Taking a deep breath, she steeled herself to read the rent increase for next year. Several stand owners who'd gotten their agreements on Tuesday had grumbled. She and the others in this front row hadn't seen theirs yet.

Fern ran her finger down the first paragraphs to— She sucked in a breath. *Impossible.* She must have read it wrong. But, no, the figure in bold print indicated her rent had tripled.

No way could she afford this. Her parents counted on her money for household bills. She'd have none left.

Russell power walked past her stand. Was he fleeing from the three stand owners with their arms out and shock on their faces?

"Could I talk to you a minute?" Fern called. "I think there's a mistake."

"No mistake," he snapped, his voice harsh. "If you don't pay it, you're out at the end of this month."

Shell-shocked, Fern stood there, the paper extended, as he passed. He couldn't be serious.

An Amish man in his early eighties shuffled over to her. "Did you get one of these?" His hand shaking, Mose Miller held up a paper like Fern's. He looked about to faint.

"Come sit down." She offered him the high wooden stool behind her counter.

"I can't believe it. I've been selling here for more than fifty years." Mose's head shook back and forth. "I understand yearly rent increases, but this?" The paper rattled in his hands. "Three times my stand rent? It's like he wants to put us out of business."

"He does," a man's voice said behind Fern. "I overheard him discussing terms with that new organic distributor. Ripley's or Ridley's or something. You know, that huge bright blue monstrosity that stands out like a sore thumb on the hill."

Nick Green, the *Englisch* candy store owner, pointed

toward his left. Although no windows allowed a view of the fields on that side of the building, they all nodded. Quite a few people had protested the prefab turquoise metal warehouse plunked down amidst acres of cornfields and white wooden farmhouses.

"I'm not about to give up my stand." Nick clenched his fists. "My grandmother started this business here in this very spot when the market opened in 1929. I have great-great-grandchildren of her first customers coming here for candy."

"I don't make enough to pay this." Mose tottered back toward his stand, looking ill.

Fern didn't want to see Mose, who used to take her hand and treat her to ice-cream cones on hot summer days when she was a little girl, lose his business. He needed his income to buy medication for his wife. "It's not fair," she burst out.

"You're darn right about that. If I had the money, I'd sue. I do plan to give him a piece of my mind." Nick had a hot temper, and his loud tone and clenched fists didn't bode well for Russell Evans.

Several other people filtered over. A few waved letters in their hands. As the number of letter holders grew to five, Nick's glower increased.

The florist in the next aisle shook her head. "Our rent went up, but not by that much."

Soon, Fern found herself in the midst of an irate crowd as other stand holders objected to their friends' exorbitant rents.

"I'm not going to let him get away with this." Nick shook his agreement in Fern's face.

"What's going on?" A tall blond Amish man laid a hand on Nick's shoulder. "Is everything all right here?"

Gideon Hartzler's deep, smooth voice had a calming effect on everyone. He placed his body between Nick and Fern as if suspecting Nick's anger was directed toward her.

At his protectiveness, Fern's heart fluttered. She'd always admired him from afar, but he never seemed to notice her.

For all the attention he paid her when she bought barbecued chicken for lunch, she could have been a piece of furniture or an extension of his counter. His impersonal *Next* always sent her pulse into overdrive, but he never even glanced in her direction as he asked, *The usual*? Then he took her money, gave her the correct change, and handed her two chicken legs with fries. At least he always remembered her order.

But right now, he appeared worried about her.

"I-I'm all right," she assured him. He couldn't know the shakiness of her words came from being near him, not from being upset. Well, she was upset, but not with Nick.

Gideon glared at Nick.

Nick held up his hands. "Hey, I didn't bother her. That did." He pointed to the paper in Fern's trembling hands.

Fern prayed Gideon would mistake her nervousness around him for distress over the letter.

When he turned his gaze in her direction, Fern's knees went weak. If she didn't sit down, she might . . .

"May I?" he asked, holding out a hand for her letter.

She extended the paper, careful not to brush the strong fingers that closed over it.

As Gideon read down the page, his jaw clenched. "This can't be right. They're charging you almost twice what I pay? For this?" He swept his hand in the direction of her small L-shaped glass case, which bordered a support pole on one side and stood about five feet from the front wall of the building.

She nodded. "But maybe your rent will be going up too."

"Not this much. I got my new rates yesterday. The increase was steep, but not like yours. It's almost like—"

"Like they're trying to evict us," Nick Green supplied. "Here's mine."

"And mine." The *Englisch* woman who sold dried herbs at the end of their row held out hers.

"They tripled the rents for this whole row." Fern glanced up at Gideon and then wished she hadn't.

Gideon squeezed his eyes shut for a moment. He'd made the mistake of looking at Fern. So small, so delicate, so in need of protection. No way would he let himself go down that path. He had enough people to protect already.

But he couldn't allow this injustice. He had to do something. Not only for Fern, but for all the vendors.

"They're trying to get rid of us."

At Nick's accusation, Gideon's eyes flew open. "But why?"

As Nick explained about the new organic farm, Gideon's heart sank. That slick outfit would probably pay these rates and more so they could have the whole front wall by the entrance. But what about these sellers? The ones who'd been here for ages?

Two stands away, Mose sat on his rickety folding chair, his head in his hands.

"Mose got one too?" he asked.

"*Jah.*" Fern's soft, sympathetic tone made him even more eager to help.

Gideon had come to work with his father from the time he was little. Mose had often treated him to his favorite candy at Nick's stand. Back then, Nick's mother had run the business, and Gideon had shared candy and played with Fern when she was five and he was six. Hard to believe that nineteen years had passed.

He and Fern had enjoyed each other's company until he became a teenager. Then they'd both become shy and awkward with each other. Later, Gideon avoided Fern altogether after his brother—

Pushing away the painful memories, Gideon focused on the situation in front of him. He had an idea of one way to help, at least temporarily, but Nick shouldered his way past.

"I'm going up there to confront him." Nick stormed toward the central staircase. "He won't get away with this."

"I don't think that's a good idea," Fern said softly.

"I agree." Once again, Gideon looked in her direction and wished he hadn't. He longed to reach out and smooth the worried frown from her brow.

He jerked his gaze away to stare after Nick, but all he wanted to do was comfort Fern.

What's the matter with you? No matter how appealing, Fern was off-limits. And so was any other woman.

"I'd better get back to work," Gideon forced himself to say. He rushed back to his stand, but he couldn't keep his mind off the problem. As much as he hoped Nick would solve the situation, Gideon suspected Nick's hot temper might only worsen it.

A short while later, shouting filtered down from the floor above. A door slammed, and Nick stomped down the steps and past Gideon's barbecued chicken stand.

Gideon didn't have to ask how the meeting went. Nick's strident tones carried through the market.

"He's impossible!" Nick shouted. "Wouldn't budge an

inch. I told him I planned to sue, and he grinned. He knows I can't afford it."

A soft voice, probably Fern's, said something soothing. Gideon was too far away to make out the words, but Nick quieted.

Gideon couldn't let Russell put everyone out of business. But he had no idea how to convince the market owner to put people's lives before higher profits.

Chapter Two

All day long, between customers, Fern scribbled figures in the back of the small notebook where she recorded each day's inventory at opening and closing, along with her total sales. She flipped through the pages.

Her *daed* did the accounting and paid the taxes, so Fern had never worried about the stand making a large profit. She turned the money over to him, and he gave her whatever she needed to buy baking supplies. They never discussed her earnings, but the money she made covered most of the household bills, especially now that Mamm's hands were too arthritic to sew quilts and Daed's stroke had confined him to a walker. They couldn't count on her brother, Aaron, for help until he returned from his mission trip assisting with the flood cleanup. He'd gone for the usual two weeks but had extended his stay. He insisted his conscience wouldn't let him leave when so much work still needed to be done.

Fern did some quick calculations. Even if she doubled or tripled her sales of baked goods, they'd end up paying more in stand rent each month than she was making.

Someone tapped at the counter, and she jumped up. Her book tumbled to the floor. "Sorry." She pushed the problem from her mind and waited on the line of customers.

She stayed busy, leaving her little time to worry. But it also meant no daydreaming about Gideon, which was probably for the best.

After speaking to Russell, Nick had clomped over, complaining loudly. She'd managed to calm him temporarily by nodding in the direction of her wide-eyed customers. She promised to talk to him after closing, but at the end of the day, he draped sheets over his candy, raced out the door, and peeled out of the parking lot in his pickup truck.

Her heart heavy, Fern called goodbye to Mose as he limped toward the door. He hadn't even packed up the leftover vegetables on his table. They'd probably go bad before the market reopened on Tuesday.

"Mose, I'm taking my leftover baked goods to the food kitchen. Would it be all right if I take your vegetables?"

He turned and waved toward his produce. "Take whatever you want." Then, shoulders slumped, he headed out the door.

In all the years she'd known him, she'd never seen Mose so discouraged. He'd always been upbeat and cheerful, no matter what circumstances he'd endured. Even now, with his wife's treatments, he praised God for each day they had together.

Lord, please show me a way to help Mose.

If she weren't about to lose her own stand, she'd ask Daed if they could help Mose. But most likely, she wouldn't have a stand at the end of this month either.

Tomorrow was Sunday, but first thing Monday morning,

she'd look into other markets to see if any had openings. Maybe she could find places for all of them.

She'd hate to leave Valley Green Farmer's Market, because she grew up here and it was close to home. Mamm would be devastated. Her mother had worked at the market stand with her own *mamm*. So many memories.

After Fern packed up her leftovers and cleaned the glass food cases at the end of the day, she couldn't help replaying Gideon's protecting her when he thought Nick was upsetting her. Her pulse still jumped at the thought that he'd cared enough to check.

The only problem was that he had no interest in her. Besides, she had enough other concerns right now. She needed to put Gideon out of her mind. But her heart refused to cooperate.

At dinner that night, Fern fidgeted in her chair as she waited for her parents to finish eating. She'd only taken a small amount and picked at her food, but she didn't want to spoil their meals. She'd let them enjoy their food before she dropped her bombshell.

Mamm glanced at Fern's plate and then inspected her face. "Are you sick, *dochder*?"

"*Neh*, I had some bad news today. I'll tell you after you've eaten."

Now Daed stared at her too. "Bad enough that you can't eat?"

Fern dipped her fork into her mashed potatoes and lifted them to her lips. The thought of swallowing them almost gagged her.

"If the news is that awful, maybe you should tell us now," Daed said.

Forcing the bite into her mouth gave her a few seconds before answering. How could she tell them she'd be out of work in two weeks? Even worse, they wouldn't be able to send money to her brother.

Mamm set her silverware on her plate. "Your *daed*'s right. Sharing burdens helps lighten them."

Often that proved true, but this news would increase everyone's pain.

"Fern?" Daed's tone demanded a response.

She choked down the gluey mass of potatoes. "Russell Evans stopped by the stands to give us our new contracts." Swallowing hard, she forced herself to continue. "He increased the rent . . ."

"We've been expecting that."

Jah, they had. "But we didn't expect the rent to triple." Mamm gasped.

"Triple?" Daed shook his head as if he'd misheard. "Are you sure?"

"Positive." She'd been handing over the rent checks every quarter.

Daed winced. "Let me see the paperwork as soon as we finish supper."

They ate in silence, and both of her parents seemed to have lost their appetites too, but they all cleaned their plates anyway. After Fern whisked the dishes off the table, she went to get the rental agreement.

Daed read through the contract. Then he slid off his glasses and rubbed the bridge of his nose between his thumb and forefinger. Finally, he spoke. "It's not the end of the world. God has a reason for this."

Although her heart agreed, Fern's mind whirled. What were they going to do?

Mamm left the dishes soaking and sank into the chair beside Daed. "What about Aaron?"

Daed met her eyes, and they shared a long, sorrow-filled look. "Unless we can get another stand set up elsewhere in the next two weeks, we may have to stop sending money to him and the mission. I pray that won't be necessary."

"We can go without things here to be sure he doesn't go hungry."

Of course. They all made do so they could send extra money to Aaron. He'd been in South Carolina since the flood, working on the mission project Fern had asked to join. Instead, her parents had decided it would make more sense for her to keep working at the market to make money. They sent her younger, rebellious brother, Aaron, in her place. As Daed pointed out, Aaron could handle the construction work that Fern couldn't.

She'd offered to go as a cook—they always needed cooks to feed the workers. But her parents depended on her income. She managed to hide her disappointment better than Aaron, who made no secret of his reluctance. None of them could believe his recent transformation. After he'd completed his two-week stint, he'd decided to stay and keep working.

Mamm had beamed as she read Aaron's letter announcing the news. "God has worked a miracle in our *sohn*'s life. Instead of getting into trouble, he wants to dedicate his life to helping others."

They all marveled at the change in Aaron and prayed for him daily. When his living expenses increased, Fern baked longer hours to make more money. They also cut corners at home so they could send Aaron extra money for building supplies to help the Mennonite mission with the cleanup and rebuilding.

Fern tried not to begrudge her brother the money and the chance to participate in the mission work she'd longed to do, but some days—like today—it proved hard. She'd be stuck in the market stand for the rest of her life. Unless she married.

Where had that thought come from? No doubt being around Gideon today had sparked that wayward idea. She shook it off. No time to think about hopeless causes—like mission trips and Gideon's love.

Right now, she needed to concentrate on figuring out how to make money to support her family.

On Monday morning, Daed took out the accounting ledgers and scribbled figures on scrap paper while Fern cleaned the kitchen after breakfast. Mamm helped when she could, but Fern could see her mother was in pain.

Guiding Mamm to the table, Fern said, "Sit down, and I'll finish."

She'd put away the last dish when Daed tapped his pen on some numbers, circled one final figure, and sighed.

"Even if you double what you're making, *dochder*, we can't pay the higher rent and send enough money to Aaron. I'll talk to Russell to see if he'll lower the cost."

"Nick tried, but Russell wouldn't budge."

"He raised Nick's rent this much?"

"*Jah*, and Mose's too."

Daed's eyebrow rose. "What's Russell trying to do? Get rid of everyone in the market?"

"Not everyone. Gideon's rent went up, but not by that much." Her face heated. Why had she mentioned his name? She was grateful Daed remained absorbed in staring at the numbers.

"So only certain stands are getting the triple rent?"

"Just the five stands closest to the front door. Nick says that new organic farm wants that whole space."

"I see." Daed stroked his beard. "Then there's little sense in trying to get Russell to change his mind."

Tears welled in Mamm's eyes. "We'll have to look for other markets."

Daed patted her hand. "I'll check with Russell first. You and your *mamm* started that stand, and Mose and Nick have been there even longer. That should count for something."

Fern doubted anyone could talk Russell out of the rent increase, but Daed should at least try. He wouldn't be as abrasive as Nick. Perhaps Russell would listen.

Maybe.

All weekend long, Gideon couldn't get Fern—and the other stand owners, of course—off his mind. Although he had to admit, no matter how much he tried to think of other things, the image of Fern's worried face crowded out all other thoughts. He had to help her.

He came up with an idea that might work, if he could get Russell to agree. Gideon waited impatiently for a chance to discuss his offer with Russell. He prayed the two-day break had given Russell time to calm down after his encounter with Nick.

Early Tuesday morning, Gideon mounted the stairs to Russell's office. He hoped to find the market owner at his desk. After a quick look around to be sure the small upstairs craft shops were still closed, Gideon headed down the hall.

He passed an older Amish man dragging his left leg along as he leaned on a walker. As eager as Gideon was to talk to Russell, he wanted to be sure the man got down the stairs safely. From the expression on his face, the man had received bad news.

"Is everything all right?" Gideon asked.

The man shook his head. "*Neh*, but God has His reasons."

"*Jah*, he does." Gideon said a quick prayer that God would help this man. Right now, Gideon had to help the man as well.

From the set of the older man's jaw, he wouldn't accept an offer of assistance down the stairs. Before the man reached the steps, Gideon hurried past him and started down the stairs slowly. If the man tripped or fell, Gideon's body would block him from tumbling the rest of the way. He tried to match his speed to that of the man behind him.

When they reached the first floor, the man gave Gideon a questioning look. He needed an excuse for coming down here.

"I forgot something in my buggy," Gideon told him. He'd get the pad and pen he'd left on the seat. He might need them when he talked to Russell.

The man nodded, but his eyes said he didn't quite believe Gideon's reason.

Gideon slowed his gait to match the man's. "Do you have space here?" Gideon asked. He hadn't seen the man before, but he could be the owner of one of the newer shops upstairs.

"*Neh*, not anymore."

Gideon wanted to ask about the man's former business, but the sadness in the older man's eyes stopped any questions. Instead, Gideon walked silently beside the man and moved ahead to open the heavy wooden market door.

He kept an eye on the man as he headed to his buggy. Gideon wanted to rush over and give the man a boost when he struggled to get in, but the man's proud demeanor warned he wouldn't accept any help.

Once the man made it safely inside and his buggy started off, Gideon grabbed his pad and pen. He raced into the market and took the stairs two at a time. He didn't have much time to corner Russell before the other sellers arrived. He hurried down the hall and through Russell's open office door.

His feet propped up on the antique wooden desk, Russell leaned back in his cushy chair, chatting on the phone. "Yep, should be able to let you move in the first of next month."

Spying Gideon in the doorway, he frowned. "Listen, I'll have to call you back. Something I need to deal with here." He hung up. "I don't appreciate being interrupted before we open."

"I'm sorry, but this is important."

"If you're here to protest your rent increase, I don't want to hear it. I've heard enough griping today. I'd hate to lose you, but—"

Of course he would. Gideon's stand was the second

largest in the market, and with his planned expansion, he'd be almost as large as Miller's Meats. Although if the organic stand took up the whole front section of the market, they'd be much bigger than Gideon's and Miller's put together.

That's what he'd come here to talk about. The organic business. "I'm concerned about the stand owners who got the triple rent increases."

Russell sneered. "What's it to you? I didn't raise your rent that high, but I could."

Gideon ignored Russell's threatening tone. "All five of those stands have been part of this market for years." He wanted to point out that Nick's family had been one of the original stand owners, but no sense in annoying Russell by reminding him of that earlier confrontation.

"Yeah, they've been around forever. Time for a change. You're modernizing your business. So should I."

"But customers count on those stands."

"They'll get over it. Plus, those old people shuffling in here with their sniveling grandchildren to buy one cupcake or a little bag of candy for old times' sake aren't the customers I want to attract."

Gideon pressed his lips together to keep from defending those old-timers. He always loved it when elderly customers remembered him toddling after his father or grandfather. And he especially enjoyed meeting their grandchildren, or even great-grandchildren. But Gideon didn't want to rub Russell the wrong way before making his proposal.

Russell lowered his feet and leaned over the desk, his eyes intense. "You're an example of the kind of forward-thinking stand owners I want. Organic chicken. People love it. Now we'll have Ridley's organic meats and specialty produce. That's what brings in the upscale customers." He rubbed his hands together.

"Your father kept a mix of both kinds of customers, and he seemed to do well."

With a wave of his hand, Russell dismissed Gideon's reminder. "Pops was too sentimental. You can't do business like that nowadays. Not if you want to get ahead."

Russell's attitude made Gideon sad. He saw nothing wrong with being sentimental or appreciating families, especially ones who'd made your business grow. But the conversation had gotten off track, and he needed to make his own point.

Taking a deep breath, he offered, "I'll give you half of the rent increase you're charging all the stands along the front wall and pay for their next quarter up front if you don't increase their rent for the next three months."

"Absolutely not."

Gideon refused to accept that flat-out rejection. "If you let me pay that reduced rate, I'll start my expansion next month at the cost we agreed on. If not, I'll look into moving my business elsewhere."

Russell's lips moved, as if silently calculating what he'd gain or lose. After a few moments, his eyes flickered. Crimson suffused his face. "This is blackmail."

Perhaps from his point of view it was, but Gideon had intended it to be a deal Russell couldn't refuse. And he hoped an immediate payment might sweeten the arrangement.

Russell's eyes narrowed to slits. "I won't settle for less than three-fourths of the rent."

Gideon did some swift mental figuring. He'd really

hoped to get his brother's debt cleared up. The exorbitant interest rate was killing him. If he accepted Russell's terms, it meant only paying the minimum payment on the loan. He'd also have to put several of his expansion plans on hold until he paid off what Thomas had owed.

"All right," he said finally.

"On second thought, let's make it one month instead of a quarter."

"*Neh*, it needs to be a quarter." Gideon hoped the organic farm would look elsewhere instead of waiting that long. He couldn't keep paying the rent after that, but Russell might be amenable to negotiating the stand rents if the big business pulled out.

"One month or nothing."

"I guess I'll be giving you my month's notice then."

Through gritted teeth, Russell spat out, "Two months." The grim expression on his face made it clear he wouldn't budge.

"All right. Two months."

Gideon regretted that he could only help everyone for two months, but it might give them a little time to find other places to sell their goods. And maybe the wait would be long enough to make the organic farm reconsider.

"And payment up front." Now that he'd gained that victory, Russell's expression slid from irritated to gloating.

"I'll bring a check for the full amount on Thursday." Gideon started for the door, then turned. "Oh, and I have one more condition."

A deeper scarlet mottled Russell's face, and he puffed up his chest.

Before he could explode, Gideon held up a hand. "All I ask is that you don't tell anyone who paid their rent."

Russell sneered. "Always the hero."

Those words cut deep into Gideon's soul. Long ago, his brother had accused him of that too, but Gideon had been powerless to save Thomas the only time his brother really needed a hero.

Chapter Three

On Tuesday morning, Fern rolled her cart full of containers into the market. Daed had decided they couldn't keep the stand in Valley Green, and her search for new market space had been fruitless.

Nick entered, a glower on his face, followed by Mose, who shuffled to his usual place, dumped his crates, and arranged them haphazardly.

"Mose," she called, waving two twenties. "I sold some of your vegetables after you left on Saturday." He didn't need to know that she was the buyer. She'd taken a few things home for Mamm and dropped the rest at the food kitchen. It wasn't much, but it was all she had left from her ingredient money for this month.

Shades of Mose's old grin crossed his face, but his smile was almost as lackluster as his produce arrangement.

After all five of them had arrived, Fern beckoned everyone over. "I contacted all the markets in the area. Only one has a tentative opening for six months from now. If any of you want to get on the waiting list, here's the name and number to call."

The two *Englisch* women took the paper she held out and jotted down the information.

Nick glowered at the note. "Six months to wait and only a possible chance? Not worth it." Then he looked at Fern and softened a little. "Thanks for trying."

Mose only shook his head. "I can't go that far from home. And six months from now? Who knows what might happen before then?"

"Don't look now," Nick said in an undertone, "but our nemesis is heading this way."

"Huh?" One of the women stared at him.

"Russell." Nick hissed out the *s*'s in Russell's name like a snake. "The evil one."

Fern cringed. As much as she disliked what Russell had done, she didn't like Nick's label for the market owner.

"We'd better hightail it back to our booths before he decides we're too lazy to finish out our last two weeks here," Nick announced, loudly enough for Russell to hear.

"Wait," Russell called. "Before you all scatter, I have something to say to the five of you."

"Besides *good riddance*?" Nick growled.

Fern's instinct was to run and hide. She had no doubt that whatever Russell planned to say, it wouldn't be good. But Gideon happened to be strolling behind Russell. Fern got so engrossed in watching Gideon, she stayed rooted to the spot until Russell reached them.

Gideon leaned casually against the wooden pillar beside Fern's stand. Close enough to hear their discussion, but far enough away not to be mistaken as part of their group. Had he come to protect them again? Would he intervene if Russell tried to get rid of them?

Looking pained, Russell cleared his throat several

times. "I, well, I've decided to keep your rent the same for the next two months so you all have time to look for other markets or jobs."

"You mean the organic place can't move in for two months?" Nick laced his words with sarcasm.

Russell's jaw worked. "For your information, they want to move in now. But I'm giving all of you extra time out of the goodness of my heart."

"The goodness of your heart?" Nick muttered. "Yeah, right." Then he raised his voice. "Thanks for nothing."

Bright red flooded up Russell's neck and splashed across his face. Teeth and fists clenched, he took two steps toward Nick.

"Go ahead," Nick taunted. "I'd love to sue you."

Behind Russell, Gideon cleared his throat. Russell whirled around.

"What are you doing here? Spying on me?" He looked prepared to advance on Gideon.

Raising both hands in a gesture of surrender, Gideon responded in a calm, soothing tone, "I'm just waiting to talk to Fern."

"Me?" At the surprised squeak in her voice, Fern's face burned. She only hoped she didn't look as flushed as Russell.

"*Jah*, you." Gideon nodded in her direction, his expression impersonal. "I have a business question."

Russell snickered. "I can imagine the business you'd like to discuss with her."

Nick's chest swelled, and he started toward Russell. "Take that back."

Gideon slipped between the two men. "It's all right,

Nick. We all know Fern. Russell never would have said that if he knew her."

Shooting a nasty glare at Gideon's back, Russell retreated.

"The market will be opening soon," Mose reminded everyone. "We should get ready."

They all headed back to their stands. All except Fern and Gideon.

Gideon gulped. Why had he said he wanted to talk to Fern? Now they'd become the center of attention. Even worse, he hadn't planned what he intended to say.

She looked up at him expectantly.

"Um, this weekend I was thinking about you." *Great, Gideon.*

That's not what he meant to say, although for some odd reason, she had figured in his dreams.

Fern's eyes widened.

"I mean all of you." He waved a hand to indicate the other four stands. *So why didn't I say I wanted to talk to everyone? That would have made more sense.*

"Oh."

Did she look disappointed? Or was that his imagination?

He needed to be clear he had a business proposition. "It really bothers me that Mose and the rest of you will be losing your stands shortly."

"Not for another two months," Fern corrected. "I don't know if you heard Russell, but he's changed his mind."

"I heard," Gideon said dryly. He'd come to make sure Russell didn't mention who'd paid the rent. Gideon should have known Russell would claim the credit. Not that Gideon cared.

Fern had her eyes fixed on him. He needed to keep his mind on the conversation. Although thinking about Russell was preferable to thinking about Fern. Something about her twisted his mind into a muddled mess.

Gideon forced his attention back to the conversation. "Two months isn't long, but I hope it'll give everyone time to find a new place."

"It'll help. I didn't find any spots at the markets in this area." Her eyes sad, Fern glanced at the other stands. "I checked all the closest markets for everyone."

Of course she did. She always thought about others. Gideon had always admired that about her. Even when she stood in line at his counter, she motioned for elderly customers and mothers with young children to go ahead of her.

"Sorry to hear that," Gideon said. "No openings at all?"

"The only opening I found is a tentative one six months from now. Autumn and Peggy are looking into it. I hope it works out for them."

"I do too." Over the weekend, he'd realized he had another way to help them after he expanded his business. "I'm taking over the space next to me when the craft business there closes at the end of the month. I've decided to add full meals, including salads, desserts, and drinks."

"That's nice. It should bring in more customers." Fern sounded kind but not enthusiastic.

Did she think he was bragging about his business when she was about to lose hers? He wasn't doing a good job of explaining this. "I had an idea for you and Mose. Possibly Nick."

Now she looked close to tears. "You'll need more people to wait on customers?"

He hadn't thought about that yet. The added business might be too much for him and his sister Caroline. Maybe his sister-in-law Nettie could help. Mamm would be happy to watch Nettie's little ones. But was Fern hinting at getting a job at his stand?

"I, um, hadn't really planned that part yet."

"I see. When you mentioned Mose, Nick, and me, I thought you meant for us to work for you."

"I did." Gideon smiled. She'd given him the perfect lead-in. "Not to work *at* the stand, but to work *for* me."

Her brows drew together. "Isn't that the same thing?"

"No. Here's what I meant."

Customers were flowing through the door. He had to explain before her stand got backed up with buyers.

"Would you be willing to sell me the desserts I need? And I want to buy Mose's produce for the salads. But everything needs to be organic. Well, except for Nick's candy, but most people make exceptions for that."

"I could do that. I'll need to talk to Daed, but it might be a good solution."

Gideon pointed to the line at her counter. "Looks like you have a lot of people eager to taste your baking."

A few young children peered into the case, drooling over the cupcakes and pastries. Behind them, several adults had lined up.

"I'll let you go now, but I'll be back to talk to the three of you after we close today."

The smile Fern flashed at him brightened even the dreary, gray day seeping in from outside the doors. He offered a tentative smile in return but spun around before he met her eyes. He'd better not take any chances.

* * *

Fern stared after Gideon's retreating back. She and Daed would have to figure out if working with Gideon would be profitable. Buying organic ingredients was costly. And he'd expect a wholesale discount.

But if she didn't have to pay shop rent, the money they took in might work out to a similar amount. They didn't have any other options nearby, so it could be their best opportunity.

Fern pushed away the frisson of excitement shooting through her at the thought of being around Gideon. That was a perk she hadn't listed, but spending more time with him definitely added to the attraction of the idea. She forced herself to concentrate on her customers, and the day flew by.

Just after closing, Gideon strode over. "Can you stay for a short while? I'll check with Nick and Mose."

Before she could nod, Gideon brushed past her stand to catch Mose, who was already heading to the exit. "Mose, wait," he called.

The old man stopped and looked over his shoulder.

"Can I talk to you over here?"

With a sigh, Mose circled back and hobbled toward Fern's stand. Gideon headed for Nick's stand and returned a few minutes later with the glowering candy seller.

All three of them stared at Gideon, who shuffled on the cement floor as if nervous or uncertain.

"I had an idea I wanted to run past all of you. I'll be expanding my stand over the next few months. If you can't find another place to sell, I wondered if you'd like to sell your goods to me."

Nick frowned. "I'm not giving up my candy business or selling my products at a loss."

"I didn't mean for you to do that. I was thinking I could give you the end of my counter space for your candy. It wouldn't be as large as your stand now, but—"

"What's it going to cost me?" Nick demanded.

Gideon smiled at him. "Whatever you think is fair."

Fern stared at him. Didn't he worry Nick would try to cheat him? Evidently not, from his easygoing attitude.

Gideon turned to Mose. "I'll pay you the regular price for your produce, if that's all right."

Mose shook his head.

Fern was as surprised as Gideon. She'd expected Mose to accept such a generous offer.

"How much more were you thinking?" Gideon asked in gentle voice.

"*Neh, neh.*" Mose's head-shaking grew more agitated. "I can't let you pay full price. That wouldn't be right."

"I'm planning to add complete meals at my stand. If I sell your produce as salads or bake your potatoes, I can make enough to cover my costs."

"If you're sure," Mose said hesitantly.

"I'm certain," Gideon answered.

"That would be a blessing." Mose's eyes watered a little. "Ever since Russell announced the rent increase, I've been worried about taking care of my wife. Without the stand rental, I should make enough to cover what she needs."

Fern blinked back her own tears as Mose headed for the door with a tiny spring in his shuffling gait. "You've made such a difference in his life." She turned appreciative eyes to Gideon.

Their gazes met in a zing of electricity. And Fern couldn't look away.

Behind them, Nick cleared his throat. "I need to close down. I'll leave you two to your, um, conversation."

As Nick hustled off, Gideon's eyes grew shuttered and cold. In a clipped, businesslike voice, he asked, "Would it work for you to make desserts for my stand? I thought your cakes might be best. Oh, and rolls to serve with the meals."

Fern concentrated on a stained spot on the floor and worked to keep her words steady. "I'll have to check with Daed."

"Of course. And like I told Mose, I'll pay your usual prices."

"But you need to make money."

"I will. If I cut a cake into eight or ten slices, I can get double or triple what I pay you."

Fern pinched her lips shut before she pointed out he hadn't accounted for overhead and paying employees and— She didn't want to criticize him. Not after he'd been so generous to Mose. Besides, he'd been in business for a long time, so he must know what he was doing. Still, she'd talk it over with Daed, and they'd figure out a fair price for themselves and for Gideon.

"Think about it and let me know," Gideon said before he headed off.

Fern remained rooted where she stood, her gaze fixed on his retreating back. He'd come up with an ideal plan, one that would benefit Mose, who grew his produce in his own garden and didn't use chemical products. And all Nick had to do was transfer his candy containers to Gideon's stand, and whatever deal they worked out—a cut of the profits or renting the space—Nick wouldn't be paying triple stand rent. The extra sales and customers would also benefit Gideon's expanded business.

The plan seemed to be good for everyone. Except maybe her. It would definitely benefit her moneywise. But if she had to interact with Gideon four days a week, could she keep her interest in him hidden? That would be a major challenge.

Chapter Four

After supper that evening, Gideon closed himself in the small room off the kitchen that served as his office. Mamm's cheerful voice penetrated the walls, along with Nettie's softer answers.

His sister-in-law had moved in with them after Thomas's death two years ago. Ever since then, she and Mamm had shared the cooking and cleanup. Mamm appreciated the company, and being with the family helped ease some of Nettie's loneliness and sorrow.

As much as Gideon loved having his nieces and nephews gathered around the table, it provided a daily reminder of not only Thomas's absence but also the weight of Gideon's responsibility. He'd taken on the task of caring for Nettie and the children. Over the past few days, he'd let concern for others blind him to those duties.

With a sigh, Gideon pulled out his account book. He'd taken a huge check in to Russell that morning and then offered to take on the other sellers' candy, produce, and baked goods. A lovely face imposed itself over the mental image of rolls and cakes. He shook his head. Doing this might not be a wise business decision. But how could he let Fern and the others lose their income?

He couldn't. Not if he could afford to help them. But it meant giving up some of his goals. He'd dipped into the cushion of savings he kept for emergencies. Plus, paying for the other sellers' products would cut into the amount he'd hoped to pay on Thomas's loans.

After all the times their father had drummed into them to avoid loans and pay outright for whatever they bought, Gideon still couldn't believe Thomas had been drowning in debt.

His brother's last words haunted Gideon. Thomas had been filled with guilt . . .

Pulling his thoughts from that horrible memory, Gideon checked the figures in the accounting ledger. On a piece of scrap paper, he tried to estimate how much Fern and Mose earned each week. He made a wild guess about Mose's income, but he'd paid closer attention to Fern's business than he'd realized.

His interest had been in more than her delicious cinnamon buns. Leaning back in his chair, he closed his eyes and imagined crunching through the thin, crisp outer crust. The soft, cushiony dough melted in his mouth, along with the sugary sweet icing and the tang of cinnamon.

He sat up abruptly. It would be a shame for customers to lose the opportunity to purchase that delicious treat, a market favorite. Gideon would miss them too. Fern had never known how addicted he was to them, because he sent his younger sister or his niece to purchase them, but he'd been one of the first purchasers every morning the market was open.

Most mornings, barbecued chicken sales really didn't start until after ten. Few people bought chicken for breakfast. But he could drive more customers to his stand in the early morning hours if he offered some of Fern's cinnamon rolls, along with milk and juice.

He'd have to be careful he didn't eat all the profits, but it would give Fern a chance to sell more of her baked goods. If he also paid full price for the sticky buns and breakfast pastries, though, he'd have to mark them up. Most customers would be willing to pay extra for organic. At least he hoped they would. He'd pay whatever Fern asked.

A soft tap on the door interrupted his planning. "Come in," he called.

Nettie stuck her head in the door. "I'm making tea for your *mamm* and *daed*. Would you like some?"

Gideon had no desire for tea, but if he refused, Nettie would be hurt. "*Danke.*"

She shot him a smile and closed the door. He sighed inwardly.

Knowing Nettie, she'd already put the water on to boil, so he wouldn't have time to do more bookwork tonight. He crumpled the papers with his scribbled figures and tossed them into the trash can beside the desk. Then he slid the account book into the drawer.

He'd already paid the deposit for his stand expansion, and he'd set aside the rest of the money for that bill. He'd make little, if any, profit on the new items he planned to add to the menu, and he'd be saddled with Thomas's loans for years, but he'd helped others. And that was more important.

"Gideon?" Nettie called softly.

He jumped to his feet and opened the door. She balanced a tray with four teacups. He took one and followed her into the living room.

"You left very early this morning, *sohn*," Daed said as he selected a cup from Nettie's tray. "Is everything all right?"

Gideon didn't usually shut himself into the office in the evenings either. "Everything's fine. I had some business with Russell this morning." Although Daed would encourage helping others, Gideon kept that morning's payment a secret. Just like he'd kept Thomas's debts—and other things—from his family. He didn't want Daed to worry.

"The stand expansion will start next week, and I've found some people to supply desserts and salads."

"*Gut, gut.* You've made some smart decisions since"—Daed swallowed hard—"you took over." With a rueful smile, he added, "Although I must say, Thomas's idea to sell organic made the expansion possible."

Cringing inside, Gideon managed a nod. If only Daed knew what Thomas's decisions had cost the business, himself, and all of them.

Tonight, Fern didn't plan to wait until after supper to mention the day's news. As soon as they lifted their heads following the silent prayer, she started to tell her parents about Gideon's offer. His generosity might erase the worry lines around her mother's eyes.

Before she could speak, though, Mamm lifted an envelope beside her plate. "We got a letter from Aaron today."

Daed stopped with his soup spoon halfway to his mouth and beamed. "What did he have to say?"

Mamm pulled out a folded page and smoothed it beside her plate. "Over the past two weeks, he's worked nonstop, and they've helped twenty families repair or replace their homes."

"That's *wunderbar*." Daed's smile grew even broader. "I'm so glad Aaron decided to stay with the mission full-time. And if he's that busy, he won't have time to get into trouble."

"*Jah*, that's true. We can praise God for that." A frown creased Mamm's brow. "But he needs more money."

Daed's forehead wrinkled to match Mamm's. "Already? How much this time?"

Mamm sighed heavily and quoted a figure.

"That's almost double what we've been sending. Are you sure?" Daed held out a hand for the letter and skimmed it. "They need a lot more money for the project." He sighed. "I wish my meeting with Russell this morning had gone better. He won't budge on the rent."

Shooting a furtive glance at Fern, Mamm shook her head. "Perhaps I should have waited to share this."

"It's all right," Fern assured them. "Maybe today's news will help."

Both of her parents turned toward her.

"First of all, Russell gave all five of us two more months at the regular rate."

Daed's pained expression eased. "That will help. I talked to your *onkel* this afternoon, and he agreed to check at the Maryland farmer's market for any openings with other stand owners. You won't make nearly as much as you do here, but it's better than nothing."

If Gideon's offer worked out, Fern could stay in Lancaster County and avoid piling into a van with her cousins at five in the morning to drive out of state. And although she had experience, working in someone else's stand meant a low hourly wage. It certainly wouldn't cover Aaron's expenses, let alone theirs.

She continued, "After Russell left, Gideon Hartzler

talked to three of us. He's expanding his chicken stand to sell full meals. He offered to buy Mose's produce at the regular price."

"No discount?" Daed squinted one eye, making it clear he didn't think much of Gideon's business sense.

"He claims he'll make money by turning it into salads or selling baked potatoes."

"Hmm." Her father stroked his beard. "I suppose he will, but it won't be a very big profit."

Fern suspected Gideon had done it out of the goodness of his heart. "I think he's trying to help Mose make enough to pay for his wife's prescriptions."

"That's kind of him," Mamm said.

"*Jah*, he seems to have a giving heart." Had Gideon offered to buy her baked goods because he felt sorry for her?

Some of the joy she'd experienced over his plan leaked away. She'd been so excited—or maybe *ferhoodled* was closer to the truth—by being around him, she hadn't considered he might see her as a charity case.

"I'm glad to know Mose will be taken care of." Daed dipped his spoon into his bowl.

"Gideon also asked if I'd be willing to supply his stand with rolls and cakes. He's adding desserts to his menu."

After swallowing his soup, Daed tapped a finger against his lip. "I suppose it depends on what he can afford to pay."

"He said full price like he's giving Mose. He thinks he'll make enough if he charges by the slice."

Daed appeared doubtful. "I don't know about that."

"I don't either. But he wants everything to be organic, so maybe he'll charge higher prices."

"Organic? We'll need to check the prices of ingredients tomorrow. Then we'll have a better idea."

"If we don't have to pay the stand rent," Fern pointed

out, "we won't need to sell nearly as much to make what we usually do."

"*Jah*, I thought about that." Daed smiled at Fern. "We can do some figuring tomorrow after we've checked the cost of ingredients, but Gideon's offer does sound promising."

Hope flared in Mamm's eyes. "Thank the Lord. Maybe we'll be able to help Aaron after all."

A flicker of jealousy shot through Fern. Everything the family did revolved around meeting Aaron's needs. She loved her brother and appreciated his mission work, but she'd remained stuck here while he'd gone to South Carolina in her place. Somehow, it didn't seem fair. Working with the Mennonite mission had been her idea and her dream.

Lord, I'm sorry. I know You must have a reason for this switch. Please help me to accept Your will for my life.

While he drank his tea, Gideon tuned out the conversation around him as his mind floated back to Fern's glowing face when he'd offered to pay Mose full price. She had such a giving heart. And he wanted to help her as much as he did Mose.

But he hadn't considered he'd be seeing her and dealing with her every day the market was open. Monday, Thursday, Friday, and Saturday glowed like beacons compared to the rest of the week. But as much as he looked forward to being around her, it wouldn't be easy.

"Gideon?"

Nettie's quiet question startled him back to the room, where his nieces and nephews lay sprawled on their stomachs under the propane lamp playing a board game.

Six-year-old Katie was helping her three-year-old sister, Sadie, beat her brothers.

"We should get the children ready for bed soon." Nettie stood and set her teacup on the tray. "Finish up the game, Katie," she said as she collected the empty cups. "Bedtime as soon as I wash these dishes."

Gideon handed Nettie his cup. Although part of him wished he had more time to daydream about Fern, he'd be better off keeping his mind on anything but her.

By the time Nettie returned from the kitchen, Katie had closed the lid to the game.

Sadie tugged at Gideon's pants leg. "I won, Gideon. I won."

He beamed down at his niece. Strands of her curly blond hair had escaped from her bob and bounced around her face as she danced excitedly.

With a superior smile, Katie handed the game box to Gideon, and he put it on the shelf. She and her brothers must have let Sadie win, because neither boy looked upset.

Nettie tried to disentangle Sadie's hands from the black fabric of Gideon's pants. "Let your *onkel* go. How is he ever going to walk with you holding on so tight?"

Sadie shook off her *mamm*'s hand. "I want him to carry me." She glanced up at Gideon with pleading eyes. "Pwease."

Gideon's heart melted. Beside him, Nettie expelled a soft, exasperated breath. Although she'd been working to make Sadie more independent, how could he resist that sweet request?

"If it's all right with your *mamm*."

Small worry lines creased Nettie's brow. "Only for tonight. If Gideon wants to, that is."

He did for sure. He bent and scooped up Sadie. She twined her arms around his neck and cuddled close. Soft curls tickled his jaw, and his heart filled with so much love his chest ached.

Lenny sidled up next to Gideon and held out a sticky palm. Gideon shifted Sadie so he could take it. At only a year older than Sadie, Lenny still preferred to have help mounting the steep stairs to the bedroom in the dark.

Nettie shooed Katie ahead of her. Five-year-old David hung back, staring longingly at Gideon's full arms. Usually Gideon held David's and Lenny's hands when they went up to bed.

"Go on, now." Nettie steered David toward the stairs.

His lower lip thrust out in a pout, David glanced back at Gideon, who lagged behind, matching his pace to Lenny's. Gideon sent David an apologetic smile.

When they reached the top of the stairs, Gideon headed into the girls' bedroom. He let go of Lenny's hand to set Sadie on her bed. Then he backed up a few steps and almost bumped into David, who stood behind him with his hand outstretched.

Gideon tousled David's hair. "You can pick the bedtime story tonight." Telling David's favorite Bible story might prevent him from feeling left out. Gideon reached for both boys' hands and led them into their bedroom across the hall.

Once they'd donned pajamas, Gideon knelt on the floor beside David's bed and wrapped an arm around each boy's shoulders. Their faces earnest, they prayed.

Tucking the blankets around David, Gideon asked, "What story do you want to hear tonight?" He really didn't need to ask. David always asked for the story of his Biblical namesake.

"David and Goliath."

Gideon straightened Lenny's covers, which had slipped

to one side. "Slide over a bit. I'll sit beside you to tell the story."

Lenny scooted closer to the wall to make room. He often shivered through the stories. By the time Gideon got to the part about David facing the giant, Lenny was trembling.

Gideon put an arm around him and held him tight. "You don't have to be frightened. God will take care of David and of us."

"I wouldn't be scared." David puffed out his chest to prove how strong and courageous he'd be, but his shaky voice gave him away.

"No matter what happens," Gideon reminded them, "we don't need to be afraid. God is always with us."

"I know," Lenny said, his words whispered and wobbly. He cuddled closer to Gideon.

David looked longingly at both of them. "I wish you'd sit on my bed sometimes."

Gideon couldn't figure out why both boys seemed more upset than usual about the story. Maybe he'd been dramatizing it too much. Sliding Lenny over more, Gideon made room on his other side. "Why don't you hop up here?" He patted the empty spot beside him.

David shot across the room and bounced onto the bed.

"Whoa, you could just sit," Gideon teased as the mattress dipped up and down.

David laughed and leaned against Gideon's chest. "Now we can all be brave together."

"Good idea." Gideon went back to the story. With one arm around each boy, he couldn't do his usual motions. No aiming a slingshot. No whirling it in the air. No loud slap to his forehead when the stone hit Goliath. No loud clap when the giant smashed to the ground.

Still, he kept his voice dramatic. So dramatic that Nettie peeked into the room.

"Is everything all right in here?"

"Gideon's just telling us about David and Goliath," David explained.

"I see." A soft smile lifted the corner of Nettie's lips.

"Maybe I'm a little too loud."

"It's all right. Sadie's fast asleep, and noises don't bother Katie."

"I'll finish in a quieter voice."

"Whatever you were doing is fine." With a tender glance at her sons that also included Gideon, Nettie backed out of the room and shut the door.

The glow in her eyes had been that of a doting *mamm*, but something about her look disturbed Gideon. Nettie seemed overly appreciative of everything he did for the children, making him uncomfortable. He hadn't taken care of all of them for praise. He'd rather fade into the background.

He'd tried to do that ever since the evening Thomas had been taken to the hospital. Gideon hadn't been trying to take their father's place that night, but Lenny and David had clung to Gideon. They cuddled close, asking questions in their two-year-old and three-year-old baby talk as they tried to understand where their *daed* had gone.

Daed will be home soon, everyone had told them. *He's sleeping at the hospital.* Gideon had begun the nightly routine that had continued ever since, because Thomas had never regained consciousness. He'd slipped from his coma into eternity.

The boys' confusion and sadness increased at the funeral. They didn't understand why their Daed didn't wake up and play with them. In the days that followed, both boys clung to Gideon as Nettie and little Katie, who shadowed her *mamm* everywhere, cared for the baby.

Many nights, Gideon held the boys, wiped their tears, and rocked them to sleep. He took Thomas's place in their lives—teaching them chores, telling them Bible stories, praying with them.

At first, Nettie had been too fragile to care for all the children. Then she'd lost the baby she was carrying, and Gideon had taken over her bedtime duties until she'd recovered.

He'd gotten so attached to his nieces and nephews, he'd find it hard to give up his role if Nettie married again. So far, she hadn't shown any interest in dating. Being a widow with four children might discourage romance.

For his part, Gideon had sometimes found the responsibility of caring for his brother's family to be heavy. That, as well as his brother's confession before his death, had dampened Gideon's desire to marry. Never would be soon enough for any relationship. But why couldn't he get Fern off his mind?

Chapter Five

On Wednesday morning, Fern drove Daed to the food suppliers, and he haggled over costs until he got the prices he wanted. Then they headed home, and Daed worked out estimates. Finally, he and Fern went over the final figures he'd copied neatly onto a fresh sheet of paper.

"I have no idea what this Gideon pays in rent or takes in from his chicken business, but I hope this will be fair for both of us. I'll need to meet with him. My main concern is whether he's upright and honest."

"He is." Fern could vouch for that. As her father studied her, Fern's face heated. "Well, he's kind and thoughtful. Look what he's done for Mose."

"He does sound like he's a caring young man, but people aren't always what they seem. And you haven't been around him enough to tell about his business practices."

If Daed had any idea how often she'd observed Gideon, he'd be shocked. And probably quite worried. Fern kept that to herself. But she could tell Daed about one observation.

"One time when I was in line there, he underpaid a man by a nickel. The customer hadn't noticed, and Gideon's older brother told him to forget it, but Gideon left the stand to give the man the correct change."

"That speaks well of him. Although if his brother isn't honest, I don't want you working with them."

"His brother died a few years ago, so Gideon runs the stand alone."

"I see." Daed cleared his desktop and set his pen on top of the paper for Gideon. "I'd like to meet him and judge his character for myself. If he doesn't seem honorable, we'll pray that your *onkel* can find you a job."

Fern had no doubt Gideon would impress Daed, the same way he'd impressed her. At least, she hoped so. She'd much rather work with Gideon than go to the Maryland market. Even if it meant dealing with her unrequited feelings.

The next morning, Daed rode into the market with Fern. They left early so Daed could catch Gideon before the market opened.

Fern unloaded her containers onto the handcart and pushed them inside. She had to walk slowly to keep everything balanced and allow Daed to keep up with his walker.

Inside the market, Daed studied the layout by the front door while she parked her cart behind the counter. "I can see why the organic business wanted this area. It's the best spot in the market. They'll have a lot of customers passing by here. Your *mammi* picked a good spot for her business."

"*Jah*, she did." Fern loved being near the front door to see all the customers when they came in.

"You know," Daed said sadly, "I haven't been here in years, but this part of the market looks the same as it did when I courted your *mamm*." He nodded toward Nick's candy stand. "I used to stop there to get those soft peppermints she loves. I can't believe all this will be gone in two months."

"I can't either." To keep her mind off that gloomy thought, she dusted her hands on her apron. "Should I take you to meet Gideon now?"

Daed nodded. "I have the paper right here." He patted his pocket, then gripped the handles of his walker, and followed Fern down the aisle.

Gideon had his back to them when they reached his counter. He was stringing chickens on a spit. He turned when she called his name. Their eyes met, and her mouth dried. All words fled.

"I know you, young man," Daed said.

Fern turned to him, startled. How could Daed possibly know Gideon?

The older man Gideon had worried about a few days ago stood beside Fern, but Gideon forced his attention away from her. "It's nice to see you again."

"I'm Ezekiel Blauch, Fern's father. You know my *dochder*?"

Her father? And Gideon definitely did know his daughter, but he stood there speechless, trying not to glance in Fern's direction. Finally, he cleared his throat. "Nice to meet you. I'm Gideon Hartzler."

"I figured." The dry humor in Ezekiel's voice indicated he saw a lot more than Gideon wanted him to. "I'm here to discuss the offer you made my *dochder*."

Had he phrased it that way on purpose? Was he jabbing Gideon over his interest in Fern? Gideon stiffened. He needed to come across businesslike. "Of course. I'd be happy to discuss it with you." He'd managed to get out a coherent sentence.

"Is now a *gut* time?" Ezekiel examined the chickens waiting on the counter. "I could come back another time."

Gideon didn't want to keep Ezekiel waiting. The poor man didn't look too steady on his walker. But the chickens shouldn't sit out on the counter. Gideon couldn't risk giving anyone food poisoning.

Fern moved restlessly beside her father. "I should get back so I can get set up before the market opens."

"You do that," Ezekiel said. "I'll take care of things here."

"See you." Gideon nodded in Fern's direction without actually looking at her. He had no desire for her father's eagle eyes to read anything into Gideon's attempt at a casual gaze. Better not take that chance.

"Why don't you get that chicken cooking first?" Ezekiel suggested. "Then we can talk. Unless you have other things to do."

Gideon had a lot of other preparations to make, but he'd do them after they'd talked. "I'll do that quickly. If you'd like to come behind the counter, you could sit down. I have a stool and a chair."

"*Danke.* That would be *gut.*" Ezekiel clunked around the corner and sank onto the wooden chair.

With Ezekiel staring at him, Gideon's movements were jerkier than usual. He slowed down to make them a little smoother. As soon as he'd put the final spit in the rotisserie and turned it on, he sat on a stool beside Ezekiel.

"First of all, we appreciate your offer. It was kind of you to help Mose and my *dochder*, but I want to be sure you are making a fair profit."

No one else had worried about that. *Neh*, to be fair, both Mose and Fern had questioned him about the prices he'd offered. Only Nick had gouged him, but Gideon had said Nick could set his price, and Gideon planned to honor that. Besides it was only one small section of his stand. Gideon would consider the small amount Nick planned to pay as extra. He'd make his profit from the rest of the business.

Ezekiel sat still, waiting for Gideon to respond. Instead, Gideon had made more of a fool of himself by wool-gathering.

He tried to make up for his silence. "Like I told your daughter, um, Fern, if I sell individual slices of cake, I'll make money."

"Will it be enough to cover your overhead, though?"

Gideon would rather not answer that question. He'd offered to take on these products to help. Profit hadn't entered into it. "The business does quite well already." Or it would if Thomas hadn't run up so much debt.

His eyes narrowed, assessing Gideon, Ezekiel pointed out, "You didn't answer my question."

"I'm sure the new products will bring in even more customers."

Ezekiel blew out a long breath. "I see you don't intend to give me a straight answer."

"To be honest, I don't know how adding all these products will affect my income. I've never offered full meals before."

"Fair enough." Ezekiel reached into his pocket and pulled out a paper. "I worked out what I think are fair prices for both of us."

Gideon's eyes widened. "Are you sure Fern—and you— will make enough?"

"We'll be fine."

"Could you also give me prices for sticky buns, cinnamon rolls, bear claws, and pastries? We do a brisk business from late morning until closing." He hoped Ezekiel didn't think he was bragging, but Gideon wanted to assure Fern's *daed* that the business made money. "I don't usually get customers until later in the morning, so I thought we could sell Fern's baked goods in the morning with coffee, juice, and milk."

Ezekiel nodded approvingly. "That's a wise idea."

"I thought Fern's regular customers would miss their breakfast treats, so if she's willing to bake those, I'm happy to sell them."

"You're a *gut* man." Ezekiel clapped Gideon on the shoulder, then struggled to his feet. "I'm sure Fern would be happy to make more."

"That's *wunderbar.*"

Fern's *daed* rounded the counter and stopped. "I don't know if Fern told you, but our youngest son, Aaron, is on a mission trip. Most of Fern's profit goes to support him, so this will let us send him more money. *Danke.*"

"I should be thanking you. You'll be helping my business grow." And giving him more time with Fern. Even though that shouldn't excite him, it did.

Fern appreciated the steady stream of customers, because it kept her mind from Daed's meeting with Gideon. They seemed to be taking a long time. What was going on?

Gideon had told Nick he'd accept whatever Nick decided. Maybe he'd do the same for Daed, but if so, her father should have been back by now. Although knowing Daed, perhaps he was grilling Gideon to see if he was upright and honest. Suppose Daed didn't agree with Fern's assessment of Gideon's character?

"Are you going to wait on me or what?" Wilma Mast stood at the counter, glaring. "Or are you too busy daydreaming to pay attention to customers?"

"I'm so sorry." Fern added an apologetic smile, but that did little to soften Wilma's expression. Most sellers called her the Pickle Lady, not only because that's what she sold but also because of her tart criticisms and sour disposition.

Something about Wilma set Fern's teeth on edge. Although Wilma's name sounded Amish, she dressed in the longer, flowered dresses most Mennonites wore, but she had no head covering. And her personality in no way resembled the quiet, sweet demeanor of the other Mennonite ladies who worked at the market.

Keeping her tone polite, Fern asked, "What can I get you?"

"You don't know my usual order by now?"

Anytime Fern picked out Wilma's usual order, a Danish pastry with cheese, before asking, Wilma snapped at Fern for not checking first. On those days, Wilma always changed her order to a bear claw. "I just want to be sure what you're in the mood for. Would you like a cheese Danish?"

Wilma blew out an explosion of air.

Fern assumed Wilma's huff meant *yes* and bent to package a Danish. Wilma didn't stop her, so Fern must have guessed correctly.

When she handed Wilma the white bakery bag, the Pickle Lady pursed her lips and counted out a pile of change, mostly pennies, while customers behind her sighed with impatience.

"*Danke*, we always appreciate change." Fern scooped up the coins without counting them.

Wilma's eyebrows rose. "Aren't you going to check that I gave you the right amount?"

"I trust you." Fern dumped the pile of pennies into the cash register and slid the two dimes and three nickels into place. Though she shouldn't get pleasure from it, she had to admit she enjoyed Wilma's dismayed expression.

"You'll be out of business pretty quickly if you trust everyone like that," Wilma said darkly as she moved off.

Actually, I'll be out of business in two months. But she didn't say that aloud. She'd rather not see Wilma's gloating expression.

The next woman in line stared after Wilma. "She's the sourest woman I've ever seen."

The man behind her said, "Yeah. No wonder everyone calls her the Pickle Lady."

"It certainly suits her." The woman looked up at Fern. "I don't know how you stay so calm and kind. I'd have been tempted to throw that change back at her."

"I truly am grateful for change. Pennies go so fast I'm surprised she didn't want them for herself."

She waited on the woman, and the man stepped up to the counter. He grinned. "You sure put that Pickle Lady in her place, but you did it so nicely you left her speechless. For a moment, at least."

Fern didn't want to gossip about another seller, so she only asked for his order.

"You Amish don't gossip, do you?"

Luckily, Fern had her back turned to get a bakery box for his cupcakes or she might have snorted.

Not gossip? No, they never did that. They only shared prayer requests and . . . Well, discussing what others were doing wrong was the best way to learn from example and avoid doing it yourself, right? And passing along information was important. And making sure people knew not to mention specific topics around certain people. And . . .

Fern turned around and concentrated on lifting the cupcakes he'd selected into the box. "Two chocolate iced, two lemon? And one strawberry?" At his nod, she added, "If you get one more, you'll be eligible for the half-dozen discount."

He glanced up at the sign. "All right. Give me one of the vanilla ones with sprinkles."

As he reached for his wallet, Daed shuffled toward the stand. Her father glanced at all the customers and raised one thumb up. Gideon must have accepted the offer.

Why did that news set her pulse thumping?

Gideon couldn't believe he'd agreed to Ezekiel's prices, but Fern's *daed* was quite insistent. Gideon only hoped Fern would make enough money from the deal. He'd have been willing to pay more.

"Gideon?" his sister said behind him. "Here's your cinnamon roll." She handed over a small white bakery bag. "Will you need me today?"

"I assume you plan to attend the antiques auction?" Caroline had recently started dating the auctioneer.

She blushed. "Zach could use some help setting things up."

Gideon hid a smile. Somehow Zach and his brothers had managed to handle the auctions all by themselves for the past seven years. Because they sold mainly furniture, it wasn't likely Caroline would be carting that around. And the brothers took turns tagging items or carrying them to the customers, so his sister wasn't needed for that either. Most likely she'd be sitting in the audience, enrapt as Zach pattered rapidly through the prices and his final *going, going, gone*.

"Please?"

When Caroline used that imploring tone, Gideon had a hard time refusing. Thursdays were their slowest days, but they still had a noon rush. "It's tough to handle the lunchtime business alone."

"I know." Caroline looked torn, but she heaved a sigh. "I'll be back." She scurried off.

Before Gideon could open the bakery bag, a man headed in his direction—the contractor who'd come to do some stand measurements and collect the next installment on the payment.

The tantalizing smell of cinnamon seeped through the bag Caroline had set on the counter, and Gideon's mouth watered. He left the roll in the bag, though, and greeted the planning contractor.

The man spread papers on the counter. "Just a final look-see to be sure this is the design you want completed, and I'll double-check the measurements."

Gideon bent his head and studied the plans and cost sheet. The estimate, which he'd agreed to two weeks ago, now loomed larger. Since then, he'd taken on three new vendors and paid a large chunk from his savings to Russell. If anything went wrong, or this cost more than he'd anticipated, he could end up in financial trouble. With four little children and their mother depending on him, one mistake could take them all down.

But if he didn't expand, three people would be out of

work, and all of them had loved ones who depended on them. No matter what decision he made, it'd be risky.

Lord, help me to make the right choice here.

"You still okay with this?" the contractor asked. "You seem a bit hesitant."

"It's a big commitment." Gideon picked up the pen to initial the sheets. The contractor had no idea how big an obligation this was. Gideon now had more than a dozen people relying on his success.

He'd have to trust God for the extra money and everyone's livelihoods. "I'm going to need to change the area at this end. We'll keep the opening to get inside the stand the same, but I want a glass display case for baked goods here. And I'd like a display case for candy beside it."

The contractor tapped his pencil on the counter. "That'll cost extra. And we already ordered the other cases. I'll have to bill you for those too." He did some quick figuring on the paper and turned it so Gideon could see the price.

Mentally, Gideon subtracted that amount from his savings. He should have calculated these costs when he'd negotiated with Nick and Fern's *daed*. If he charged them more, they'd lose money. Fern needed to support her brother and her parents. And Nick had a family. How could he not help them?

The contractor broke into Gideon's thoughts. "You change your mind?"

"*Neh*, I'll pay whatever it costs." And he'd trust God for the money to cover it.

"Would have made more sense to decide this weeks ago."

"I know." But Gideon had only learned of Russell's plans last week.

"I'll put in a rush order on these two new display cases, but those will have to wait. No idea how long it'll take for them to come in."

"As long as it can be done within two months, that'll be fine."

"Hmm, I'll see what I can do." The contractor stepped aside so Gideon could wait on a customer.

After the customer left, Gideon asked, "Do you need a deposit for ordering the new display cases?"

"I have to check the prices first. I'll add it to your next payment."

"Thank you." That gave Gideon a little breathing room, but he'd have to sell a lot of chicken between now and the due date of the next payment.

"The installation team will start on Saturday as soon as the market closes. You got permission for them to come in the employee entrance?"

Gideon nodded. Russell wasn't too happy about it, but he'd agreed to give Gideon a key to lock up after the workers left.

"They could get this done much faster if you'd let us work on Sundays."

"*Neh*, no Sunday work." Gideon never worked on Sunday, and he'd never encourage anyone else to do so.

The contractor shook his head. "It's your call, but it'll take longer."

"We agreed to Saturdays after our early closing and all day on Mondays and Wednesdays." Gideon set a check on the counter and filled it out. "Here's the payment I owe you today." He slid the check across the counter.

"Thanks. The guys will see you Saturday, then."

"I'll plan to stay while they work and lock up afterward," Gideon promised.

After the contractor left, Gideon realized he'd miss putting the boys to bed. He'd have to figure that out. Perhaps Daed or Mamm could take his place. They could talk it over at supper tonight.

Right now, he had a cinnamon bun calling his name. As he bit into it, he floated off into daydreams. A beautiful baker pulled a pan of freshly baked rolls from the oven and turned to him with a smile. And the rolls and her smile were all for him.

Chapter Six

As Russell unlocked the entrance door on Friday morning, Fern finished hanging a huge cardboard sign on the wall behind her stand to announce her move to Hartzler's Chicken Barbecue in two months.

Her first customer of the morning stared at the sign. "What do you mean you're moving? Why?"

"A new stand is taking over this whole space." Fern waved toward Nick and then in the opposite direction toward Mose and the *Englisch* sellers.

"Nooo," Margery Witmer moaned. "Not Nick. He's going out of business? My children love to pick out treats there. I did too, when I was small."

"Don't worry. Nick's not going out of business. He'll be moving to Hartzler's too."

"Where in the world will both of you fit? That stand is pretty big, but there's no room for anyone else."

"Gideon's expanding his stand, so he'll be making space for us."

"I'm glad you'll both still be here, but I don't want to see this market changed. It's been the same for ages."

Fern bit her lip. It pained her to think of this whole area

being altered. Her family had been in this spot for years. In a choked voice, she asked, "Did you want a dozen sticky buns?"

"Yes, as usual." Margery smiled. "I don't know what I'd do if you closed. Who'd feed my family's sweet tooth four days a week?"

After Fern handed over the bakery box, Margery turned to the next person in line. "Did you see that sign? The new owner's putting Fern out of business. Isn't it terrible?"

Roy Zimmerman shook his head. "His father never would have done that." He faced Fern. "Do his parents know?"

Fern shrugged. She had no idea whether or not Mike Evans had been informed, although she suspected he hadn't. Somehow, she couldn't see him agreeing to get rid of Bertha's Candy Cupboard. Nick often told the story of how his grandmother Bertha and Mike's mother had become best friends.

As Roy was leaving, he pointed out the sign to others and bemoaned the new business moving into that end of the market. All morning long, Fern fielded questions about the move. Some people were sad; others, indignant. But everyone assured her they'd still buy from her.

In the late afternoon, a teen boy stomped through the door in heavy black boots. Fern tried not to stare at his nose ring and tattoos. He headed straight for Nick's stand.

Nick, who'd bent down to wait on three towheaded sisters, straightened up. He looked taken aback. "Aidan? What are you doing here?"

Aidan? Nick's son? Fern hadn't seen him since he was twelve or so. Back then, he'd been a quiet, shy boy who sometimes accompanied his dad to work on the weekends. For the past five years, Nick had complained about Aidan's rebellious attitude and claimed his son hung out with a wild gang.

The teen clomped closer to the candy display, and the three small girls edged away.

"Hang on," Nick said. "You're scaring these kids."

"Sorry," Aidan muttered. He stepped back and waited for the children to make their purchases. As soon as they clutched their small bags of candy and scurried off, he approached the counter, his fists and jaw clenched. "Mom told me about the stand. I'm not going to let that Evans jerk do this to our family."

Nick crossed his arms. "And exactly how do you plan to stop him?"

Aidan wilted a bit under his father's scowl, but his chin and eyes remained defiant. "Me and my friends can teach him a lesson."

"Leave your friends out of this." Nick's raised voice carried through the aisles. "If you get arrested for assault and battery, I'm not going to bail you out."

The hate-filled glare Aidan shot at his father made Fern shiver.

"You'd be the last person I'd call." Aidan whirled around.

"Get back here this instant." His father's words cracked the air like a whip.

Aidan ignored the order and started toward the central staircase. He'd barely gone a few steps before Russell barreled toward them.

"What's going on here? I was up in my office"—Russell waved one hand toward the ceiling over Nick's stand—"and I heard a commotion. Do I need to call the police?"

"No need for the police." Aidan sneered. "And you're just the person I wanted to see." Legs spread and arms crossed, he frowned at Russell. "What do you think you're doing putting my family out of business?"

Russell's eyes narrowed. "Your old man put you up to this? Creating a scene on our busiest day of the week?"

"*He* has nothing to do with it." Aidan strode forward until he was almost toe-to-toe with Russell.

In the next aisle over, Gideon hurried toward Fern's stand. "Is everything all right? I heard shouting."

"Nick's son is upset with Russell," she whispered.

Gideon glanced in the direction she indicated, and his eyes widened. "That's Aidan?"

"*Jah.* I never would have recognized him. I haven't seen him for years."

"He looks really different. I'd better see if I can help." Gideon hurried toward them. As much as Fern wished he'd stay and talk to her, she trusted him to calm everyone.

As Gideon reached them, Russell pulled his cell phone from his pocket. "I'm calling the police."

"For what?" Aidan taunted. "You scared I might beat you up?"

"A little punk like you?"

Gideon's arm sliced between them. "Hey, Aidan. I haven't seen you in a while."

"Yeah, Gid. I'll talk to you later. I'm busy with this, um, guess I'd better not say that word in front of you, but he's an—"

"Why don't we head back to your father's stand and talk?" Gideon slung an arm over Aidan's shoulder.

Aidan shook it off. "Later, man. I got business to take care of first."

"This may not be the best way to do it. Maybe we could wait until after the market closes to talk to Russell."

Fern loved Gideon's use of the word *we*. It signaled that he was on Aidan's side.

"Naw, man, this don't concern you. Just me and Russell here." Aidan leaned forward threateningly and glowered at Russell. "You can't close Bertha's Candy Cupboard. My great-grandma started it. It's been in our family almost a hundred years." Aidan's voice cracked.

Fern's heart ached for him. As angry as he was toward his father, he still cared about his family and their traditions.

Rather than sympathizing with Adian's pain, Russell shot back, "Not that I have to answer to a juvie, but your pop's not going out of business."

"Don't call me that. I ain't never been arrested."

"Only because you haven't been caught." Russell waved a derisive hand toward Aidan's piercings and tattoo. "You sure look like one."

Gideon inserted an arm between both of them again. "Perhaps you could talk in the office. Some customers look scared."

Russell glanced around. When he saw people gawking or scurrying in the opposite direction, he straightened up and spun around. Acting as if he hadn't been involved in an altercation with the teen, Russell smiled at everyone. "Nothing to worry about, folks."

His reassurance didn't erase the wary glances many customers directed at Aidan. With his furious face and tense body, he appeared about to go ballistic.

Russell sauntered through the milling crowd and gestured toward the stands. "Enjoy your shopping."

Aidan's shouted curse words echoed around the market. Russell kept walking, but he yelled over his shoulder right before he reached the stairs, "If you're not quiet and out of here in five minutes, I'm calling the cops to haul you off for disturbing the peace."

When Aidan opened his mouth to scream a reply, Gideon draped an arm around the teen's shoulder and drew him in the opposite direction. "Don't give him the satisfaction."

Aidan's angry expression crumpled, and his shoulders slumped.

Fern wanted to reach out to him. As a small boy, he'd always loved her bear claws. Not that food could heal the wounds he was dealing with, but maybe a treat would help. And she could show she understood his feelings.

"It's not easy to accept." Gideon walked beside Aidan. "But Russell won't change his mind."

"But he put my old man, my whole family, out of business."

"Your dad will still be working here at the market."

"It's not the same. I was going to take over the candy store."

Fern pulled out the tray of bear claws and waved to get Gideon's attention. He steered Aidan in her direction.

"Somehow, I gotta make him pay." Aidan stopped speaking when he saw the bear claw.

Fern used bakery tissue to hold out the pastry. "I'm sorry about your family's stand."

Aidan patted his pockets, and his lips turned down. "Sorry. I got no money on me." But he eyed the bear claw hungrily.

"It's free. I just wanted to let you know that all of us feel this situation with Russell is unfair." Fern extended her arm closer to him and added a *go-ahead-and-take-it* smile.

Although Aidan hesitated, after he accepted the sweet pastry, he gobbled it down.

From behind him, Gideon's eyes conveyed his thanks. Fern almost drowned in the approval reflected there. She lowered her gaze and shakily inserted the tray in her case, praying her eyes hadn't given her away.

Gideon sighed inwardly. Good thing Fern broke the connection between them. No matter how difficult it was, he had to be careful not to get involved.

Aidan brushed his fingers off on his black jeans with their strategically torn holes. "That was good. Thanks, Fern. Next time I come in, I'll pay you."

Fern waved away his offer. "No need to pay. I don't charge you."

"I ain't a child anymore." Aidan's cheeks brightened. "Can't believe you gave me all those bear claws free when I was little. I owe you."

"No, you don't. I always make extra for the children. And you were always one of my favorites. That hasn't changed."

Gideon's heart thumped faster at the sunny smile Fern gave Aidan. What he wouldn't give to have it shine in his direction.

He gave himself a mental shake. He had no business wanting smiles or anything else from Fern, but that didn't stop him from wishing.

To distract himself, Gideon concentrated on Aidan. He'd devoured that pastry in a few seconds. Maybe the kid was hungry.

"How about some barbecued chicken, Aidan?"

Aidan licked his lips. "I don't have money, man."

"Don't worry about it. Sometimes I don't cut the chickens exactly right and have pieces I can't sell. If you don't mind seconds, you're welcome to those."

The sideways flick of Aidan's eyes showed he didn't believe Gideon. Then Aidan looked from Gideon to Fern. "Why are you guys always so nice? You give to everyone."

Fern's sweet smile made Gideon's stomach flip. "It's what God wants us to do," she said.

"God?" Aidan practically spat out the word. "There's no such thing. If there was a God, He'd never let Russell take away our family's candy business."

"We don't always know why God allows things to happen to us, but He always has a purpose. We just have to trust."

Fern's gentle, soothing words fell like balm on Gideon's heart. If only he could believe it about his brother. Every day when his mind wandered to that day on the roof, he questioned why God had let it happen. He struggled to believe God had a hand in his brother's death. He'd never had these doubts until that horrible day two years ago.

Fern's confidence in her faith almost made him accept even that tragedy as God's will. Was taking care of Nettie and the children also fulfilling God's purpose? And dealing with Thomas's debts? And, worst of all, living with his guilt?

As Gideon and Aidan walked off, Fern worried about the deep sadness in Gideon's eyes when she'd mentioned God's will. He seemed to be carrying a heavy burden. She didn't know him well enough to ask about personal matters, but the fact that he was unmarried made her wonder if he'd lost the woman he'd loved. She understood pining over a lost love.

Fern shook off thoughts of Gideon to wait on customers. Answering each person's questions about the business closing made her usual lines even longer. The lunchtime rush didn't end until two.

By that time, her stomach was growling. She'd forgotten to bring her lunch in from the buggy, and Daed had driven off. She didn't like leaving the stand unattended.

Usually Nick or Mose would keep an eye on her stand if she took a break. But Mose sat staring off into the distance, his eyes so sad and faraway, she hesitated to disturb him. And ever since Aidan had left, Nick had been withdrawn and groused at everyone except the small children who came to buy candy. With them, he was only gruff.

Fern propped a hand-lettered sign against the register and headed for Gideon's stand. Before she got there, she stopped and drew in a sharp breath as a pretty blonde shot him a dreamy smile and exited the stand.

Then her pulse quieted as she recognized Gideon's sister Caroline. The same Caroline who loved Fern's cinnamon buns so much, she bought one almost every market day. For a minute, Fern had mistaken Caroline, with her enraptured smile, for a possible rival for Gideon's heart.

Rival? What was she thinking? *Rival* implied fighting, something she should avoid. Besides, she couldn't be in competition with anyone over Gideon. Not when he'd never shown any interest in her.

She exhaled a slow, aching breath. She'd need to let go of these feelings when she and Gideon worked together. Determined to be businesslike, she headed toward his stand, but the minute his gaze flicked in her direction, her resolve melted.

Gideon's lips curved into a welcoming smile, and she lost her grip on common sense altogether.

He seemed to be concentrating on her rather than on the man giving his order. "Three wings, two thighs, four fries?"

The man stared at him. "You got the numbers right, but I wanted four wings, three thighs, and two fries."

Gideon broke his gaze and jotted on the pad lying on the counter. "Coming right up."

A short while later, he returned and handed the man an insulated bag and a brown paper bag with slight grease stains.

Before he paid, the man opened both bags and counted the contents. "Hope you don't mind, but I want to be sure I got what I requested."

"Everything all right?" Gideon asked.

The man nodded, reached into his pocket, and paid. Then he turned and spotted Fern. "Aha, no wonder you were so distracted." He laughed. "I'd be distracted too, if I were your age and Amish."

Fern's cheeks burned. She wished he hadn't called attention to her. Would the man's remarks make Gideon aware of her interest?

Gideon appeared as flustered as she was and stared at her without speaking for a few moments. Several people lined up behind her moved restlessly.

Gideon cleared his throat. "Your usual?"

Not trusting her voice, Fern nodded.

He slid open the doors to the heated glass case and took out her chicken. She enjoyed sneak peeks at him.

When he brought her food, she focused on the bags rather than him.

Their hands brushed as she took them from him, and her fingers burned from more than the hot chicken. She steadied herself before she gave him the money. This time, she held out her hand for the change, and he avoided touching her as he dropped the coins into her outstretched palm.

She didn't want to leave without saying anything. "How did everything go with Aidan?"

"He was hungry." Gideon's eyes twinkled. "Good thing I had trouble cutting several chickens today."

"That was nice of you."

Gideon waved away the compliment. "You're the one who gave me the idea. I could see how much he liked that pastry."

"I hoped it might get him thinking about something other than Russell."

"It worked. I managed to convince him that fighting Russell wouldn't be a good idea." Gideon glanced off into the distance. "I think his anger will boil up again. I hope he won't do anything foolish."

"I do too." Poor Aidan. To lose the family business had to be hard.

"Right now, he's rebellious, and he's furious at his dad and Russell. Plus, he has friends who get into trouble. He promised me he'd stay away from illegal stuff, but he's impulsive. I'm praying God will protect him."

"He used to be such a quiet, gentle boy."

"He still is, underneath his tough outside."

"Excuse me," a voice behind Fern interrupted. "I'm in a hurry here. I only get fifteen minutes for my break."

"I'm sorry." Her face burning, Fern stepped aside so the woman could reach the counter.

While Fern had been talking to Gideon, she'd completely shut out everything around her. Everything except him.

Without looking in his direction, Fern waved goodbye and scurried off. She couldn't believe she'd taken up so much of Gideon's time and blocked his customers from ordering. And she'd also left her own stand unattended all this time..What was wrong with her that she made such a fool of herself whenever she spent time around Gideon?

Chapter Seven

Yesterday Fern had promised herself she'd act more businesslike around Gideon, but when she entered the market early Saturday morning, he waited by her stand. Her heart leapt, and her mouth went dry. So much for that plan.

Gideon held out a hand-drawn sketch. "This is what our stand will look like. Let me know if you want any changes."

Our? Her heart fluttered like a trapped bird. He'd included her in his business. Too tongue-tied to speak, she reached for the paper, careful not to touch his fingers.

She sucked in a breath. Was the paper warmer where his fingers had touched it? Or was that her imagination?

Fern forced herself to read the labels. The precision and strength of the black block printing fascinated her. The writing matched Gideon's character and personality.

"Will that work?" He waited expectantly for her answer.

"What?" Fern ducked her head so he couldn't see the heat rising in her cheeks. She hadn't even found the spot he'd designated for her baked goods. Sliding her finger over the paper—the paper he'd touched—she pointed to the far end of the rectangular counter. "It looks perfect." Her words came out breathless.

"I'm glad. I hoped you'd like it."

"I do." Not that it mattered, because she wouldn't be working there, but he'd been kind to ask.

Gideon shuffled his feet. "I should check with Nick before we open."

Ach! She still held the plans. "Sorry." She thrust the paper in his direction. "*Danke.*"

With a brisk nod, he took the sketch. "See you."

Before she could form a response, he hurried to Nick's stand. Fern stayed where she was, staring after him. She shook herself. All of her baked goods still had to be unloaded. She had no time to stand here mooning over a man who had no interest in her.

But he'd said *our* as if he considered her part of Hartzler's Chicken Barbecue. He had no idea how much that meant to her. She'd always dreamed . . .

Nick caught her staring after Gideon and smirked. Fern busied herself with arranging the pastries and didn't even glance in Gideon's direction once, despite an internal battle. She was counting change into her register drawer when a girl approached the counter.

"Are you ready to open?"

Fern smiled at the customer who always bought a cinnamon roll right before they opened. Caroline, Gideon's sister. Fern wished she hadn't been reminded of Gideon so soon after Nick's knowing look.

"I'm almost done here." Fern cracked open a roll of pennies and counted them. She added up the amounts on her tablet and jotted the total in her book. "Now what would you like?" she joked as she reached for a cinnamon roll.

"Could I have two?"

Fern stopped. "Two?" Would she give one to her brother? The thought of Gideon enjoying one of her cinnamon rolls thrilled Fern.

Caroline's cheeks flushed. "I'm getting an extra one to share with someone special."

The way she said the last two words made it clear she wouldn't be giving this roll to her brother.

Caroline must have thought Fern's raised eyebrows implied she was questioning her, because her tone turned defensive. "Zach has to come in really early on auction days, so sometimes he skips breakfast."

She must mean Zach, one of the auctioneers. "That's kind of you." Although she shouldn't tease, Fern couldn't help asking, "Are his brothers hungry too?"

Caroline jerked back a bit. "I—I don't know. I never asked. I mean . . ." Her already pink face deepened in color until she almost matched the cherries decorating Fern's fruit tarts.

"It's all right." Fern hadn't meant to embarrass Caroline. "Two cinnamon rolls coming up."

"Could I, um, have them in separate bags?" Caroline's voice came out hesitant and uncertain.

Fern kept her curiosity under control and did as Caroline had asked. She made change and handed over both bags. But she couldn't help wondering why Caroline wouldn't eat hers with her boyfriend. Maybe she was just shy.

As Caroline walked off, Gideon's word echoed in Fern's mind. *Our.* How foolish she'd been. He hadn't been including her in the business. His *our* referred to him and his sister. Her fragile daydreams shattered.

* * *

"Here, Gideon." Caroline thrust the white bag in his direction. She held a matching bag in her other hand. As soon as he took the bag, Caroline whirled around and headed off.

"Wait," he called after her.

"I don't have time." She lifted the bag in the air. "I have to deliver this while it's hot."

"Come right back," he yelled at her departing back, but the door swung closed behind her.

Gideon sighed. He had no idea if she'd even heard him. For the past few months, he'd been on his own in the mid-mornings, when he most needed help. He needed to talk to her, but lately she'd been so preoccupied that she barely acknowledged conversations around her.

Not that he had any room to criticize. He kept his hands busy, but he had little control of his thoughts, which immediately drifted to Fern. That is, when he wasn't worrying about expenses or squirming with guilt.

After the late-morning rush began, he had no time to think of her. Instead, the only female on his mind was Caroline.

As the clock inched toward noon, Gideon kept waiting for his sister to appear. By twelve thirty, his concern grew. It wasn't like her to be late. She always helped to serve the lunchtime crowds.

He kept an eye on the doors that led to the auction building across the parking lot. Suddenly, they banged open, and Aidan stumbled in. He staggered toward Gideon's stand with a fistful of dollars.

"Just a minute," Gideon said to the woman he was waiting on.

He rushed from the stand and grabbed Aidan's arm

before the teen toppled into a small pyramid of apples at a nearby produce counter. Aidan must be either high or drunk. Gideon propelled him to his stand and set him on a stool.

"I came to pay you, man," Aidan slurred. He waved the money at Gideon.

"Later. I have all these customers to wait on." And no Caroline to help.

"I can do that." Aidan tried to stand and almost pitched forward onto his face.

"Stay there until you get your balance." Gideon had enough to worry about without Aidan sprawled out on the floor. Gideon raced from one customer to the next.

"One whole chicken and three orders of fries."

Gideon dropped a chicken into a bag, then headed for the fries. *Ach!* Caroline usually handled the fries. He scooped out two containers, but he didn't have enough for three.

He rushed back with the man's order. "I'm afraid I don't have enough fries for three orders. It'll be about five minutes until they're ready."

With an exasperated look, the man made a show of glancing at his watch. "I can't wait that long. Besides, the other fries will get cold." He exhaled a put-upon sigh. "Seems like you'd do a better job of keeping up with your orders."

Gideon wouldn't blame Caroline. He should have paid closer attention to the fryer. "I'm sorry. I'll give you a discount on the chicken to make up for it."

After he settled the bill, he apologized to the next person in line. "I'll be right back." He headed for the fryer, but Aidan was supporting himself against the metal towel railing with one hand and lowering the fryer basket with the other.

Gideon's heart practically stopped. "What are you doing?"

"I worked at Fast Fries and Burgers a few years ago. I know how to make fries."

How did Gideon tell Aidan he didn't want him near hot oil? "It's dangerous, especially when—"

Aidan cut him off. "I can do it. I used to go into work like this all the time."

"That isn't safe."

"Go wait on the customers, man. I'll be fine."

Gideon wasn't so sure about that. But other than shoving Aidan out of the way, he had little choice.

Several minutes later, Aidan drained perfectly cooked fries, dumped them in the warmer, and salted them. Although he remained unsteady on his feet, he even scooped them into containers.

Just as the lunch rush was settling down, Caroline breezed in the back doors, her eyes and face apologetic. "I'm so sorry. I lost track of time."

Gideon swallowed his irritation. "We've been swamped with customers."

His sister hung her head and rounded the corner. She stopped short when she spotted Aidan at the fryer.

"Who's that?" she hissed. "Did you replace me?"

"I needed help, and he showed up at the right time." Gideon kept his voice low to say that, but then he raised it on purpose. "Aidan's been a big help."

Aidan's head jerked up. "Aww . . . I didn't do much. Just kept up with the fries."

"That was a major job today. I couldn't have done it without you."

Gideon hadn't meant to jab his sister, but Caroline pressed her lips together.

"I really am sorry, Gideon."

"I believe you."

His sister had a soft heart, and she'd always been helpful. Until she met Zach. Ever since then, she'd been acting forgetful and dreamy. Although Gideon had to admit he understood exactly how distracting it could be to fall in love.

Wait a minute. Where had that thought come from?

Caroline may have fallen in love, but he certainly hadn't.

As the lunch crowd dwindled, Fern had a hankering for barbecued chicken. She always packed her lunch to save money to send to Aaron, but the memory of eating at Hartzler's yesterday made her mouth water. Or was it more than chicken she had a hankering for?

Fern brushed aside that thought. For all she knew, Caroline would wait on her today. That didn't mean Fern couldn't catch a glimpse of Gideon. Leaving her lunch bag under the counter, Fern headed down the aisle for the barbecue stand.

When she neared, Caroline waited outside the stand, looking upset. Fern hoped nothing had happened to Gideon.

"Is everything all right?" she asked.

Caroline whirled and pressed her hands against her heart. "*Ach*, you scared me."

"I didn't mean to." Behind Caroline, Gideon stepped closer, and Fern's breath hitched. He wasn't hurt. In fact, he looked fine—in more ways than one. She made herself concentrate on Caroline. "Are you all right?"

Caroline's brows drew together. "I'm gone for part of the morning, and my brother replaces me."

"No, I didn't." Gideon's response echoed around them. His deep bass voice gave Fern the shivers—in a good way. He seemed to be including her in their family squabble.

"What happened?" Had Gideon really hired someone else?

Although Fern had directed her question to Gideon, Caroline answered, "Gideon has someone else working in the stand."

"Aidan helped out during our busiest time."

Fern sighed inside. He'd used the word *our* again. He definitely meant his family's business.

"I was late," Caroline admitted. "I didn't keep an eye on the time."

Fern tried to understand what had Caroline so upset. "Aidan's taking your place permanently?"

Caroline said *jah* at the same time as Gideon replied *neh*.

Fern looked from one to the other. One of them seemed to be mistaken, and Fern guessed it was Caroline.

"Unless you don't want to work here," Gideon added, studying his sister.

"Of course I do." Her words sounded a bit shaky.

"Then why don't you go and wait on that customer?" He pointed his chin at the lady with two small children approaching the counter, and Caroline scurried off.

"Is Aidan really working here?" Fern asked.

"*Jah*, for today." Gideon shifted to one side, revealing Aidan propped up near the fryer.

Aidan looked pretty wobbly, and Fern gasped. "Is he all right?" She didn't want to question Gideon's judgment, but should Aidan be so close to hot grease?

Gideon moved nearer and leaned toward her, making it even harder for her to breathe. Could he hear the rapid pattering of her heart?

* * *

Gideon clenched his fists and stuffed them in his pockets. Getting close enough to whisper had been a mistake. He swallowed hard and only managed to mouth the words, *I think he's high or drunk. I didn't want to let him drive like that.*

"I could take him home." Fern spoke so softly he could hardly hear her.

"*Neh*, that's not safe." She shouldn't be alone with anyone under the influence. Although Aidan had handled the French fries, Gideon didn't trust the teen with Fern. Or with his sister, for that matter.

A quick glance over his shoulder reassured him Aidan remained focused on cooking fries and hadn't noticed Caroline. Then Gideon turned back to Fern, who looked about ready to protest.

He backed up a few steps. "If he falls, how will you pick him up?"

Fern was petite and barely reached Aidan's shoulders. Considering her dainty and delicate figure had been unwise. So had looking into her eyes.

Gideon struggled to get his thoughts under control. *Focus on Aidan, not Fern.* He turned and gestured toward Aidan. "As you can see, he's very unsteady."

Caroline reached past Aidan for some fries, and he jerked backward.

"Whoa, gorgeous, where'd you come from?" He grabbed for the metal ledge surrounding the fryer and missed. He flailed his arms in Caroline's direction. Eyes wide, she jumped back.

Gideon dashed toward them and grabbed Aidan around

the waist before he toppled into Caroline. After hauling Aidan upright, Gideon guided him to the chair.

"Sit there for a minute until you're steady," he ordered, gripping Aidan's shoulders to steady him.

"Nothing wrong with my balance," Aidan muttered. "She surprised me." His mouth curled into an appreciative smile. "Not that I minded."

"She's my sister." Gideon's sharp tone made it clear Caroline was off-limits.

"Aww . . . Ya can't bother guys' sisters." A long, martyred sigh escaped Aidan's pursed lips.

"Exactly." Gideon added a stern look to reinforce the clipped word.

He let go of Aidan's shoulders and straightened to find Fern still in the stand entrance, staring at him, her cheeks flushed.

"I wanted to be sure he's all right." Fern ducked her head and scurried around the counter to order.

Gideon rushed over to prepare her order. He wanted to do it himself. And he'd have it ready for her now, even though she was behind five other customers. He waited impatiently while Caroline served the others and helped out when he could, but he practically elbowed his sister away from the counter when Fern stepped up.

"The usual?" He lifted the bags he'd kept in the warmer.

Fern's delighted smile flipped his stomach upside down. Gideon froze, still holding the bags in the air. Caroline's raised eyebrows and curious look broke the spell.

"Here." He thrust the bags toward Fern.

At her soft *danke*, he swallowed hard. "You're welcome." Was he grinning like a fool?

She held out her money. Gideon longed to brush her fingers with his, but he took the bills gingerly to avoid any contact. He had enough trouble keeping his thumping heartbeat under control.

After he dropped the change into her outstretched palm, he stayed mesmerized as she walked off until Caroline nudged him.

"Are you going to wait on customers?" A teasing smile played around her lips. "Or do you only have time—and eyes—for one special customer?"

"She's not special." He focused on the next person in line. "What can I get you?"

But Caroline's "Really?" echoed around him.

She's not, he wanted to insist, but he couldn't utter those words, because they'd be a lie.

Chapter Eight

Caroline's voice carried, and Fern's face burned. Just because Gideon knew her usual order and had it ready for her didn't mean he was interested in her. But Caroline had called attention to Fern's longing.

Had Gideon realized her feelings for him? His gruff answer stabbed her through the heart.

She's not special echoed through her mind as she hurried to her stand. She'd already known that truth, but to hear the words from his mouth had been painful.

Blinking back tears, she slipped into her stand. Several customers stood waiting.

"I'm so sorry." Fern picked up the sign she'd propped by the cash register, promising she'd return by two fifteen. She'd spent so much time watching the interaction between Gideon and Aidan, she'd stayed almost twenty minutes longer.

One of the women who'd been waiting stepped closer to the counter. "I'd like—" She stopped and peered closely at Fern. "Is everything all right?"

"I-I'm fine." Fern's shaky voice revealed her fib.

"If you're sure." The woman didn't look convinced, but she gave her order.

Fern handed over the coconut cupcakes and collected the payment. She moved by rote to fill bags and bakery boxes for her other afternoon customers, but her mind kept returning to Gideon.

She admired how he'd handled Aidan. Gideon had been so considerate and caring. He had a kind heart. Look how generous he'd been about sharing his stand. That made his remark about her even more cruel.

If Nick had said it, Fern would have brushed it off, because Nick grumbled and complained about everyone. Until today, she'd never heard Gideon criticize anyone or make unkind remarks. For him to snap back at his sister like that, he must have been extremely provoked.

Esther Groff reached out and patted Fern's arm when she handed her a bakery bag. "Whatever's making you so upset, God is in control."

Fern couldn't believe she'd been so obvious. "You're right." She needed to turn this over to God, but how did she release her attraction to Gideon?

Customers trickled off as closing time drew near. Caroline stared at the exit, and Gideon sighed. Whenever the door opened and closed, his sister paid less attention to the orders and focused more on the auction building outside.

He understood the longing. Luckily, Fern worked at the opposite end of the market, and the huge stairway to the second-floor shops blocked his view. But if Caroline's yearning matched his, he couldn't deny her the chance to spend time with her crush.

As Caroline repeated a customer's order twice without taking her eyes off the open door, Gideon nudged her aside. "I'll take care of this. Why don't you take off now?"

Her mouth open in surprise, she studied him. "But the cleanup?"

"Go on," Gideon urged. "Aidan can help."

Caroline's eyes narrowed. "You said he wasn't taking my place."

"He's not." Gideon flicked his eyes in the customer's direction. "We'll talk later." Ignoring his sister's squawk of protest, he hurried over to fill the customer's order.

By the time he returned to the counter, Caroline had scurried out the door. Gideon had no idea how much help Aidan might be, but his sister would be even less if she didn't keep her mind on the job.

"You wouldn't mind helping with the cleanup, would you?" Gideon asked as he passed a bleary-eyed Aidan.

"I know how to clean. Night-shift workers had to do that at Fast Fries and Burgers."

"Good." Gideon took another order. "That'll be a big help."

"Your sister don't seem to pay much attention to working."

"She used to, but she has other interests now." Gideon handed two hot bags with whole chickens to the customer and made change.

Behind him, Aidan let out a snarky chuckle. "Yeah, I can tell. She's really hot for some dude outside in the auction, huh?"

Gideon wouldn't have phrased it like that, but Aidan was right. "Seems so." He squirmed a bit inside. He shouldn't be talking about his sister like this.

Holding on to a counter edge, Aidan pulled himself up. "What do you need me to do?"

To Gideon's surprise, Aidan proved to be a competent worker, although a bit unsteady on his feet. He wiped counters and mopped the floor while Gideon waited on the last few customers and then cleaned the equipment and stored the food.

Gideon debated about offering to pay Aidan for his work today but worried he might use the money for drugs or alcohol. The kid looked half-starved, so giving him something to eat might be better.

"Want some more chicken?" Gideon waved toward the pieces piled in the warmer. He'd made a little extra to feed the workers installing the refrigerated display cases tonight, and Aidan certainly deserved some for all his assistance. "Help yourself to some fries and soda."

"Sounds good. Thanks, man." Aidan pulled crumpled dollars from his pocket. "I forgot to pay you earlier."

"*Neh*, you don't owe me anything. Not after all the work you did."

"You sure?"

"Positive." Gideon owed him more than two meals.

"You ever need help around here, call me anytime."

"I might do that." Once the stand expanded, he'd need more people to wait on customers.

"Really?"

"Sure. You did a great job today."

Aidan sat up straighter. "Ya think?"

The eagerness in Aidan's eyes revealed how much he needed reassurance. "I couldn't have done it without you. You really came to the rescue with the French fries."

"I guess." Aidan swallowed hard. "I'm not always a—"

He clapped a hand over his mouth. "Better not say what my dad calls me."

"Neh, you're not." Whatever Nick called him was sure to be negative. "You're smart, helpful, and—"

His face flushed, Aidan stood abruptly. "I gotta run to the can."

As he wobbled off, Gideon prayed he didn't intend to take more drugs. If Caroline were still here, he'd follow Aidan to be sure.

Soon after Aidan left, the remaining Saturday afternoon shoppers dispersed, and Russell locked all the doors except the employee entrance. Then the market owner, a scowl on his face, headed to Gideon's stall.

Russell handed over the key. "You'd better not lose this. And keep your eye on all your workers. Nobody better be wandering around anywhere in this market."

"I'll watch everyone." Gideon planned to stay and help the workers when they installed the new counters. He doubted they'd have any time—or desire—to get into trouble. What mischief could they get into anyway?

"See that you do."

Gideon headed around his counter. "I'll go outside to let the men in. After they finish for the night, I'll lock up after them." He followed Russell to the door and locked it behind them.

When Gideon stood in the parking lot to wait, a worried look crossed Russell's face. "Don't make me regret this," he snarled.

"I won't," Gideon assured him. What would it be like to be so distrustful of others?

As Russell zoomed out of the parking lot, someone pounded on the side door. Gideon rounded the building. The banging came from inside.

"Hey, let me out!"

Ach! Russell had gotten Gideon so flustered, he'd forgotten about Aidan.

"I'm coming," Gideon called. He hurried back to the employee entrance and unlocked the door. "Sorry, Aidan."

"Man, I thought Russell locked me in." Aidan appeared slightly more sober. "At least I'd have a few things to eat." He patted the cell phone in his pocket. "And my homies woulda busted me out."

Gideon blew out a breath. Thank heavens, Russell was gone. He'd have exploded if he'd discovered Aidan here.

Aidan glanced around at the empty building. "Where's Russell?"

"He left a few minutes ago." And Aidan should have too. But Gideon still worried about letting Aidan drive. When Fern had asked earlier, Gideon should have let her take Aidan home. *Neh*, he'd never want to put her in danger.

"So what's going down?" Aidan stared at Gideon with a puzzled expression.

"I'm expanding my stand, and the men are installing some of the new counters today. Can you hang around until they're done?"

"Well . . ."

"I'll feed you dinner and drive you home. All you have to do is stick around my stand." Gideon didn't want Aidan snitching food from other stands.

"You don't trust me?" Aidan gazed at Gideon with hurt puppy-dog eyes.

"It's not that. I promised Russell—"

"To keep an eye on me?" Aidan spat out.

"Not you. Russell has no idea you're here. No one's allowed to wander around the market after hours." Gideon beckoned Aidan to come with him. "Speaking of that, I need to let the workers in." He hoped they hadn't been sitting outside long.

"Sure, I'll stay. I don't have nothing to do until later tonight." Aidan followed Gideon to the employee entrance. "So Russell didn't know I'm here, huh?"

Aidan's devilish chuckle gave Gideon shivers. He turned and gave the teen a warning frown. "No trouble."

Once again, Aidan looked wounded. And totally innocent.

Was that an act? Or did people misjudge Aidan because of his appearance and tough-guy attitude?

Gideon decided to give Aidan the benefit of the doubt. "I trust you."

"You do?" Aidan examined Gideon's face as if expecting to discover a lie.

But deep inside, Gideon believed those words. Aidan might be lost and wild, but he had a good heart. "I don't say anything I don't mean."

Except when it came to Fern. He'd told Caroline a terrible lie today.

Aidan whipped his head around but not quickly enough to hide a glimmer of tears.

Had Gideon made a breakthrough?

Rapping on the door interrupted them, and Gideon opened the door for the workers. For the rest of the evening, Aidan helped by carting in tools, holding wires, and handing out chicken and fries. As the drugs or alcohol wore off, though, he grew jittery.

Concern about Aidan led Gideon to stop the workers a little earlier than planned. "You can come back on Monday. The market's closed all day."

He and Aidan helped pack up tools and carry things to the truck. Then Gideon returned to the building to turn out the lights and lock up.

"Ready to go?" he asked.

Aidan's eyes registered shock when Gideon led him to the small barn where he kept his horse. At least Caroline had fed and watered the horse. He assumed Zach had driven her home.

Aidan gasped when he spied the buggy. "You expect me to ride in that? My friends'll—"

Gideon cut him off. "Think you're special?"

Aidan gulped. "Yeah, right."

But after watching Gideon hitch up the horse, Aidan climbed in and stared around. "Kinda weird to sit on the left. Feels like I should be driving." His eyes twinkled. "I can help out if you want."

With a smile, Gideon clicked to his horse. "Not today, but thanks."

When they reached Aidan's place, he turned to Gideon, his eyes serious. "I meant it when I said I'd help you if you needed it. I'll even do it for free." He laughed. "Well, maybe for some chicken."

"Sounds good to me."

"See you Tuesday, then," Aidan said as he climbed out.

Tuesday? Gideon had meant sometime in the future, when he had a larger stand. He should explain. But at Aidan's eager face, the words dried up in his throat. The teen looked as if Gideon had thrown him a lifeline. How could he tell Aidan not to come?

He couldn't.

He'd added another person to his list of responsibilities. Helping Aidan would be a huge one.

As the teenager slouched up the walk to his front door, Gideon sat motionless. What had he gotten himself into now? Would he end up regretting it?

Chapter Nine

As Fern steered her full cart to the market door on Tuesday morning, heavy boots pounded the asphalt behind her.

"I can get that." A teen sprinted past her and yanked at the door.

She stopped so suddenly her boxes wavered. He reached out to help her steady them.

"Aidan?" Fern almost didn't recognize him.

Instead of scruffy clothes, he had on jeans without holes. He looked as though he'd cleaned up, although he still had stubble on his jaw. And his T-shirt had a psychedelic pattern featuring a group of monsters—or were they humans?—with their mouths open in screams.

"Need help, Fern?"

Still in shock, she managed to shake her head. "I'm all right. Just surprised to see you here so early." Nick constantly complained that Aidan stayed out most of the night and slept until noon.

"Yeah, it wasn't easy." Aidan's rueful smile indicated he'd had a rough time getting up. "I didn't want to be late for my first day on the job."

"You're working here?"

Hurt flashed in Aidan's eyes. "Don't sound so shocked."

"I didn't mean . . . That is, I thought you and your dad, well . . ."

The mean, sarcastic laugh that spilled from Aidan's mouth didn't bode well for him and his father.

"You thought I'd be working for my dad?" His last word ended in a screech. "I'd never work for him. Not in a million years."

"But then who are you working for?"

"Hartzler's Chicken Barbecue, of course."

"You're working with Gideon?" she asked faintly.

"I helped out on Saturday."

"*Jah*, you did." She refrained from pointing out he hadn't been in the best shape for assisting anyone. He'd barely been able to stand without swaying.

What had Gideon been thinking? Aidan was a hazard. Or at least he had been. What had prompted Gideon to offer Aidan a job?

Maybe it would work. Aidan had risen early and gotten cleaned up. Those changes were significant.

"You don't think it's a good idea, do you?"

"Of course it is." At least for Aidan. But what about Gideon?

To avoid more questions, Fern pushed her cart inside. "Want a bear claw before work?"

"Yeah, sure." Aidan followed her to the stand. When she handed him the pastry, he held out some bills.

Fern waved it away. "You don't have to pay me. Like I said before, I always make extras."

"For the kids." Aidan straightened. "I'm not a kid anymore."

Fern smiled at him. "I know. But I also give free treats to special friends."

Aidan's cheeks turned pink, and he ducked his head. "Thanks." He sounded as if he had a frog in his throat. "I'd better go." He hurried off.

Lucky Aidan. He'd be around Gideon all day long.

Caroline had just left to get Gideon's daily cinnamon roll when Aidan strolled over to the counter. Gideon hadn't really expected the teen to show up. How would he explain this to his sister when she got back?

Aidan stopped and crossed his arms. "You don't look too happy to see me." Despite his defiant posture, his eyes revealed his vulnerability.

Gideon couldn't turn Aidan away. Pasting on a welcoming expression, Gideon motioned toward the food prep counter. "I can use help getting chickens into the rotisserie."

He demonstrated the procedure, which Aidan picked up quickly. Once they'd done the first row, Gideon kept glancing nervously toward the aisle. He needed to catch Caroline and explain. He wanted to avoid hurt feelings for both Caroline and Aidan—or, worse yet, an explosion.

Aidan looked up from the chickens he was brushing with barbecue sauce. "Something wrong?"

"Umm, I need to talk to my sister."

Suspicion flared in Aidan's eyes. "About me?"

"That and other things." Like asking Caroline not to say anything to make Aidan feel unwanted. "Think you can handle the chickens while I find her?"

"Of course." Aidan ducked his head but not fast enough to hide his pleased smile. "You sure you trust me?"

"Anyone who handled the French fries the way you did can certainly manage a few chickens."

This time Aidan didn't bother to conceal his pride. He

threw back his shoulders and beamed. "Take your time. I'll get it done."

"Great." Gideon took off at a rapid clip. Caroline was threading her way through a chattering group of older women who were blocking the aisle. He held up a hand to slow her down.

She skidded to a stop, then eased around the ladies. "What are you doing here?"

"I need to talk to you."

Her eyebrows arched. "And you left the stand unattended?"

"Not exactly."

"What does that mean?"

Best to get it over with. "Aidan showed up expecting to work. He misunderstood a comment I made on Saturday."

Caroline narrowed her eyes. "A comment about me being undependable?"

"*Neh*, nothing like that."

"You told him you wanted to replace me?"

Gideon shook his head. "I don't want to replace you. And certainly not with Aidan."

"Then why don't you tell him that? Nicely, of course."

"I can't. He seems to need help. Maybe working with us can keep him out of trouble."

Caroline's face softened. "Then I guess he should stay. But we shouldn't leave him in the stand alone." She hurried off.

When Gideon reached the stand, Caroline started to hand him a bag. "I'm sorry I didn't know Aidan would be here. I could go back to Fern's for another roll."

"Actually, he prefers bear claws." At her surprised look, Gideon shrugged. "That's what Fern said."

"Fern?" The inflection in Caroline's voice hinted at her curiosity.

Gideon refused to give her any satisfaction. He pretended to be indifferent to Fern's name, but it took a lot of willpower. Gideon indicated the bag his sister held. "I can't eat that in front of Aidan. Why don't you take it to share with Zach?"

After Caroline left, he'd slip down to Fern's stand for a bear claw. That would more than make up for missing his morning treat.

Caroline grinned. "I have a better idea." She handed him the other bag she held. "This one has two. Give the extra one to Aidan."

His sister must have planned to eat that roll. If she gave it up for Aidan, she must not resent him working there. Gideon relaxed. And, thanks to Caroline's generosity, he could enjoy his roll.

He tamped down his disappointment. It also meant he didn't have to buy a bear claw from Fern.

When the after-lunch lull began, Fern forced herself to open her small lunch cooler. One peek at the contents, which had seemed so appetizing that morning, made her long for a hot meal. Crisp chicken skin, juicy meat, and more tempted her. Plus, she wondered how Aidan was handling the work.

It wouldn't hurt to mosey by and check. She tucked a few bills into her pocket. Not that she needed that money. She had no intention of stopping to buy chicken. None at all.

So why, a few minutes later, was she standing in line, staring hungrily at Gideon?

Tongue-tied when she reached the counter, she only nodded when Gideon asked, "Your usual?"

While he filled her order, she berated herself for her foolishness. She'd only planned to stroll past the stand to check on Aidan. Now she struggled to keep her mind on that. She rehearsed her question internally several times— just to prevent herself from forgetting her intention when Gideon returned.

Before he even handed over her bag, she blurted out, "How's Aidan doing?"

Gideon hesitated and glanced over his shoulder. "Real well. He's been a big help already."

"That's good." Not able to think of anything else to say, she stepped aside so the man behind her could order. Reluctant to leave, she stayed while Gideon waited on the customer until Caroline pinned her with a knowing smile. Fern turned and hurried off.

Why had she made her interest so obvious? Especially after Caroline had teased Gideon the last time? And even more so, knowing how Gideon had responded.

Her cheeks still burning, Fern ducked into her stand and tucked the chicken behind the counter to wait on customers, trying to forget her shame.

Nick spied the bag. "Going to Hartzler's again? You're making that a regular habit," he called over.

Fern pretended not to hear him and concentrated on filling a box with the two dozen chocolate chip cookies a customer had requested. *Twenty-one, twenty-two* . . .

"You sweet on that Hartzler boy?" Nick's booming voice had people glancing from him to Fern with curious eyes.

Could her face get any hotter? Not only had all the customers heard, but so had many stand owners. And what if

Nick's question had carried to Gideon's stand? Or if someone repeated it to Gideon? Or to his sister?

Fern stared down at the cookie in her hand. She'd lost count. Was this twenty-two or twenty-three? Rather than counting again, she added four more cookies.

"Hey, Fern, you ignoring me? What's with this sudden interest in Hartzler's?" Nick waggled his eyebrows in a suggestive manner.

She had to stop him before market gossip reached Gideon, but what could she say? Clearing her throat, she called across the aisle, "I had a business question." Asking about Aidan counted as business, didn't it?

"Business?" Nick's tone took on a sharp edge, and he narrowed his eyes. "You trying to take over my space in that stand?"

Fern sighed. She couldn't win with Nick. "I was wondering about your son."

"My son?" Nick's face paled. "What about him? Is he in trouble again?"

"No, he's not." Fern motioned toward her line of customers with her chin. "Why don't we talk later?" Much later.

A mother with four children approached Nick's stand and distracted him. Perhaps if Fern were lucky, Nick would forget all about it.

But it sounded as if he didn't know Aidan was working in the market today. How sad that their relationship was so fractured. Fern wished she could do something to help them heal it.

God could work miracles in situations like this, but Nick had made it clear he wanted nothing to do with God. Fern did the only thing she could think of to help. She prayed the two could forgive each other and be reunited.

Nick eyed her during the last-minute flurry of crowds before the market closed. As soon as Russell shooed the final few customers out the door and locked up after them, Nick strode over to Fern's stand.

"What's my son done this time?" he demanded. "Although if he and his gang beat up Russell, I'd cheer him on." He raised his voice so Russell, who was passing by, could hear.

"If your juvie kid so much as steps a foot in this market again," Russell snapped, "I'm calling the cops to have him arrested."

Nick spun around. "Oh, yeah? Well, let me tell you something—"

Fern put a hand on Nick's arm. "Just ignore him," she whispered, but he shook off her hand and charged toward Russell. As much as Fern wanted to stop him, she couldn't step between the men, who were standing almost toe-to-toe. Right now, she needed to warn Gideon and Aidan before Russell reached that part of the market.

Gideon had begun showing Aidan how to clean the rotisserie when Fern dashed toward the counter. Her chest rose and fell in rapid breaths.

He handed Aidan the bottle of degreaser. "Is everything all right?"

She inhaled deeply, and then her words rushed out. "Russell's threatening to have Aidan arrested."

That didn't make sense. Aidan had been here all day. "For what?"

"For being in the market."

"I got a right to be here," Aidan growled. "He ain't got no business throwing me out of a public place."

"He's arguing with your dad." Fern turned a pleading gaze to Gideon.

His heart picked up its beat. Unsure if he was responding to her concerns or her presence, he pushed aside his reaction. He fought to keep his tone soothing and neutral. "Aidan's been working hard all day. I can tell him that."

"I don't think Russell will listen to reason." Worry edged her soft words.

Russell could be as hot-tempered as Nick, and if Russell had been provoked, he'd never listen.

Aidan dropped his cleaning supplies and balled up his fists. "Russell better not mess with me. He wants to tangle, I'll give him what he's asking for."

Fern shot a troubled look in his direction. "I don't think . . ."

Caroline, who'd been washing warmer pans at the sink at the other end of the stand, shut off the water. "This isn't only about you," she said to Aidan.

"Sorry," Aidan mumbled. "I don't want to get you in trouble, man."

Gideon understood Fern's sense of urgency. "Listen, why don't you go now? I'll smooth things over with Russell." He hoped Aidan would agree to sidestep the macho attitude.

Aidan puffed up his chest as if to protest, but then he glanced from Fern to Gideon. "I'll do it for you." His thundercloud expression showed he'd rather confront Russell.

"I appreciate it." Stepping aside so Aidan could pass, Gideon pointed to the back wall. "Russell locks those doors last."

Aidan hightailed it to the exit.

Gideon smiled. For all of Aidan's bravado, he seemed

eager to escape. At least he had an alibi for running away from a fight. He could claim he did it for Gideon's sake.

Fern released a soft sigh. "I'm glad he decided to go. After fighting with Nick, Russell will be in a foul mood. I hope Aidan's gone before Russell heads this way."

"I'd better slow him down, just in case." Gideon started in her direction.

She moved to one side so he didn't need to brush past her. He schooled his face not to show his disappointment. But then she fell in step with him as he headed down the market aisle, close enough that he could reach out and take her hand.

Where did that thought come from? He thrust his hands into his pants pockets.

"I hope they haven't come to blows." Fern's voice trembled a little. "Nick's really angry."

"I know." They'd all witnessed Nick's confrontation with Russell when he announced the rent increase. Gideon could only imagine how that had festered. Venom spewed from Nick's lips at any mention of Russell's name.

"And Nick has no idea Aidan's working for you."

"He didn't tell his father?"

"I guess not."

Gideon shook his head. "Hard to believe. They must really be at odds."

"I can't imagine a father not knowing what his son is doing."

"I can." The words popped out before Gideon could stop them. They were torn from the depth of his pain. Daed had never known the truth about Thomas.

Fern stared at him, a question in her eyes. He wished

he'd kept his mouth shut. "Teenagers can be rebellious and secretive."

"You're right." She bit her lip. "My brother Aaron was before he went on a mission trip. That brought him back to the faith."

Although the ending she'd mentioned was a happy one, her eyes held a deep sadness. Gideon started to ask why, but shouting interrupted him. "I'll see if I can help." He sprinted off.

Fern followed close behind.

"Hey, Russell," Gideon called, "some customers are coming in the side doors." He hadn't made it up. Two people had just entered.

Russell stopped mid-scream. "Don't think you've won," he warned Nick before striding down the aisle.

"You haven't heard the last of my complaints," Nick yelled after him.

"No, we never do. You've been complaining from the day you were born."

"Leave my mother out of this."

"Nick," Gideon cut in, "I think that lady wants some candy."

"We're closed." Nick's sullen voice carried, and the woman changed directions. With a contrite expression, Nick hurried after her. "I'm sorry. If you'd like candy, I'm happy to help."

Gideon marveled at Nick's rapid change. Like a chameleon, he'd shed his fighting skin and donned his salesman manner.

Fern stared up at Gideon with shining eyes. "You did a great job distracting Russell and Nick."

Too bad he couldn't distract himself. Gideon stayed

cool on the outside as he deflected her compliment, but inside he was a hot mess. Nick wasn't the only chameleon.

"Should we ask Russell about Aidan?" Fern pressed her fingers against her lips. Why had she said *we*?

"Huh?"

Gideon appeared lost in thought. Maybe he hadn't heard her.

She rephrased her question. "Would this be a good time for you to talk to Russell?"

Instead of looking at her, Gideon stared at Russell as he chained and padlocked the double doors. "Is there ever a good time to talk to him?"

"He has to know about Aidan if you plan to keep letting him work at the stand."

"Right." Gideon shook his head as if tossing off bothersome thoughts. "I guess I'd better do it now."

Russell tested the locks twice before strutting across to the doors on the opposite side. Gideon started toward him. "Russell?" he called.

Unsure whether to accompany Gideon, Fern stayed still. It really wasn't her business. And Gideon had been so disinterested in her that he hadn't even faced her when she talked to him.

He'd gone only a few steps before he turned. "Coming?"

Fern's heart leapt, even though he hadn't looked directly at her. "I guess." In trying to act nonchalant, her words came out uncaring.

For a fleeting moment, Gideon looked wounded. "You don't have to. I know you have to pack up."

Why had she said anything? She should have kept quiet

and joined him. "It's all right. I want to support Aidan." *And you.*

Gideon's *Of course* sounded flat.

She must have hurt him. She didn't trust herself to say she was concerned about him too. He might read more into that than she'd like. Or, worse, he might realize her true feelings.

Catching up with him, she said, "I'm so glad you're giving Aidan a chance. Having a steady job and a good example—" Heat crept from Fern's neck to her face. Every time she spoke, she hit a new pitfall.

"I'm glad you think so." Gideon's dry laugh sounded as if he didn't believe he'd be a positive influence.

"I do," she insisted.

They'd reached Russell, so Gideon didn't answer.

An impatient look on his face, Russell stood waiting. "I need to get these doors locked. Can't this wait?"

"Why don't we walk with you while we talk?"

Fern admired how skillfully Gideon changed the tone of the conversation. Without a word, they fell into step with Russell as he headed toward the side doors.

While Russell turned the bolts and threaded the chains, Gideon cleared his throat. "I'm planning to hire a new employee."

"What's that got to do with me?" Russell growled. "It's your stand. Hire whoever you want." He clicked the padlock in place. "As long as it's not a criminal."

"I'm pretty sure he's not a criminal, but I can check to be sure."

Russell snickered. "You'd run a background check on a market employee?"

"I hadn't been planning to, but—"

After a quick yank on the lock to be sure it was secure, Russell dropped it into place with a clank.

Fern jumped at the sudden clatter, but Gideon squared his shoulders. Her pulse fluttered.

"I'm hiring Aidan Gr—"

"That juvie?" Russell screeched.

"He's not a juvie," Fern protested, and Gideon shot her an appreciative look that made her quiver.

"You can tell by looking at him that he is."

"I don't think you can tell criminals by their clothing," Gideon said, his tone mild. "Aidan said he's never been arrested."

"You trust that hoodlum to tell the truth?"

"I do." The strength of Gideon's conviction came through in his firmness.

Fern sent him a supportive smile. They both believed in Aidan, despite outward appearances. And being around Gideon would be a wonderful example for the teen.

"That juvie better not set foot in this market." Russell stalked off.

Gideon followed him. "He already has. He worked for me today and did a great job."

Russell whirled around, his face contorted.

Before he could say anything, Fern spoke softly and soothingly, "You did say Gideon could hire anyone he wants."

Fiery darts shot from Russell's eyes. If she'd been kindling, she'd be ablaze. Gideon stepped closer as if to protect her.

"I've already hired Aidan. I'll keep a close eye on him. But I did want to let you know."

Russell stood there with his mouth flopping open and closed, but no words came out as Gideon turned.

"Ready, Fern?" he asked. Then he motioned for her to precede him as he headed back toward his stand.

When they were out of Russell's earshot, Gideon smiled at her. The admiration in his eyes took her breath away. "*Danke* for what you did back there. I appreciate it."

Fern longed for Gideon's admiring gazes. But not for arguing with Russell or defending Aidan.

Chapter Ten

The next two months passed quickly, and Fern said her last teary goodbye to the stand she'd known as a child. She could hardly believe she'd never work in this market again.

Mose packed up the last of his vegetables and carried them over. "I'm not sad to close down. These last two years have been hard. I'll be glad to spend more time with Alma."

"She'll like having you at home, but I'll miss you, Mose. You were always here when I came here to help Mamm." Fern choked back the lump rising in her throat. "*Danke* for all the candy and ice cream you bought me over the years."

"*Ach*, you were such a little bitty thing. I'm surprised you still remember."

Fern would never forget. Not any of it. She'd miss him.

"Don't look so glum. We'll see each other on market days when we drop off our food at Hartzler's."

"That's true." But it wouldn't be the same. They wouldn't have time to connect, to smile at each other during the day, to chat when business was slow, to share about their families and troubles.

Mose set the vegetables on the counter. "Take those to the food pantry. If you're going today, that is."

"I am."

"*Gut.* I'm grateful to God for Gideon, aren't you?"

Fern hesitated. *Jah*, she was grateful, but how did she say it without gushing?

Mose cocked his head, a question in his eyes.

When she opened her mouth to speak, Nick came up behind her.

"Judging from how many barbecued chicken legs she's bought over the past few months, I'd say she's very grateful." His laugh shook his belly under his candy-striped apron.

Fern wished she could shrink into the ground.

As if sensing her distress, Mose smiled at Nick. "Are you moving your candy to Hartzler's now?"

"Yeah. Whatever can fit, that is." Nick had been selling most of his stock for half price the past month. "I still can't believe I'll have to take that down." He gestured toward the wooden sign saying, *Bertha's Candy Cupboard, est. 1929.*

Fern couldn't tell if it was a trick of the light or a glimmer of tears in his eyes. "*Ach*, Nick."

"Gramps painted and hung that sign two days before this market opened. I have a picture of Gram here with my mom when she was little. I never thought . . ."

This time moisture definitely formed in his eyes. Fern blinked back wetness of her own.

Nick gulped. "My wife even said the kid's upset about it. Never thought he'd care."

"You mean Aidan?" Nick had seen his son's confrontation with Russell, so why did he think Aidan wouldn't care?

"Yeah, Aidan. That kid's hated me from the time he

turned thirteen. My wife's always saying I come down too hard on him. I think she's way too soft."

Fern tended to agree with Nick's wife. Nick always had been hard on his son. Fern had heard Nick berate Aidan when he was younger.

"That's the problem with having a late-life baby. She wants to pamper him. He needs to toughen up."

"I'm not so sure that's—"

Mose interrupted Fern. "Need any help moving your stock, Nick?"

"Nah, I can get it. But thanks, Mose."

"I'm happy to help too." Fern snapped the lid on the carrier she'd been filling.

Nick waved a hand. "You have cleanup to do. I'll be okay."

"I'm almost done."

Nick's expression switched from melancholy to snide. "I'm sure you're dying to help me. Maybe you have an ulterior motive?"

"Hey, now, that's no way to treat Fern. She only offered to help," Mose chided Nick.

Although she appreciated Mose's support and she did want to help, Nick had hit on the truth. She did have an ulterior motive—spending more time around Gideon.

As the clock inched nearer to closing time, Gideon stepped back to let Caroline wait on customers. Aidan pulled the last basket from the fryer to let it drip. Gideon moved to Aidan's side.

"You want to leave now?" Gideon kept his voice low.

Aidan's head snapped up. "Why?"

"I thought you'd rather not be around when your dad carts the candy over here."

"You thought right. When will he be here?"

"Market closes in twenty minutes."

Aidan dumped the fries into the warmer, salted them, and tore off his black chef's apron. "I'm outta here."

Gideon had expected that reaction. "See you on Tuesday, then?"

"Of course. I plan to help with the candy."

"You do?" Gideon had been expecting Aidan to quit. If he planned to stay, he and his dad would have to do some serious talking before the market opened on Tuesday.

"It is my family's business."

"I know. It's just that—" Gideon struggled for a diplomatic way to point out his animosity toward his father.

"Don't worry. I won't let my feelings for my old man get in the way of business."

"That's great." Relief coursed through Gideon. He'd spent the past few weeks dreading an explosion when Nick moved to the end of the counter.

"I'm glad you agreed to take on the candy." Aidan bit his lip. "It's not the same as having great-grandma's stand, but maybe someday we'll drive that organic place out of business and get our spot back."

Gideon hoped Aidan didn't have any actual plans to get rid of the new business. Before he could issue a warning, Aidan raced off.

Caroline waited on the last customers, but as Russell headed to lock the doors, she squeezed past Gideon. "I'll be back to help clean up."

"Wait, I need you. Nick's moving in today."

"I won't be long," Caroline called over her shoulder. "Tell Aidan I'll be there to help him shortly."

"Aidan's not here."

Caroline skidded to a stop. "Where is he?"

"He went home about twenty minutes ago." His sister had been dreamy all day, but she hadn't noticed Aidan leaving?

"Why?"

Caroline hadn't been around for the blowup between Aidan and Nick months ago. "I'll tell you later, but I need help now."

"But Zach—"

"I'm sure Zach will understand."

Caroline's sullen expression said otherwise.

"If he doesn't, then maybe he's not the right one for you."

"What do you have against Zach?"

"Nothing." Nothing except rumors. And Gideon knew better than to trust hearsay. He did have to admit that may have colored his opinion of Zach.

"All right." Caroline rounded the counter, but her heavy sighs as she emptied the warming pans made her annoyance clear.

Gideon busied himself wiping down the counter for the candy.

"You're not going to help here?" Caroline's petulant tone grated on Gideon.

Until she'd met Zach, Caroline had been sweet-natured and kind. Now, she often acted impatient and irritable. That added to Gideon's distrust of Zach.

"I planned to help Nick cart his stuff here. Unless you want to do it."

"*Neh*, you can." She turned her back on Gideon.

"I'm sorry." And he was. Sorry he was keeping her

from her boyfriend. And sorry he'd stuck her with all the cleaning.

With a loud, put-upon exhale, she clunked the empty warming trays into the sink. "Go ahead. I'll take care of everything here."

Water gushing into the sink drowned out Gideon's *Danke*. He started toward the far end of the building but hadn't gone far when he met Nick pushing a teetering cart.

"Need help?"

"Nah. Why don't you go help Fern? She's bringing another load. I'm sure she'd appreciate your brawny muscles." Nick winked. "In more ways than one."

Gideon wished Nick would stop making suggestive remarks. First of all, because Fern had no interest in him, and second, because Gideon didn't want Fern to think he was attracted to her. Even if he was.

"Need any help?"

The deep voice behind Fern made her jump. The boxes she was loading almost tumbled from her arms. Gideon reached out to steady them, and Fern forgot to breathe. She squeezed her eyes shut for a minute to calm her nerves.

"*Ach*, Gideon, I didn't know you were there."

"Sorry. I wasn't trying to scare you."

"It's all right." She hoped he'd assume her breathlessness came from being startled.

"Nick suggested I help you."

"Oh." He hadn't come to be with her. Where had she gotten such a silly idea?

Maybe from the intentness of his stare? From the light in his eyes? A light that flickered and died. A businesslike expression descended over his face.

"What do you want me to do?"

Fern wished he hadn't asked that question. She was tempted to say *Take me in your arms*.

Nick. Think about Nick.

"Um, we're supposed to move this candy."

"I know."

Of course he did. Why was she prattling on? To cover up her reaction to him and because she couldn't think straight anytime he was around.

She pointed to a row of boxes. "Those go next."

Gideon glanced around. "Is there another cart?"

"I haven't loaded mine yet. We can use that." Without waiting for an answer, she hurried off. Better to stay as far away from him as possible.

For the next hour, they ferried carts full of candy to Gideon's stand, while Nick arranged them and Caroline cleaned up. Then Fern transferred her bakery boxes, bags, and tissue to the spot Gideon pointed out before he and Nick hung the *Bertha's Candy Cupboard* sign at the far end of the counter and replaced Gideon's old luncheon menu with the new one. Before they'd finished, Fern waved and hurried off.

She needed to pack up and drop everything off at the food pantry. She'd also discovered that working so close to Gideon could be heart-stopping. From now on, she didn't need to worry about that. She'd only see him for a few minutes when she dropped off her containers of baked goods or picked up the empty boxes.

Gideon held the sign aloft to hook it to the chain, but he stared after Fern. Nick adjusted his end, and Gideon wobbled on the stool.

Caroline giggled. "You'd better pay attention, or you'll topple onto your nose." Once again, she gave him that knowing look.

He tore his gaze from Fern and tried to act nonchalant. But fire started under his collar and burned up his neck and onto his face.

Nick had hooked his side of the sign. "You putting yours up or what?"

Gideon hoped Nick hadn't noticed his attention wandering. Hastily, he lifted his side higher and attached it. "Thanks for the help."

"Sure." Nick threw out his gruff response as he descended the ladder. "And thank *you* for this." He waved a hand toward the other end, where his candy sat in neat rows. "And for what you've done for my son. My wife said you had him working here temporarily over the past month or so, and it helped to straighten him up."

"I'm happy to have you here. And Aidan's been a big help."

"Yeah, well, he's a handful at home." Nick kept his back to Gideon.

"He's well-behaved and polite here."

"Hard to believe." Nick's voice grew thick. "I've tried to stay down at the other end of the market. I figure if he doesn't see me, well . . ."

Once again, Gideon wished he could smooth things over between father and son. "Perhaps with both of you working here that'll change."

Nick's head whipped around. "He's gonna keep working here?"

"That's what he said today."

"Maybe he doesn't hate me as much as he says." Hope flickered in Nick's eyes.

"I'm sure deep down he loves you." Gideon shoved the stool and ladder they'd been using back into place. "Sometimes teens get rebellious. My brother did, but he came around." Or they all thought he had.

"I've pretty much given up on Aidan."

"You might be surprised."

"Let's just say my son always surprises me, but not in a good way." Nick headed for the exit. "See ya Tuesday."

Gideon waved, then rushed over to help Caroline.

His sister squirted glass cleaner on the rotisserie door. "Aidan usually does this. I didn't realize how much work he's been doing."

"He does a lot. I'm glad he'll be here on Tuesday. We'll be busy keeping up with the baked goods plus the new, expanded lunch menu."

"Nettie said she'd come if we want. Mamm will watch the little ones."

"It'll be crowded, but we may need her. One of you can handle Fern's section of the stand. I'll keep Aidan at this end."

"That's a good idea. We don't want a family fight."

"I still can't believe Aidan agreed to come in."

"Neither can I."

Gideon prayed Nick would be pleasantly surprised. Maybe there was hope for the family after all.

"Why didn't you ask Fern to handle her own stand?"

"I, um, didn't think about it." That wasn't true. He thought about it all the time. "When I first asked everyone about selling their goods, I just thought about adding them to our stand. Not about who'd be selling them."

"Uh-huh." Caroline sounded as if she didn't believe him. "Too much of a distraction?"

Gideon refused to take the bait. "Speaking of distractions,

you can't be running off to see Zach until we see how the first day of business goes."

"Trying to change the subject?"

"We're talking about how many workers we need for the stand."

"*Neh*, we're talking about Fern and why you can't keep your eyes off her."

"That's not—"

Caroline held up a hand. "Don't try to deny it. What I want to know is why you don't date her?"

"I have too many responsibilities to even think about it. And Fern wouldn't be at the top of the list if I did have time." She'd be the only one on the list.

Chapter Eleven

On Tuesday, Fern hitched her horse to his usual spot in the small lean-to. But nothing else about today would be usual.

She loaded her folding pushcart with about half of her usual amount of baked goods. It had taken her twice as long to make them, though, because she experimented with her recipes to be sure the organic versions tasted as close to her regular products as possible.

As Fern walked through the doors, a rush of memories flooded through her. Mamm had worked with her mother here, and Fern had worked at the market stall since she was a child. She'd arrange the rolls and pastries on the lower shelves while Mamm set out cakes and cupcakes in neat rows on the top shelves, which Fern could only reach on tiptoe. Over the years, she'd taken over as Mamm's arthritis grew worse.

Now when she entered, the stand that had been so much a part of her life and growing up would be gone. And she'd never work here at the market again.

Taking a deep breath and blinking the mistiness from her eyes, she pushed her cart toward the pair of entrance doors. As she reached for the handle, one of the double doors banged open, and an *Englischer* rushed out. She stepped aside to let him pass.

If he was here this early, he must have a stand here, but she didn't recognize him. He clicked open the door to a huge refrigerated truck with *Ridley's Organic Meats & Produce* painted on the side.

Fern bit her lip. That must be the business taking her place. She steeled herself to walk inside. As she always did, she pressed her back against the door and struggled to drag her cart through.

"Hang on, little lady," a voice called. The man who'd gone to the truck hurried in her direction. "Let me get that door for you."

All she wanted to do was run the opposite way, but he grabbed the edge of the door and held it open.

"*Danke,*" she mumbled.

"No problem. Where's your stand? Will we be neighbors?"

A little unnerved by his scrutiny, Fern stared at the cement floor of the market. She had to be polite, but she could barely push out the words. "*Neh,* I'm just delivering these to . . . another stand." *Because you took over mine.*

"Aww, too bad. I was hoping to get to know you." He sounded genuinely disappointed.

Maybe she'd misjudged him. Just because he'd wanted to expand his business didn't mean he deserved to be labeled bad or uncaring. Maybe he didn't even realize what Russell Evans had done to push out the smaller stand owners.

"I'd better get these to Gideon before the market opens." This time, she made her thanks more heartfelt.

"Gideon Hartzler of barbecued chicken fame? I'm

hoping to do business with him too. Well, maybe I'll see you around."

Fern couldn't believe it. Gideon was partnering with the man who'd driven her out of business? After all the fighting he'd done for her?

She forced herself to push the cart through the door. But as the man let the door swing shut behind her, she stopped. Her feet automatically took her in the direction of her stand.

Even before she reached it, she sucked in a breath. All the old stands had been replaced with gleaming glass cases filled with meats. At the far end, where Mose had sold his garden produce, bright turquoise bins bloomed with colorful vegetables—purple asparagus, white radishes, black carrots, purple broccoli, and orange or green cauliflower.

And the prices? Who would pay that much for vegetables in such strange colors when they could get them in regular colors for a quarter of the cost?

She shook her head. That thought helped lessen the pain of seeing her childhood market stand demolished. Somehow this shiny modern row made the market appear surreal and took away from the homey feel. Even the cement in front of these counters had been scrubbed clean, making the market floor everywhere else appear dingy, worn, and gray.

Except by Gideon's stand. His newly expanded counter space gleamed, and the floor had no chewed gum stuck in the small cracks between the floor and the bottom of the counter. Fern had often come in early to scrape the gunk that collected under her stand edges. She'd always disliked that task, but now knowing she'd never do it again made her eyes sting.

Gideon's space also looked pristine. Although old stains

splashed the cement floor surrounding the counters, the freshly washed floor inside the stand still gleamed with damp mop lines.

His back to her, Gideon threaded whole chickens onto a spit. She waited until he'd adjusted the rod in the broiler and brushed a large paintbrush dripping with thick red paste over the skin. He rotated the skewer to slather the other sides of the chickens with barbecue sauce. As he reached for the next spit, Fern cleared her throat, and he jumped.

He whirled around. "Sorry. I wasn't ignoring you. It's just that I, well—" He gestured to the glass door of the rotisserie.

Why did he have to look so handsome, with his bangs hanging slightly to one side as he tilted his head to look down at her? Her breath caught in her throat. She forced herself to respond. "It's all right. You were busy. I brought the baked goods."

"Great." Gideon glanced over his shoulder at the chickens. "I'm a little late getting these started. Would you mind putting them in that case? Your displays always looked so pretty." Red crept from his neck to his cheeks.

He'd studied her counter? He'd said *always*, which made it sound as if he'd checked on her stand on a regular basis. She'd never seen him there buying anything.

Maybe he'd strolled past sometimes, and she hadn't noticed him. Was that even possible? Whenever he headed down a nearby aisle, her whole body went on alert, and she sneaked glances at him as he passed.

Gideon shuffled his feet. "I'm happy to pay you for your time."

He must have interpreted her hesitation as reluctance.

"*Neh, neh.* I'm glad to do it." Did that sound overeager? Now it was her turn for burning cheeks.

"If you're sure?"

"I am." Fern turned around to lift the first large plastic bin.

"Let me get that for you." Gideon slid by her, almost grazing her as he passed.

Fern sucked in a breath. They'd be awfully close to each other in this small space. Although she liked being so near him, she backed up to Nick's end of the counter so Gideon had room to maneuver. And for her own good.

Gideon inhaled a long, slow breath to calm his racing heart. He should have waited until she'd moved out of the way. He'd slid by her with only inches to spare.

After hefting the first box, he hesitated for a moment, trying to appear cool and casual. If only he could calm the current zinging around inside.

Behind him, Fern skittered away. When he turned to set the container on the counter, she had her back plastered to the far end of Nick's counter. Her message was clear: Keep away from me.

"I'm used to carrying my own containers." Her voice shook a little.

Had she misinterpreted his actions? Maybe she thought he'd done that on purpose to be close to her. He hadn't, had he?

"I only wanted to help." He tried to make his voice businesslike.

"*Danke*, but I can do the rest myself." Her gaze strayed to his half-filled rotisserie. "You have work to finish."

"*Jah*, I do," he said abruptly and strode to the opposite end of the stand.

Concentrate on the chicken rather than her.

But that proved almost impossible.

The soft swish of her skirt distracted him. Gideon slopped sauce onto the chicken with jerky movements. The doors of the case squeaked as she slid them along the track. Even though he wasn't facing her, just sensing her presence behind him made breathing difficult. His hand slipped, and he nearly dropped the spit. It took him two tries to put it into the slots.

Behind him, Fern unsnapped a container lid, and the aroma of cinnamon teased him. "That smells delicious." The words popped out before he could stop them.

"Would you like one?"

Of course he would. He loved them. "I'd better not eat the profits."

She laughed. "I won't charge you for this one."

"*Neh*, I'll pay for all of them." He wouldn't deprive her of any of her money. He'd wait until she'd gone before he snacked on one.

"These are my first batch of organic cinnamon rolls. You might want to sample one to see if they taste right."

Gideon shouldn't have turned, but he did stop himself from moving closer to the smell. And to Fern. "I'm sure they're delicious. As usual."

"You shouldn't sell something without testing it first. What if it's awful?" She held one out.

How could he resist?

In his brain, alarms buzzed. *Stay where you are. Don't move any nearer. You're being lured into a trap.*

Despite the warnings, Gideon stepped closer and closer

as if under a spell. What was that *Englisch* fairy tale about a poisoned apple?

This wouldn't be poisoned. At least not literally. But taking an offering from Fern's soft, delicate hand meant giving in to temptation. If he couldn't resist one small cinnamon roll, how would he fight off even greater longings?

He shook his head. *Stop making such a big deal about such a tiny thing.* He made a mental note to pay her for the roll. He'd keep this a business transaction.

"You don't want it?" A look of hurt flashed in her eyes, and she started to turn away.

"Wait." She'd misinterpreted his head-shaking. He hadn't meant to hurt her feelings. "You're right. I should try the foods I'm selling. And I really want to taste that." Even though he shouldn't move any nearer. Especially not when the smile that lit her face drew him to her.

Ignoring the signals to keep his distance, he stepped toward her and reached out for the iced bun, careful not to touch her fingers. That meant taking it by the top and bottom, one finger buried in the icing. Could he have handled this any more awkwardly?

Fern waited while he took a bite, her gaze focused on his mouth. Usually, Gideon closed his eyes and savored the taste. But with her staring at him so intently, he concentrated on the cement floor.

Too stiff to relax and enjoy the cinnamon roll, he chewed and swallowed the bite quickly. "Delicious," he murmured through the sticky sweetness still clinging to his teeth and tongue. He turned back to his chicken, but not before he registered her disappointment.

Once he was no longer looking at her, he added, "It tastes every bit as good as your regular cinnamon buns."

Ach, *why did I say that?* Now she'd know he'd eaten them often enough to know the difference.

Her worried "Are you sure?" made it clear she was more concerned about how it tasted than whether he'd eaten any of her baked goods before.

He needed to focus her attention on something else. "The customers will love them. And speaking of customers, it looks like Russell is heading over to unlock the doors. We'd better get ready."

"I'm sorry. I shouldn't have distracted you." Her voice sounded small and uncertain.

"It's not your fault." It had been his. He should have kept his mind on the chicken.

She didn't answer. Only the clatter and slide of metal trays revealed how quickly she was filling the cases.

Gideon wanted to lift the other containers for her, but he had to get these chickens on the spits or he'd have none ready for his early customers. He rarely had customers when the market first opened, but as soon as they realized Fern's baked goods were here, the counter would be flooded with buyers.

"Looks like Nick's here," Caroline said behind him. "As soon as Fern's done, I'll take her place before Aidan arrives."

"Sounds good. He doesn't usually get here until close to opening time. That'll give Nick some time to get set up."

"Nettie'll be in soon, so we should have enough help."

Gideon would prefer to have Fern stay, but for his peace of mind, he'd be glad when she finished stocking the shelves so he could concentrate on his work.

"*Ach*, there's Aidan." Caroline pointed to the side door. "He's early."

Gideon braced himself for some fireworks. At least

Fern stood between Nick and Aidan. Gideon couldn't think of a better buffer, but he should warn her Aidan was heading their way.

Although Fern was facing away from Gideon, she sensed his every move. She froze as he headed in her direction again. She needed to finish filling these shelves and leave.

"Fern?" Gideon whispered.

Her name on his lips strummed a chord deep inside her. If only— She jerked her mind away from the fantasies.

"Aidan's coming."

"Now? Here?" She kept her voice as quiet as Gideon's. He must not want Nick to hear. She could understand why.

When Gideon nodded, she asked, "To work? When his father's here?"

"Seems so."

"Maybe Nick will stay busy with those customers until Aidan's down at the other end of the counter."

Nick had gone outside the stand and squatted down to talk to a small girl and hand her a lollipop.

Fern swiveled her head as Aidan approached the chicken side of the counter, a broad smile on his lips. "That looks great." He pointed to the array of side dishes Caroline had arranged in the glass case. Coleslaw, chow chow, and red beet eggs sat in metal pans next to potato, broccoli, and macaroni salads.

"Thanks." Caroline smiled at him. "Missed you Saturday night during cleanup."

Aidan shuffled and hung his head. "Yeah, well, I didn't want no heat from my old man."

"I had to do most of the work while Gideon hung the signs."

"No wonder you missed me." Aidan grinned. Then he glanced up at the sign at the far end and swallowed hard. "Doesn't seem right to see that hanging here."

"I know," Caroline sympathized.

"Well, it is what it is. Can't change it now. I guess I get to take the family business in a new direction. Kinda fitting, don't you think?"

Was Aidan hoping to work at the candy counter? He and his father must have ironed out their difficulties.

Fern checked to see if Nick had noticed Aidan's arrival, but he was still talking to the small girl. She flung her arms around Nick's neck and hugged him.

His face softened for a moment. "Enjoy your lollipop."

"I will." She skipped off beside her mother, and Nick watched her.

"Hey, Gid," Aidan called. "I got here early in case you needed me to help with the candy."

Beside Fern, Gideon tensed. "Um, that's great. I think we're all set with that, but I could use help with the chick—"

Nick rose and started to enter the stand. He stopped dead when he saw Aidan.

"What's he doing here?" Aidan stared openmouthed at his father.

Fern needed to do something to defuse the situation, but she wasn't sure her explanation would help. "He moved the candy here on Saturday."

"I know *that*."

Fern ignored Aidan's sarcasm. "He'll be selling here now."

"I thought I'd be doing that." His eyes reflected his

betrayal. He narrowed his eyes at Gideon. "Why didn't you tell me he'd be here?"

"I thought you knew."

"How would I know that?"

Nick glared at his son. "Maybe if you talked to us once in a while instead of grunting and complaining, you'd have known."

His words sharp as a knife, Aidan stabbed back, "I do talk to Mom. At least she listens. She said"—his voice broke—"you were turning the stand over to Gideon."

"That was the original plan." Gideon's calm response cut through the tension. "Your dad decided he wanted to keep an eye on the business."

"But he never bothered to tell Mom. All he cares about is himself." Bitterness dripped from each syllable. "I thought I'd finally have my chance . . ."

"Oh, Aidan." Fern wanted to reach out to him. He'd been desperate to prove himself. He looked so devastated. So lost.

Aidan shot her a quick look. "Save your pity. He's the one who needs it." Aidan flicked his hand in his father's direction. "All his kids hate him. Even my *perfect* older brothers."

Fern sucked in a breath. Poor Nick. To have his son turn on him so savagely. And poor Aidan. To be filled with so much pain.

Aidan glared at Gideon. "I can't believe you'd do this to me, man. I thought you were my friend." He whirled around and stalked off.

Fern waited for one of Nick's critical comments about Aidan, but when it didn't come, she turned to see him slumped on his stool behind the counter, his eyes glassy.

"*Ach*, now what?" Caroline said. "Customers are lined up by Fern's stand already, and Nettie won't be here for another hour. The chicken's not in the rotisserie, and—"

"I can stay and wait on customers," Fern offered.

"Would you?"

The relief in Gideon's eyes melted her. She swooned inside.

"I'd be happy to pay you," he said.

"No need for that. I'll help out until your other worker gets here."

"*Danke,*" Caroline called.

Fern was the one who should thank them. She smiled at some of her favorite customers lined up in front of her counter. *Neh*, not hers. Gideon's. She'd never have her own counter again.

Pushing aside that sadness, Fern waited on one customer after another. For as long as she could, she'd enjoy these interactions. And she'd enjoy being in the same place as Gideon, even if he acted as if she didn't exist.

Chapter Twelve

It took all of Gideon's willpower to keep his eyes on the chicken. But he couldn't force his mind not to stray. His hands moving by rote, he slid one chicken after another onto the spits and brushed them with barbecue sauce.

But his senses tuned in to Fern's sweet voice chatting with the customers. Everyone seemed to love her. He could understand why. And she seemed to know each one. If only he could find a way to keep her here.

If Aidan chose not to return, maybe Fern would stay. He shook his head. Even if she'd agree, asking her would be a big mistake. He'd never be able to concentrate on the business. And right now, with the debts he needed to pay off and all the people depending on him for support, he needed to focus on making this new expansion profitable.

As Gideon set the last spit into place, he sneaked a quick peek at the far end of the stand. Fern had a long line. Maybe she could use some help. People wouldn't start lining up for chicken yet.

"Fern?" An elderly woman's quavering voice sounded confused. "What are you doing here?"

"Another stand went in my space, so Gideon offered to sell my baked goods here."

"Oh, that was nice of him. But what was the market owner thinking to move you out of your rightful spot? I intend to have a word with him."

Although Gideon doubted one older lady's censure would have any effect on Russell's judgment, he hoped other customers would protest. Maybe Russell would think twice about closing other businesses.

"Have you been all right?" Fern's caring tone toward the customer plucked a lonely chord inside Gideon. "I missed seeing you the past few months."

"I took a tumble. Broken bones take a while to heal at my age. I'm ninety-two, you know."

"I remember. Your birthday's in July."

Gideon stood there stunned. Did Fern recall everyone's birthday? She made a lot of cakes, but did she keep track of each person's birthday?

Although Mrs. Vandenburg hadn't been a fan of barbecued chicken, he'd seen her in the market for years and knew her by name, yet he'd had no idea of her age and birthday. He doubted he knew that much personal information about any customers who frequented his business.

Mrs. Vandenburg obviously appreciated the kindness. She beamed at Fern. "How sweet of you to remember!"

"Would you like your usual?" Fern asked.

"Yes, dear. Oh, there goes Russell." Although her voice wavered slightly, she hollered, "Russell? Russell Evans, get over here now."

Russell stopped in his tracks. A sickish look crossed his face. He pasted on a fake smile as he turned to greet her.

Gideon closed the rotisserie door and checked the settings before glancing over his shoulder to watch Mrs. Vandenburg challenge Russell. Slightly unsteady on her feet, the hunched-over, white-haired lady waved her cane at Russell. "Get over here now," she demanded.

The market owner cringed. It seemed impossible, but Russell's cowed shoulders and his darting eyes revealed his reluctance to face this senior citizen who looked like she'd blow over in a strong gust of wind. What hold did she have on him?

As Mrs. Vandenburg swished her cane through the air, Fern sucked in a breath and prayed the elderly woman wouldn't topple to the ground. Shoving aside the plastic bins blocking her way, Fern rushed out to support the sweet old lady. The last thing Mrs. Vandenburg needed was another broken bone.

Gideon dashed over to help, but Fern sped up and slipped through the narrow exit first so they wouldn't collide.

Just before Fern reached her, Mrs. Vandenburg swayed. Fern dove forward and grasped Mrs. Vandenburg's forearms to steady her. She was so frail, Fern worried about bruising the crepey skin covering the elderly woman's brittle bones. Once Mrs. Vandenburg seemed a little steadier on her feet, Fern loosened her grip a little.

Gideon stopped beside them, arms outstretched. He must have thought the two of them might fall, and he planned to catch them. Fern imagined sinking back into the protection of his muscular arms, feeling their warmth wrap around her. Her heartbeat quickened, and she sucked in a soft breath.

Concentrate on Mrs. Vandenburg, not Gideon.

Fern exhaled slowly, hoping to calm her racing pulse,

and kept a gentle hold on Mrs. Vandenburg, who still seemed to be wobbling. "Are you all right?" she asked.

"I'm fine, dear, if you're talking about my balance. But I'm not fine with what this young whippersnapper is doing to his father's business." She leaned against Fern as she brandished her cane at Russell Evans.

Russell cowered as if Mrs. Vandenburg might lunge at him. Fern doubted the lightweight woman could do any damage. Despite that, the market owner's eyes held fear.

"What were you thinking when you took away this young woman's stand?" Mrs. Vandenburg's regal tone belied her feeble limbs.

"We have a new business coming in that will pay well." The whining, almost pleading note in Russell's voice conflicted with his usual superior manner.

Why was he so scared of Mrs. Vandenburg? She posed no threat. Even if she whacked him with her cane, it would barely sting.

"Profit above loyalty? This girl has been a faithful renter for years. As were her mother and grandmother."

Instead of answering, Russell's face paled.

Mrs. Vandenburg's voice rose. "I've been coming to the market since your grandfather owned it, and I don't like seeing familiar businesses eliminated."

Nick strode out of the stand. "That's right, Mrs. V. Preach it!" He shot Russell a nasty glare.

Russell returned it with an ugly one of his own, which he erased when Mrs. Vandenburg gave him a cross look.

"Hello, Nick," Mrs. Vandenburg said. "How are you today?"

"Terrible. What can you expect after what he did?" He flung an arm in Russell's direction, almost hitting him.

A puzzled frown creased Mrs. Vandenburg's brow. "What do you mean?"

Nick had been about to reenter the barbecue stand, but stopped. "You don't know? But you just said you didn't like seeing our businesses axed."

"Our?" she echoed faintly. "More than one?"

Fern's heart melted at Gideon's sympathetic look. He seemed to understand how disorienting this would be to an elderly customer who had been following the same routine for years.

He stepped from behind them to explain in a quiet voice, "Five businesses closed."

His response so close to Fern's ear set her tingling. If she took one step sideways . . .

"Five?" The word exploded on Fern's other side and jarred her from thoughts of Gideon. "Russell, what have you done?"

"I'll show you what he's done." Nick rushed inside the stand and pointed to his end of the counter. "Here's what's left of Bertha's Candy Cupboard."

Mrs. Vandenburg gasped. "Bertha's is gone? But—but that was one of the original market stands. Children loved it." Her chest heaved as if she were hyperventilating.

Fern stepped even closer and prayed Mrs. Vandenburg wouldn't collapse.

"I demand you give all five of these owners their stands back immediately." Mrs. Vandenburg's voice rang through the market.

"I—I can't," Russell said miserably. "Ridley's Organics has taken over that space."

"Tell them their contract is canceled. Kick them out the way you kicked these sellers out."

"That's impossible." Russell's mumble could barely be heard.

Poking her cane in his direction, Mrs. Vandenburg declared, "Nothing is impossible."

As much as it pained her to defend Russell, Fern wanted Mrs. Vandenburg to understand. "Ridley's tore out our stands and put in glass meat cases all along the front wall."

"Tell me that's not true." This time Mrs. Vandenburg's cane came close to poking Russell in the stomach. He jumped back.

Fern shouldn't be glad that Mrs. Vandenburg had almost clipped him, but a tiny part of her felt a little punishment in this case was justified. Later, she'd ask God for forgiveness.

Mrs. Vandenburg's power over Russell confused Gideon, but she'd brought up some of the same points he'd tried to make when he'd talked to Russell. Everyone stood in silence as the elderly woman's icy stare made Russell squirm. He looked like he might be sick.

Customers were streaming into the market. Gideon wanted to smooth things over and help Mrs. Vandenburg adjust to the changes that had her upset. "What Fern said is true." He tried to say it soothingly, for Mrs. Vandenburg's sake.

"I can't believe this." Mrs. Vandenburg fanned herself with one hand.

Gideon was glad she'd rested her cane on the ground to do that. He'd been expecting her to thrust it into Russell's stomach. Or for her to pitch forward onto the floor.

"It can't possibly be true, can it?" She turned teary eyes to Gideon.

"I'm so sorry." If she'd come in the front door, she'd have seen it right away. Maybe it was better she'd had some time to prepare. "You came in the back way?"

She nodded, looking completely disoriented. "My daughter always lets me off there. It's flatter and easier to walk. She's expecting to meet me at Fern's stand." She hesitated. "Her real one. She's probably already there, wondering where I am. And wondering where Fern's business is." She frowned at Russell.

Gideon held out his arm. "If you'd like, I can take you down there to meet your daughter." She didn't look as if she could totter the length of the market, and she might need some physical support when she saw the changes.

Mrs. Vandenburg squinted up at him. "If you don't mind. I want to see what's happened." Then she turned in Russell's direction. "You stay here," she snapped. "I'm not done with you yet."

He'd started to scuttle off, but he froze at her sharp rebuke.

A crowd had gathered around Fern's counter, and Nick waited on children lined up in his section.

"Fern?" Gideon gestured toward the milling customers. "Could you keep waiting on people until I get back?"

"I'd be glad to."

"*Danke.* You can make change from my cash register if you need it. But keep whatever money you make while I'm gone. That's only fair."

Fern shook her head, but Gideon wouldn't let her go without pay. The baked goods were hers, and she deserved the profit.

He should move, but he remained mesmerized as she returned to the stand. He admired her easy camaraderie with her customers. She greeted everyone by name, and they all seemed to adore her. He could stand here all day staring at her, but Mrs. Vandenburg tugged at his elbow.

He had to take her to the other end of the market now. Her daughter was probably concerned. And he didn't want anyone to misread his interest in Fern. He was only fascinated by her relationships with the buyers, and he could learn some tips by studying her interactions.

"She's good with people, isn't she?" Mrs. Vandenburg asked.

"Definitely." Gideon tore his attention away from Fern. "Should we go?"

"I don't know. Should we?" Mrs. Vandenburg inspected him closely. "Seems like you'd prefer to stay right here."

"No, no. I just wanted to be sure Fern—and Nick—would be all right on their own."

Mrs. Vandenburg chuckled. "You can't fool me. Fern's been working the market for years. She doesn't need to be supervised. Besides, I've seen many lovebirds in my time."

Gideon gulped. *Lovebirds?* She was totally mistaken. At least, he hoped she was.

By the time Gideon and Mrs. Vandenburg headed down the aisle, Fern had waited on six customers. Sensing Gideon's gaze on her, she'd tensed. He'd examined her as she worked. Was he evaluating whether or not he should leave her alone in the stand?

She breathed a sigh of relief when he moved out of sight. Then she relaxed back into her usual bantering with customers. Many were old friends, but being in this new spot in the market, quite a few unfamiliar people approached the counter. And if she answered the question once, she answered it twenty times.

What are you doing at this end of the market?

Although she'd hung a sign several weeks ago to let customers know she'd be moving, it seemed few people had read it. Or if they had, they hadn't noted the date. No one expected the familiar old stands to disappear between close of business early Saturday afternoon and the following Tuesday morning. And the replacement of small, well-worn stands with a gleaming wall of metal and glass had to be as disorienting for them as it had been for her.

Speaking of disorienting, working here in a different place with many of the same customers made her equally *ferhoodled*. She could hardly believe she was inside the stand she'd always approached with a rapidly fluttering pulse. And she'd almost brushed against Gideon more than once this morning. Good thing she didn't actually work here. She'd find it difficult to breathe.

"Fern?" Wilma Mast waved a hand to get Fern's attention. "Open mouths attract flies."

Had she been standing here with her mouth gaping as she daydreamed? *Neh*, her lips remained firmly closed. And not as tightly pinched as Wilma's. A permanent frown had gouged a deep canyon into the older woman's brow. Fern tamped down the irritation that often rose in her whenever she spoke to Wilma. Although Fern tried not to think of Wilma as the Pickle Lady, the older woman's biting comments made it difficult.

"I'm sorry." She should have been paying attention to customers instead of daydreaming. "What would you like?"

Wilma bent to examine the small price tags Gideon had clipped to his trays before Fern had arrived that morning. They reflected the prices he'd agreed on with Daed.

A sharp gasp made it clear Wilma disliked the increase.

None of the customers before her had complained. A few had even thanked Fern for going organic.

"What do you think you're doing charging prices like this? Are you trying to cheat customers?" Wilma's indignant tone put Fern on the defensive.

After all, she hadn't decided on the final cost. Gideon had set these prices and made the signs. Fern wanted to defend him. "Gideon sells all organic now. That means we have to use more expensive ingredients."

A loud huff escaped Wilma's lips. "Well, I'm not paying those prices. I'm sure I can find sticky buns just as good elsewhere in the market."

"I understand." At her own stand, Fern could lower the prices if someone couldn't afford her pastries. But this was Gideon's business now.

Besides, even if she were in her own place, she wouldn't give Wilma a reduced rate. The Pickle Lady made money hand over fist. At least she always bragged she did. That meant she could afford her usual Danish.

"You done yet?" the little boy behind her muttered.

"Actually, I am. I won't be buying anything here. That's for sure." Wilma whirled around and headed off. "Don't bother waiting," she said to the customers she passed. "Her new prices are a rip-off."

A few people looked hesitant, but nobody stepped out of line. Fern took a deep breath and focused on the small boy in front of her.

"One bear claw." He handed her his usual amount.

She didn't have the heart to disappoint him, so she wrapped up the bear claw. "Here you go, Beckett." She'd pay the extra

Explaining the change in prices to some customers, especially the small children who came with a handful of coins that matched her previous prices, proved difficult. Fern noted how much she owed for the treats she gave away at lower prices.

Nick seemed to be as busy as she was. Only one person stopped to inquire when the chickens would be ready. Caroline was mixing another salad in a large bowl at the prep center behind the cooking area, so Fern checked the rotisserie timer and answered the man's question.

Until then, she'd been too busy to notice, but Russell still remained where Mrs. Vandenburg had told him to stay. He leaned against the refrigerated glass display case with his arms crossed, his face sullen and drawn. Behind him, Caroline's neat rows of side dishes were lined up in a colorful array.

The broccoli salad reminded Fern of the garish colors from Ridley's Organics. She pictured Gideon's display filled with salads made from purple broccoli or orange cauliflower. Would people buy it if he mixed the colorful vegetables into the sour cream–mayonnaise dressing and dotted it with cheddar cheese and bacon? The thought made her snicker.

Russell's head whirled around, and he narrowed his eyes. He must think she was mocking him.

Overcome with giggles, she turned her back and tried to stifle them, but that only made her shake harder.

"What's so funny?" Nick demanded.

"Nothing."

He stared sideways at her. Fern didn't want to hurt his feelings too.

"I was just imagining Gideon's salads made with the purple broccoli or orange cauliflower at Ridley's."

As soon as she said the name *Ridley's*, Nick's fists and jaw clenched. His whole body stiffened, and he looked about to explode. But when he glanced at Fern's comical expression, he snorted. Then he joined her, his belly laughs jiggling his stomach and chest.

Russell's expression grew darker.

"We. Should. Stop," Fern managed to say between giggles. "Russell . . . thinks . . ." She gasped in a breath. ". . . we're making . . . fun of him."

"Let him," Nick replied savagely. "He deserves it."

Fern sobered. As upset as she'd been with Russell about the stand closing, she shouldn't hold a grudge. "God would want us to forgive him."

"Forgive? You've got to be kidding me. No way will I ever forgive that—" Nick clamped his mouth shut. Then he muttered, "Sorry. It's hard to watch my language with him around."

Fern's conscience chided her about being unkind. She headed over to reassure Russell. "We weren't laughing at you, Mr. Evans."

His scowl made it clear he didn't believe her. Before she could explain, his expression changed into a tight smile. Fern turned in the direction of his gaze.

Gideon was leading Mrs. Vandenburg toward them. Fern's stomach did a little flip. She fought to keep her lips from curving up too much. Her smile probably looked as stiff and wooden as Russell's. Then Gideon's eyes met hers, and her self-control crumbled.

Chapter Thirteen

Gideon made the mistake of staring at Fern. He broke his gaze and concentrated on the tiny woman propped on his arm. Mrs. Vandenburg had had quite a shock when they'd reached the front of the market.

At first, she'd studied the gleaming cases and the long signboard hanging over Ridley's long stand. Then she blinked several times, her eyes damp.

"I've been coming to this market since I was a young girl. My dad always bought me a lollipop at Bertha's Candy Cupboard." Her hand trembled as she pointed to the spot where Nick's stand once stood.

"I'm sorry," Gideon said softly.

"So am I." She sounded on the verge of tears. "And I remember when Fern's grandmother opened her stand. I was a brand-new mother. I bought my son's first birthday cake there."

No wonder Fern knew Mrs. Vandenburg so well. Mrs. Vandenburg had known Fern's family for decades.

"And Mose? I didn't need his vegetables back then,

because I had my own garden. But we always spoke in passing."

She lifted her cane to point and wobbled. Gideon moved closer to keep her steady. She lowered her cane and leaned heavily on it.

"It's not easy growing old. You lose so many friends. Things change. And worst of all, you have to depend on others for so much."

Gideon's heart went out to her. She looked so lonely. If only he had a way to comfort her.

"Look at that stand." Mrs. Vandenburg grew indignant. "Raised up so high like they're royalty or something. And all that metal and glass."

Until then, Gideon had avoided looking at Ridley's stand and his sign. His heart preferred to hold the image of Fern with her small glass cases. Nick's candy display. Mose's cheerful greeting. Somehow the market wasn't the same without them.

Mrs. Vandenburg tipped her head toward the sign. "Organic meats? That's just ridiculous. If you want organic meat, raise your own." She looked up at Gideon. "That's what you do with your chickens, isn't it?"

"When my dad owned the business, we did. After Thomas took over, he grew the business and started buying from a supplier. My nieces keep chickens for the eggs now."

"Your sign says *Organic* too, doesn't it?"

After what she'd said, Gideon disliked admitting it. "Yes, it does. Thomas thought customers would prefer it." And his brother had anticipated they'd pay more. Thomas hadn't considered how much more he'd have to pay for the meat.

"Russell thought the same thing." She gripped Gideon's arm so hard her nails dug into his skin. "Talking about Russell, I need to go back there to give him a piece of my mind."

"Mom!" a shrill voice called. "There you are. I've been looking all over for you."

"That's my daughter," Mrs. Vandenburg explained. "She worries about me."

Gideon could understand why. Her mother wasn't too steady on her feet. Several times he'd been afraid she'd take a tumble.

Mrs. Vandenburg's daughter rushed over, red-faced and out of breath. "Fern's at the other end of the market. So is Bertha's Candy Cupboard. Only it's tiny now."

"I know." Mrs. Vandenburg lifted her chin and pulled her bent back almost upright. Then, her spine almost ramrod straight, she grasped Gideon's arm even more tightly. "And I intend to give Russell Evans a piece of my mind."

"But we have shopping to do."

"You do the shopping and meet me at Fern's when you're done. I'm going to have a discussion with Russell."

"But—"

"I'll be fine. Just go. Gideon will take good care of me."

Her daughter looked to Gideon, a question in her eyes.

"Don't worry. I'll watch out for her."

She bit her lip. "If you're sure?"

"He's sure," Mrs. Vandenburg intervened. "Now, Gideon, let's go."

Grasping his arm in a vise-like grip and using her cane to support her other side, she marched back to the barbecued chicken stand.

Whatever power she had over Russell must have been strong, because he still remained in the same place where they'd left him. Usually as soon as he unlocked the doors in the morning, he bustled through the market, barely taking time to greet people, and headed straight for his office.

When Russell spotted Mrs. Vandenburg, he straightened from his slouch and pasted on a fake smile that didn't erase his petulant expression. But his eyes gave away his nervousness.

Despite her unsteady gait, Mrs. Vandenburg strode straight to him. "When your father asked me to lend you money, I understood it would go to expansion. Not to putting people out of business."

Aha. That explained her hold on Russell. No wonder Russell had been so anxious and eager to please.

"I thought you'd be happy I'm making more money so I can pay off the loan faster." Russell tried to bluster, but with his voice shaking, he didn't quite pull it off.

"People's lives and livelihoods are more important to me than the money. I'm warning you—this better not happen again. If it does, I'll call in the full amount of the loan immediately."

Russell swallowed hard. "You'd put me out of business?"

Mrs. Vandenburg didn't hesitate. "Exactly." Her voice crisp and clear, she raised her eyebrows. "Isn't that what you did to Fern and Nick and Mose?"

"But they're still here." Russell's protest was barely audible.

She must not be hard of hearing, because she snapped

right back, "That's only because someone was kind enough to offer them space. And where's Mose?"

From behind the counter, Fern piped up, "He's at home with his ill wife, but Gideon is buying his produce for salads."

Gideon's face burned. He wished she hadn't told everyone that. He'd done nothing special. Anyone would have done the same.

"Thank heavens for Gideon." Mrs. Vandenburg acted as if he was a hero while Russell was the villain.

"Oh, yes, Gideon is quite the man." Russell's snide tone implied the opposite.

"Yes, he is" came a sweet voice from behind them.

Fern said that? Gideon longed to turn his head to see if she meant it, but he stayed facing Russell.

"I quite agree." Mrs. Vandenburg lifted her cane and swayed toward Gideon, who kept supporting her. "From now on, you'll run all future plans through me, Russell. I'm not going to have anyone else put out of business. Do you understand?"

"Yes," Russell mumbled. When she dismissed him, he slunk away with an unhappy expression and downcast eyes.

After he headed off, Mrs. Vandenburg expelled a heavy sigh. "He's definitely not the man his father was."

"That's for sure." Nick's angry response carried to them. He must have been listening to the whole conversation.

"I'm sorry, Nick. I wish I'd known soon enough to prevent it." With Gideon's assistance, Mrs. Vandenburg turned and headed for his counter. "But don't write him off. God can work miracles, and people can change."

"Not him," Nick muttered.

Nearby, Fern took money from a customer and handed over a white bakery box. Then she smiled at Mrs. Vandenburg. A smile that—even though it hadn't been directed at him—jump-started Gideon's pulse.

Fern had set aside Mrs. Vandenburg's usual order. "I packed this up for you." She held up the white bag.

Mrs. Vandenburg beamed at her. "You're so sweet."

"Yeah, she is." Nick plopped two giant jawbreakers into a small brown bag for a child.

Startled, Fern almost dropped Mrs. Vandenburg's order. Nick complimenting her? Those were the first positive words from his mouth that day.

Evidently, Fern wasn't the only one he'd surprised. A smile played at the corner of Mrs. Vandenburg's lips as she studied him. For some reason, Gideon was frowning.

Noticing all the eyes on him, Nick shrugged. "What? It's the truth."

Mrs. Vandenburg laughed. "You just proved my point about people changing."

Nick turned his attention to the small boy counting up his change and pointedly ignored her. "Is that it?" he asked the boy and then busied himself with totaling up the purchases.

Quietly enough that Nick couldn't hear, Mrs. Vandenburg said, "You're a good influence on him, Fern. Now that you'll be working together, you'll have plenty of opportunities to soften him up."

Fern didn't contradict her, but as much as she wished she could spend time here, she'd have to leave whenever Nettie arrived. While she'd filled the cases and waited on new and familiar customers, Fern could pretend she was still in business. But she was in Gideon's stand. Not hers. She'd almost forgotten that as she slipped into her old role of chatting with customers and boxing up their purchases.

A deep sense of loss washed over her. She'd really miss her customers. She loved hearing about their lives, baking cakes for their special occasions, watching their babies grow up.

Tears stung her eyes, and she blinked to hold them back. She'd lost more than a business. She'd lost friends. Friends who'd become like a second family.

Mrs. Vandenburg let go of Gideon's arm to reach out and pat Fern's hand. "I'm sure it's hard not having your own stand, but you'll get used to it. God always has a reason for these upheavals."

Fern managed to choke out, "I know." But she couldn't tell Mrs. Vandenburg that today would be the last time she'd ever wait on her.

Gideon, who no longer needed to support Mrs. Vandenburg, didn't correct her either. Instead, he said abruptly, "I'd better check on my chickens. I don't want them to burn."

Staying far away from Fern, he rushed behind the counter and headed for the rotisserie. Although his avoiding her was for the best, she couldn't help being disappointed.

Gideon's gruff voice rose over the clatter of metal spits clanking against the counter. "Mrs. Vandenburg's order is on the house."

"No, no. I insist on paying," Mrs. Vandenburg said. "I'm not about to be the reason another stand goes out of business. I feel guilty enough about what happened to the other five. Or at least the three of you. I'm not quite as worried about the candle and herb ladies. They have other options."

"Yeah, you don't need to be." Nick weighed a bag full of hard candy. "They opened an online business together."

"Good to know." Mrs. Vandenburg reached into her pocket and pulled out a small change purse stuffed with bills. "How much do I owe you, dear?" When Fern told her the price, she bent and squinted through the glass at the card clipped to the bakery tray. "Is that what it says?"

"I can sell it to you for your usual price." If Mrs. Vandenburg wouldn't accept Gideon's offer, Fern could reduce the cost. She'd add the extra into all the other prices she'd been jotting down.

"These old eyes aren't what they used to be. I'll have to believe you." Mrs. Vandenburg counted out her money and handed it to Fern.

Fern made a quick note on the pad beside the small box she'd been using to hold the cash. It saved running back and forth to the register each time. So different from the old-fashioned manual cash register her grandmother and mother had used. Dad had insisted on keeping that cash register in the family. It sat on a shelf in the basement, a sad reminder that Fern no longer had her market stand.

She schooled her face into a smile as she handed Mrs. Vandenburg her change. "I hope you enjoy it." Changing to organic ingredients had slightly altered the taste, and Fern hoped customers would think they tasted better.

"I have no doubt I will. Things are usually as good as you make up your mind they'll be."

Fern had to agree with that. Maybe it was time for her to make up her mind to see the good in her new job status.

Mrs. Vandenburg leaned in closer. "I'm so sorry you've lost your stand, dear. Please know if there's ever any way

I can help you, I will." Then with a sly look at Gideon, she simpered. "Although maybe things have worked out well for you after all."

As much as Fern wished it were true, Gideon's indifference told a different story.

Gideon hacked up several chickens before placing the parts in the warmer. What had he been thinking asking Fern to stay and take care of customers? She'd become a total distraction. He could barely keep his mind on his work.

And he should never have let Nick's compliments about Fern get under his skin. In addition to being an *Englischer*, Nick was way too old for her. And he was married. She'd never be interested in Nick. So why had Gideon given away his jealousy by his abrupt manner? Had Fern figured out what caused his fit of pique?

Time to focus on business instead of her. He had no idea how he'd wait on the unending lines for baked goods and keep up his chicken business. He'd asked Nettie to come in today to chop lettuce and make garden salads. She could help over the busiest lunch hours, but what had he been thinking when he'd expanded the business without factoring in his need for extra help?

Maybe Fern would be willing to assist them just for this week. Once he had a chance to see how much extra business the full lunch menu added, he could figure out what to do for next week.

He headed toward the foot of the L-shaped section, where she and Nick waited on long lines. "Fern?"

She jumped and almost dropped the cupcake she'd been about to place in a bakery box.

"I'm sorry. I didn't mean to startle you."

Her flushed cheeks and slightly parted lips did strange things to his insides. He jerked his attention back to business.

"It's all right."

Her soft, sweet tones added to his inner chaos. "I, um, that is, I didn't expect so much business. I'll need to figure out what to do about staffing. For today, though, would you be willing to stay and wait on bakery customers?" Before she could answer, he added, "Like I said, you can keep all the money that comes in."

"I couldn't do that, but I'd be glad to help." Her pink cheeks grew rosier, and she looked as if he'd just handed her a special gift.

He hadn't thought about it, but maybe she missed her business. Buying her baked goods had helped her financially, but he'd never considered how much she'd miss her interactions with customers. She seemed to have such close relationships with many of them.

Gideon's fists clenched. Russell had taken away not only her livelihood, but also her friendships. Before Gideon could worry about the consequences, he blurted out, "In fact, if you'd like, you could keep your business going like Nick's doing and pay me a small percentage of the profits."

She blinked at him, and tears welled in her eyes. "I'd love to do that. But are you sure?"

If it made her that happy, he was more than certain. He couldn't say that, so he only nodded.

"Gideon?" A woman's voice behind him jolted him back to the stand.

He turned to find Nettie studying him, her lips pursed

as if she were upset. She had Lenny and David by the hand. "You did say you needed me today?"

"I do." He wanted to wipe the uncertainty from her eyes. "I'm so glad you're here." He flashed smiles at his nephews. "And you too."

Nettie's gaze flicked to Fern. "You didn't say you'd hired other workers."

"I haven't." Now Fern had a worried look in her eyes. "I mean, this is Fern. She owns the baked goods business, and she'll be selling down here with Nick." He rushed on. "Fern, this is Nettie. She'll be helping me fix lunches."

Fern's tense smile was polite enough, but she and Nettie eyed each other warily. "Nice to meet you, Nettie." Squatting in front of the children, Fern asked, "And who are you?"

"I'm David," his nephew answered. "And this is Lenny. He's four. I'm five. Mamm says we're old enough to help."

"I'm sure you are. I started helping my *mamm* at the market when I was five."

Fern's wide, generous smile and sparkling eyes took Gideon's breath away. Nettie cleared her throat and broke the spell.

"*Gut* to meet you, Fern, but we'd better get to work. Come," she said to the children.

As they turned to follow their mother, Fern reached into the case. "Would you each like a cookie?" Then she hesitated. "If it's all right with your *mamm*, that is."

"I suppose one cookie wouldn't hurt." Nettie seemed reluctant to give permission.

Gideon had never seen her limit her children's snacks before, and he hoped his sister-in-law's lukewarm response hadn't hurt Fern's feelings. At least David and Lenny responded with enthusiasm.

David jumped up and down as Fern pulled out the tray and extended it toward him. He reached a tentative hand toward a sugar cookie.

"Only touch the one you plan to eat." Nettie's rebuke halted his hand in midair.

While his brother deliberated, Lenny slid a hand under David's arm and snatched a chocolate chip cookie. "*Danke.*" He bit into it. "Yum. This is *gut*." He spoke with his mouth full, earning him a warning look from his mother.

David grabbed the largest cookie dotted with sparkling blue sugar. Nettie frowned, but prodded, "What do you say?"

Her son's mouth was too full of cookie to answer. Nettie thanked Fern for him and herded her children down the narrow aisle toward the chicken.

Gideon lingered behind, his attention on Fern as she returned the tray to the glass display case. They hadn't really finished their discussion before Nettie arrived. Now, while she and the children were washing their hands in his small sink, might be the best time to make sure Fern did plan to stay.

Part of him eagerly awaited a *jah*, but the rest of him dreaded it. How would he keep his mind on business with Fern here every day?

Fern straightened after inserting the tray and almost bumped into Gideon. She hadn't been expecting him to stay. She'd assumed he'd follow Nettie.

Gideon cleared his throat. "I just wanted to be sure we, um, have a deal. You can decide what percentage you want to pay."

"I need to discuss it with Daed, but I'm pretty sure he'll agree."

Giving Gideon a percentage of sales would cut into their profits, but she could sell a lot more than the amount he'd requested each week if her regular customers realized she'd relocated here. She understood the caution behind his smaller-than-usual order, but she had a better knowledge of her buyers. And she could continue making birthday cakes, something Gideon hadn't requested.

She had no idea how the price increase would affect sales. So far, she'd only lost two customers who'd refused to pay the higher prices. She didn't count the Pickle Lady.

Gideon still stood there as if waiting for her to say more.

"Can I let you know when I come in to work on Thursday?"

"That'll be fine." He shuffled as if he wanted to say more.

"What do you want us to do first, Gideon?" Nettie called.

"I'd better go, but we can talk more on Thursday." He scurried down the aisle.

Nick jerked a thumb in Nettie's direction. "That his girlfriend?"

Fern shrugged. "I don't know." She'd been wondering the same thing.

"Sure acts like it. Or maybe more like a wife. Except he doesn't have a beard, so he can't be married." He cocked an eyebrow in Fern's direction. "Right?"

"*Jah.* He's not married." But if Nettie's behavior were an indicator, Gideon soon might be.

"Well, one thing's for sure, she's jealous of you." Nick chuckled.

"Of me?" *Why on earth would Nettie be jealous of me?* If anything, it was the other way around.

"Yes, of you. And she has good reason to be. You're younger, prettier, and not saddled with two young'uns."

What was with Nick and the compliments today? But he'd misread the situation. Nettie had nothing to worry about. Gideon barely even spoke to Fern, and when he did, his words came out cold and stilted.

As much as she wished Nick's assessment were true, common sense warned her not to lose her heart to a man who could never return her love.

Chapter Fourteen

"Where's the vegetable peeler?" Nettie asked.

Her question shattered Gideon's daydreams. Whenever he started drifting off, Nettie interrupted. Although he appreciated her help with the salads, he hadn't anticipated she'd bombard him with questions all day long. After all, she'd helped Thomas in this stand before they married, so she should be able to figure out most of these things on her own.

"How much salad do you want us to make?"

Lenny and David stood beside their mother, shredding lettuce into one of the huge mixing bowls he'd bought last weekend.

"I have no idea. Today's the first day we're offering it." Gideon passed them to wait on his first customer of the morning.

"Well, I need to have some idea." A hint of impatience colored Nettie's words.

Not that he blamed her. He'd been struggling to concentrate and make decisions because his mind—and his gaze—kept straying to Fern.

Besides, he couldn't answer most of Nettie's questions.

He'd never sold any of these things before. Maybe nobody would buy them because they weren't used to him offering full meals. Or perhaps they'd have huge crowds who'd love to have organic salads for lunch.

Nettie's sigh made it clear she was still waiting for an answer.

"Why don't you fill that bowl for now? If we find we need more, we can always make it," Gideon said over his shoulder before turning to his customer.

The *Englischer* waved toward Fern. "Your wife said—" He stopped speaking as Nettie passed behind Gideon with the two little ones. Confusion in his eyes, the man asked, "Or is that your wife?"

Most *Englischers* in the area could tell he was unmarried, but this man had a Southern drawl. Gideon rubbed his clean-shaven chin. "Neither one is my wife. I'm not married."

"You have your own little harem, then?" The man chuckled, but when Gideon didn't, he choked back his laughter. "Sorry. Guess you wouldn't consider that humorous."

Gideon kept his expression neutral. He didn't like to offend customers, but he didn't want to encourage disparaging remarks about Nettie or Fern.

"That lovely lady there—" The *Englischer* once again indicated Fern.

Despite Gideon's best efforts to avoid glancing in that direction, he automatically followed the man's sweeping hand gesture and then wished he hadn't. Fern, her expression soft and caring, was listening to an old man, who seemed to be rambling on.

"Hate to interrupt you there," the man said, "but I don't have a lot of time."

Gideon forced himself to concentrate on the customer in front of him.

"Not that I blame you." The *Englischer* arched his eyebrows. "She's quite a looker."

Those words made Gideon's blood rise.

"Well, anyway, she told me the chickens would be done by"—he glanced at his watch—"fifteen minutes ago."

"*She* was right." Gideon was reluctant to let the man know Fern's name. How had she known what time the meat would come off the spits? Gideon pointed to the chicken parts displayed in the warmer. "The chickens are ready. What would you like?"

"It's early yet, so no meal, although those look good. Just two whole chickens to go."

Gideon turned away to hide a smile. Why did the *Englischer* add the words *to go*? Gideon certainly wouldn't expect the man to sit at the small tables scattered nearby and eat both chickens. Perhaps he'd only been trying to emphasize the need to hurry.

But as Gideon slid each chicken into an insulated bag, his mind wandered to Fern. By sheer willpower, he focused on handing over the chickens and making the correct change. Then he allowed himself one brief glance in her direction.

She was leaning over the counter to hand a cookie to a small boy in a baseball cap. The boy's gap-toothed grin and shining eyes thanked her.

Was she giving away another cookie? It seemed she'd found the secret to children's hearts.

Gideon's chest ached. She not only affected young hearts—she'd managed to win over an older, hardened one too.

* * *

Fern couldn't resist the apple-cheeked grin from one of her favorite youngsters. "Here, Liam." She held out a pink-iced heart. "Take this cookie to your sister."

Liam eyed the cookie hungrily. Fern wagged a finger at him, but softened it with a smile.

She pointed to his half-eaten chocolate chip cookie. "You already have one."

Luckily, business being so brisk had prevented Fern from checking on Gideon, but he was never far from her thoughts.

After she'd waited on the next woman in line, an *Englisch* man with an *I-know-I'm-handsome-and-you-should-too* attitude leaned one elbow on the counter. Although Fern had to concede he was good-looking, his smarmy smile made her skin crawl.

"You must have a pretty popular business." He looked at her with an appreciative gleam in his eye that had nothing to do with her sales.

"I do have a lot of regular customers." Fern dipped her head and pretended to be absorbed in moving her unsold baked goods to the front of the case. His intense stare made her squirm.

She also wanted to keep busy because she realized she'd seen him earlier that morning. He was the man who'd held the door open for her. The one who worked for the organic market that had put her out of business.

"I thought you said you didn't work here."

"I don't. I mean, I didn't. I'm helping Gideon today." He made her so uncomfortable, she didn't want to let him know she might have a job here.

"I hope he'll decide he needs you to stick around permanently. Then we can get to know each other."

Getting to know him was the last thing Fern wanted to do, so she stayed silent.

He didn't seem to notice her reluctance to talk or that a line of customers had formed behind him.

"My name's Bo Ridley. I own the organic market on the hill." He waved in the direction of his blue monstrosity. "And you must be Fern Blauch."

How did he know her name? She nodded, slid the tray she'd arranged back into place, and pulled out another one.

"Don't you want to know how I know who you are?"

Although she did, she'd rather not engage in conversation with him. And she'd much rather wait on customers.

Her silence didn't deter him. "I also know you're quite popular, Fern, judging by the number of people who came to my stand today looking for you. I spent more time answering questions about your location than I did selling anything."

"I'm sorry. I did let people know I was moving. The ones who missed the sign and flyers must have been confused not to see me in my usual spot."

"They definitely were. And some were quite upset. They said they'd been coming to your stand for years. And Bertha's Candy Cupboard too." He smiled in Nick's direction.

"You're a Ridley?" Nick snarled.

"Sure am. I'm *the* Ridley of Ridley's Organics."

Fern cringed. Bo Ridley seemed to have no idea he'd just lit the fuse of a bomb. A bomb that was about to detonate.

"Then you're the one who put us out of business," Nick

growled, his face almost purple. He clenched his hands into fists and started in Bo's direction.

"Nick," Fern warned softly, "you have three little girls who want some candy."

He looked over his shoulder, and his expression softened. "I'd better deal with them." Before he did, he glared at Bo. "Don't think I'm done with you."

After Nick turned, Bo said quietly, "I guess he's upset that I took over his space."

"We all are." Fern had to be honest. "Most of us had been there for generations. My grandmother started the bakery business. Nick's stand was one of the original ones. His family owned it since the first day this market opened."

Bo's eyes widened, and to his credit, he even looked a little guilty. "Sorry, I didn't know. I just saw that space had some older stands, and Russell said he wanted to modernize. I guess I didn't think about the people who'd be affected."

Fern dipped her head to acknowledge he'd spoken, but she didn't answer. She couldn't. Her throat had tightened, and her eyes stung. She didn't want to feel sorry for Bo, but he hadn't taken over that space to hurt them.

Bo sighed. "I'd hoped to talk to Gideon. It'll have to be another time. I see he's swamped with customers."

"Lunchtime is the busiest time for all of us. People in the nearby businesses all stop by to get lunch and do their shopping."

"Oh." Bo glanced behind him. "I didn't realize I was holding up your customers. Sorry. I seem to owe you a lot of apologies today." He straightened up. "If lunchtime is as busy as you say, I'd better get back to supervise my workers."

Relief coursed through Fern as he hurried away. But a small ache remained.

Bo had wanted to talk to Gideon. Earlier that morning Bo had mentioned doing business with Gideon. It hurt to think of Gideon supporting the man who'd taken over her spot in the market and put her out of business.

As busy as he was, Gideon couldn't help noticing the *Englischer* flirting with Fern. He'd seen that man in Ridley's Organic Meats earlier. The way the *Englischer* leaned his elbow on the counter and acted so chummy made Gideon's blood boil.

Fern would never be interested in an *Englischer*, would she? Although logic told him she was with the church and would never leave the faith, his irritation simmered. He was tempted to go down there and point out that the man was holding up all the other customers.

Caroline shot him a sly look as she passed. "Something bothering you, *bruder*?"

Gideon almost growled at her but caught himself in time. If he did, she'd know her teasing had bothered him. And she was smart enough to figure out why.

Luckily, the *Englischer* moved back and let other customers surge toward the counter. Some of the tension in Gideon's chest eased. Caroline was still staring at him, waiting for an answer.

"What makes you think something's wrong?"

She shrugged. "You don't normally hack chicken with the back of the blade."

Gideon glanced down at the cleaver. He flipped it over and brought it down with a loud *thwack*. But the noise wasn't loud enough to drown out Caroline's soft snicker.

His sister's mocking looks, along with the steady flood of crowds, kept Gideon focused on his own counter and customers. "I guess adding salads and full meals was a good idea," he remarked as he danced between lowering batches of fries into hot oil, reloading the rotisserie, and asking Nettie to mix up more bowls of salad.

"I guess." Caroline's mouth twisted into a pout. "Except it means I can't eat with Zach."

A teasing comment flitted through Gideon's mind, but he bit it back. No sense in annoying his sister when he could barely fill the orders, even with her help. He really needed Aidan.

The long lines continued until closing time. When they'd waited on the last family, Gideon breathed a sigh of relief.

Neh, here came one more. An *Englischer* leaned on the counter.

"You closed?" he asked.

As soon as Gideon recognized the man, he was tempted to say yes, but his customary politeness prevented him from being rude. "What would you like?"

"To talk to you."

Gideon had been unprepared for that answer, and he gaped at the man.

"You have a little time now?"

He had no more customers, but he did have work. And he'd much rather clean than talk to this flirt who'd chatted up Fern earlier. Gideon shot a questioning glance at Caroline, who was hovering nearby, perhaps to eavesdrop on the conversation.

His sister frowned. "You're sticking me with the cleanup again?"

His sister's complaint probably had more to do with

missing Zach than with doing the work, but guilt niggled at Gideon. This business was his responsibility. *Jah*, it supported the family, but he shouldn't leave Caroline with all the work. Before he gave in and offered to do everything himself, Nettie shepherded the children toward them.

"It's all right, Gideon. I can stay to help Caroline." Nettie's usual sweet smile had returned. "David and Lenny know how to do chores."

Gideon's tight lips relaxed into a broad grin of thankfulness. "*Danke* so much." His overenthusiastic response kindled a flame in Nettie's eyes that made him wary. She always appeared overly grateful for every little thing he did, which made him uncomfortable.

No time to think about that now. He needed to find out what this man wanted and end their talk quickly. If Gideon followed his instincts, he'd stay far away from anyone connected with Ridley's. Especially someone who made eyes at Fern.

Crossing his arms, Gideon returned to the counter to face the man he'd already come to resent without even knowing his name.

"Hey, I'm Bo Ridley. I just opened Ridley's Organic Meats & Produce." He waved toward the far end of the aisle.

This was even worse than Gideon had thought. He'd assumed Bo worked at Ridley's, not that he owned it. Standing in front of him was the man who'd caused Fern and the others to lose their stands. But God would want him to forgive Bo. In some ways, Gideon would find it easier to let it go if it had happened to him. But Fern? That was a different story.

"Welcome," Gideon said through clenched teeth. "I'm Gideon Hartzler."

"I know. I've heard a lot about you. So, what all do you sell here?"

Gideon resisted the temptation to point to his menu, hanging a few feet from the man's head. All Bo had to do was glance up to see.

Biting back a sigh, Gideon opted for politeness. "Mainly barbecued chicken, although we're expanding to add full meals."

"I see you do organic too."

Gideon nodded. So Bo *had* read the sign. Why did he ask what they sold? Maybe he was only trying to start a conversation.

Gideon shouldn't be so judgmental. The man was only being neighborly. And Gideon shouldn't hold a grudge because Bo had pushed Mose, Fern, and the others out of their stands. Most likely he had no idea of the havoc and pain he'd caused for them and for their regular customers.

Bo tapped a finger on the glass. "It's smart to mark your produce organic, so you can double or triple the price."

Did he mean to imply Gideon was lying by labeling his foods as organic? It almost sounded like it, but maybe he'd misunderstood. He made his answer noncommittal. "A lot of people are looking for organic now."

"Exactly, which is why we have it in large letters on our new sign."

Gideon had glimpsed that sign when he'd accompanied Mrs. Vandenburg to the front of the market. Most people had five-foot wooden signs over their stands. Ridley's stretched the length of the whole row. The row that used to contain the small stands he'd put out of business. Gideon and Mrs. Vandenburg had gaped at the gleaming glass cases and bright turquoise bins brimming with odd-colored vegetables. Gideon wondered if people considered them appetizing. He'd prefer vegetables the color God originally made them.

The word *ORGANIC* had been printed in huge, red capital letters right over the spot where Fern's stand once stood. Gideon's stomach clenched.

At the end of the sign, where Mose should have been, in small cursive letters, the sign said, *Est. 1919*.

What?

They'd had an organic business for more than one hundred years? Did people even care about or know about organic foods back then?

Gideon had been so lost in thought, he jumped when Caroline bumped his shoulder as she pressed the tab on the cash register drawer.

"Sorry to disturb you," she said. "I need to count the money."

Caroline didn't sound the least bit repentant. Gideon smiled to himself. His sister had hoped to eavesdrop. Except he'd been so busy mentally picking out Bo's faults, they hadn't started talking yet.

The whole time, Bo had stood there, patiently waiting. Now, though, he leaned forward, curiosity flaring in his eyes as the drawer slid open.

"Just a sec," Gideon said to him. "Things are busy at closing." Normally, they counted the money in the drawer, but Bo's avid stare made Gideon uncomfortable.

He lifted out the till and handed it to Caroline. Her eyes widened in surprise, but she got the message. She carried it behind the cooking area, out of Bo's sight.

Before Gideon turned back to Bo, he struggled to get control of his temper and his critical attitude. *Lord, forgive me for judging. Give me an open mind and heart.*

"Looks like you do a good business here," Bo remarked.

They'd had an exceptional day. The expanded menu had brought new customers flocking to the stand. "Today was our first day selling full meals."

"Really? Well, they seem to be a hit. I stopped by earlier to talk to you, but you guys were hopping."

So he'd decided to flirt with Fern instead? Bo hadn't seemed eager to speak with anyone else.

"I noticed the candy and baked goods at the other end of your stand. Fern told me they used to be in my spot. I didn't mean to bump anyone out."

"I see." If Bo meant that, why had he taken over their spaces?

"Russell led me to believe those stands were closing down, but so many people asked about Fern's baked goods today, it didn't seem she was going out of business. And she had long lines when I came by." Bo looked genuinely guilty.

Gideon had misjudged Bo. The man hadn't been heartless. Russell had lied to him.

"I'm not sure what to do about it now." Bo spread his hands in a helpless gesture. "I can't give them back their stands. I'm glad you took care of them."

"*Jah*, well." Gideon wished Bo would get to the point of his visit.

"Anyway, we both sell organic," Bo said, "but you sell cooked meats and prepared salads."

Gideon nodded. They'd already established that.

"Glad we won't be rivals." Bo flashed Gideon a toothy

smile. "And just so you know, I can give you a good deal on chickens. You'd be better off getting them from us than your usual supplier."

"Thanks. I appreciate the offer." Gideon didn't want to get entangled in a business arrangement with someone he'd spent so much time resenting. Besides, it might hurt Fern.

Maybe God was nudging him to let go of his grudge. After all, Bo had only made a smart business decision. And he claimed he'd had no idea he was putting people out of business.

"I'd better get going, but I think you'll find we'll make you an offer you can't refuse," Bo said over his shoulder as he headed off.

Up to that point, Bo had seemed friendly. Why did his parting comment sound more like a threat?

Chapter Fifteen

As Bo Ridley strode off, Caroline slid the till into the cash register and tucked the money bag with the bank deposit on the shelf beneath it. "Who was that guy and what did he want?"

"Bo Ridley. He's the one who opened the new stand."

"The one who put Nick and Fern out of business?"

"*Jah*, that's him. But he said Russell told him those businesses were closing."

"What?"

Caroline's screech hurt Gideon's ears.

His sister's eyes narrowed, and she studied him. "So why did he come here? To check to be sure Fern and Nick are okay? Or did he just want to meet the other stand owners?"

Gideon didn't answer. Bo's parting comment had indicated his visit had a hidden meaning. He wanted to sell his chickens, but did he intend to twist Gideon's arm if he refused?

"Hey?" Caroline waved a hand in front of his face. "You've been staring off into space all day. First Fern, now this."

"Listen, I can take over the cleaning so you can run out to see Zach before he leaves."

"Trying to get rid of me so you don't have to answer questions?"

"Of course not." He only wanted to be left in peace so he could daydream about Fern.

"There you go again," Caroline accused. "You have that faraway look in your eyes."

Gideon blew out a long, martyred breath. "I have a lot on my mind."

"I know. Fern, Fern, Fern, and more Fern." She giggled.

Nettie stood nearby helping David clean the rotisserie door. At the mention of Fern's name, she frowned in their direction, then scrubbed furiously.

One more worry. Something about Fern upset Nettie. Gideon couldn't imagine why. Or maybe he could, but he didn't want to go there.

Caroline straightened her apron and *kapp*. "I'm going to see Zach, but first, I want to know what Bo—what kind of name is that?—Ridley wanted."

"He wants us to buy his organic chickens."

"You're not going to do that, are you? Not after he put Nick and Fern and Mose out of business."

"*Neh.*" Gideon had no intention of doing business with Bo. And he certainly didn't want to hurt Fern. Or Nick and the others. Besides, he was locked into the contract Thomas had negotiated, and that still had a year to go.

"Good." Caroline flounced off.

Finally, Gideon could retreat back into reminiscing over all the details he'd stored away about Fern. The way she leaned over the counter, her eyes sympathetic as the old man recounted a long story. The way her eyes sparkled when she handed children free cookies. The way she bent over gracefully to lift baked goods from the tray. The way she—

"Gideon?"

Nettie's sharp voice interrupted.

"Did you want me to make more of the salads you're low on?"

"Caroline will be making them tomorrow so they'll be fresher for Thursday morning." When Nettie looked hurt, Gideon added, "I'm sure she'd be glad to have help tomorrow."

"I put all the pieces from the rotisserie into the sink to soak."

"*Danke*," Gideon said absentmindedly, wishing he could head back to his imagination. "I can clean those so you can go."

"You didn't want me to do the counters or—or . . .?" Nettie looked as if she were about to burst into tears.

"I'd be happy for your help. I just thought you'd want to be home when Katie gets back from school." As soon as he said it, Gideon realized Katie would have gotten off school an hour ago.

"Katie has her scooter, so she can get home. And Mamm's there with Sadie."

Caroline stuck her head in the door and called out, "You don't have to wait for me. Zach'll drive me home after we finish."

We? Gideon was tempted to throw that word at her Again, he doubted Caroline would be much help to the auctioneers, but he'd disliked her teasing. He shouldn't return it.

The door banged shut behind his sister.

If she'd been going off with one of her buddy bunch from the church youth group, Gideon would have called after her, *Have fun!* But that wouldn't be appropriate. And he didn't want to encourage her relationship with Zach. Not until he had a chance to investigate some of the rumors swirling about the new auctioneer.

Maybe he should go after Caroline and insist she ride home with him rather than Zach.

"Gideon," Nettie said behind him. "The refrigerator's a little messy. Should I clean it out?"

"Do whatever you think is best." He hadn't meant to act impatient, but Nettie had worked in the stand before she had the children. She had as much knowledge about what needed to be done as he did.

Nettie retreated into sullen silence. He'd never seen her act like this before. She'd always been calm and sure of herself. Instead, all day long, she'd asked question after question about what she should do next. And she'd also overcorrected the children's small mistakes. She usually wasn't so critical.

What bothered him most were her glares. The majority of them had been targeted at Fern's back. But several times, Fern had turned unexpectedly, and Nettie had rapidly rearranged her features into a semipleasant half smile. As far as he could tell, Fern had done nothing to deserve Nettie's animosity.

Pushing his worries aside, Gideon cleaned all the rotisserie parts and put them in place while Nettie wiped out the refrigerator. He indulged in recalling each sneak peek he'd taken of Fern.

"I'm finished," Nettie announced. "Do you need anything else?"

"*Neh. Danke* for all you've done today. I'm sorry for being so *mürrisch.*"

"It's all right. You had a lot to deal with today. The business did well, didn't it?"

Caroline had cashed out the register, so Gideon didn't know for sure. They had been extremely busy. "I'd say so." He'd find out when he deposited the money.

"I'm glad." Nettie's face relaxed into the first real smile Gideon had seen all day. "I always worry we're a heavy burden for you."

Gideon hoped he hadn't done or said anything to give her that impression. "*Ach*, Nettie. Never think that. I'm happy to take care of all of you." *Jah*, it was a weighty responsibility, but he'd taken it on willingly.

"If you're sure?" Once again, Nettie appeared uncertain. "I thought maybe, well, that caring for us might be keeping you from courting."

"Not at all." Gideon busied himself with reinserting the center shaft and side wheels so he didn't have to meet her eyes. "There's no one I'm interested in dating."

Nettie hissed out a breath. With his back to her, he couldn't tell if she was relieved or disapproving. It almost sounded like a little of both. He didn't turn around to check.

He could have added, *Thomas warned me against falling for a woman.* Gideon would never make his brother's error of saddling himself with a wife and large family before he could financially support them. Thomas and Nettie had been so madly in love, they'd made a foolish mistake. They'd only been baptized a few months when she discovered she was in the family way. A hasty wedding, and four children over the next four years, had overwhelmed Thomas. Learning Nettie was expecting baby number five had broken him.

"Gideon? Are you all right?" Nettie studied him, anxiety in her eyes.

Not really. But he couldn't share his concerns with his sister-in-law. She had enough to handle. Losing her husband and her fifth baby within months of each other, raising four little ones alone. Well, it wasn't really alone when you lived with family, but Nettie bore most of the burden.

"I'm tired," he admitted, although that was only part of the truth.

He avoided her searching gaze by putting the grease deflectors and fan covers back in place. Then he checked the door gaskets. They were spotless. "Excellent job on these."

Nettie beamed. "I did the top, but David did this one. He did work hard to get all the grease off."

David peeked his head around the corner. "I did good."

"You sure did." Gideon gave his nephew a special smile.

Lenny joined his brother. "I helped too." He ran his hand along the counter. "I cleaned this."

"*Danke.*" Gideon gave them each a grateful smile. They'd behaved well and had avoided getting underfoot as the adults rushed around. They'd even carried salads to customers. "You both did a good job today."

David's small chest puffed out, but Lenny ran over, threw his arms around Gideon's legs, and hugged hard. "I like being with you all day. I miss you when you go to work."

"We all do." Nettie's eyes rounded, and she clapped a hand over her mouth. "I mean . . . the, um, boys do. And the girls too," she stammered, her face flushed.

A warning flutter started in Gideon's stomach. He'd pushed Nettie's dislike for Fern out of his mind, but now uneasiness set in. He hoped Nettie didn't think that his decision to take care of her and the children and help with bedtime routines meant he intended to . . . Nettie couldn't possibly suppose . . .

Had asking her to work in the stand given her the wrong idea? How could he correct that impression? He needed her help.

After Nettie left, Gideon collected the money bag. He'd deposit it on the way home. When he arrived at the bank parking lot, he unzipped the bag to check the deposit slip. Gideon stared at the numbers Caroline had printed.

They'd taken in double their usual amount. Of course, their expenses ran much higher now that he had to buy salad ingredients, but maybe he'd make enough to get some of those debts paid off.

After he finished in the bank, he sat in the parking lot, mulling over the help he needed for the stand. He couldn't afford to hire many workers, so Nettie and Caroline would have to do. Unless . . .

Gideon clicked to his horse and turned in the opposite direction from home. He'd probably get a *neh*, but he could at least ask.

He pulled in front of the house he'd come to a few months ago. He hoped what he planned to do wouldn't start a family battle.

Lord, please direct my steps and my words.

Throwing back his shoulders for courage, Gideon strode onto the porch and knocked.

A tired dishwater blonde in her late forties opened the door. "You here to see Nick? Come on in."

"Actually, I wanted to talk to Aidan. If he's around."

"I think he just headed up to his room."

"Stomped is more like it." Nick bit into a thick sandwich as he walked into the room. He stopped when he saw Gideon. "What're you doing here?" he asked with his mouth full.

"Hoping to talk to Aidan."

Nick frowned and gulped down his bite. "You're not planning to ask him to work at the market after what happened this morning?"

"Nick," his wife pleaded.

Ignoring her, he picked up the remote from the coffee table and clicked on a show. She glanced at him, a hurt look in her eyes.

"I don't think . . ." she said. Her gaze flitted from her husband to the door.

Gideon didn't want to make her any more uncomfortable. She obviously wanted him to leave. But he hadn't come all this way to go without speaking to Aidan. Even if it was only to apologize.

When Gideon didn't take her subtle hint, she pinched her lips together. With one last exasperated glance at Nick, she beckoned for Gideon to follow her down the hall and into the kitchen.

"I'm sure you know Aidan and his dad don't get along."

With a nod, Gideon took the chair she indicated.

"I'll run up to see if he wants to talk to you. I'm not sure he will. This morning he slammed into the house complaining about being betrayed."

"I'm sorry. I didn't know Nick hadn't told him about working there."

"Yeah, well, it's not your fault. Most people would assume a father and son would talk to each other." With a deep sigh, she added, "Aidan hasn't spoken civilly to his dad since he became a teenager. I can't say Nick's been any better."

All Gideon could think of to say was *I'm sorry*, but he'd already said that. His *daed* and Thomas had had a strained relationship when his brother rebelled during *Rumspringa*, but Thomas had never spoken disrespectfully, no matter how many times he'd broken the rules and his parents' hearts.

"Listen, I'll do my best. Sometimes I can get Aidan to listen to reason." Nick's wife left the room.

The TV blaring from the living room didn't drown out the banging and scuffling overhead.

"Please, Aidan." His mom's desperate voice filtered downstairs. Loud thumps of a bass drum filled the air, followed by screechy guitars and what Gideon supposed was intended to be music.

"Turn down that caterwauling," Nick screamed, "before I come up and bust that—" His next words were muffled, as if he realized Gideon was still there.

After turning the music to earsplitting decibels, Aidan banged down the stairs. His mom, with an apologetic glance at Gideon, entered the kitchen behind her son.

"What do you want?" Aidan's set jaw and crossed arms didn't bode well for Gideon's request.

"I came to say I'm sorry. I should have told you about—"

Aidan cut him off by chopping a hand in the air. "Not your fault, man. I guess where you come from kids talk to their *fathers*." Aidan spat out the last word as if it were poison.

"We still should have talked about it," Gideon had been aware of the tense relationship Aidan had with his dad.

"I'm not all that mad at you," Aidan admitted. "I just

spent the past few weeks thinking I'd get to take over the stand."

"That was my fault," his mom broke in. "Your dad did say Gideon would be running the business. After he changed his mind, I should have told you. It's just that I had no idea what you'd been planning."

Aidan sank into a chair at the table. "Shoulda told you, I guess. It's just that I loved working there with Grandma." Bitterness colored his tone. "She'd still be around if the old m—"

At his mother's warning look, Aidan snapped his mouth shut.

Then a defiant glare entered his eyes. "Well, she'd still be around if it wasn't for *him*. He's the one who put her in that nursing home. She lost her will to live after that."

"I don't think Gideon wants to hear us air our dirty laundry."

Aidan's sullen *Sorry* didn't sound the least bit apologetic. "Thanks for stopping by, Gid. I knew you were real." He started to rise, but his mom reached out and put her hand over his to stop him.

"I think Gideon has something else to ask you."

"We were swamped today," Gideon said. "I could really use your help."

Aidan shook his head. "Work there with my old"—he ignored his mother's hissed out breath—"man? No way."

"You could stay at the end by the fries. Caroline and I would be between you and the other end of the counter. Fern would be there too."

"I'd puke if I had to see him every day. That wouldn't be good for your business."

"Aidan!" His mother sounded shocked.

"What, Mom? It's not like I don't say stuff like that all the time."

"I know, but he's Amish."

"Don't worry. He's pretty cool."

Gideon hid a smile. Nice to know Aidan considered him cool. "Caroline will be disappointed. She missed you when she had to clean up alone."

"Caroline? Naw, man. She hates me."

"That's not what she said when she got stuck with the cleanup."

"Really? You serious?"

"I think she realized what a big help you are. I know I wished you were around all day today. Nobody was there to make sure I didn't forget the French fries."

A tiny smile played at the corner of Aidan's lips. "Yeah, there is that."

"Will you consider coming back?"

"I don't know, man. It'd be tough."

"But you're tougher."

Aidan laughed. "You're good, man. Okay, I'll try."

"I appreciate it. And I'll talk to Fern and Caroline to be sure someone's always between you and the far corner."

"You don't have to do that. Like you said, I'm tougher. I'm tougher than my problems. And I'm definitely tougher than my old man."

Gideon wasn't so sure about that, but he was grateful Aidan had agreed. Now all he had to do was make sure they kept a buffer between Aidan and his dad at all times. The last thing they needed was for the tensions between them to flare.

Chapter Sixteen

"Fern?" Gideon stopped her as she entered the stand with her baked goods on Thursday morning. "I need to talk to you, but first, do you want help?"

Gideon's voice saying her name had punctured the calm she'd talked herself into that morning. "I can do it."

"I know you can. I asked if you'd like me to help."

She was torn between agreeing and enjoying his company or turning him down and controlling her runaway emotions.

Without waiting for an answer, he lifted the top two containers and carried them to her section of the stand. Fern waited until he returned to pull her cart into the narrow aisle.

He backed up as she passed, which both relieved and disappointed her. Then he stood there, waiting.

Oh, right. He'd said he wanted to talk to her. Maybe he wanted to hear her decision about working in the stand. Or . . . did he plan to tell her he'd changed his mind?

She hoped not. She'd been looking forward to this since Daed had agreed. Better get it over with.

"Daed came up with what he hopes is a fair way to divide the profit. That is, if you still wanted to do that."

"Of course I do. I'm glad you're willing to do it."

If so, why did his words come out so stilted and hesitant? He didn't sound pleased. Instead, he seemed almost wary. Did he worry he couldn't count on her?

"Listen, before Nick gets in, I wanted to tell you that Aidan's agreed to work here."

"*Wunderbar.* I'm so glad he and his dad worked things out."

"Um, *neh*, that's what I need to talk to you about. They aren't getting along at all."

"But then why did Aidan decide to come back?"

"I think I talked him into it. Or maybe pressured him."

Fern couldn't imagine Gideon pressuring anyone.

Her skepticism must have showed in the tilt of her head, because Gideon said, "I convinced him he needed to be tougher than his dad."

"I imagine Aidan agreed with that."

"He did. But it's true. He needs to be strong to handle Nick's criticism."

"That's for sure." Aidan had endured the sharp edge of his dad's tongue from the time he was young.

"The reason I wanted to talk to you is because I made Aidan a promise that I'd keep people between him and his dad."

"That's such a shame." Fern couldn't imagine having to ask people to stand between her and Daed.

"It is, but if I'm going to keep Aidan, we need to keep the two of them separate."

Poor Aidan. And poor Nick. How sad that his son refused to be around him.

"The way the stand's set up, you already box Nick in

down here. Caroline and I can block the chicken aisle. I want to prevent arguments."

"I understand." But keeping Nick and Aidan apart would add a lot of tension. "I hope Nick won't say mean things about Aidan." Nick had a habit of criticizing his son's attitudes and actions to his customers.

"Me too." Gideon looked up. "Here comes Nick. I guess I should let him know about Aidan." He headed out to meet Nick.

Fern didn't envy him that job. A few minutes later, Nick pushed past her. He appeared to be steaming. Fern vacillated between making conversation or letting Nick stew for a while. She finished unpacking her cookies and pastries while Nick removed the sheets he draped over his counter each night.

The envelope from Daed lay in the bottom of the last container. Fern tucked it under the cash box. She'd give it to Gideon later.

"Good morning, Nick," she called as he refilled an almost empty glass jar of giant jawbreakers.

"Is it?"

"Well, it's sunny outside for a change."

"Great." His clipped, sarcastic answer made it clear he didn't want to talk to her.

Fern left him alone and finished arranging cupcakes on the top shelf. She'd even brought a birthday cake. Two of her regular customers had family birthdays today, so she hoped one of them might want it.

As she set it in the display case, Aidan headed down the aisle, his walk stiff and face tight. Should she call Nick's attention to his son? Or would it be better to let Aidan slip past unseen?

Beside her, Nick tensed. He must have spotted Aidan. Nick turned his back and rummaged through one of the boxes.

Aidan glanced up at the Bertha's Candy Cupboard sign. For a moment, his expression softened, and he reverted to the young boy he'd been when Fern had first met him. Then he stared at his father's back. Hurt and longing warred in his eyes.

With a toss of his head that sent his greasy bangs flying, Aidan's jaw hardened, and his look and stride turned macho. He nodded at Fern as he passed and avoided looking in his father's direction.

Caroline shifted so he could get by. "Glad you're here. We missed you Tuesday."

"I bet."

"We really did. Until you were gone, I didn't realize what a big help you are."

Adian shot her a skeptical look. "You serious?"

Beside Fern, Nick sounded like he was choking.

"Are you okay?" she whispered.

His face contorted into disgust as Gideon patted Aidan's shoulder.

"My sister doesn't lie," Gideon said. "I'm glad to have an experienced French fry maker take over for me."

Aidan's proud grin lit up his whole face. "Aw, thanks, man. What do you want me to do first?"

Gideon's eyes met Fern's, and they shared a relieved smile. Everything had gone more smoothly than they'd expected. When her pulse erupted into a rapid patter, she broke their gaze, hoping her eyes hadn't given her away.

Nick was still ripping through the box of candy. He

seemed more intent on destruction than on finding a certain kind. He muttered something.

Fern was unsure if he meant for her to hear or if he was talking to himself. To be polite, she asked, "What, Nick?"

He glanced up at her, his eyes brimming with anger. "I didn't say anything to you."

Fern backed up a step. "Sorry."

"What are you sorry for?"

"I didn't mean to upset you."

"*You* didn't upset me." He pushed out each word between his teeth.

"I see." Fern slid the cookies she'd been arranging into the display case.

"*I see. I see,*" Nick mocked. "Why do you people always say that? You don't see anything. You don't understand anything."

"I'd like to try."

Nick's features remained twisted, and he spluttered. With his red face, blazing eyes, and outstretched hands, he looked as if he planned to throttle her.

Fern stood motionless. Her natural instinct was to apologize or soothe, but that might add fuel to the fire. Better to let Nick rage. Maybe he'd release some of his pent-up anger.

"Is everything all right?" Gideon came up behind her.

Fern tensed at his nearness. Caught between Nick's fury and Gideon's warmth, she couldn't breathe. Her heart banged against her ribs so hard they ached.

Nick spun to face Gideon. "No, it is NOT all right. You people are treating that son of mine like he's some kind of royalty. Praising him for showing up to do a job he skipped out on Tuesday." Nick's voice raised to a shout. "What he needs is a good thrashing!"

"And you'd love to give it to me, wouldn't you?" Aidan yelled. "Except I'm too fast for you to catch me."

"Aidan?" Gideon's quiet question cut through the tension-filled air. It served as a reminder they were in a public place. Customers had already started entering.

The teen glanced around at the people coming through the doors. "Sorry, man," he mumbled. He whirled around and returned to brushing the chickens with barbecue sauce.

"I'm sorry this upset you," Gideon said to Nick.

Gideon's breath so close behind Fern made her shiver. His strength gave her a sense of protection. If Nick went wild, Gideon would step in and save her.

Nick glowered at Gideon. "Did you ever think how this would make me feel?"

Neh, he hadn't. His only concern in keeping Nick and Aidan separated had been to help Aidan. He'd assumed Nick, as a parent and an adult, would handle the situation. Gideon had figured wrong.

When Nick took a step toward him, Gideon reached for Fern to move her out of the way. He had to protect her.

But he hadn't counted on the softness of her arms. Touching her did strange things to his insides. And her quick intake of breath made him ache with longing.

He didn't have time for yearning. He moved her to one side, let go of her arms, and slid in front of her.

Nick's bark of laughter echoed through the market. "You don't trust me? You think I'd harm Fern?"

"*Neh.* You'd never hurt her." Although Gideon hoped that was true, he was filled with uncertainty. Mostly, he wanted to calm Nick.

"Then why are you standing in front of her like some knight in shining armor?"

"I didn't want her caught in the middle of our discussion."

"Yeah, right."

If Gideon had closed his eyes, he'd have mistaken Nick's sarcastic comeback for one of Aidan's. Their tone and inflection matched exactly.

"Look, Nick"—Gideon spread his hands in a conciliatory gesture—"I wish I'd asked you about this. I had no idea it would upset you this much."

"Upset me?" Nick's voice was a screech. "You've heard me rant day in and day out about my son's rebellion, his nastiness, his troublemaking. And you didn't think it might bother me? Or infuriate me?"

"I guess I should have known."

"You're darn right you should have."

"Nick?" Fern's soft voice came from behind Gideon. "Isn't it a good thing that Aidan's working? You always said you wanted him to have a steady job."

Nick growled deep within his throat and ripped off the candy-striped apron he always wore. "*Ack*! I can't stand this." He gestured toward Fern and then the rest of the stand.

"Can't stand what?" Fern's gentle question had a soothing effect on Gideon. He hoped it would calm Nick.

Nick tossed his apron onto the boxes he'd been unpacking. "I can't work here with all this goodness and light."

Goodness and light? All Gideon had noticed so far today had been tension and irritation.

His tone a mocking falsetto, Nick minced out his words. *"Ooh, Aidan, we're so glad you're here. Ooh, Aidan, we couldn't run this stand without you. Ooh, Aidan, you're the most wonderful worker in the universe."*

Although Nick was exaggerating their comments, he sounded almost jealous of the compliments they'd been giving his son.

"What am I? Chopped liver? I've been coming here faithfully for over thirty years. Day in and day out. Whether I was sick or well. Did that little louse ever appreciate my sacrifices?"

"Nick?" Fern pointed to the customers lining up at his stand and the people standing around gaping.

Gideon repeated Nick's name, but he ignored both of them.

"I put food on the table and a roof over his head. And what thanks do I get? A disobedient, rotten, self-centered brat who breaks every rule, talks disrespectfully—"

"Nick." This time Gideon made his warning firm and clear. "Fern needs to wait on her customers, but—" He motioned with his chin to show Nick was blocking her counter.

"What?" Nick snarled. "I'm in her way? Well, guess what? I'll get out of everyone's way." He shoved past Fern, knocking her into Gideon. "You can have my worthless son instead."

Aidan stared after his father in horror as Nick strode to the exit and slammed out the door. "I-I'm sorry," he stammered. "I didn't mean to make trouble for you. I'm the one who should go."

Gideon shook his head and moved so he stood between Aidan and the stand exit. "I can't afford to lose you too. I hope your dad will calm down and come back."

"You don't know my old, um, my dad. He never backs down."

This time it wasn't just a father-son fight; it was Nick's livelihood. "Until he does, someone needs to wait on the customers. Would you do that?"

"Me?" With a stunned look on his face, Aidan stared at Gideon. "You want me to take over the candy business?"

"You were ready to do it on Tuesday," Gideon pointed out. "And the chicken's in the rotisserie, so we don't need help there yet."

"All right." Straightening his shoulders, Aidan headed to that corner of the stand.

He bent and picked up the apron his father had discarded and held it out in the air with two fingers as if he wanted nothing to do with it. Making a face, he looped it over his head. He had to wrap it around his waist twice before he tied it.

Gideon swallowed hard. Except for his thinness, Aidan looked much like his father had years ago when Gideon was small. Fern must be remembering that too, because she got teary-eyed when Aidan leaned over the counter to help the first customer.

She had such a loving, tender heart. The more time he spent around her, the more he wanted to be with her all the time.

What was he thinking? He had Nettie and the four children to care for, as well as the rest of his family. Plus he'd taken on responsibility for Aidan, Mose, Fern, and Nick— whether or not he returned—along with Thomas's debt.

Fern blinked back the moisture in her eyes. Aidan used to stand on a stool beside his father, wearing a miniature version of that candy-striped apron, to hand customers their change. Now he'd taken his father's place.

She made the mistake of meeting Gideon's eyes. They were both bursting with pride over Aidan's businesslike manner. But Nick's abrupt departure had left a gaping hole. She only hoped Nick would simmer down soon and return to the stand.

Something shifted suddenly in Gideon's eyes. They went shuttered and blank.

With a sigh, Fern turned toward her first customer and pasted on a cheery smile. "I'm sorry to keep you waiting."

Mary Ann Kemp leaned in close and whispered, "What's going on, Fern?"

"I'm not sure."

"What's with Nick's big scene? Aidan's taking over for his dad?"

How did Fern answer questions without spreading gossip? The regular customers would be curious.

"I'm really not sure," Fern repeated. She had no idea what might happen. "What can I get you?" she asked Mary Ann, whose face fell over missing out on juicy rumors.

"Can you package up that cake for me? My mom's in town, and her birthday's tomorrow."

Fern wished she'd made more cakes. Now she didn't have one for either of the other customers who might want one. But since she'd be working here, she could start taking cake orders again.

The woman behind Mary Ann sighed. "I'd been hoping to get that cake. Our anniversary's on Saturday."

"I can make one for you and have it ready tomorrow or Saturday," Fern offered.

"That's okay. I'll just take some cupcakes."

Fern stayed busy all morning. Beside her, Aidan laughed

and joked with customers. When people asked where his dad was or wondered if Aidan planned to take over the business, he only shrugged.

"I don't know what to say," Aidan confided to her as he fielded those questions again and again. "Do you think my old, um, my dad will come back?"

His eyes looked so vulnerable. They reminded her of his childlike admiration of his father. Aidan used to follow Nick around and imitate his every move. What had changed in their relationship?

"I don't know." Fern had to be honest. "I hope he changes his mind once he's calmer. If he doesn't, though, you're doing a great job with the business."

"Ya think?"

"People enjoy your friendliness and caring. It shows how much the family business means to you."

"Family, huh? We haven't been a family in ages. Grams would be turning over in her grave if she could see what things are like between us. And us being here in someone else's stand. She'd be livid after her mom kept the business going during the Great Depression."

"I hope you and your dad can work things out," Fern said.

"Fat chance. He's too hardheaded." Aidan hurried over to wait on a customer.

Although she didn't say it aloud, Fern had noticed a resemblance between Aidan and his father in that charac- teristic. Aidan, though, seemed more pliable than Nick, except in his reactions to his dad. Once again, Fern prayed the two of them could find peace.

"Hey, Aidan?" Gideon stopped near Fern. "I could use help with the lunchtime rush. It'll be starting soon."

"Oh, man, what'll I do about these customers?" He indicated the long line waiting for candy.

"I can handle it," Fern volunteered.

"Would you? That'd be great."

"Sure."

Gideon smiled at her, sending her into a slow burn. "I'm sorry you have to keep pinch-hitting for my business. I promise I'll work out the staffing problems."

"You couldn't have known Nick would walk out today." Fern didn't add he'd also had no idea Aidan would disappear Tuesday.

"Whatever your *daed* put in the proposal is fine with me. I'm happy to give you whatever you want."

Gideon hurried away with Aidan on his heels. Fern stared after him. He'd give her whatever she wanted? What if she asked him to give her his heart?

Chapter Seventeen

Over the next hour, Aidan rushed back and forth between cooking fries and assisting Fern whenever he could. All sides of the counter were so busy, Gideon had no time to think. Or glance at Fern.

Instead, he smiled at the woman who was next in line.

"I'll have a garden salad and unsweetened iced tea."

Salad? Nettie should've been here by now.

"It'll be a few minutes for the salad. We're making it fresh." Frantically, Gideon signaled Caroline with his eyes before she waited on the next customer. *Salad*, he mouthed.

Caroline glanced around the stand. "Where's Nettie?"

"I don't know." Gideon hoped nothing had happened to her. He lowered his voice so the customer couldn't overhear. "Could you take care of this lady's salad?"

Caroline nodded and leaned over the counter to talk to the customer. "If you wouldn't mind stepping to the side, I'll be right back with your salad, ma'am."

As Gideon asked the next person in line for his order, Nettie came rushing in, her eyes brimming with tears.

"I-I'm sorry I was late."

"What's wrong?"

Nettie waved off his question. "It can wait. It looks like you're swamped."

"*Jah*, we are. Can you take over the salad-making from Caroline? And once you've done that, Fern could use help with candy sales. I need Aidan back here."

Nettie craned her neck to see the candy counter. "Where's Nick?"

"Long story. I'll tell you later."

When Nettie's gaze passed over Fern, her nose wrinkled. Although it bothered Gideon, he had no time to worry about it. They were much too busy.

The new lunch menu had attracted more business than he'd anticipated. He had to plan for extra staff, especially if Nick didn't return. And that seemed like a real possibility.

As soon as Nettie caught up on salads, Gideon suggested, "Why don't you help Fern now?"

But Nettie balked. "Aidan can do that. I can do the fries."

Aidan's brows rose. "You need me to show you how?"

"It's been a few years, but I used to do them all the time."

"If you're sure?" Aidan shook the basket he'd lifted from the oil.

Nettie cast a sideways look at Fern. "I'm positive."

Once again, it upset Gideon that Nettie went out of her way to avoid Fern. But wasn't he trying to avoid Fern too? For a totally different reason.

Fern bounced between baked goods and candy, trying to be fair to the long lines of customers at each place.

"Where's Nick?" several people asked.

"He's not here today." Fern had no intention of describing Nick's blowup or his angry departure.

"I hope he's not ill."

"No, he's fine." Or as fine as he could be after he'd moved his family business to someone else's stall, fought with his son, and stalked off in a snit.

"That's good. I'm sure the move's been hard on him."

"Yes, it's not easy."

"Oh, that's right. You moved too. I'm so sorry, dear."

"*Danke,*" Fern mumbled.

A woman at the bakery counter waved for her attention. "Yoo-hoo, Fern. Are you going to be waiting on us over here?"

"In a minute." She checked with the woman who'd been so busy talking she hadn't selected any candy yet. "Can I get you anything?"

"I'm still thinking. Go ahead and wait on her since she's so impatient." The woman sniffed. "Honestly, some people."

"I heard that, Mabel. You're holding up a long line so you can gossip."

Mabel narrowed her eyes and gave the other woman a scornful scowl. "Asking about someone's health is not gossip, Rosemary."

Fern glanced over her shoulder. Gideon must have heard the argument. He motioned for Nettie to head to that end of the counter. Fern didn't have time to see more.

"We should be getting more help in a minute," she called to the people shuffling and sighing behind Mabel.

Fern preferred not to deal with Nettie's animosity, but Fern could barely keep up with her own customers, let alone Aidan's. She'd be grateful for Nettie's help and try to stop complaining inside.

But it wasn't Nettie who slipped in beside her. Aidan greeted Mabel, parried her questions about his dad, and sent her off with a lot more candy than she'd come to buy. He was even smoother than his father. Or maybe he was more successful because he was young and cute. Swarms of teen girls gathered near the counter, stood around giggling, and then nudged each other to buy candy. Preteen girls also seemed to buy a lot more than usual.

With Aidan working, Fern could concentrate on her own customers and have time for quick peeks at Gideon whenever she reached behind her for boxes or bags. But that didn't last long.

"Aidan," Caroline called, "Nettie needs to make more salads, and we're almost out of fries."

"Be right there." With a wink, he handed one of the giggling girls her small bag of candy, which set her friends tittering. "Could you wait on the rest?" he asked Fern.

She nodded, and Aidan rushed off. By the time Fern finished packaging a dozen cupcakes, the crowd of girls had dispersed. Most likely, they'd return when Aidan could wait on them.

He pitched in whenever he could, running from one end of the stand to the next, never seeming to get winded. Only once did Nettie take his place.

"Excuse me." Her tone polite, but cold, Nettie zigzagged around Fern to reach the candy counter.

If Fern were more assertive, she'd confront the situation and ask what she'd done to offend Nettie. Instead, she bit down on her lower lip and tried to stay out of Nettie's way.

A large crowd of girls had congregated at the stand. Their faces fell when Nettie arrived to wait on them. Most of them drifted off, but one of the younger girls, her cheeks the color of her fuchsia hoodie, asked for a giant jawbreaker.

"I guess I disappointed them." Nettie's half-laughing comment made her sound friendly.

If she plans to get along, I should be nice back. Fern smiled. "I think Aidan is a big draw for the business."

"*Jah,* young girls are often foolish." Nettie sighed. "I should know."

Fern had no idea how to respond to that. She'd been that young when Nettie had worked at this market stand with Gideon's brother Thomas. Rumors had circulated through the market after the young couple had been shunned, but the adults had hushed their whispering whenever Fern neared, so she'd never learned why. Now that she was older, she suspected the reason was why Nettie and Thomas had married soon after that, at only seventeen.

Nettie pinched her lips together for a moment. "That foolishness doesn't change much when we get older, does it?"

Before Fern could respond, Nettie turned her back and hurried to help another customer. Fern stood staring after her. Had Nettie been referring to herself? Or was she calling Fern foolish for her crush on Gideon?

Usually Thursdays were slower than the weekends, but the rush continued until closing. Gideon heaved a huge sigh of relief when Russell locked the side doors.

Caroline rushed past him. "I didn't get a chance to talk to Zach at all today. I cleaned up for you the other night, and you have a lot of help today."

Gideon added finding out the truth about Zach to his

mental checklist of problems. First, though, he needed to know if Nick intended to return, and he had to come up with a plan for getting Nick and Aidan back together. Then he had to discuss payment arrangements with Fern, find out what had upset Nettie, and discover why the kids hadn't come with her today. Oh, and hire at least one more employee, preferably by tomorrow. And that meant coming up with money for a salary.

Aidan had agreed to work for free in exchange for help paying off his motorcycle—after he got his suspended license back in six months. Gideon had been happy to make the deal. It gave him time to come up with the money, but more importantly, it kept cash out of Aidan's hands. Cash that might otherwise be spent on drugs or alcohol.

But Gideon's stressful day hadn't ended yet. Bo Ridley strode toward the counter, and Gideon tensed. Did the organic meat man intend to make another play for Fern?

Bo breezed by Fern with a toothy smile and a flip "Hello, doll."

Gideon ground his teeth. Fern deserved more respect. On the bright side, though, Bo hadn't lingered to talk to her.

"You have a few minutes to talk?"

"Now? We have a lot of cleanup."

"*We?* Aren't you the owner? That means someone else can handle the dirty work, right?"

"I clean too."

Bo pursed his lips. "You don't trust your people?"

"Of course I do. But I clean too. That's only fair."

"Whatever. Okay if I stop by after you're done?"

"Gideon?" Nettie interrupted them. "How do you want to do this?"

Rather than annoying him, Nettie's question came as a

welcome relief. "Excuse me," he said to Bo and went to help Nettie.

Once again, Nettie could have easily figured this out on her own, but Gideon was so grateful at having escaped Bo's pressure campaign, he didn't mind. Besides, this way, he faced Fern. He angled his body for the best view of her packing up.

She stowed everything in neat rows in the bins. Not that she had too much to pack. She'd been busy all day, and customers had emptied her shelves of most of her baked goods. Without being asked, she straightened the candy counter and covered the open bins with sheets. That was so like her. She always cared for others.

"Gideon?"

Nettie's plaintive tone dragged him back to the cleanup. His face burned as she followed his gaze. Her mouth pursed into a narrow line. Was she worried he'd date Fern and abandon his role as caretaker to her and the children? He'd tried to ease her mind over that, but doubt niggled at the edges of his mind.

Once again, he mulled over the possibility that Nettie wanted something more from him. It would explain her dislike of Fern. *Neh*, Nettie, at five years older, had always viewed him as Thomas's little brother. Surely that hadn't changed. At least, he hoped it hadn't.

Gideon tried to hide his interest in Fern, confining himself to brief sideways glances until she pushed her cart out of the stand and down the aisle. When she left, his day darkened, as if a flickering flame had been snuffed out.

Aidan had cleaned the rotisserie and taken care of the fryers. "Need me to do anything more?"

"You've done plenty. You can go."

"Thanks, man. I still need to do the candy."

Gideon waved toward the spotless area. "Fern took care of that."

"She did? I didn't even thank her."

Neither had Gideon. She'd done a huge share of the work today at both the bakery and candy counters. And he'd never even said *danke* or goodbye.

"You can thank her tomorrow." And so would Gideon.

After Aidan scooted down the aisle, Gideon checked the rest of the stand. Nettie had done most of the salad cleanup and storage. He'd wipe down the rest of the counters and count the money.

"Why don't you go too, Nettie? I can finish up here."

Her eyes filled with tears.

"Nettie?"

"I-I'm sorry. I didn't mean to do that. I've been holding it in all day."

She'd come in late that morning and had been crying. "What's the matter?"

"You'll think I'm silly. Katie's teacher stopped me this morning to schedule a conference for tomorrow afternoon."

"Is she having trouble in school?"

"I don't think so. At times like this, I miss Thomas so much. I don't have anyone to talk things over with. Or to go with me to the conference."

"I'm always ready to listen. And if you need company at the conference, Mamm or I could go along."

"Would you? That would be such a relief." Nettie gave him a quick hug.

Had Gideon just dug himself in deeper?

"*Ahem,* hope I'm not interrupting something here." Bo Ridley strolled toward the counter with an *I-caught-you* grin on his face.

"*Neh*, you're not. Net—my, um, sister was just leaving."

Of all the people to see that, it had to be Bo. The gleam in Bo's eyes indicated he planned to use that fact.

"Sister-in-law," Nettie corrected.

"*Oh-ho*, does your brother know how, um, friendly you are with his wife?"

"My husband's dead." The tears that had filled Nettie's eyes earlier threatened to overflow.

Gideon wanted to protect her from any more of Bo's harassment, but Bo surprised him.

He wiped the smirk off his face and replaced it with genuine concern. "I'm so sorry. I didn't mean to make you cry."

"You didn't. I already was." She swiped at her eyes. "Gideon was trying to be helpful."

"By offering his shoulder to cry on?" Bo's snark had returned.

"Gideon's a good man. Honest and upright and—"

Bo held up a hand. "I get it. He's a paragon of virtue. Anyone who rescues damsels in distress deserves a medal."

Nettie eyed him suspiciously as if not sure if he was serious or mocking. Gideon had no doubt Bo had intended it as a snide comment.

"If you ever need another shoulder to cry on," Bo told her, "I'm always available. Just stop by the front of the market anytime. Ridley's Organics. You can't miss it."

"Oh, you're the one who took over Fern's and Nick's stands."

"Guilty as charged. I hope you'll forgive me if I tell you I didn't know those stands were occupied. Russell made it sound like they weren't."

"I see." Nettie sounded as if she didn't quite believe him.

Neither did Gideon. But shouldn't he give others the benefit of the doubt? Yet something in Gideon's gut told him not to trust Bo Ridley.

After Nettie left, Bo moved closer and kept his voice low. "I don't mean to play hardball here, but I do know the truth."

The truth? About what?

When Gideon didn't respond, Bo leaned over the counter. "About the fake organic."

Bo made no sense. Was he implying Gideon had lied about his food being organic? "I don't know what you're talking about."

"You may be able to convince your customers of that, but I know better."

"What are you trying to say?"

"Stop playing games. We both know Q & Z Organic Farms is a fraud."

"I don't believe you." Why would Bo say something like that?

"You know it's true."

"I don't know any such thing." But Bo had planted doubts in Gideon's mind. Maybe that had been his purpose. Get Gideon to doubt his supplier so he'd switch to Ridley's. If that's what he'd planned, it wouldn't work.

Bo reached into his pocket. Paper crinkled as he pulled out a folded newspaper clipping. He unfolded it and slammed it down on the counter between them. "Look familiar?" he taunted.

Gideon stared at the bold black headline from a Southern newspaper: *Q & Z Organic Farms Investigated for Fraud.*

Their chicken supplier. His heart sank as he read the date. This hadn't happened recently. In fact, it had occurred around the time Thomas had begun buying from them.

"Cat got your tongue?" Bo's gloating face floated above the newsprint as Gideon tried to piece together the truth.

Had his brother known? The day Thomas died he'd nattered on about his sin with Nettie, about the pressure of having so many children so close together, and about his guilt. Gideon had always assumed Thomas had meant guilt over having to get married, but what if he'd meant this?

"Your brother made a deal with them after they'd been cited. He'd even been warned."

"You didn't know my brother, so you have no proof."

"I have my sources. And I know someone who'll testify to it in court, if it gets that far."

Court? What did Bo have in mind? Putting Gideon out of business? They weren't competitors. Or was he doing all this to force Gideon into buying Ridley's chicken?

"I doubt we need to go that far. All it takes is a call to the USDA. In case you aren't familiar with the penalties . . ." Bo whipped another paper from his pocket, laid it on top of the newspaper clipping, and poked a well-manicured finger at the first paragraph.

Under the headline *Fraudulent Organic Certificates*, the sentence just above Bo's fingertip read, *Punishable by fines of up to $17,952 for each violation.*

The words blurred before Gideon's eyes. All this time, he'd been cheating his customers. They thought they were buying organic chicken. But he'd been committing fraud. Who'd believe he was innocent?

And did that mean he'd owe that amount for each chicken he'd sold? Even if it was a onetime fine, it could put him out of business, especially since he'd need to make things right with all the customers he and Thomas had cheated.

Bo set a pricing sheet with his business logo and phone number on the counter. "So, are you ready to do business with Ridley's?"

Gideon shook his head. He couldn't believe this.

"You're turning me down? You'll regret it." Bo let the threat hang between them.

"I need time to think." Gideon sank onto the stool closest to the counter.

"Sure, man. I'll give you time. But two weeks is my limit. Then I go public. Your customers will never buy from you again."

Gideon didn't care about Bo's threat. He'd tell his customers himself. He couldn't go another market day living a lie. Or could he?

Chapter Eighteen

As Fern packed her containers into the buggy, she couldn't get Nettie out of her mind. Nettie always acted so helpless and needed Gideon to rescue her. And all day long, she'd done her best to get his attention. She narrowed her eyes if Gideon paid any attention to Fern. Not that his attention meant anything.

Whenever Fern wondered if Gideon's stares held meaning, she reminded herself of his derisive comment to Caroline. Nettie had no competition.

Instead of fretting over Nettie, Fern needed to concentrate on building her business in this new location and find ways to ease Gideon's staffing issues. The bakery stayed busy, but maybe she could go in before they opened and help by setting up trays and portioning out side dishes into takeout containers they could store in the refrigerator rather than dipping out each order one by one.

She'd go in early tomorrow and suggest it to Gideon. That would save a lot of time. Even if Gideon found another worker, she doubted anyone would be ready to start the next morning.

Ach! She'd forgotten to give Gideon the letter from

Daed. She'd been so preoccupied over Nettie, she'd rushed away instead of talking to Gideon after work. Would he still be there cleaning if she returned?

Only one way to find out. Fern turned her buggy around at the next intersection and headed back to the market. If Gideon hadn't left, it most likely meant facing Nettie and enduring her glares.

When Fern reached the market, she tied her horse to a hitching post near the employee entrance. She wouldn't be long.

As she headed through the door, she almost ran into Bo Ridley, who appeared to be in a snit. The minute he spied her, though, his expression transformed into a smile—a *wolf-licking-his-lips-over-tasty-prey* smile.

"Hey, beautiful, did you come back to see me?" He opened his arms as if he expected her to walk into his embrace.

Englisch men and women might casually hug one another, but Fern had no desire to be anywhere near this overbearing man. She sidestepped his embrace. "*Neh.* I'm here to see Gideon." Not that it was any of this man's business, but letting him think Gideon was expecting her might make him back off.

"Wow, he's one lucky guy. First, the cute brunette sobbing on his shoulder. Then as soon as she leaves, you show up."

Cute brunette? Nettie? Bo made it sound like Nettie and Gideon had been doing more than cleaning. *Her* head on Gideon's shoulder? The thought made Fern sick. Had they been spending special time together? Or had Bo exaggerated? He seemed to like getting people riled up.

"Hey, sorry. I didn't mean to upset you." Bo moved

closer. "If you and Gid are an item, don't worry. You're much prettier than her."

Fern skirted around him and spoke stiffly. "I'm not worried."

"Well, if he's two-timing you, I'm great at comforting jilted ladies. Just saying."

Gideon couldn't jilt her, because they'd never had a relationship. But it did hurt to picture him close to Nettie. Now Fern couldn't erase the image of Gideon and Nettie in an embrace. It played over and over in her mind.

After Bo left, Gideon buried his face in his hands. What was he going to do? He could ignore Bo's warning and keep selling his chicken, the way he had in the two years since Thomas's death.

Neh, now that he knew the truth, he couldn't pretend his meat was organic. But how could he possibly switch everything by tomorrow morning?

"Gideon?"

Fern's soft voice made him jump. He hadn't heard her enter the stand. He lifted his head and pasted on a neutral expression to cover his concerns and hide his quickening heartbeat. "What are you doing here?"

Gideon could have kicked himself. He sounded unwelcoming and accusatory. "I mean, I thought you went home." His explanation did little to erase the hurt in her eyes.

"I started to, but I forgot this." She went over to her counter and came back with a letter. "Daed wanted you to look over his ideas on payment for the stand."

As he reached for the envelope, Gideon winced. He

might not even have a stand for her unless he could come up with a solution to this chicken dilemma.

"What's wrong?"

Sadness replaced the hurt on her face. She must think he was reluctant to be around her. Well, he was, but not for the reasons she might be imagining.

Their fingertips brushed as he took the letter, and sparks shot through him. What was it about Fern that turned him upside down and inside out?

She stood, silent and downcast, still waiting for an answer. An answer he couldn't give. He didn't want to tell anyone about the fake organic chicken or possibly going out of business or . . .

But he couldn't let her go on believing his reaction was related to her.

Taking a deep breath, he admitted, "I just got some bad news."

Her soft, inviting expression encouraged him to share more. She'd find out soon enough. He may as well be honest.

"Bo Ridley stopped by."

Fern recoiled, and despite his dilemma, Gideon's heart danced. So she hadn't been charmed by Bo. Not that it mattered to Gideon. Or, at least, it shouldn't. But it did.

At the mention of Bo's name, Fern's stomach clenched. The man gave her the creeps. And, worse yet, her suspicions had been right. Gideon and Bo must be working together despite Bo putting her out of business.

"I'm in a big mess. You may as well hear it now."

She scrunched her brow. Had Bo put Gideon out of business too? Did he plan to take over the whole market?

Gideon cleared his throat. "Bo threatened me with newspaper clippings showing Q & Z Organic Farms, the distributor for my chickens, is not certified organic."

"What?" Fern was positive Gideon would never deliberately deceive people. "You didn't know that, did you?"

Giving her a grateful look, Gideon shook his head. "*Danke* for thinking the best of me. *Neh*, I had no idea, but who'll believe me?"

"I do." Fern suspected most of his customers would too.

He stared at her like a drowning man being thrown a life preserver. "I appreciate that, but if Bo goes to the USDA, I have no defense."

"Can't you say you just found out?"

"I could, except Bo says he has proof Thomas knew. Who'll believe my brother never told me? I think he planned to."

Gideon's face twisted into a mask of anguish, and Fern longed to comfort him. If only she had the right to reach out and . . .

He groaned and lowered his face into his hands. The rest of his words were so muffled, Fern could hardly make out what he said. "Thomas started to confess his guilt. But he died before he could finish."

"*Ach*, Gideon. I'm so sorry."

"Thomas knew the chicken wasn't organic. That's what had him so upset. That and other things."

Fern waited for him to go on, but he only sat silent, his shoulders heaving. She wished she could put a hand on his shoulder, but she shouldn't. What a terrible burden to bear. "What's Bo going to do?"

"He demanded I buy chickens from him. He gave me

two weeks to think about it before he notifies the USDA. If he does, the fines are huge."

"What are you going to do?"

"I could pretend I didn't know and keep the business going like it is. We're making good money. That would give me time to work out a new supplier."

Gideon would let his customers believe a lie? That didn't match his strong morals. What happened to the boy who'd been upset about keeping a nickel too much?

He kept his head bowed and rubbed his forehead. "I can't do that. I'd never cheat my customers that way."

Fern exhaled a soft sigh. She should have known he'd do the right thing.

"So I either paint out the word *Organic* on my sign and lower my prices, or I have to accept Bo's offer."

"I'm sure he'll ask more than he should."

"What choice do I have? If I don't agree to his costs, I'll have to change my menu tonight."

"Are there any Amish farms around here that sell organic chicken?"

Gideon's head shot up. "I hadn't thought about that. I've spent all my time focusing on Bo's threat. Maybe I can work out an emergency delivery with the Amish co-op and get enough chicken to take care of tomorrow and Saturday."

Gideon was grateful for Fern's suggestion, but why hadn't he considered other options besides Bo Ridley's offer? He'd been blindsided by Bo's information and mired in the past. Everything about the switch to organic reminded Gideon of Thomas's death.

"*Danke* for the idea. I, well . . ." He shouldn't make

excuses, but her caring expression made him want to share. "This whole thing's hard for me because of my brother."

"I can imagine."

Neh, she couldn't. She had no idea of the depth of his guilt. Or the reasons for it.

Gideon still had one other heavy burden in addition to the circumstances surrounding Thomas's death, but he didn't want to keep Fern any longer. He appreciated the help she'd already given him.

Fern studied him. "You look upset."

Her gentleness made him long to confess. Not about Thomas. He wasn't sure he could ever confide that to anyone. Not even to Nettie. But Fern deserved to know his concerns about the business, because it might affect her future.

"If I switch to all organic from now on, I don't know if the USDA will still fine me. If they do, it could put us out of business." Fern and Nick had just lost their stands, and now Gideon might have to close them down again.

"Do you think they would?"

"I don't know. But the USDA's not the worst of it." A knot of anxiety tightened his stomach. "I've been cheating people for two years now."

"You didn't know."

"That doesn't make it right. I owe it to people to tell them the truth. I can't just quietly switch to real organic chickens and hide the past. I also feel like I should pay them back. But how?" *And where will I get the money?*

"Finding all the people who bought your chickens would be impossible, wouldn't it?"

"I need to at least try. And what about all the people

who bought organic for health reasons? I hope I didn't make anyone sick."

"*Ach*, Gideon. You can't blame yourself for something you didn't know."

But he did. And for a whole lot more.

Gideon looked so downcast, Fern wanted to ease his mind, but she could think of nothing more to say. He hadn't done this on purpose. Even if his brother had known and kept silent, people would understand it wasn't Gideon's fault.

If he had to work out the organic chicken order tonight, he'd probably have no time to think about hiring anyone. Maybe her idea would lighten his load a little.

"I had a suggestion for making tomorrow easier."

Gideon's eyes lit up. "You do?"

She'd suggested Amish suppliers for chickens. He must be expecting a brilliant way to handle the chicken crisis. "It's only a small change that might make staffing easier."

He pinched the bridge of his nose. "I can't believe I forgot all about getting more workers."

"You have a lot on your mind," she said gently. "You won't have time to do that tonight. You have enough to worry about with getting chicken. We'll all do what we did today."

"I can't expect people to keep working like that." Gideon looked as if she'd added to his concerns instead of helping.

"We managed fine today."

"Thanks to you."

Fern hadn't done anything special. "*Neh*, thanks to Aidan. He jumped from job to job."

"He certainly did. He always managed to be where we needed him most."

"*Jah*, he did. I wondered if I could come in early and package up salads in to-go containers. If they were made ahead of time and stored in the refrigerator, it would be easier to fill orders."

"That's brilliant. It would also cut down on us blocking the aisle when we're dipping out salads."

"I also thought we could prepare stacks of trays with silverware packets and napkins before the market opens. The less work you need to do at lunchtime, the faster you can serve customers."

"That would make everything easier and faster, but you don't have to come in. Caroline can handle it. And maybe Nettie could come early too."

Fern hid her disappointment. She'd imagined herself working with Gideon in the morning before anyone else arrived. She pushed that fantasy from her mind. It still hurt that he didn't want her around.

"I'm happy to help." She hoped she didn't sound as if she were begging to be included.

"You've done more than enough already." For the first time since she'd arrived, Gideon's face relaxed into a smile. And his eyes . . .

She shouldn't read anything into the admiration shining in them as he thanked her. She'd given him two suggestions that helped, so naturally he was grateful and relieved. But she couldn't resist dreaming of more.

Chapter Nineteen

After Fern left, some of the excitement of the last few minutes leaked away. Whenever he spent time with her, she set his pulse on fire. He rushed through the rest of the cleaning and then counted out the cash drawer.

Thank you, Lord!

Again they'd had high sales. If they could maintain that level of income, he'd be able to make headway on Thomas's debts. Except now he'd have to pay more for his chicken.

On the way home, Gideon stopped to deposit the money in the bank and then swung by the Amish co-op. He hadn't counted on such a high price for organic chicken. It would be easier and cheaper to stick with their present distributor. As fast as the thought flitted through his mind, Gideon rejected it. He had to do the right thing starting now.

But that meant reducing the amount he'd been paying on the debt. Would he ever be free and clear of his brother's obligations?

By the time Gideon arrived, the family had already gathered at the table, but they'd waited for him. He hurried to wash up and then slipped into his place for the silent prayer.

Afterward, he picked at his food and tuned out the conversations swirling around him. Right after the meal ended, he hurried into the study and shut the door. He'd have to call Q & Z. He dug out the contract and skimmed it to see their cancellation terms.

Gideon groaned. Thomas had locked them into an automatic delivery contract. One of the clauses made it clear if he broke the agreement, he'd still be responsible for paying the monthly amount for the next two years. If Gideon owed for it anyway, he may as well take the chickens. But what would he do with all the extra meat?

That contract would siphon off all the extra money coming in. He'd have nothing left to pay down the debt. And he still needed to make enough to cover at least one more employee.

He also had to figure out how to make up for all the people who'd been cheated. An idea came to him. It might not be fair to those who missed out on his offer, but he'd attempt to make amends. He swiveled his chair toward the typewriter to create a flyer. They could hand them out starting tomorrow. Only one problem: he had no idea how he'd pay for it.

He'd finished the heading when Nettie tapped at the door and stuck her head in.

"Would you like some tea?"

"Not now." He hoped he didn't sound too curt, but he didn't want to lose the phrasing he'd worked out in his mind.

"I wanted to talk to you." Her plaintive tone added to his guilt.

"Can it wait?"

"Not really. It's about tomorrow."

"Tomorrow?" Gideon lost his train of thought. He stopped typing. "You can work, can't you?" The last thing he needed was to lose another worker when they were already shorthanded.

Nettie wrung her hands together. "For most of the day, but Katie's teacher wants to talk to me after school. I wondered if you'd go with me to the meeting."

"We don't have enough people at the market."

"Please, Gid. I can't do this alone. And now that I don't have Thomas . . ." She dissolved into tears.

How could he refuse her pleading? Besides, wasn't he partly to blame for Thomas not being here?

Although Gideon intended to have Nettie and Caroline do the preparations, Fern arrived extra early.

When she pushed her cart into the stand, Gideon stopped speaking to Caroline. "I said you didn't have to come in."

"I know, but I thought you might need more help."

"We'll be fine." Nettie snapped her mouth shut on the last word, her expression making it clear Fern was unwelcome.

Gideon frowned at Nettie, but Caroline smiled warmly at Fern. "I'd be happy for more help."

"To give you more time with Zach," Nettie muttered.

Ignoring her, Caroline added, "Come join us whenever you're done unpacking your baked goods."

Fern rushed through filling her trays and took the empty containers out to her buggy to give everyone more room to maneuver. Then she headed toward the spot that always drew her attention—anywhere Gideon stood.

"Glad you're here." Caroline scooted over to make room for Fern. "Gideon says this was your idea. We all think it's a great one."

"It is." Gideon slid a large stack of papers from a brown paper bag. "It'll save a lot of time."

The admiring glance Gideon directed at Fern did not go unnoticed. Nettie studied him with narrowed eyes.

Although Fern appreciated his affirmation, she shuffled her feet, uncomfortable under Nettie's and Gideon's scrutiny, but for different reasons. Fern shifted her attention to Caroline, but that turned out to be a mistake.

Gideon's sister flashed him with a mocking, knowing look. A look that brought back memories of Caroline teasing Gideon about his interest in Fern. A look that brought back memories of Gideon's crushing remark.

Fighting back tears, Fern tried to act perky. "What would you like me to do?"

"I'll let Caroline answer that while I set out these flyers." Gideon started to crumple the brown paper bag in his free hand.

"Wait." Fern grabbed for the bag before he crushed it. "There are still some white papers in there." She extracted them, conscious of her closeness to him and of all the eyes on her.

"*Danke.*" He reached for the paper. "I paid enough to have these printed, I wouldn't want to waste any."

His grateful smile set her pulses jumping. She broke their gaze and focused on the paper in her hand.

Shocked, she skimmed the flyer. Gideon had issued an apology to all his customers and offered reduced prices on meals for anyone who'd purchased nonorganic chicken unknowingly. It was beautiful and heartfelt, but . . .

"So, this is what you decided to do?" she said.

He nodded. "It won't pay back everyone, but I had no other way to make things right."

"You have no records of who bought your chickens. How do you know people won't cheat you?"

"I'll have to trust them."

"*Ach*, Gideon. Won't doing this put you out of business?"

"That's what I said," Nettie chimed in. "But how did you know about this? Gideon only told us this morning."

"I told Fern about it last night when she made these suggestions." He waved a hand toward the trays Caroline was stacking on the prep counter.

Nettie's deflated *Oh* spoke volumes. Then suspicion flared in her eyes. "Is *that* why you were so late getting home last night?"

"One of the reasons."

Inside, Fern shriveled. Did Nettie keep such close tabs on Gideon that she knew when he got home from work?

Behind Nettie's back, Caroline flicked her head to one side and raised her eyebrows, signaling for Fern to disregard Nettie.

But Fern couldn't do that. Her joy at being near Gideon took a nosedive.

Caroline's cheery chatter did little to smooth things over between Nettie and Fern. Nettie brushed past Fern with a haughty look whenever she passed, but Fern pretended not to care. If it had been anyone else, she'd have done her best to make friends, but jealousy hardened her heart.

Under Nettie's watchful glare, Fern couldn't even enjoy sneaking peeks at Gideon as he put chickens in the rotisserie.

About ten minutes before opening time, Caroline declared

they'd prepped enough side dishes and trays. Fern had no further excuse to hang around the chicken counter.

"*Danke*, Fern," Gideon said as she passed.

Her heart sang. "I hope it helps."

"I'm sure it will."

Fern hugged his words of praise close as she prepared for the market to open. Facing away from Nettie's censure, Fern could indulge in daydreams. Daydreams that shattered when Aidan came rushing in.

His eyes bloodshot, he looked like he'd just tumbled out of bed. "Whew. I made it. Had a rough night last night. Could barely drag myself out of bed this morning."

"I'm glad you're here. You were such a big help yesterday."

"Ya think?" Aidan said it flippantly, but pride shone in his tired eyes. "Hope I'll be able to keep up today."

"You'll do fine."

Aidan had started removing the sheets draped over the candy, but he stopped and stared at her. "You're not going to lecture me?"

Fern finished counting out the cash in her box to be sure she had the correct amount and jotted it on the tablet she kept on the counter. "About what?"

"About staying out too late? About hanging around with the wrong crowd? About drinking too much? About wasting my life?"

"It sounds as if you know enough to give yourself your own lectures."

"Huh?" Aidan stared at her for a moment, dumbfounded. Then he laughed. "You're right. I could." Then he sobered. "You know, if my old man kept his mouth shut, I might even listen to those inner lectures. Maybe I wouldn't be so rebellious."

"Really?"

"Yeah. Mostly I do it to get under his skin." Aidan stared off into the distance, his eyes sad. "I don't like it all that much. But if I give it up, he wins."

Fern wrinkled her brow. "So you're hurting yourself to get revenge on your dad?"

"When you put it like that, it sounds kind of stupid."

Fern didn't respond, but only met his eyes with a steady gaze.

"I guess it is dumb. I just don't want to give in."

"It's not easy." Fern should know. Hadn't she been nursing a grudge against Nettie? And against her brother? Part of Fern didn't want to give in. Not for either one. But maybe God had just given her a wake-up call.

Aaron was too far away, though, and she didn't have time now to make any friendly overtures toward Nettie. Russell had unlocked the doors, and people streamed toward her stand. Fern turned to greet them as they approached and caught the malevolent glare Russell sent Aidan.

Fern shivered. She'd been complaining inwardly about Nettie, but Russell outdid Nettie by a mile. *Neh*, by ten miles, one hundred miles, or more. At least Aidan hadn't seen it. Russell looked as if he wanted to kick Aidan out of the market. Or worse.

She had no time to think about it because, once again, they were so busy she barely had time to breathe. Or even to glance at Gideon. Well, she did manage that, but not as frequently as she'd like.

During the midafternoon lull, she took a short break to eat the meal she'd packed.

Caroline called to her, "Your idea worked well. We just ran out a few minutes ago. We'll make a few more to take care of the before-supper crowds."

"What's she talking about?" Aidan asked.

Fern explained why they'd come in early.

"I can come in tomorrow to help."

"I'm sure they'd appreciate it." Fern couldn't help teasing, "But it means getting up even earlier than you did this morning."

Rather than smiling, Aidan tilted his head to one side as if he were thinking. "You're right. And that means I can't go out tonight. On a Friday night? Not sure that's possible, but I'll come in early no matter what."

Fern was so focused on praying for Aidan, she didn't hear Gideon approach. His deep voice behind her sent tingles up her spine.

"Can I ask you two to help Caroline wait on customers later this afternoon? Nettie and I have an appointment."

Nettie and I? Those three words cut through Fern's fantasies. *Nettie and I* echoed through her brain, stabbing into her heart.

"Sure." Aidan's eager answer startled Fern from her self-pity.

Gideon stared at her, waiting for a response. But Fern couldn't bring herself to say yes. If she didn't help, would Gideon stay and let Nettie go to the appointment alone?

"Fern, is everything all right? I don't want to impose on you. Not after you already came in early."

Now he thought she was unwilling to help. "It's not that." She pinched her lips together before she gave herself away. She had to force words past her dry mouth. "I'm happy to help."

"You don't have to."

"It's all right." *At least about helping with the work. Not about Gideon and . . . and Nettie.*

"*Danke.* I know I've been overworking both of you. I'll try to have more help by Tuesday." He hurried off to deal with a line of customers.

"Are you okay?" Aidan asked after Gideon left. "You don't look so good. I can help Caroline and try to keep up with everything here."

Fern choked back the lump in her throat. "*Neh*, you don't have to do that. I'll be fine." Her conscience nagged at her for telling a fib. If Gideon and Nettie were together, would she ever be fine again?

An hour later, as Gideon and Nettie were exiting the stand, he turned and called to his sister, "Caroline, if we're not back by closing, could Zach drive you home?"

Before Caroline could answer, Fern said, "If he can't, I'd be happy to take her."

When Gideon turned to smile his thanks, Nettie tugged at his elbow. "We don't want to be late."

"*Neh*, we don't."

As the two of them left together, Nettie directed a triumphant smile in Fern's direction. A smile that said, *He's mine, not yours.*

Caroline sidled up next to Fern. "Don't mind Nettie."

But Caroline hadn't seen Nettie's gloating expression. And no matter how much Fern told herself she didn't mind, she did. She minded that Nettie would spend the rest of the afternoon with Gideon. She minded that Nettie had Gideon's time and attention. And most of all, she minded that she'd never have the right to take Gideon's arm and stroll off with him. Not today and not ever.

Chapter Twenty

After the school conference, Gideon went into the house and sat at his desk to do some figuring. He had to find a way to pay the co-op invoices and decide what to do about the Q & Z chicken shipments.

When he emerged from the office for supper, Nettie had a worried frown. "Katie's supposed to feed and water the horses, but I haven't seen her since we got back from school."

"Maybe she's in her room. I'll take care of the horses." Gideon headed out the door before Nettie could protest. She always insisted the children do their own chores without help, but they could give Katie a break for one night.

When he reached the barn, the door stood partway open. He'd shut it after he pulled the buggy inside. Had Katie done her chores and forgotten to close it?

Muffled sobs came from one of the stalls. Gideon hurried over to find Katie, her arms wrapped around the pony's neck, crying into his mane.

"Katie, what's the matter?" Gideon let himself into the stall and squatted beside her.

His niece threw her arms around his neck. "I'm not stupid."

"Of course not. I think you're smart."

"You do?" Her words had a suspicious edge.

"Of course. You help Sadie win card games, you add up everyone's scores quickly, and you can even figure out how to let your brothers win."

"You knew about that?"

"Don't worry. I won't give away your secrets." Gideon took her shoulders and moved her back a little so he could look directly into her eyes. "What's going on?"

"Teacher Esther talked about me today."

"And you thought it was because you're having trouble with schoolwork?"

Katie nodded.

"She said you're doing well."

"Even in reading?"

"She did ask us to see that you practice for a little while every night. But that's not a problem—everyone needs help sometimes."

"You don't."

"You'd be surprised. Yesterday, I had two big problems at work to solve. And one of my friends helped with the answers."

Katie tilted her head to one side and stared at him, a skeptical look on her face. "What friend?"

Gideon hesitated. He'd rather not mention her name, but Katie needed to hear it to believe he wasn't making this up. "Her name's Fern."

"The Fern that works at your market stand?"

Now, how did she know that? He'd never mentioned Fern's name.

"I don't think Mamm likes her. Do you?"

Did he ever. More and more each day. But how did he answer Katie's question? "She's a very nice lady. I think you'd like her."

Katie frowned. "Mamm says you pay too much attention to Fern."

"I see." But Gideon didn't see. Or maybe he was trying not to see. Because Katie's statement led his thoughts to a place he didn't want to go. It confirmed what he'd suspected. He'd hoped he was wrong, but if Nettie really was jealous of Fern . . .

Gideon stood abruptly. "We'd better get the horses fed. It's almost time for supper."

Katie threw her arms around his legs and hugged hard. "I love you."

He put his hand on her head. "I love you too."

A short while later, after they'd said their silent prayer at mealtime, Katie turned to her grandparents. "Gideon said I need to practice reading."

"I'm glad Gideon talked to you about that." Nettie smiled at him with more than gratitude in her eyes.

The chicken pot pie he'd been enjoying a few minutes earlier curdled in his stomach.

Katie prattled on, but Gideon didn't hear her until she turned to her *mamm*. "I know you don't like Fern, but she helped Gideon with his problems. And he really likes her a lot."

Nettie's fork clattered to her plate. Her cheeks flushed, she stood abruptly and turned away from the table. "Would anyone like more milk?" She headed to the refrigerator.

Considering everyone's glass was three-quarters full, it only reinforced what Katie had told him in the barn. He'd tried to make it clear to Nettie that he had no interest in dating *anyone*. Including her.

When Aidan came strolling in early the next morning, he surprised Fern with his clear eyes and jaunty attitude.

"You look good today," she exclaimed without thinking.

He laughed. "Guess that means I usually don't?"

"*Neh*, I only meant you look—" If she said *better*, she'd imply he normally looked bad. And *cheerful* might indicate he generally looked glum.

"It's okay," he assured her. "I know what you meant."

"Sorry," she mumbled.

"No problem. I took your advice and listened to my inner lecture to go to bed early. My homies kept texting, but I turned off my phone and ignored them. Not sure I can keep this up, but one night didn't hurt."

"Good for you." Fern moved closer to her counter so Aidan could get by.

He folded the sheets covering his stand and put them away. "I figured out how to bug my old man so he didn't realize I was giving in to his advice."

Too bad he felt he needed to do that, but Fern was glad Aidan had taken some steps in the right direction.

"I just turned my music up full blast and pretended I couldn't hear my old man banging on my bedroom door and screaming for me to turn it down." A self-satisfied smile spread across Aidan's face. "Actually, hearing him getting steamed like that was almost more fun than going out. Almost."

"I'm sorry you and your dad don't get along."

Aidan ducked his head, but not before Fern glimpsed

the wetness in his eyes. "Yeah, me too." His voice gruff, he added, "When I was little, he was my hero."

Fern finished setting the last row of pastries in place. "It's a shame things have changed."

"Yeah, well . . ." Aidan kept his back to her and shuffled his feet.

Maybe it was time to change the subject. "I'm going over to help Caroline set up trays and package side dishes. Want to come?"

"In a second." Aidan rearranged the large display jar filled with huge swirled lollipops, but it didn't look any different when he finished. Then he took a quick swipe at his eyes with the backs of his fists.

Fern turned away and waited until he joined her. Then they both headed over to help Caroline and Nettie. Caroline suggested setting up workstations on each side of the prep counter.

Fern positioned herself so she'd be looking across at Gideon while he loaded the rotisserie. Nettie's face fell, but Fern pretended not to notice. She could have moved and given Nettie her place, but she ignored the still, small voice inside prodding her to be kind.

Time flew by, and when Caroline declared they'd done enough, Fern regretted not giving up her spot. She'd spent most of the time sneaking peeks at Gideon while Nettie gave her the side-eye.

Several times Gideon had been looking in her direction when she glanced in his. Most of the time, he immediately busied himself with the chickens or other work. But twice he'd smiled at her. She hoped Nettie couldn't tell how that accelerated her breathing and heart rate. Spending more than an hour staring at Gideon had filled Fern with joy.

Again, he thanked her as she slipped past him to get to

her counter, and Fern's spirits soared. She hummed as she recounted her money and greeted the first customers.

Aidan leaned over to whisper, "You sure are cheerful today. I mean, you always are, but you're especially happy today."

Fern hit on the first response that came to mind. "It's such a lovely day."

"Really? Last I looked, the sky was gray and cloudy."

Oops. "Any day God makes is a good day."

"If you say so."

Fern heaved a sigh of relief when they both had too many customers to talk. The rest of the morning, Aidan raced between his candy counter and the French fries. And Fern alternated between the bakery and candy counters.

"What are you doing here?" a harsh voice demanded as Fern shifted back to the candy customers.

"Can I help you?" Fern asked the Pickle Lady.

Wilma studied Fern through slitted eyes. "I don't know. Can you? What are you doing here, and what'd you do with Nick?"

"I'm filling in temporarily. Aidan has taken over for Nick, but he's busy at the moment." As soon as she said it, Fern regretted giving Wilma fodder for gossip.

"Aidan? I can't believe Nick let that troublemaker take over the business. Did you know he threatened Russell? Kids these days have no manners. If he were my kid . . ."

Fern had no interest in hearing what Wilma would do to Aidan. "Did you need something?"

Wilma snorted. "No, I don't *need* anything, but I did *want* some lemon drops."

Fern measured them out, handed Wilma her change, and moved over to wait on bakery customers. But not before she caught the muttered comment of the woman in line behind Wilma.

"Lemon drops? Perfect for a sourpuss like her."

"I'll be right back," Fern told the lady.

Fern exhaled a long sigh of relief when the midafternoon lull began. Aidan came back to work the candy counter and offered to keep an eye on her stand if she wanted to take a late lunch break.

That sounded perfect. Fern had started to agree when Caroline called to Gideon, "We're down to the last two chickens. Are you cooking more?"

"I don't have any more."

"You mean we ran out?" Caroline's shrill tone carried as several people stopped to stare. She didn't seem to notice she was attracting attention. "But we always have a run on takeout chickens right before we close. What are we going to tell customers?"

"I'll figure something out."

Gideon headed in Fern's direction. Though she shouldn't, she waited for him.

"Is everything all right?" she asked when he was close enough.

"*Neh*. As much as I dislike doing it, I'll have to ask Bo Ridley for some chickens."

Fern could only imagine the humiliation he'd face because he'd turned Bo down the other night. Maybe she could spare him that embarrassment. "I'm heading that way on my break. If you'd like, I can ask him."

"I couldn't do that to you, but he'd probably say yes to you faster than he'd say it to me."

Fern could imagine Bo making Gideon grovel before

agreeing to sell him the chickens. "Just tell me how many you need. I don't mind doing it."

Gideon's eyes held pain. "I'm sure you don't."

Was he implying that she liked Bo's flirting? Fern bristled and almost told him to get his own meat. Then she looked into his eyes and couldn't say anything at all.

He broke their gaze. "I have no idea how many chickens we'll need. People have been passing that flyer around, so we've been flooded with customers who want the super-reduced price."

That's what had worried Fern when she'd read the flyer. How would Gideon keep the business afloat?

"We usually sell a dozen or two late Saturday afternoon, but we might have more customers than usual."

"Why don't I ask him for thirty?"

"That would be good, but are you sure you want to do this?"

When she nodded, Gideon stared at her with admiration. "I can't thank you enough. It's hard enough buying Bo's chickens, but having to order them directly from him . . ."

"I understand." She'd do anything to help Gideon.

Gideon's heartfelt *danke* set her whole body on fire. But Nettie craned her neck and targeted Fern with a glower that quickly doused the flames.

"I'll be back soon." Fern scurried away.

Although she'd assured Gideon she didn't mind, her steps slowed before she reached Ridley's. She disliked facing Bo's creepiness.

But this wasn't about her. Gideon needed her help. Steeling herself to face Bo, she forced herself to march to the counter where he stood.

"Well, hello, doll. What a pleasant surprise! You coming to take me up on last night's offer?"

"I'm here to buy some chicken."

Bo's eyebrows shot up. "You don't get *enough* where you work?" He colored his question with a suggestive tone.

Fern recoiled. If she hadn't been doing this for Gideon, she would have whirled on her heel and stalked off.

Only by reminding herself of Gideon could she keep her words civil. "I'd like to buy some whole chickens if you have them."

Bo waved toward his workers. "Any of them would be happy to help you."

"I'd prefer to deal with you."

"Oh, well, if it's personalized service you require, I'm happy to oblige." He flashed her an *I'm-going-to-have-you-for-dessert* smile. "You said chickens. How many do you want? Two?"

"Thirty."

Bo squinted at her. "I assume these are for Gideon?" When she nodded, he waved a dismissive hand. "Tell him to come see me in person and we'll work out a deal. I knew he'd come around eventually."

"*Neh*, I promised him I'd get the chickens."

"And you always keep your promises?"

"I try to."

"Will you make me a promise?"

"Depends on what it is." Her clipped tone made it clear she'd rather not agree to anything he'd suggest.

Bo pressed his hands against his heart and made an overly dramatic disappointed expression. "You wound me. Don't you like me? Even just a little?"

"God commands us to love everyone."

A gleam lit his eyes. "You have to love everyone, eh?"

Before he could get out what she suspected he planned to say, Fern said, "Do you have thirty chickens to sell or not?"

"I might if you ask nicely enough."

"Pretty please, may I have thirty chickens?" Although her words dripped with honey, they sounded fake. A reflection of the truth in her heart.

Resting his elbows on the counter, he studied her. "I guess that's the best I'm going to get, huh? Oh, all right. I'll see what I have left." He disappeared into the huge walk-in refrigerator that stood where the candle lady used to have her stand.

When he emerged, he said, "Sorry, I only have twenty-two. I don't want to take the ones in the display case. I'm sure we'll sell those."

"That's fine." She suspected Gideon would be happy to have any amount of chickens.

"You don't plan on carrying them, do you?" Bo said as she stood there. "I'll have one of my guys bring them down soon."

"Thank you." Fern even managed a smile.

"Now we're getting somewhere," Bo said. "Who knew chickens were the key to your heart?"

Bo was wrong. Not counting God, her family, and her community, only one person held the key to her heart. And he didn't seem to care to use it.

Chapter Twenty-One

Gideon paced back and forth so many times, Caroline snapped, "What's making you so antsy?"

He didn't answer, but his mind kept conjuring up pictures of Bo leaning over the counter, leering at Fern. Right now, they could run out of chickens, for all Gideon cared. All he wanted was to keep her away from Bo.

"I'll be right back," Gideon told his sister as he started to exit the stand.

"Wait a minute. Where are you going?" Caroline demanded. "You left us stuck yesterday afternoon. You're not going to do that again."

"Nettie can help at the counter. We should have enough salads for the rest of the afternoon."

"But—but . . ."

Gideon took advantage of his sister's sputtering to head off. He had to save Fern. She must have fallen into Bo's clutches. Poor, innocent Fern was no match for sneaky, worldly Bo.

He'd only made it partway to the front of the market before he spotted Fern heading toward him. Without Bo. And without chickens.

Gideon didn't care. He'd rather have Fern safe than all the chickens in the world.

In his relief, he might have smiled too broadly. Fern lit up in response. *Ach*, what that did to his heart. He had to get himself under control before he reached her.

The closer she came, the wider Fern's grin stretched.

Be still, my heart.

"Gideon, he says he only has twenty-two chickens, but he'll be bringing them down in a little while."

"You did it!" Gideon wanted to take her hands and dance her around in circles like they'd done when they were small. He managed to restrain himself.

"I'm sorry it wasn't thirty."

"Twenty-two is great." Gideon was relieved to get any at all. He had a sneaking suspicion that if she'd turned up with only two chickens, he'd be just as elated.

"We'd better get back to the stand so we don't miss Bo."

"Right." If Fern hadn't reminded him, he'd probably have stayed rooted to this spot, staring at her.

He fell into step beside her and resisted the urge to take her hand. Was he grinning like a fool? His lips were tugging at the far sides of his cheeks, so he must be. But he couldn't seem to help himself.

As they reached the stand, Nettie's displeasure washed over him like a cold bucket of water. It wiped the smile from his face.

"*Danke,*" he said softly as he let Fern enter first. "I really appreciate you doing this."

"I was happy to."

"You're back." Caroline greeted him with an exasperated look, which was better than Nettie's look of betrayal.

"Thanks to Fern, chickens are on their way."

"Of course, everything's thanks to Fern," Nettie muttered. Gideon frowned, and she subsided.

A cart clanked down the aisle. Bo walked beside the young worker pushing it. With his usual swagger, Bo approached the counter. "Where do you want these, Gid?"

Only people who knew him well called him "Gid." Something about Bo doing it set Gideon's teeth on edge. "I'll take them right here. Thanks for bringing them."

"You mean they're going straight into your rotisserie? You ran out?"

"Not quite," Caroline answered for Gideon. "We have one chicken left and, of course, a selection of pieces. But we've been so swamped with customers, it's been hard to keep up."

Gideon hid a smile. Leave it to Caroline to put Bo in his place.

"I thought maybe you'd decided to take my advice about switching suppliers." After flicking his eyes in Caroline and Nettie's direction, Bo gave Gideon a secretive glance.

"I did take your advice. All the chickens I had today and yesterday were certified. Thanks for letting me know."

Bo appeared taken aback. "You sure?"

"Positive."

"Well, good for you. But I'm disappointed. I hoped you go with us."

"I may need you from time to time if we run out. As Caroline said, business has been brisk."

Bo motioned for his worker to transfer the chickens. "Just so you know, the prices I gave you the other day only apply to bulk orders. If we're doing emergency shipments, they double."

Bo's prices already were high—much higher than Gideon could afford. If he didn't need the chickens, he'd tell Bo to take them back.

"That's not fair," Fern burst out. She left her counter and came charging toward them. "If you give someone a price, you need to stick to it."

Bo smiled. "Ooo, I love women with tempers."

Then he leaned on the counter and said to Gideon, "Tell you what. I'll make you a deal. Ten percent off my emergency price if you send Fern to do the ordering."

Gideon's jaw worked. He wanted to tell Bo to take his chickens and leave. "Fern is not part of any deal." He'd pay more than double the price to keep Fern away from Bo.

Bo shrugged. "Your loss." He nodded to his worker, and they both took off.

Fern waited until Bo was out of earshot to say, "I can do the ordering if it'll get you a better price."

"*Neh*, it's not worth it." Gideon would not let Fern get near Bo again if he could help it. "I don't trust him, and I wouldn't want anything to happen to you."

Her grateful expression made him want to take her in his arms and—

What was wrong with him? What was he thinking?

With a soft *danke*, Fern returned to her counter, but Gideon stared after her.

"Um, Gideon, we do need those chickens cooked." Caroline pinched her lips together as if pressing back a smile.

"I'm on it." But he couldn't resist one more glance in Fern's direction. Having her here in his stand had been a mistake. How would he ever keep his mind on work when she was proving to be such a distraction?

* * *

Fern couldn't believe she'd interfered in Gideon's business, but Bo's unfairness upset her. She couldn't let him cheat Gideon.

At least Gideon hadn't seemed to mind her interference. He'd even thanked her. And she'd felt his gaze on her as she left. If only . . .

She had no right to wish for things like that. Especially not when it seemed he and Nettie had a relationship. She'd probably incurred Nettie's wrath. Again.

The more she tried to push Gideon from her mind, the more he intruded into her thoughts. She gave up. Between waiting on customers, she replayed the scene of him defending her. And when he said it wasn't worth it, her heart fluttered as much now as it had then. He sounded as if he cared about her.

She sighed. He would have done the same for Nettie or Caroline. As much as she'd like to dream, it hadn't meant anything special.

Boots clumping and chains clanking, a group of rough-looking teens surrounded the counter, interrupting her daydreams. Fern took a step back, but they surged closer to Aidan's end. Several customers who had been heading toward the candy counter swerved away.

A tall, skinny guy with a scruffy beard and a snake tattoo curling up his neck and onto his face smacked a hand on the counter. "Hey, dude. Where you been?"

Aidan lifted his chin. "Working. I took over my old man's candy shop."

"Here? Thought he was at the other end of the building." Scruffy Beard jerked a thumb over his shoulder.

"Yeah, he used to be there. Some m— Well, umm, somebody put him outta business."

"What?" the one with the nose ring screeched. "You gonna stand for that?"

"You oughta make them pay," Scruffy Beard said. "Need some help?"

Aidan held up both hands. "Nah, Cogan. I don't want to start no trouble."

Cogan ignored him. "Let's go see about this dude. Put a little scare into him."

"Don't, Cogan," Aidan called after them. "I mean it."

The group traipsed after Cogan.

"Fern?" Desperation in his voice, Aidan asked, "Could you watch my stand? I gotta stop them. When they get going—" He tore off the candy-striped apron and sprinted down the aisle.

As Aidan disappeared, Gideon rushed over. "What's going on? Where did Aidan go?"

Fern's heart, which had already been thumping as the gang surrounded the stand, kicked up several notches. She squeezed her hands together and struggled to calm herself.

Two of the families who had given the gang a wide berth approached the counter.

"Are you okay?" one of the mothers asked. "They looked pretty scary."

"And furious," the other one added. "They weren't upset with you, were they?"

Fern shook her head and swallowed hard. With Gideon so close behind her, she could barely breathe, let alone come up with a coherent sentence.

"I'll be with you in a second," she managed to say. Aidan needed to be protected, and someone had to stop those teens before they caused trouble. Maybe Gideon could help.

She took a deep breath, and the words tumbled out.

"Aidan went chasing after his friends. They plan to go after Bo for taking Nick's spot."

A loud commotion came from the other end of the market. Gideon dashed from the stand. "I'll see what I can do."

Fern turned back to wait on the ladies, but they'd disappeared. Like magnets, all the shoppers streamed toward the shouting and chanting. Fern followed.

As she passed the stairwell, Russell came stomping down. "What's going on?" He brushed past her and ran toward the noise.

By the time Fern arrived, the teens were all yelling at Bo. Some of his workers cowered against the wall. Customers scrambled away like frightened ants as the teens surged toward the counters chanting, their words unintelligible.

Cogan screamed the loudest. "You had no right to take this dude's stand."

Where was Gideon? Fern tried to locate him in the chaos.

Russell charged into the crowd and tried to outshout the teens. "YOU HOOLIGANS! GET OUT OF HERE NOW OR I'M CALLING THE POLICE!"

"Call away, old man," Cogan practically spat in Russell's face. "You the owner of this joint?"

"Yeah, he is," someone in the crowd called out.

"Then you deserve the same as him." Cogan pointed at Bo.

Aidan grabbed Cogan's sleeve. "Come on, dude. This guy'll get you put in jail."

"He don't scare me." Cogan advanced toward Russell,

who was dialing his phone. "We don't need no cops. Put that away."

"SEND THE POLICE," Russell shrieked into the phone. "There's a riot here. Valley Green Market."

Cogan reached out to snatch Russell's phone, but Gideon stepped between them.

Fern sucked in a breath. If Cogan swung those chains clanking on his vest, he'd do serious damage to Gideon.

"You don't want to do that," Gideon said in a calm, persuasive voice. "It'll get you in trouble."

Cogan sneered. "Who's this Amish dude?"

"He's my boss." Aidan tugged at Cogan's arm. "Leave him alone."

"He one of the good guys?"

"Yeah. He gave my old man a stand when that crook gave away my dad's space." Aidan indicated Russell, who remained hidden behind Gideon.

"So he's the one we should be going after?"

"Not right now," Aidan pleaded.

"When, then?" Cogan demanded.

"Later," Aidan said, his voice edged with desperation. "We'll talk later."

"No talk. Just action." Cogan edged around Gideon to face Russell. "Who do you think you are?"

Russell straightened his back and jutted out his chin, but the fear in his eyes gave him away. "I'm the owner of this market, and I demand you all leave now."

"And if we don't, whatcha gonna do?"

"I'll have you all hauled off to jail." Russell's threat sounded shaky.

"Cogan?" Gideon's calmness contrasted with Russell's irritation.

"What?" Cogan looked at Gideon but kept the sneer on his face.

"Can we take this outside so we don't disturb the customers?"

"And let him"—Cogan pointed at Russell—"and him"—he flung an arm in Bo's direction—"make money when my man here"—he slung an arm around Aidan's shoulders—"lost his business? No way."

Gideon nodded. "I know you're upset because it doesn't seem fair, but maybe Bo would come outside to talk." He sent a questioning look to Bo.

"Sure." Bo sounded nervous, but he stepped from behind the counter and headed for the front doors.

The teens, still chanting, followed him. Gideon stayed beside Cogan and Aidan. Russell didn't move.

Fern walked over to him. "You're going to be part of the discussion, aren't you?"

She'd trapped him. A sickish expression on his face, Russell trailed after the noisy group.

As she and Russell exited, Gideon said to Cogan, "Can you get your friends quiet so we can talk?"

Cogan inserted two fingers into his mouth and whistled—a noise so shrill Fern had to cover her ears. Complete silence descended.

Gideon addressed Cogan. "Maybe Aidan should speak first."

Aidan faced his friend. "Cogan, I hate this guy." He flipped his chin in Russell's direction. "But come on, man. I don't want to lose this job. It's my great-grandma's business."

Cogan planted his hands on his hips, making his chains rattle. "I'm not letting this dude diss you."

Beside Fern, Russell's jittery movements revealed his

fright. Fern was also scared, but for Gideon and Aidan. If the gang chose to turn on them . . .

In the distance, sirens whirred, getting louder.

"Cops. I'm outta here." Cogan motioned for his buddies to join him.

They all raced for their cars or motorcycles and careened out of the parking lot.

Russell stepped toward Aidan with a threatening look. "Don't think you're getting away with this."

Aidan stood his ground. "I didn't do anything."

"You'll be charged with disturbing the peace."

"I was not. Gideon, tell him. I was trying to stop them."

Gideon put an arm around Aidan's shoulders. "I know. And I think Russell knows that too. That's why we're all going to go inside and forget it happened. It's over."

Russell turned on Gideon. "You think I'm gonna drop this, you're crazy. I'm gonna put every one of those punks behind bars if it's the last thing I do."

Fern moved closer to Gideon and Aidan. Gideon tried to signal her with his eyes and a head toss to stay away, but she ignored him.

"The boys didn't do any damage," she pointed out.

"Scaring my customers is plenty. I'll drag them into court and sue them for every penny. You think people will come into this market now? Customers will be afraid they'll be mobbed by a gang."

"And you"—Russell jabbed his forefinger toward Aidan—"I'll make sure the cops drag you out of here in handcuffs."

"He didn't do anything," Fern pointed out.

Russell turned a blistering glare on her. "Stay out of other people's business."

"Fern is a witness," Gideon said. He motioned for her to come stand beside him.

She scooted close, grateful for his protection and strength, as the police cars, sirens blaring, screeched to a halt around them.

One officer emerged from a car and approached the group, while another stood, hand on holster, observing everyone. Several others got out and formed a circle around them.

"What seems to be the problem?" an officer asked.

Russell explained that he owned the market, dramatized the scene that had just occurred, and then pointed to Aidan. "That's the ringleader."

"No, I'm not." Aidan's defiant shout didn't go down well with the officer, who studied him with narrowed eyes.

"He didn't do anything," Fern spoke up.

As the officer studied her, Gideon backed her up. "She's right. Aidan is innocent."

"Don't believe them," Russell shouted. "They're liars. That boy works for them, and they have a vendetta against me."

The officer and his backup all glanced from one to the other. Then he turned to Bo. "Who are you?"

Bo stood at attention, his back rigid. "Bo Ridley, sir. I own the stand where the protest occurred."

Russell glared at Bo. "Protest? It was a RIOT."

"Seems there's a difference of opinion here." The officer nodded to Bo. "Why don't you tell us what happened?"

To Fern's surprise, Bo's account downplayed the event. Then he added, "Look, I can understand why the kids are upset. I understood the stands I replaced were going out of business."

"They were," Russell blustered.

"Only because of a steep rent increase." Bo turned his attention back to the officer. "The kids—"

"Kids?" Russell shrieked. "Those were no kids. They were hoodlums, delinquents . . ." He stuttered to a stop when the officer glared at him.

The officer nodded for Bo to continue.

"Anyway, the kids are upset that his dad"—Bo waved a hand toward Aidan—"lost his business. I don't blame them for being upset."

"You concur with Ridley's story?" the officer asked Gideon.

"I do. The kids may have gotten a bit rowdy, but they did come outside when I asked them to."

"Gideon's right," Fern said. "They calmed down when he spoke to them."

Russell narrowed his eyes at Fern, and Gideon moved closer. Although she'd been on edge during the confrontation, now every single nerve ending jumped and tingled. She forced herself to focus on the conversation.

The officer directed his question to Gideon. "Where are these teens now?"

Hands clenched in fists and jaw tight, Russell erupted. "They all fled like the rats they are the minute they heard sirens." He poked a finger toward Aidan's chest, one that didn't connect. "He can give you all their names and addresses. He put them up to it."

"That's not true. I was trying to stop them." Aidan leaned forward aggressively.

Gideon shifted, and Fern noticed he'd tightened his grip on Aidan's shoulders. Aidan relaxed his puffed-out chest.

"Could we all get back to our businesses?"

Fern was shocked to hear the request coming from Bo.

"We don't want to press charges or anything. It's all

over, and I'm sure Aidan's friends won't do that again. Right, Aidan?" Bo's tone carried an implicit threat.

"I hope not," Aidan mumbled.

Fern tried to smooth things over. "I'm sure Aidan will explain to them that you didn't put us out of business on purpose." Fern wasn't totally convinced of that herself, but they all needed to get back inside before the final hour's flurry of customers.

"I agree with Bo," Gideon said. "We all need to get back to work."

The officer slid the pad he'd jotted notes on into his pocket.

"Wait," Russell yelled, "I want to press charges. This is my market, and I want all those kids arrested for disturbing the peace."

Wearily, the officer pulled out the pad. "Duly noted. I'll get names and addresses from this young man here."

"Young man?" Russell snarled. "He's a juvie."

"Sir," the officer said in a stern tone, "I think it'd be best if you went inside. Some of the officers will come in to gather some eyewitness accounts and get your signed statement."

As Russell passed Fern, she said too low for the officer to hear, "I wonder what Mrs. Vandenburg will think. She's been good friends with Nick's family for decades."

Russell's head snapped up. "You wouldn't . . ."

Fern smiled sweetly.

Russell stalked toward the building, then turned abruptly. "I've changed my mind," he called to the officers. "Drop the charges."

Beside Fern, Gideon choked back a half snort and changed it to a cough. Then he glanced down at Fern, his eyes shining. "Remind me never to fight with you."

His grin made her heart take flight.

* * *

Gideon couldn't believe Fern had stopped Russell with two simple sentences. She was amazing. Simply amazing. He smiled down at her, which was a mistake. Next thing he knew, he was drowning in her eyes. Going down deeper, deeper.

The officer cleared his throat, breaking the spell. "You're all free to go."

But Gideon was not free at all. He'd fallen into a trap he'd tried to avoid.

"Fern?"

Her breathless *jah* set his pulse pounding harder.

"I, um, that is . . ."

"Hey, guys?" Aidan's question punctured the mood. "Shouldn't we go help Caroline and Nettie?"

"Right." Gideon blew out a long breath, grateful he'd been saved from making a major mistake.

The police cars spit gravel as they zoomed out onto the road. Gideon stared after them, trying to get his racing pulse under control.

From the opposite direction, a delivery truck rattled into the parking lot, a huge Q & Z logo on its side.

"*Ach*, no. I forgot about the chickens."

Fern stared at him in dismay. "You forgot to notify Q & Z?"

Another trap Gideon had gotten caught in. It seemed as if they were closing around him. "I can't cancel. Under the contract, I have to pay the monthly fee even if I don't take deliveries."

"That's so unfair."

Gideon loved how Fern championed him. Even in the worst circumstances, she remained on his side.

Aidan looked from one to the other. "What's going on? Why don't you want chickens? Especially since you almost ran out today?"

"It's a long story."

"Did you see Gideon's flyers?" Fern asked.

"Those papers on the counter?"

She nodded.

"It looked like a long letter, and I don't read so good."

Fern gave him a quick overview of what the letter contained.

Gideon took over the explanation as the truck pulled up to his outside refrigerator. "I have to go, but Q & Z chickens aren't certified organic, so I can't use them anymore." He turned to Fern. "Can you two go inside and help Caroline and Nettie?"

As the two of them headed toward the building, Aidan's question drifted to Gideon. "How's he gonna afford all that?"

Gideon couldn't hear Fern's answer, but the only one he had was to trust God. He had no other choice.

After the chickens had been unloaded, Gideon hurried to the stand. As he passed Bo, he called, "Thank you for what you did out there."

Bo nodded. "No problem. The last thing those kids need is an arrest record." His face twisted into an ironic smile. "I should know."

Interesting. Bo had a record? Gideon only hoped it wasn't for selling noncertified organic meats. He should have checked into Bo's business before buying chickens today.

Fern's smile when he reached the stand brought back all the feelings he'd tamped down earlier. How would he ever keep his mind on work?

"What are you going to do with all the chickens?" she asked.

"I have no idea. I'm not sure I can resell them. Most people won't pay the price Q & Z charges when the chickens aren't organic. I'll have to sell at a loss or give them away."

Aidan finished waiting on a candy customer. "Me and some of my buds hang out in the 'hood. There's a church down there that feeds the poor and homeless. People line up around the block to get a meal at lunch and dinnertime. Maybe they'd want some."

"Would you ask them if they can use forty-pound packages of whole chickens?"

"Me? Go into a church? No way."

Gideon would have to make time to do it himself. He didn't have enough storage space in the refrigerator for more than two deliveries.

"Aw, don't look so disappointed. I'll do it." Aidan gave him a cheeky grin. "I suppose a little religion can't hurt."

He started to head off but turned to face them. "If I hang around the two of you much longer, it might rub off on me." He swallowed hard. "Thanks for sticking up for me."

Fern's sweet smile flipped Gideon's insides. She'd been so loving to his nephews and now to Aidan. With her kindness and caring, she'd be a great mother. And wife. But with his present financial difficulties, he couldn't even consider it.

Chapter Twenty-Two

On Tuesday morning, Aidan was opening the employee entrance door when Fern pushed her cart across the parking lot. As soon as he spotted her, he stopped and waited.

"Need any help?" he called.

"*Neh*, I'm fine. Thanks for getting the door."

While they walked to the stand, Aidan chattered about his weekend. "Oh, and you're not going to believe this," he said as he stepped aside to let her go into the stand first. "I stayed home on Saturday night too."

"You did? That's great."

"Well, I didn't do it on purpose. I was worn out from all that stuff with Russell. I fell asleep before dinner and didn't wake up until like ten on Sunday."

"You must have been tired."

"I guess." He removed his sheets, rearranged some candy, and then waited until Fern had set out her baked goods. "You ready to help package?" he asked.

The two of them joined Nettie and Caroline, who'd already begun setting out trays. As they passed Gideon, Aidan stopped.

"I did what you asked, man." He pulled a slip of paper

from his pocket. "Like I told Fern, I slept in late on Sunday. By the time I got to the church, the service had ended. But I caught the minister and asked him."

Gideon slid the last spit into the rotisserie and turned it on. Then he took the paper. "Thanks."

"That woman"—Aidan gestured to the paper—"buys groceries and collects donations for most of the food programs in the area."

"Buys food?" Fern asked.

"Yep, I told him you needed to make money. He said they get good deals, but she can pay."

"That's *wunderbar*." Fern smiled up at Gideon. "Isn't it?"

His face broke into a wide grin. "It sure is. Thanks, Aidan." In a quieter voice meant only for Fern, he added, "I don't mind if part of it is a donation. At least it'll offset some of the cost."

"I prayed about it all weekend. I'm so glad it worked out."

"*Danke*." The softness in his eyes seemed to be for her alone.

Fern wanted to burst into song, but then she turned. Nettie's pinched face and pursed lips changed Fern's joy to guilt. And Nettie had positioned herself in Fern's favorite spot—the best one for watching Gideon.

Fern tamped down her disappointment and set to work. She'd packaged only a few side dishes when sirens split the air.

Aidan's hands shook. "What's that?"

"Police cars? Sounds like it's out front."

Fern stepped closer to Aidan. After Saturday's encounter with the police, the sirens seemed to be making him nervous. "I'm sure it's all right," she whispered, hoping that was true.

"Maybe I should see what's happening," Gideon said. "They may not realize we're in here."

A loud banging on the front doors echoed through the building. Gideon had started out of the stand when someone clattered down the stairs.

"Coming," Russell yelled.

"Maybe we should stay here," Aidan suggested.

"Good idea." They shouldn't interfere in Russell's business.

Gideon transferred his weight from one foot to the other several times, as if undecided.

"Look at what they did." Russell's scream echoed through the empty building.

Low murmuring came from that end of the market, interspersed with loud curses and complaints.

Most of the conversation remained garbled, until Russell yelled, "That's not all. Come upstairs."

Several pairs of boots and shoes clomped up the stairs.

"I should have pressed charges on Saturday."

Aidan froze. *Saturday?* he mouthed.

A ball of dread grew in Fern's stomach. Had Aidan or his friends done something over the weekend to get back at Russell?

Aidan had made it a point to tell her about staying home on Saturday night. Had he lied? What if he did it hoping she'd back up his alibi?

"What do you think happened?" Aidan's face creased into worry lines.

He sounded innocent. But Russell had called Aidan a juvie. Did Aidan have a criminal record?

Doubts floated through Fern's mind. Yet what about the teen's actions when he worked here? He'd been kind, dependable, hardworking, giving, caring, honest. He'd even tried to stop his friends from causing trouble. *Neh*, she refused to believe he'd done anything wrong.

Gideon moved to the exit. "While they're upstairs, I'm going to see what happened."

"I want to go with you." Aidan pressed a lid onto the container of applesauce he'd filled.

"I do too." Fern put the plastic cover over the coleslaw and set it in the refrigerated display case.

"Let's all go." Caroline put the serving spoon back in the bowl of broccoli salad and stored it.

Together they traipsed to the front of the building. They stopped in shock an aisle away from Ridley's stand.

Fern gasped. Aidan moaned what might have been *Nooo*. The horror in his eyes convinced Fern he'd had nothing to do with this.

Every one of the glass cases had been painted black. Red graffiti had been sprayed over the black. Red and black squiggles and swear words covered the walls behind the counter. Some places said, "Get out" or "You don't belong here." Others read, "Thief" or "Cheater."

"I shoulda told them about Bo." Aidan looked sick. "Gideon, instead of paying for my motorcycle, can we use the money to clean this up?"

Motorcycle? Gideon promised to buy Aidan a motorcycle? Still shaken by the vandalism, Fern stood still, stunned and unable to ask that question.

Gideon was too dumbfounded to reply to Aidan's request for the money. As much as Gideon had been bothered by Bo's flirting with Fern and his threats over the chicken, Gideon never wanted to see this disaster happen to anyone.

Even worse, Bo had been kind and refused to press

charges against Aidan's friends. Would the teens have done this if they'd known?

Aidan stared at Gideon with pleading eyes. He'd been relieved not to owe Aidan his pay for six months. Gideon had hoped the extra time would allow him to stabilize his income. Instead, he'd been plunged into deeper financial turmoil. But how could he refuse Aidan's request?

"We can work it out," Gideon managed to respond.

But he had no idea how. With his apology discount for customers cutting into the profits, the higher cost of organic chickens, and paying Q & Z's monthly fees, he'd have little left. He'd depleted most of his savings paying rent for Fern and the others for the last two months, plus he'd had the expansion costs. But if Aidan wanted his salary to help with this, Gideon would do what he could.

Fern moved closer. "Is something wrong? I mean besides this?" She waved toward the mess in front of them. "You seem, I don't know, worried and distracted."

Gideon couldn't believe she was so perceptive. He didn't want to hurt her feelings, but he couldn't share his financial concerns. "*Danke* for noticing. It'll be all right." One more thing to leave up to God.

"They must have done something to Russell's office too." Aidan's statement ended on a squeak.

"You're probably right," Gideon said. "We should get back to the stand before they come down."

But his suggestion came too late. The stairs behind them vibrated with footsteps. Seeing them here would make Russell furious. But if they scurried away, they'd look guilty.

Gideon faced Russell and the police officers flanking him. "I'm sorry this happened."

"I bet you are," Russell said through gritted teeth. "You probably put that little punk up to it."

"Now, Mr. Evans," the woman officer said in a soothing tone, "it's understandable to be upset, but let's not accuse anyone until we've completed our investigation."

"I know who did it." Russell rushed at Aidan and would have grabbed him by the collar if Gideon hadn't stepped between them.

"You let that juvie in here. I bet you made a copy of the key and gave it to him."

"No, I didn't." Gideon couldn't believe Russell would make such an accusation. "And Aidan didn't do this. He was as shocked as we were to see it."

"You're a liar. And, of course, he'd pretend he didn't do it. I'm sure he's quite an actor."

The policewoman cleared her throat. "Mr. Evans, I wouldn't suggest attacking people in front of us." She frowned. "Or when we're not around."

Dodging around Gideon, Russell aimed a glare of hatred at Aidan. Stabbing his finger at Aidan, Russell growled, "I can save you a lot of trouble. Arrest him. He's the culprit."

"You have any proof?"

"Look at his expression. That proves he's guilty."

"We can't arrest people based on their expressions. If we did . . ."

Aidan snorted. "Guess they'd have to lock you up."

Gideon signaled for Aidan not to add fuel to Russell's flaring temper. To Gideon's surprise, Aidan pinched his mouth shut, but he didn't muffle his snickers.

"Question him." Russell thrust his finger in Aidan's direction again. "He and his gangster friends did this."

"Do you know anything about this?" the officer asked Aidan.

Aidan faced her with a defiant look. "I know my rights. You can't question me without my parents and a lawyer."

"Told ya he was a juvie. How many kids know to ask for a lawyer? And if he's innocent, why would he need a lawyer?"

The officer held up her hand. "Mr. Evans, I'd like you to go with Officer Perez to give him your statement. He can also look at your surveillance videos."

"I was so rattled after the Saturday afternoon riot, I, um, forgot to double check that the cameras were turned on." Russell's eyes drilled into Aidan, as if blaming him for the security lapse. "But, don't worry. I'm sure I can find eye-witnesses to prove you and your friends did this."

"I'd be careful with threats, Mr. Evans."

The officer's sharp rebuke made Russell jut out his jaw. "That kid may look smug now, but I'll find proof."

Fern moved closer to Aidan and Gideon. "We know you didn't do it," she whispered.

Gideon loved her use of *we*. "We'll do whatever we can to help." If she could say *we*, so could he. They were in this together.

Fern beamed up at him, and Gideon was lost.

The officer's voice snapped him back to the situation at hand. Looking at Aidan, she said, "I would like to speak with you."

When Aidan bristled, she added, "I'm not accusing you of anything. Please come to the station with a parent or guardian. You're also welcome to bring a lawyer. Be there at three this afternoon."

"I can't." Aidan turned pleading eyes to Gideon. "Tell her I have to work."

"It's all right," Fern said. "I can take your place."

Aidan shook his head. "Why should I skip work for Russell's lies?"

"What time do you get off?" the officer asked.

"The market closes at four. Then I help with cleanup."

"I'll see you at five, then." She headed over to direct two officers who were cordoning off the area with yellow caution tape.

"I didn't notice that before, but there's grease all over the floor." Gideon had been so focused on the graffiti, he hadn't spotted what looked like vegetable shortening smeared all along the aisle.

"Oh, man. They really wanted to get that dude."

"You sure it was your friends?" Gideon kept his voice low enough that the officers couldn't hear.

"Who else could it be?" Aidan said miserably. "And that lady cop was here on Saturday. She didn't get out of her car, but I saw her. She'll never believe I didn't do this."

Gideon slung an arm around Aidan's shoulders. He wished he could offer more comfort, but he feared Aidan might be right. The situation looked bad. Especially after Saturday's confrontation.

"Come on." Gideon tried not to let his uneasiness show. "Let's all get back to work. We don't have much time before the market opens."

Fern stayed close to Aidan's other side. Gideon loved how she supported Aidan. She had such a caring heart. If only he were in a position to date.

* * *

Fern walked beside Aidan, conscious of Gideon's big, strong hand on Aidan's shoulder. So close she could touch it. Her heart fluttered. What would it be like to have the warmth of his palm pressed against hers, to have their fingers entwined?

She shook off her imaginings. They needed to help Aidan. "Should you call your parents?"

Aidan stopped dead. "Call my old man? He'd kill me."

After seeing Nick in a temper several times, Fern had no doubt he could be scary. "What about your mom?"

"She'll think it's her duty to tell my old man." The bitterness in Aidan's tone revealed his feelings of betrayal.

Fern couldn't even fathom what it would be like if she couldn't rely on her parents for support. No wonder Aidan came off so abrasive and rebellious. She'd seen his true heart when they worked together, but he kept that softer side hidden. His rebellious act only covered up his vulnerability.

Aidan scuffed his toe on the cement floor. "I have to call somebody, though." He brightened. "She did say guardian. Could you two come as my guardians?"

"I wish we could, but I think they'll need your real parents. Do they know any lawyers?"

Although she listened for Aidan's answer, part of her mind wandered off into a fantasy where she and Gideon, hands still entwined, became Aidan's guardians. Her picture also included several small children—hers and Gideon's.

"I don't know. Maybe Mom does. She gets off at three today. I'll call her afterwards. I don't want to upset her at work."

"Good idea." Fern met Gideon's eyes, which were burning with a strange light. Had he guessed what she'd been thinking about him? About the two of them? Her face heated, and she lowered her lashes.

Fern needed to push aside her daydreams. She could indulge in them later. But no matter how hard she tried, thoughts of her and Gideon as a couple kept intruding.

Chapter Twenty-Three

Just before the market closed, Nick burst through the side door, a bleached blonde following on his heels, and marched over to the stand.

Beside Fern, Aidan emitted a whimper. "I told her not to tell him. Now I'm in for it."

Judging by the thundercloud on Nick's face, Aidan had guessed right.

Fern stepped in front of him as he barreled into the stand. "Hi, Nick, good to see you." She hoped to deflect some of his anger.

He ignored her greeting and pushed past her. "What did I tell you would happen if you ever got in trouble?" Nick's furious words echoed around the market, and the last straggling shoppers turned to stare.

Although his legs quivered, Aidan stood his ground. He met his father's question with defiance. "I didn't do anything."

"Sure you didn't. That's why the police want to question you? Because you're innocent?"

Aidan's mother laid a hand on his arm. "Let's hear his side of the story first."

Nick shook off her hand. "I'm sure we'll hear his alibi after we get to the station."

"Alibi?" Aidan's voice cracked. "You don't even know what happened, and you already don't believe me." He turned pleading eyes to his mother. "Mom?"

"I'll trust you to tell us the truth." Although she spoke sternly, her eyes displayed gentleness.

Aidan shifted so his back faced his father, and he spoke to his mother. "Someone vandalized the new stand. Bo Ridley's."

At the name, Nick's fists clenched. "What did they do to it?"

"Sprayed it with graffiti telling him to get out of the market and stuff like that."

A little smile played around Nick's lips. "He deserved it."

"Nick!"

At his wife's sharp exclamation, he rearranged his expression to a more neutral one, but his eyes danced with glee.

Aidan shot his father a look of disgust. "Bo Ridley's a nice man, and he didn't know he was putting people out of business."

"Yeah, right. He assumed all the stands were vacant? Fern and Mose took their stuff home, but our candy was completely stocked. And so were the candles and herbs."

Aidan blew out an exasperated sigh. "Russell told him all the stands were going out of business."

"Only because the sneaky, conniving little—" His wife's warning look silenced the cursing. "He pushed everyone out."

"Yeah, he did."

Fern couldn't believe Aidan had agreed with his father. The look he gave his mother begged for understanding.

"That's why Russell thinks I'm guilty. They messed with his office too."

"I hope they destroyed it all."

Nick's wife turned to him with a look of exasperation. "We don't have much time before we have to leave for the police station. Can we hear Aidan's story?"

"Story?" Nick snorted. "Sounds like you don't believe him either."

"Please, Nick, this is hard enough for all of us without your—"

"*My* what?" Nick exploded. "Our kid's in trouble, and you're blaming me?"

"I'm not getting in the middle of this." Aidan stalked off. "Gideon, what do you need me to clean?"

Gideon had been about to tell Aidan he didn't need to help, but the desperation in the boy's eyes made him reconsider. "Why don't you clean the rotisserie?"

He'd already turned it off and let it cool down. And a hard, time-consuming job might get Aidan's mind off his parents' bickering. But Gideon didn't want Aidan to feel obligated to finish.

He said in a low voice, "Just do whatever you can before you need to go. I'll finish the rest."

Aidan removed the center shaft, side wheels, grease deflectors, and fan covers, and set them in the sink to soak. He'd started wiping the glass with baking soda and water before his parents settled their disagreement.

Nick glanced over at Aidan, and his eyes glowed with both surprise and pride. Nick must be impressed that Aidan knew all about disassembling the rotisserie and that his son was a hard worker. Gideon wished Aidan had seen his father's expression, but Aidan's attention was fixed on the glass door as he removed all the grease and splatters.

Aidan's mother slipped in front of Nick. Although Nick's face reflected his annoyance, he kept his mouth shut. But it appeared to be a strain.

Gideon reached for the cloth in Aidan's hand. "You've done a great job so far. I can take over from here. I know you need to go."

With reluctance, Aidan handed Gideon the rag and turned to face his mother. He pointedly ignored his dad.

"Aidan, we need to go," she said. "You don't want to be late."

"Yes, I do."

His mother shook her head. "You don't mean that. Before we leave, though, we need to know everything that happened."

"What's there to know? Russell's blaming me for something I didn't do."

"But what does he claim you did?"

"Like I told you—the vandalism and his messed-up office."

"Do you know when it happened?"

"He thinks Saturday night."

"And you were out with your friends then?"

"Mom! You sound like you believe him."

She sighed. "All I'm trying to do is find out the facts. I certainly hope you wouldn't do something like this."

Gideon couldn't watch this deteriorate into another argument. "I know your son didn't do this. He was as shocked as the rest of us when we saw the damage."

Nick interrupted. "Kids can put on an act and pretend to be innocent."

The same thing Russell had said. Poor Aidan. Not only

had he been falsely accused by Russell. Now his own father doubted him.

"Great to see you have faith in your own kid." Aidan's hostility oozed out of every word. "For your information, I have an alibi."

"Good. Let's hear it." Nick crossed his arms and assumed an *I-don't-believe-it* expression.

"I was in my room, tired after working, and fell asleep. I didn't go anywhere on Saturday night." Aidan didn't add *So there*, but his tone made it clear.

"With your music blaring? A likely story. Many nights you leave that on and sneak out with your friends."

"I didn't go anywhere on Saturday night." The stubborn line of Aidan's jaw indicated another blowup was brewing.

Gideon smiled as Fern moved closer and intervened. "I'm sure Aidan's telling the truth."

Aidan sent her a grateful glance, but Nick exploded, "What would you know about it? This kid lies all the time."

Gideon wasn't about to let Nick get away with attacking Fern. "Hey, Nick, calm down here. Fern's only trying to help."

Nick turned on Gideon. "You're the cause of all this. If you hadn't given him a job—"

Gideon held up his hands to stop Nick's tirade. "What's past is past. It's more important to help Aidan."

"If you two do-gooders want to help him, go right ahead. As far as I'm concerned, they can lock him up and throw away the key. Maybe it'll teach him a lesson." Nick whirled on his heel and stalked off.

"He didn't mean that." Fern's sweet voice cut through the shocked silence. "He's upset and angry. I'm sure he'll get over it."

Aidan stared after his father with hurt eyes. "You don't know my old man."

Gideon suspected Aidan often faced his father's fury. If only there were a way to make things right between the two of them.

Lord, please give me the wisdom to say and do the right thing.

Setting a hand on Aidan's shoulder, Gideon said words he hoped he wouldn't regret. "I'm, I mean *we're*"—he checked with Fern to be sure she agreed and then had to tear his gaze away—"on your side. Whatever it takes, we'll do our best to help."

"You two are the greatest." Aidan swallowed, his tough-guy demeanor slipping. He looked like a small, lost boy.

But Gideon had to be sure of Aidan's story. "I want you to look me in the eye and tell me again what happened. I'll believe whatever you say is the truth." He prayed he could count on Aidan's honesty. "I'm sure your mother will too."

Aidan's mother nodded.

His eyes shiny with unshed tears, Aidan lifted his chin and met Gideon's gaze. "After Russell kicked everyone out, my homies were steaming. They came back to pick me up after work, and they wanted to wait outside for Russell and—" Aidan swallowed hard. "Well, it wouldn't have been pretty."

Beside Gideon, Fern flinched. He wanted to reach out to her, but he kept his eyes locked with Aidan's.

"I convinced them not to mess with Russell, but they wanted revenge."

Although Gideon disagreed with violence, he understood why Aidan's friends wanted to get back at Russell. They shouldn't have hurled insults and threats at Bo Ridley and his employees, but Russell's behavior had been even more despicable.

Instead of calming everyone, Russell had incited the teens by humiliating and taunting them.

"Cogan was so mad, he wouldn't listen to anything I said. I didn't even get to tell him about Bo dropping the charges. By the time they left me at my house, I thought Cogan understood it made no sense to stir up more trouble. I never thought they'd do something like this."

Fern shifted a little closer to Gideon, and he had trouble keeping his eyes on Aidan.

"Sometimes when people are hurt or angry, they say and do things that don't make sense," she pointed out.

Aidan glanced at her. "Yeah. They do." The look on his face made it clear he'd gotten her underlying message about his father.

Gideon exerted all his willpower not to turn his head in her direction. If Cogan had decided not to get revenge, why had he changed his mind? Maybe anger simmering under the surface had erupted.

His mom studied him. "You said you didn't go out with them on Saturday night."

"I didn't. I fell asleep. I even told Fern about that. Didn't I, Fern?"

Earlier, Fern had worried that Aidan had confided in her so he could use her for his alibi. Now that had come true. But this time, she was convinced Aidan was innocent. She only hoped she wasn't making a mistake.

"*Jah*, Aidan told me about falling asleep early on Saturday. He said he slept until ten on Sunday."

His mom looked thoughtful. "I didn't hear him leave, although I often don't. He sneaks out quietly to avoid his dad. And I did hear him in the shower just before I left for brunch with my friends a little after ten."

If one part of Aidan's account turned out to be true, perhaps the rest was as well. For Aidan's sake, Fern hoped it was, but he couldn't count on his parents for an alibi. And, although Fern backed him up here, she could only take Aidan at his word. She had no proof.

"We need to leave." Aidan's mom nodded a goodbye.

"I hope it goes well," Fern whispered as Aidan passed her. "We'll be praying."

"Yes, we will," Gideon added.

"Thanks." Aidan's wan smile showed he was unconvinced prayer worked.

"I wish we could do more for him." Fern said. "But God can do what we can't."

She was rewarded with a special smile. A smile that made her insides go all soft and mushy.

"We can back up Aidan's story about Saturday afternoon, but we have to trust God to reveal the truth."

Gideon was right about Saturday afternoon. Russell had claimed Aidan had incited his friends to violence. She and Gideon both knew that was untrue. So did Bo, but would he testify? Maybe after seeing the vandalism, he'd refuse to help Aidan.

"What are you thinking?" Gideon asked.

"Will Bo tell the truth about Saturday now that his stand's been destroyed?"

"That's a good question. He didn't press charges, but he might regret it."

"Maybe I should talk to Bo."

Gideon's face darkened. "I don't think that's necessary."

"I might be able to convince him Aidan wasn't involved."

"I'm sure you'd be persuasive."

His sarcasm cut Fern deeply. They'd been getting along so well, she'd almost dared to hope. But with one remark, he'd destroyed her dreams.

When hurt flared in Fern's eyes, Gideon regretted snapping at her. The thought of her even talking to Bo had made him nauseous. And what would she do to convince Bo? Lean close, smile at him, beg in her sweet voice.

The more Gideon pictured it, the more agitated he became. But he had no right to cause her pain because of his jealousy.

"I'm sorry." Could he be honest without revealing the whole truth? "Thinking about you—or any woman—being around Bo makes me sick. He's so, so—"

"Sleazy," Caroline supplied. "That's what Zach calls him."

Jah, that fit. Gideon had avoided telling Fern he cared about her. Bo being around any woman, especially an Amish woman, would upset Gideon, so he hadn't lied. Not exactly.

His conscience chided him, *If it's not the whole truth, it's a lie.*

Gideon came up with excuses. It wouldn't be fair to let Fern know of his attraction. Not when he couldn't date or marry.

Chapter Twenty-Four

On Thursday, Aidan arrived a few minutes before the market opened.

Fern, who'd already helped Caroline and Nettie package the side dishes, had been wondering if he'd be coming in. "How did everything go on Tuesday?"

Gideon turned on the rotisserie and hurried over. "I want to hear too."

He stood so close behind Fern, his body heat warmed her back. Her breath caught in her throat. If she swayed a bit, she could lean against his chest. Could he hear her tiny gasp for air?

Aidan folded a sheet. "I think they believed me about sleeping all night on Saturday." He turned his back to remove another sheet and added, "Might be because my old—my, um, dad got belligerent."

"With the police?" Gideon's breath tickled the hairs on the back of Fern's neck, making her shiver.

"Yeah. He has no class. But he told them I can't drive and he woulda heard loud engines roaring in the driveway if one of my friends came to get me."

So Nick had stood up for Aidan? Fern didn't agree with

Nick's fibbing. When he'd been here at the market, he'd questioned Aidan's truthfulness. But then he'd misled the officers about the very thing he refused to believe.

"He complained about my blaring music and didn't even mention that I often did that on nights I sneaked out. I think I'm in the clear."

"I'm glad." Although Fern felt uncomfortable with how that had happened, she was sure Aidan hadn't been part of the vandalism.

"Then the cops tried to get me to give them names, but I refused to rat out my friends. I hope they can't figure it out." Aidan refilled a jar with peppermint puffs.

"Looks like Russell's opening up." Fern pointed to Russell approaching the side doors. "Guess we need to get ready for customers." Reluctantly, she stepped away from Gideon to put her cash drawer in place and set her tablet and pencil on the counter.

"Oh, wait." Aidan stopped Gideon from leaving. "I didn't tell you the weirdest thing. Cogan and the rest of them went to a party Saturday night, got smashed, and passed out on the basement floor. I checked with other people at the party, and they said the same thing."

"Would the party host lie to give them an alibi?" Gideon asked.

"Nah. The girl, well, she likes me." Aidan's face reddened, and he looked down at the floor. "She'd tell the truth. Plus, she was pretty mad 'cause they messed up the house."

Gideon tapped a finger against his lower lip. "Are they sure the break-in happened on Saturday night? The market was closed Sunday and Monday too."

"The lawyer my dad hired found out Russell forgot to

turn on the security cameras on Saturday. He remembered on Sunday and activated them."

That didn't make sense to Fern. "Wouldn't he have seen the vandalism when he came in'?"

Aidan shook his head. "He can control them remotely. Oh, and he claimed a lot of stuff in his office was stolen. Big stuff. Like twenty thousand dollars' worth. He tried to blame me for that too."

"What?" Gideon stared at Aidan incredulously. "I've been in his office. The antique desk and his computer were the only valuable things in there."

"Yeah, well, the lawyer thinks he's trying to get extra insurance money." Aidan scrunched up his face like he smelled a terrible stench. "Speak of the devil. Here he comes."

Russell passed the stand to open the back doors. When he spotted Aidan, he stopped. A scarlet flush rose from his neck and splashed across his face. He advanced toward the stand. "What are you doing here'?"

"What's it look like? I'm working." Aidan used a belligerent tone guaranteed to irritate Russell.

Russell's face grew two shades darker. "They were supposed to put you behind bars."

"You need evidence for that."

At Aidan's flippant words, Russell's voice rose almost to a shout. "Don't get smart with me. I found three witnesses who'll pick you out of a lineup. You and that kid with the snake tattoo. Pretty stupid tattoo for a criminal. Easy to identify."

"He didn't do anything either. He has an alibi."

Russell sneered. "Sure he does. Who's gonna back him up? Your punk friends? My lawyers will rip them to pieces."

Turning to Gideon, he said, "Get that troublemaker out of here. I don't want a criminal working in my market."

"Innocent until proven guilty," Aidan taunted. "And you'll never prove me guilty, 'cause I'm not."

"My eyewitnesses will swear they saw you."

"How much did you have to pay them?"

Russell's eyes bulged. He reached over the counter as if to throttle Aidan.

"That's enough." Gideon's firm voice halted Russell's hands in midair. "This is my stand, and I won't have any of my employees harassed."

Turning his fury on Gideon, Russell announced in ringing tones, "This is my market, and I can decide who comes in here. I want him out now."

Many of Fern's usual customers skirted around the stand. "Russell," she said in soothing voice, "the customers can't order."

He turned to her with a furious glare, but she only gestured to the people who were gawking at or rushing away from the confrontation.

Russell's eyes burned with rage. But he mashed his lips together. "You'll pay for this," he muttered, his tone threatening. "And get rid of that thief."

"I will," Gideon said, "once I see proof of his guilt. Until then, he stays and works with me."

Fern leaned forward and called to a customer who was race-walking away from the stand. "Did you want your usual sticky buns, Margery?"

Margery turned with a wary look. "I do, but . . ." She cast a frightened glance at Russell.

"He's just leaving," Fern assured her.

With a wrathful scowl, Russell backed away from the

stand. As soon as he headed down the aisle to unlock the back door, customers flocked to Fern's and Aidan's stands.

Behind her, Gideon chuckled. "You sure do know how to deal with Russell."

As she turned around to get a bakery box, Fern's lips twitched. She tried hard not to smile or laugh, but how could she help joining in Gideon's mirth? Her whole body shook with suppressed laughter. Not over Russell, but because Gideon was staring at her with delight. If only it meant more than the fact that she'd sent Russell packing. If only it meant more than a temporary sense of relief. If only . . .

Gideon couldn't believe how Fern's soft and gentle ways had vanquished a bully. The more time he spent around her, the more he admired her. And if he were honest, the more his attraction increased.

Before it could get out of control, he cleared his throat. "I'd better get back to work. *Danke* for what you did for Aidan."

"You stuck up for him too."

Aidan filled a small brown bag with an assortment of candy. "You're both awesome. I really wish you were my guardians."

Gideon swallowed hard. Aidan's words touched him, although at twenty-five, he'd be much too young to be a seventeen-year-old's guardian. Unfortunately, Aidan had brought up Gideon's recent longing to become a parent. And to share parenting responsibilities with Fern.

"Happy to help," Gideon said gruffly, before hurrying over to check on the chickens and face Caroline's teasing.

* * *

Two hours later, as Aidan drained French fries, a foghorn blared from Aidan's pocket. "Oops. Sorry. Thought I turned down my phone." He pulled it out. "It's my mom. She wouldn't call except in an emergency."

A few minutes later, his face ashen, Aidan faced Gideon. "I gotta go when my mom gets here."

Aidan's pallor worried Gideon. Had something happened to Nick? "Is everything all right?"

"Naw, man. It's wrong, all wrong. I have to go to the police station. They said three people are saying they saw me breaking in on Saturday night."

"What?" Had Aidan been lying to them all along? Gideon didn't want to believe that. "You didn't do it, did you?"

Aidan's hurt-puppy-dog eyes accused Gideon of betrayal.

He held up a hand. "I didn't mean I think you did it. I was just asking to—" *To what? To get confirmation that it's a false accusation.*

"Yeah, I know. It looks bad. But how could they see me when I wasn't there?"

Gideon wondered the same thing. "Maybe they saw someone who looked like you?"

"Or," Aidan said bitterly, "Russell convinced them—or bribed them—to say they saw me."

Would Russell go that far? Maybe he'd insisted to people they'd seen Aidan when they'd really seen someone else. He might have made them doubt their sightings. But bribing?

"Look, I gotta go. I don't like leaving you right before

the busiest time, but my mom'll be here soon." He gulped and appeared to be holding back tears. "What about Fern?"

"I'll explain to her. Go ahead and meet your mom. I'll be praying."

"Wish I believed in that stuff, 'cause that's about the only thing that can save me now."

Gideon followed Aidan down the aisle. Fern stared in surprise as Aidan exited the stand.

"Would you be able to take care of Aidan's customers?" Gideon asked her.

"Of course, but what's going on?"

Gideon explained Aidan's phone call.

Fern's brow creased. "But that doesn't make sense. How could anyone have seen him if he slept through the night?"

"I wondered the same thing. Aidan thinks Russell convinced or bribed them to lie."

"Do you think he'd do something like that?"

"I hope not, but he does seem to want to convict Aidan for some reason."

"I noticed that." She stared off into the distance, a thoughtful look on her face. "Do you think Aidan's telling the truth?"

"My gut's telling me he is." Although his gut was also sending signals about being so near Fern, so maybe his internal messages were confused.

"I believe him too. Is there anything we can do?"

"I guess we'll have to wait to find out what happens."

"And we can pray."

"I've already been doing that, but I'm glad you'll be praying too."

Fern smiled up at him, setting his world on fire.

* * *

Heart beating wildly, Fern let herself be drawn into Gideon's gaze. She might have stayed connected to him all day if Nettie hadn't called out.

"Gideon, we need help over here." Her petulant voice shattered the special moment.

"I'd better go." Gideon rushed back to help Nettie and Caroline, leaving Fern bereft.

"Ahem." A man at the counter cleared his throat. "I'd like some pastries to go."

Fern tore her gaze from Gideon's departing back to face the customer. "What would you like?"

With the long lunchtime lines, she had little chance to moon over Gideon again. But her mind kept replaying the way he'd stared down into her eyes. Had his gaze held a spark of interest? Or had she only imagined it?

She bounced back and forth between the bakery and candy counters. After packaging a birthday cake, she returned to the candy counter.

Mrs. Vandenburg waited her turn. "Hello, Fern. Where's Nick? My daughter said Aidan was helping to run the stand now."

"He has been."

"Well, where is he? I haven't seen him since he was a little boy. He was always so kind and thoughtful."

"He still is." *Except when he's around his dad*.

"He used to offer to carry my packages for me. And that was back when I was still young and spry."

Fern hid a smile. Mrs. Vandenburg would have been in her mid-eighties then. "You're still young and spry."

"You're such a sweetie. But I am getting old. It's hard to move now."

"You do a wonderful job of getting around."

"I suppose. But you haven't answered my question. Where are Nick and Aidan?"

"Well, Nick isn't working here anymore."

"He retired already? He's still a spring chicken. That's what makes people grow old. Sitting around with nothing to do. Keep busy, I always say. It keeps the creaky hinges greased." She leaned heavily on her cane and rotated her arm in a circle.

Some of the people in line behind her huffed impatiently, but she paid no attention.

"And Aidan?"

"He, um"—Fern struggled to keep her voice steady, but didn't accomplish it—"he's at the police station."

"For what?"

"They think he vandalized the Ridley's stand and Russell Evans's office."

"That sweet young boy? They think he did it? I don't believe it." She lifted her cane and set it down with a thump.

If Mrs. Vandenburg saw Aidan now, would she still call him a *sweet young boy*? "Gideon and I don't believe it either."

"Not that I'd blame anyone who did spray that stand. That modern metal-and-glass monstrosity has no place here. My daughter said someone sprayed it with graffiti." She smiled ruefully. "Not that I'm advocating destroying property."

"I know."

Mrs. Vandenburg struck Fern as an upright, law-abiding citizen.

"What makes them think it was Aidan? I hope they didn't catch him on those cameras they have all around."

"*Neh*, the cameras weren't working. Russell has eyewitnesses who claim Aidan entered the market that night."

"Russell, *pah!* I wouldn't trust a thing he says."

Although Fern agreed with Mrs. Vandenburg, she kept her mouth shut.

"Any good lawyer could tie Russell up in knots. Wish my late husband were still around. He'd set that whipper-snapper straight."

Nettie blew out an irritated breath, and Fern jumped. She hadn't realized anyone had come up behind her.

"Gideon suggested I take care of the rest of the customers since you're so busy." The sickening sweetness of Nettie's words turned them into an insult.

"I'm sorry," Fern responded automatically.

"I'm the one who's sorry," Mrs. Vandenburg's voice quavered. "I'm holding you up."

"It's all right."

"Would you be a dear and get me some cupcakes? My great-niece will be visiting tomorrow with her little ones."

"How nice. How many would you like?"

"Half a dozen." After Fern reached for a bakery box, Mrs. Vandenburg said, "Wait. Make that a dozen. I can send the extras home with them."

After Fern handed her a larger box and her change, Mrs. Vandenburg leaned in and said in a conspiratorial whisper, "Can I come back later to talk to you and Gideon about Aidan?"

Fern nodded. "We'd have time after the market closes."

That comment earned her a broad smile from Mrs. Vandenburg and a withering scowl from Nettie. Fern brushed it aside. She wouldn't let Nettie's displeasure keep her from the joy of helping Aidan. Or from spending time with Gideon.

Chapter Twenty-Five

Gideon waited on customers, but his mind stayed focused on Fern. And Aidan. When Aidan hadn't returned by the end of the day, Gideon's concern increased. His spirits lightened when Fern walked toward him right before closing.

"Would you have time to talk with Mrs. Vandenburg? I think she wants to help Aidan."

Gideon had no idea how a lady in her nineties might assist Aidan, but he'd do whatever he could. The bonus of being around Fern sweetened the deal. He turned to Caroline, who made a face, and Nettie, whose brows had drawn together in a frown.

Evidently, the idea wasn't popular with either of them. Gideon sighed internally.

Caroline pressed lids onto containers with savage snaps. "It's my turn to see Zach tonight."

"It also leaves us shorthanded." Nettie dumped empty metal pans into the sink with a clatter.

"I can help with the cleanup later," Fern offered.

Nettie's mouth tightened. "That won't be necessary. I can do it all alone if Caroline wants to visit Zach."

"That's not fair." Gideon didn't want to be responsible for Caroline missing a meeting with her boyfriend or for Nettie being a martyr.

Nettie barely managed to conceal her small, triumphant smile. She must be expecting him to stay and work with her. She definitely wouldn't like his plans.

Russell had just locked the doors. "Why don't you both go now?" Gideon suggested. "If Fern doesn't mind, we can take care of everything after we've talked to Mrs. Vandenburg."

"I don't mind at all." Fern's sunny smile assured him she was telling the truth.

Fern's cheeriness contrasted with Nettie's gloom. "I'll finish washing these."

Without waiting to hear any more, Caroline waved and scurried off.

Gideon and Fern headed out the employee entrance to find Mrs. Vandenburg seated at one of the outdoor picnic tables.

They'd almost reached her when Bo Ridley came out the door. Gideon felt terrible. He didn't realize Bo had been in today. Gideon wished he'd gone down to tell Bo how sorry he was about the damage.

"Hey, Bo," he called.

"Yeah?" Bo veered in their direction.

Gideon suspected Fern provided the draw. That irritated him, but Bo deserved some kindness. "Sorry about what happened to your stand."

"I am too," Fern said.

Bo's haggard face lit up at the sight of her. "Thanks. It's been a disaster to clean. I've had a crew at it since the police let us start yesterday. It'll take a while to get things back to normal."

"Gideon, is that Mr. Ridley?" Mrs. Vandenburg called. "I'd like to speak with him."

"Do you have time to meet her?" Gideon asked Bo.

"Not really, but as I always say, you should never turn down a lady. Right, Fern?"

Beside Gideon, Fern stiffened. Maybe Bo bothered her as much as he bugged Gideon.

Mrs. Vandenburg studied Bo as Gideon performed the introductions.

"You're the one whose stand got vandalized?"

"Yes, ma'am."

"I'm sorry that happened. Do you have any idea who did it?"

Bo shook his head. "I'm guessing someone who didn't like me putting the other stands out of business."

Fern jumped in. "Russell told Bo we were all going out of business."

"So you didn't know you were displacing those five businesses?" Mrs. Vandenburg watched Bo closely.

"No, ma'am. If I'd known that, I wouldn't have taken those spots."

"Well, that's good to know. I have one other question for you. Do you think Aidan Green did it?"

"You mean the kid who works in Gideon's stand?"

"That's the one."

"I suspect it might be his friends. Aidan seemed to be trying to stop the trouble last weekend."

"Last weekend?"

Fern explained about the incident and Aidan's attempts to calm his friends. She also mentioned Bo's refusing to press charges. To Gideon's annoyance, Fern made Bo sound like a hero.

"Hmm." Mrs. Vandenburg looked thoughtful. "These friends may have done it?"

"We don't think so, do we, Gideon?"

Fern gazed up at him with such a trusting look in her eyes, he would have said yes to anything she'd asked. But he really did agree with this.

"It seems Aidan's friends have an alibi for that night," Fern told Mrs. Vandenburg and Bo. "At least, Aidan says they do."

"And you've found him to be truthful?" Mrs. Vandenburg looked from Gideon to Fern.

They both nodded.

"Bo, I don't want to keep you," Mrs. Vandenburg said. "I did wonder, though, if the cleanup is expensive."

"More than I anticipated, but insurance is covering most of it."

"Won't it increase your premium?"

"For sure. I hate to think about how that'll skyrocket. It's a brand-new policy."

Mrs. Vandenburg rummaged in her purse and pulled out a business card. "Send all the bills here instead of to your insurance company. If the police catch the culprit and you get reimbursed, you can pay the money back. If not, don't worry about it."

Bo stared at her in shock. Then he glanced at the card in his hand. "You're part of the Vandenburg Charity Foundation?"

She chuckled. "I own it."

"Wow! Thanks so much." He bent, took her hand in his, and kissed the back of it.

"Go on with you, young man. You're quite the charmer. I'm sure the ladies fall all over you."

"Most do." Bo grinned. "Well, except for this one here. I can't even coax a smile from her." He indicated Fern.

"Leave her alone," Mrs. Vandenburg advised. "Her heart belongs to another, doesn't it, Fern?"

A swift, sharp pang shot through Gideon as Fern's cheeks reddened.

"Don't look so glum." Mrs. Vandenburg poked at Gideon with a gnarled, bony finger. "You're acting like you don't know the only one she's interested in is you."

Me? Fern's interested in me? Was Mrs. Vandenburg right? From time to time, Gideon had glimpses of hope. But he'd never been sure.

He barely heard Bo's parting comments. "Lucky man." And "What did I tell you about never turning down a lady?"

Fern stood there, mortified. If only she could run away and hide. Why had Mrs. Vandenburg exposed her this way?

Beside her, Gideon had frozen in place. She could only imagine his horror. Now she could never face him again. How would she ever work at the stand?

Mrs. Vandenburg laughed. "If you two could only see yourselves. You're both standing there with scarlet faces, not even looking at each other. There's nothing shameful about falling in love."

Juh, there was, if the other person didn't return the feeling. Poor Gideon's red face must be from realizing she had a crush on him.

"I hate to be the one to break the news," Mrs. Vandenburg said, "but when I see two lovebirds afraid to admit their feelings for each other, I can't stand by and watch."

Speechless, Fern stared at the ground. Could this get any more uncomfortable?

Beside her, all Gideon's muscles tensed. "I don't think . . ."

"No, you've done too much thinking," Mrs. Vandenburg scolded gently. "Time for admitting your true feelings, Gideon. Why don't you ask Fern out on a date?"

"I can't . . ." Gideon's words sounded strangled.

Fern peeked at him from the corner of her eye. He looked red-faced and wretched. "Please, Mrs. Vandenburg," she begged, "stop teasing Gideon. He has no desire to date me."

"I don't believe that. Why don't you look him in the eye and ask him?"

Fern gave her a reproachful stare. "I would never put him on the spot like that when he's too polite to say no."

"It's not that," Gideon admitted miserably. "I'd be honored to court you, but I can't."

If he truly felt that way, why did he sound so dismal?

"Oh, for heaven's sake, would you two at least face each other when you're talking?" When neither of them moved, Mrs. Vandenburg swirled a hand in the air to indicate they should rotate. "Come on now, turn."

Fern dreaded looking up. What if Gideon read her true feelings in her eyes? She wasn't sure she could mask them. And it hurt to know he'd been polite enough to say it would be an honor to go out with her. But he had other commitments. Like Nettie.

"Chin up, Fern," Mrs. Vandenburg commanded.

Even without her order, Gideon's presence drew Fern's gaze upward. His strong jaw, slightly shadowed at this time of day, his firm lips, his . . .

She sucked in a breath. The gentle caring in his eyes

held her like a magnet. And she responded, letting her own emotions overflow and spill into her eyes.

Fern's sharp inbreath touched a place deep inside of Gideon. Her eyes revealed her loving spirit. Was that meant for him?

Forgetting Mrs. Vandenburg was there, he cleared his throat and said the words that lay heavy on his heart. "Fern, I have responsibilities that prevent me from dating. But if I didn't, I would ask you out."

When their eyes first met, Fern's eyes shone, but as he spoke, they dulled. She did care about him. His spirit took flight.

"Pin him down, Fern," Mrs. Vandenburg prodded. "Make him tell you what responsibilities are holding him back."

Fern lowered her gaze. "It's all right. You don't have to tell me."

"I want to."

She looked up at him in surprise.

He wanted to unburden his soul. He wasn't ready to share the depth of his feelings for her, but he could alleviate the hurt that had flared in her eyes when he mentioned responsibilities. It would be painful to admit, but she deserved the truth.

Taking a deep breath, he began, "I have to take care of my family. Nettie and the children need my support. I also have debts to clear away, and until my income covers the stand expansion and . . ."

"The organic chicken costs." She finished his sentence for him. "And the discounts you're giving people and the Q & Z contract."

"*Jah.*" Gideon couldn't believe she'd paid that much attention to all the details of his business.

"Is there another woman in the picture?"

Gideon had been so focused on Fern, Mrs. Vandenburg's question startled him. "Of course not."

"Well, that's reassuring, isn't it, Fern?"

Fern stared at the ground. Her quiet *jah* sounded joyful.

Had she thought he was interested in someone else? Why would she think that? Nettie? Had his sister-in-law given Fern the wrong impression?

Mrs. Vandenburg broke into his musing. "If money's the only problem . . ."

Gideon cut her off. "Bo might accept charity, but the only money I'll take is what I earn myself."

"Admirable, but who knows what the future holds? Don't you believe in God? Have you prayed about it?"

Actually, Gideon had been praying nonstop about his financial problems and about Aidan. As for Fern, although she entered his dreams at night and his every waking thought during the day, he'd only prayed for her health and well-being. He'd never asked God if he should date her. An omission he planned to rectify immediately.

If God seemed to be leading him in that direction, he'd talk to Fern privately. Not with Mrs. Vandenburg directing their actions.

They'd been like puppets, and she'd controlled the strings. Gideon had answered her questions and done what she'd said. He'd been respectful to an elder. And, if he were honest, he appreciated her pushing him to get over his awkwardness. He and Fern could handle it from now on without assistance.

Mrs. Vandenburg gave a satisfied smile. "Well, I'm

glad that's settled. Or at least, it's out in the open. But we've strayed far from the original purpose of our meeting."

They certainly had, and Gideon wasn't sure he could keep his mind on Aidan, not when he wanted to explore the possibility of a relationship with Fern.

"Sit down. Sit down." Mrs. Vandenburg waved toward the bench opposite her. "Let's discuss Aidan."

Fern's shoulder grazed his as she sat beside him on the bench. What if he had the right to take her hand in his? What if she . . .?

Once again, Mrs. Vandenburg broke into his daydreams. "Okay, you two, I know you'd rather focus all your time and attention on each other, but Aidan is in trouble. Tell me everything you know about Saturday night."

Gideon and Fern took turns telling the story, although Gideon spent most of the time conscious of Fern's soft, warm presence. When they finished, she sat for a moment, her knobby fingers tapping the picnic table.

"Doesn't it seem odd that Russell didn't turn on the security cameras?" she asked.

"I thought the same thing," Fern said. "Especially after what happened with Aidan's friends. Wouldn't he be extra careful?"

"Exactly." Mrs. Vandenburg pinned Gideon with a searching gaze. "And you said he didn't have much of value in his office?"

"Not that I saw."

"The two crimes seem so different."

Gideon had thought the same thing. "Vandals destroy. Would they also plan to steal?"

"It wouldn't surprise me, but vandalism seems more like a teenage crime. A crime of anger and revenge."

Fern nodded. "Aidan's friends seemed furious when they took off."

"Yes, that much is clear." Mrs. Vandenburg's eyebrows drew together. "I can see them tossing Russell's office and maybe taking cash if they found it, but as for the rest . . ."

"It doesn't make sense," Fern said. "They ride motorcycles. How would they cart off big items?"

"Good point." Gideon had avoided looking at her to prevent being distracted. Now that he had, he struggled to take his eyes off her. Good thing she was focused on Mrs. Vandenburg.

"Was Russell's computer new or expensive?" Mrs. Vandenburg asked, drawing his attention back to her.

"I don't know that much about computers, and I didn't look at it closely, but it didn't seem new or special."

Mrs. Vandenburg leaned forward. "It might be insurance fraud."

That made sense to Gideon. "Maybe once Russell saw the vandalism, he decided to claim things were stolen."

"So you believe Russell is lying about the thefts?" Fern glanced from him to Mrs. Vandenburg and back again. "Aidan suggested that too."

When their gazes met, Gideon's insides danced. Would God have given them these feelings for each other if He didn't mean for them to be together? Even if that was God's plan, Gideon could see no way of overcoming the obstacles. It would take a miracle. Gideon's only hope was trusting God's promise that everything works together for good.

Chapter Twenty-Six

Looking into Gideon's eyes had been a mistake. Fern needed to concentrate on the conversation, but how could she do that when the tenderness in his eyes mesmerized her? She tried to tune in to Mrs. Vandenburg's answer to the question about Russell lying.

"Russell has certainly lied before. There's only one way to find out." Mrs. Vandenburg pulled out her phone. "I'll call my daughter to pick me up. I'm tired and need to go home."

"But what about Russell?" Fern didn't want Mrs. Vandenburg to leave without deciding on a solution.

"I'll take care of Russell."

"How?" Gideon asked.

"A private investigator will get to the bottom of this." Mrs. Vandenburg tapped a number on her phone and told her daughter she was ready to go.

Fern waited until Mrs. Vandenburg hung up to ask her question. "Will the police be all right with that?"

"Technically, I own more than half of this market until Russell pays back what he owes. They can't fault me for protecting my investment."

Nettie exited the market. Her eyes lit up when she spotted Gideon, but then she noticed Fern sitting close to him, and her expression moved from sunshine to storm clouds.

This time, instead of being jealous of Nettie, Fern sympathized. She'd experienced the same roller coaster of emotions. Now, though, she had the reassurance Gideon cared for her. Even if they couldn't date for a long while, Fern clung to that hope.

Gideon shifted uneasily. He must have caught sight of Nettie. "She's just leaving? She must have cleaned everything. I should have been in there helping."

He shouldn't feel guilty. "You told her she could go."

"I should have known she wouldn't leave work undone."

"Gideon, she wouldn't have taken care of it if she didn't want to." Fern wished he wouldn't worry so much about Nettie. "Haven't you done all the cleanup by yourself?"

"*Jah*, but it's my responsibility."

Mrs. Vandenburg interrupted them. "You know, Gideon, I wonder if you take on too many responsibilities that aren't yours."

Fern agreed. But she kept silent.

Gideon jumped up. "I'd better go check to see if everything's done before Russell locks the employee entrance for the night."

"Do you want help?" Fern started to get up.

"*Neh*, we can't leave Mrs. Vandenburg alone."

Fern should have thought of that. Once again, Gideon's first instinct was to care for others.

"Yes, I'd like you to stay, Fern, if you don't mind. I'd be fine on my own, but I did have a few questions for you."

Fern sank back down on the bench, but she'd rather be walking beside Gideon as he strode across the parking lot.

"I guess there's no point in asking you anything until he enters the building." Mrs. Vandenburg laughed. "I'm so glad you two straightened things out. I kept picturing you working together as you reached my age, still casting surreptitious glances at each other, but hiding your true feelings."

As grateful as Fern was to Mrs. Vandenburg, she didn't want to encourage her matchmaking.

"All right, now that I have your full attention, I'd like you to tell me about Gideon's obstacles to marriage."

"I didn't know he was supporting Nettie and her children. I guess he's been doing that since his brother died two years ago."

"Yes, I remember hearing about that tragic accident. Supporting a family of five is a heavy burden."

It certainly was. No wonder Gideon had avoided dating. Fern didn't want to be an additional burden.

In response to Mrs. Vandenburg's prompting, Fern explained about Gideon's other financial troubles.

Mrs. Vandenburg rummaged through her huge purse. "Do you know how the Q & Z investigation turned out?" She pulled out a tablet and pen.

"*Neh*, Gideon didn't say."

"So this distributor not only committed fraud by labeling their products organic, but they also locked Gideon into an unbreakable contract?" She jotted the words *fraud* and *organic* beside Q & Z's name.

"It seems so. Gideon will donate those chickens to a food program. According to Aidan, the program will pay for the meat."

"I'm sure the food program is expecting a bargain price. They depend on local churches for funding, from what I understand."

"Gideon will make a little toward the cost. He originally planned to donate the chickens for free."

"That boy has a big heart. Perhaps too big. I hope God rewards him well for his generosity."

"So do I." Gideon deserved so much for all he'd done and given. She could hardly believe this wonderful, upright, honest, and generous man had fallen for her the way she'd fallen for him.

When Aidan didn't show up for work the next morning, Gideon hoped he hadn't been arrested.

"Do you think he's all right?" Fern asked as she took care of preparing the candy stand.

"I don't know. I wish I had a way to find out."

A few minutes before the market opened, Nick strolled into the stand, donned the candy-striped apron, and counted out the cash box as if he'd never been absent.

Fern, who'd been helping Caroline package side dishes, stared in amazement, then hurried back to her part of the stand. "Nick? What are you doing here?"

"Working. What's it look like?"

"Where's Aidan?"

"On probation. Thanks to that—" Nick bit off the next word. "That liar."

"They think Aidan's guilty?"

"What else could they think when he sends in three stoolies who pretended to be eyewitnesses?"

Gideon came over. "Is Aidan all right?"

"Not when he's been falsely arrested. And that—that—" Nick pointed to Russell, who was unlocking the side doors.

"He's in jail?" Gideon looked shocked.

"Nah, they don't usually do that to juveniles. He's on probation. He's allowed out of the house for school and work. That dirty rat Russell also tried to get a restraining order to keep Aidan off market property." Nick ground his teeth together. "That, um, cretin didn't succeed, but he threatened Aidan with more charges if he enters the market."

"Mrs. Vandenburg wants to look into Ru—"

Gideon elbowed Fern, stopping her mid-word. Surprised, she stared up at him. He tilted his chin to her right. Russell was passing by the stand.

"*Danke*," she whispered. They didn't need to alert Russell to Mrs. Vandenburg's plans.

Russell spied Nick. "You have a lot of gall coming in here after what your thieving son did."

"Aidan didn't do anything. You framed him."

Gideon stepped closer. "I don't want my customers scared off by arguments."

Russell settled for spiteful glare, which Nick returned.

"I should have gotten a restraining order against you," Russell said in a low, cruel tone.

"Just try it." Nick matched his nastiness. "We're going to prove your scheme."

"You wish. I'm going to see your son locked up. Stealing forty thousand is a felony." Russell hurried off before Nick had time for a comeback.

"Forty thousand?" Fern must have misheard. "Aidan said twenty."

"That liar claims he had another twenty in cash in his safe that's missing."

"He kept twenty thousand in his safe?" Gideon sounded incredulous. "For what?"

Fern met Gideon's eyes. "This story is getting more unbelievable."

"I agree." As customers approached, Gideon said in a low voice to Nick, "Mrs. Vandenburg's hiring a private investigator. I hope they'll find out the truth."

"Bless her," Nick said. "She's been a good friend to my family, but my guess is Russell's covered his tracks."

"Gideon and I are praying." Fern turned to greet her first customer.

Nick's face stayed glum. "Hope it helps."

Instead of retreating to his chicken counter, Gideon stayed nearby until Fern had a break between customers.

"Can I tell you a secret?" he asked.

Fern turned to him eagerly.

"I've been addicted to your cinnamon buns for years. Every morning, I sent Caroline to buy them."

"Those were for you?"

"*Jah.* I didn't want you to know it, so I asked my sister to get them."

"But you haven't had any since I started working here. Except for one that very first day."

"I know, and I've been craving them."

"Why didn't you ask?" She reached into the case with bakery tissue and handed him a cinnamon bun.

Gideon took a bite and closed his eyes. "Mmm." He finished chewing. "Delicious. I missed these."

"I'll give you a bun every morning from now on, but you didn't answer my question."

"I didn't ask because I was too busy fighting my attraction to you. I had to avoid you."

What about what he'd said to his sister? "You told Caroline you had no interest in me." She didn't use his exact words about her not being special.

"You heard that?" Gideon ached inside to think he'd hurt Fern. "I didn't mean it. I tried so hard to deny it to myself, but back then, I'd already fallen for you."

"You had? I wish I'd known. I've had a crush on you for so long."

"I guess it's good I didn't know. I would have pushed you away even harder."

"Because of money?"

"That's a big part of it, but there's more. A deeper reason. I really need to talk to you. Maybe tonight after work?"

Fern nodded. But as Gideon took off to wait on his own customers, her mind churned.

Another reason they couldn't be together? Gideon had told her yesterday in front of Mrs. Vandenburg he had no other woman. It couldn't be that. But what other reason could he have to keep them apart?

Gideon could barely keep his eyes off Fern. He dropped a fully loaded spit, and most of the chickens slid off, splattering barbecue sauce everywhere, including all over the front of his shirt.

Luckily, the chickens landed on the clean counter. He strung them all on again, recoated them with sauce, positioned the spit with extra care this time, and shut the door. Then he went to the sink. Nettie, her expression sad and defeated, moved aside so he could wash off his shirt.

"Need help?" she asked.

"*Neh*, I can do it."

"I see." Her words were laced with disappointment, and she obviously meant more than a simple *I understand*.

Gideon needed to talk with Nettie too. He'd been shutting

himself in the office every night to work on financial plans, but daydreaming about Fern had stolen most of his working time.

He'd barely seen Nettie at home the past two weeks. Only at the dinner table and right before they split up to care for the children. Whenever the girls fell asleep first, she'd peek in on him, reading to the boys. Last night, after a brief good night accompanied by a wounded look, she'd fled to her room.

After seeing him with Fern yesterday, she must think he'd lied to her about not wanting to have a relationship. But he'd also been lying to himself. He had to get everything straightened out with Nettie and with Fern. You couldn't tell a woman that you'd fallen for her but moving forward in the relationship was impossible, could you?

Somehow, Gideon didn't think it worked that way. But he needed to be honest. It was only fair to Fern.

Right now, though, he needed to smooth things over with Nettie. He tried to think of a neutral subject that would get her mind off him and Fern. "I miss having David and Lenny here."

"You do? I was afraid they were getting in everyone's way."

"Not at all. They tried to be helpful." They didn't always succeed, but they were learning. And Gideon was more than happy to teach them.

"I can bring them if you want."

"I do. Maybe they could fill side dish containers."

Nettie smiled, her first genuine one of the day. "Thanks, Gideon. I like having them around."

"So do I." He went back to the counter, humming under

his breath. He'd rather whistle, but he might startle the customers.

Things might not be perfect, but he'd smoothed over the situation with Nettie for the time being, and he'd enjoy having David and Lenny here. But knowing Fern cared for him brought him the greatest joy.

Caroline elbowed him as she passed. "Wow, you're cheerful today."

"*Jah*, I am." He couldn't stop his lips from curving up into a broad smile.

"Does it have anything to do with a certain person you claimed wasn't special?"

Gideon disliked admitting she'd been right all along, so he kept his answer noncommittal. "It might."

His sister laughed. "You can't fool me. You're in love."

The word *love* smacked Gideon in the face. *Love?* He'd labeled his feelings as *attracted to*, *fallen for*, *interested in*—but *LOVE?* That carried an extra weight of responsibility, of commitment, of permanence.

"Don't look so scared." Caroline's teasing expression became serious. "It's not the end of the world."

But wasn't it? His whole world had shuddered to a stop.

Fern had just faced in Gideon's direction to get a bakery box when his face altered. He'd been smiling and joyful as he headed past his sister. Then Caroline said something, and Gideon's happiness melted into—what? Shock? Despair? Terror?

What had Caroline said to cause such a dramatic transformation?

"Fern?" Margery called. "I'd like to add a birthday cake to my order."

For a few seconds, Fern stood there holding the box, unable to remember what she was supposed to put in it. She tamped down her first instinct to run to Gideon and ask him what was wrong. But she struggled to focus on her work.

Fold the box, Fern.

She took a deep breath and let her hands do the work they'd done so many times before. Bend the cardboard sides into place, insert the flaps into the slots. Try to remember the order.

Turning to face Margery, Fern asked, "Sticky buns, right?"

Margery stared at Fern as if she'd lost her mind. "I've been coming here every market day for the past five years. My order has never changed."

Margery. A dozen sticky buns. Fern's mind brought up the details, but then it rebelled. Gideon's face filled her thoughts. She wanted to know what had caused his pain. Could she do anything to alleviate it?

A small part of her counted out twelve sticky buns, but the rest of her—body, emotions, and spirit—remained focused on Gideon.

Fern slid the box across the counter. "You wanted a cake too?"

As soon as she packaged up the chocolate cake and handed Margery her change, she checked on Gideon, but he had his back turned.

"You plan to drool over him all day?" Nick asked. "You do have customers, you know."

With great reluctance, Fern returned to her work. And

an hour later, Gideon slid behind her and handed Nick a check. She stopped placing cookies in the bag she held.

Nick stared at the check. "What's this for?"

"It's your percentage of the sales for last week."

"I didn't work last week."

"Right." Gideon smiled at him. "But Aidan did."

"You mean to tell me my son made twice as much as I do? That's impossible."

Although Fern should mind her own business, she laughed. "Aidan seems to attract plenty of teen girls. That might account for the extra sales."

Nick's face darkened, but then he smoothed the apron over his burgeoning belly and threw back his shoulders. "He must be a chip off the old block. I used to be quite a lady-killer myself."

Fern hid a smile. She had a hard time picturing Nick as a suave young man. In her first memories of him, from when she was six, Nick's scowling face, as round and red as a balloon, had scared her. His explosive temper had petrified her.

"I guess I'm getting old." His face drooped. "Maybe I should let the kid take over full time." Then he gritted his teeth and scowled. "If it weren't for that jerk Russell. First, he destroyed my family's stand. Now, he's destroying my chance for a better income. I should sue him."

"I hope Mrs. Vandenburg's investigation clears Aidan," Fern said.

Gideon smiled down at her, and she admired the laugh lines around his mouth, the sparkle in his eyes, the caring look on his face. She forgot all about Nick, her customers, and the market. She only wanted to bask in the sunshine of his smile.

* * *

Gideon appreciated Fern's positive viewpoint. She always found the best in every situation. But smiling at her might have been a mistake. He lost his train of thought. He'd planned to say something to Nick, but he couldn't remember what.

"Get a room, why don't ya?"

Nick's sarcastic comment cut through Gideon's preoccupation with the beautiful woman gazing at him adoringly.

"I should get back to work."

"Ya think?" Nick slid the check into his pocket.

The check reminded Gideon of the response he'd planned to make after Fern tried to soothe Nick. "Like Fern said, I hope Mrs. Vandenburg finds a way to make things right for Aidan. I really miss him. He's a *gut*, hard worker."

Fern noticed Nick bristling and added, "You and your wife raised him well."

Immediately, the tension on Nick's face dissolved. His lips twitched as if he were wrestling a smile into a neutral expression.

Gideon marveled. How did Fern always know the best way to defuse tense moments and bring joy to everyone around her?

Nick's smirk spurred Gideon into action. He couldn't stand around all day enamored. He needed to get back to work.

His sister's cry startled him. "*Ach*, Gideon, is something wrong with the rotisserie?"

"What do you mean?" He hurried over, expecting smoke

or an explosion, to find the glass door stone-cold. The spits stayed still; the chickens remained raw. He checked the connections, but all the hookups appeared fine.

Replacing the rotisserie would be a huge expense. That's the last thing he needed. He'd already been picturing the excuses he'd need to make to Fern, but he hadn't anticipated another major bill.

"Um, Gideon?"

With his future plans crashing around him, his sister's mocking tone aggravated him. "What?"

"Might help if you turned it on." She burst into laughter.

Had he really forgotten to do that? Sheepishly, he started the rotisserie, relieved that he'd escaped another crushing cost, but humiliated that Caroline had discovered his absentmindedness.

"You know, *bruder*, maybe you should keep your mind on your work instead of on certain people who definitely don't hold your interest."

He could be petty and remind her of how flighty she'd been since she started spending time with Zach, but Gideon might not fare well in the contest of who'd been acting the most besotted.

Chapter Twenty-Seven

Anticipating the closing-time talk with Gideon made the day drag on. Fern usually enjoyed chatting with her customers, but today she wished everyone would go home and leave her alone with Gideon.

Near the end of the day, Mrs. Vandenburg shuffled up to the candy counter. "Nick? I thought Aidan would be working here."

"Sorry to disappoint you. I seem to have done that to a lot of young ladies today."

Fern smiled. Nick had been referring to the bevy of girls who'd peeked around the corner, spotted Nick, and hurried away.

Mrs. Vandenburg laughed. "Flattery will get you everywhere." She leaned close and confided, "The doctor says I have the heart of a seventy-year-old. I don't tell him I still feel twenty inside. That's the secret of staying young."

"Maybe I should try it." Nick's melancholy expression revealed he didn't believe it would work. "I feel more like one hundred."

"You look it too."

Evidently, Mrs. Vandenburg's beliefs about flattery

didn't apply to her own comments. She glanced around. "Is Aidan helping Gideon?"

"Of course not. He's on probation. And when that moron"—Nick flipped a hand toward the ceiling overhead, where Russell had his office—"couldn't get a restraining order, he forbid my son to come into the market."

"That's ridiculous." Mrs. Vandenburg's annoyance rang through her words. "We'll see about that." She fumbled around in her purse and pulled out a cell phone. She held it out to Nick. "My eyes aren't the best. Do me a favor and push seven. My daughter put Russell on speed dial."

Nick did as she asked, then thrust out the phone as if holding a dead mouse by its tail.

"Be careful," Mrs. Vandenburg scolded. "I need that phone if I have a medical emergency."

He switched to a gentler hold and waited while she rebalanced herself on her cane. Then she reached out for the phone as a squawking *Hello? Hello?* came through the receiver.

As she lifted it to her ear with a shaky arm, the voice grew belligerent. *Is anyone there? I'm hanging up.*

"Don't you dare hang up on me, Russell Evans."

Once again, the man's tone underwent a major alteration. *Mrs. Vandenburg, how, um, nice to hear from you.*

"Really, Russell? I don't like lies. I'm downstairs at Hartzler's waiting for you."

I'll be right there.

Nick didn't bother to hide his smile. "You really make him nervous, Mrs. V. Good for you."

"The only language Russell speaks is money. Having wealth gives me a lot of power. Over him, anyway. Not all people bow down that way."

"Most people do," Nick said.

Mrs. Vandenburg waved toward Gideon, who'd drifted over to stand near Fern. "He, for example, refused my money yesterday, while young Bo seemed only too eager to take it."

"You're giving out money to stand owners?" Nick looked as if he wanted to beg for some.

"Only for certain purposes."

"Like what?" Nick must be hoping to apply.

"Oh, there's Russell already. That was quick. Money calls."

Several customers on Fern's line watched avidly as Mrs. Vandenburg, one hand propped against the candy counter to hold herself up, waved her cane in the air.

"Get over here, Russell," she commanded.

Russell scurried over.

"Where's Aidan?" she demanded.

Russell shrugged.

Nick narrowed his eyes. "You dirty liar."

"I understand you forbade Aidan to enter this market." Mrs. Vandenburg jabbed her cane tip toward Russell to emphasize each word.

"Not exactly," Russell began. "But you have to understand how concerned I am about the customers' welfare."

"Really?" Mrs. Vandenburg's eyebrows inched upward toward her sparse, permed bangs. "What do customers have to fear from a teen?"

"He's a thief, and he vandalized the market. If you saw what he did, you wouldn't want him back here either."

"That boy didn't do what you've accused him of. You framed him."

"I did no such thing," Russell blustered.

"You and I both know that's a lie." Mrs. Vandenburg

poked her cane in his direction again, this time more threateningly.

Russell jumped back.

Before he could open his mouth to protest, she forestalled him. "I expect to see Aidan here waiting on customers when I come in tomorrow."

Moving out of cane distance, Russell tried to put on a brave face, but his words came out whiny. "The kid's on probation. I don't want a juvie, er, juvenile delinquent, waiting on customers. How do you know he won't cheat?"

"I want him right here, Russell." She tapped her cane against the candy counter. "First thing tomorrow morning. No excuses."

Russell strode off, muttering, "Don't blame me if every one of these stands is robbed."

Mrs. Vandenburg thumped her cane on the ground. "That takes care of that." If Mrs. Vandenburg hadn't been leaning on her cane, she might have dusted her hands together.

"I'll be back tomorrow to be sure Russell's complied. Good day, everyone." After a quick wave to people inside and outside the stand, she hobbled away.

Nick stared after her. "I'm glad she put that weasel Russell in his place, but what am I going to do?"

Fern finished waiting on a customer. "What do you mean?"

"I can't work here with my kid. And he sure won't work here with me."

"You know, Nick," Gideon said, "you two just might be the answer to my prayers."

Nick snorted. "Yeah, right."

"I'm serious. Like I told you, Aidan's a terrific help. I need more staff, but I always feel guilty when Aidan's handling the fries, because then Fern's down here alone, handling both counters."

"I don't mind," Fern assured them both. Besides, she'd do anything for Gideon.

As usual, Fern showed how much she cared about others. But Gideon didn't want to overwork her. "You're gracious about it, but we definitely need more people."

"And we've been hoping you'd come back, Nick," Fern added. "I've missed you."

"Aww, go on." But Nick's smile showed that her compliment had pleased him.

How did Fern always know the right things to say?

While Nick waited on two customers, Gideon leaned close to whisper, "I think you may have charmed him into staying."

"I hope he does. My only concern is whether or not the two of them can get along."

"That could be a problem. I've been praying about that."

"So have I. Maybe having them both in the stand together is the answer to our prayers."

"Let's hope so."

Nick crossed his arms. "What are you two whispering about?"

"About how much we both hope you and Aidan will work here." Fern added a sweet smile that Gideon wished had been directed toward him.

"You sure know how to soft-soap a guy. I'm willing to stay, but I don't know about Aidan. He's furious with me."

"Sometimes anger can cover hurt." Fern's gentleness

didn't make it seem like she was criticizing Nick. "I've often found an apology can defuse even long-held resentment."

Her words seemed to have made an impression on Nick. His eyes glimmered with unshed tears. "Yeah, well." He turned away and fiddled with some of his display jars. His voice husky, he said, "I always wished my dad had apologized to me for some of the stuff he did. It's too late now."

"But it's not too late for you and Aidan," Fern pointed out.

"I guess."

"One thing I know for sure," she said, "is that Aidan loves you. I remember how he always followed you around when he was little."

Nick cleared his throat and kept his back to them. "Yeah, he kind of hero-worshipped me. That's long gone."

"No, it isn't. Aidan really appreciated you standing up for him with the police."

"Oh, that." Nick flicked a hand dismissively. "Any parent would've done the same. No one wants their kid to go to detention or whatever."

"Still, Aidan was grateful. Maybe that'll help you rebuild your relationship."

"I don't know about that, but maybe we can get along for one day. At least for Mrs. V's sake. She's some lady." Nick didn't turn around, but he added, "And so are you."

"I agree," Gideon said, low enough that Nick couldn't hear. He had so much more he wanted to say, but not in front of Nick.

Fern's face turned the prettiest shade of pink. Gideon longed to run a finger down her cheek. He clutched his suspenders to keep his hands from following that impulse. He pivoted abruptly. He had to get back to work before he did something foolish.

As usual, a flurry of customers lined up at the stand during the last two hours before closing. Gideon had little time to glance at Fern, but it didn't stop him from alternating between anticipation and dread. As much as he longed to spend time alone with her and talk to her, he didn't want to tell her the things he needed to say.

After Nick had gone home and Fern closed down her bakery counter, she headed over to Caroline. "Can I help with anything?"

Gideon sucked in a breath. Having Fern so near brought back his earlier desire to touch her. He scrubbed hard at the glass.

"Gideon," Caroline scolded, "are you trying to break the rotisserie door?"

For the first time ever, Gideon wished his sister had gone to meet Zach. He eased up on his pressure. The last thing he needed was shattered glass.

With Fern's help, the women cleaned up faster than usual, but Gideon had barely gotten halfway through cleaning the rotisserie. He might have been finished already if he hadn't sneaked so many glances at Fern.

Several times, Nettie caught him. Her eyes filled with reproach, and her lips pinched into a tight line.

Gideon had another talk to face. One that might be even harder than his conversation with Fern. Two women he cared about in different ways, but he'd end up hurting both.

As soon as Caroline had finished, she thanked Fern and took off to meet Zach, leaving Fern alone with a scowling

Nettie. A short distance away, Gideon scrubbed the inside of the rotisserie, his jaw set and a stern look in his eyes.

Maybe she should have gone home instead of agreeing to wait. It didn't look as if Gideon welcomed the idea of talking to her.

"Can I help with that, Gideon?" Nettie's honeyed question made Fern long to flee.

"If you could wash the parts I left soaking in the sink, that'd be a big help."

"Of course," Nettie practically cooed.

Fern stood there, uncertain over leaving or staying. Gideon had told her he wanted to talk, but he may have changed his mind.

"I can handle this, Fern." Nettie's faux-friendly statement clearly meant *It's time for you to go.*

Gideon must have gotten the same message, because he stopped scrubbing the metal interior. "You're not leaving, are you?" He appeared almost alarmed.

"Not if you still need to talk to me."

"I do." His clipped words made it sound as if they'd be having a businesslike conversation.

Had he done that for Nettie's benefit, or had she misinterpreted his earlier request? She'd thought they'd established a special bond after yesterday. But maybe he'd been putting on a show for Mrs. Vandenburg, who'd seemed to be compelling him to say what she wanted to hear.

Nettie's scrutiny made Fern uncomfortable. "I'll take my containers out to my buggy and come back."

"Sounds good," Gideon said without looking in her direction.

If he were that disinterested, did she really want to stick around?

Fern took everything out to her buggy, then stood there

for a while, debating. She'd rather not go back in and face Nettie. But she shouldn't be cowardly.

Lord, Gideon doesn't seem to want to spend time with me. Please show me what to do.

In her prayers last night, God had seemed to be leading her in a certain direction. Now, though, she wondered if she'd mistaken her own desires for God's will.

She bowed her head. *Not my will, but Yours. I'll trust You and do whatever You want me to.*

Even if it meant giving up Gideon. Even if it broke her heart. She'd do God's will.

With her heart and soul in the right place, she returned to the building, ready to face whatever God had in store for her.

Gideon and Nettie didn't seem to hear Fern approaching. Nettie handed Gideon pieces that he installed in the rotisserie. They worked like a team who had done this many times before, making Fern an outsider. As she approached, she couldn't help overhearing their conversation.

"Nettie, please tell Mamm I won't be home for dinner."

Nettie stared at him in shock. "What? You'll be home to put the boys to bed, won't you?"

"I'm not sure."

"Not sure? But David and Lenny count on you."

"Perhaps Mamm or Daed could tuck them in tonight."

"But Gideon"—Nettie sounded close to tears—"you promised me . . ."

Fern's stomach churned. She hadn't realized Nettie lived in the same house and that Gideon took care of his nephews. No wonder they'd clung to his legs that day they'd come here.

And what promise had he made to Nettie? Would that get in the way of Fern and Gideon being together? Maybe that's what he intended to tell her. Fern wasn't sure she could bear to hear it.

Chapter Twenty-Eight

Gideon hated hurting Nettie's feelings like this, but he had to make it clear he'd fallen for Fern. Telling his sister-in-law had to wait, though. First, he had to discuss everything with Fern. Even if he could never be with the woman he loved—and *jah*, that word, which had once scared him, now made him realize his true feelings for Fern—he could never enter a relationship with anyone else. Not ever.

"Nettie, we'll talk later. Please just let Mamm know about dinner."

"I will," she said in a strangled voice. Then she fled.

She almost ran headlong into Fern, who stood there staring from one to the other, her mouth open.

Ach! How long had Fern been standing there, and what had she heard? From the look on her face, she'd misinterpreted his conversation with Nettie.

As Nettie rushed past Fern and dashed out the exit, Gideon froze where he stood, wondering if all his hopes had smashed around him. He'd been afraid of breaking the rotisserie door, but that could be replaced. How did you replace a shattered heart?

"Fern?" He hadn't meant for his voice to come out so

hesitant, so uncertain. But dreams were fragile. And he might have just destroyed his. And maybe hers.

"Gideon, if you need to go after Nettie, I understand."

He shook his head. "*Neh*, I can talk to her later tonight or another day. I need to speak with you first. I have some things to explain."

Fern headed toward him as if toward an execution. Was she expecting him to hurt her too?

Gideon had spent most his life, and especially these past two years, trying not to hurt anyone. And now in one night, he'd hurt two women he cared about. And he hadn't meant to cause either of them pain.

When she reached the stand, Fern took a deep breath, and her words came out in a rush. "Please don't feel you owe me any explanations. I know Mrs. Vandenburg can be intimidating. Her commands made me feel like a puppet, and I understand she forced you to say things you wouldn't ordinarily have said. So—"

"Wait," Gideon pleaded. "Are you telling me you said things you didn't feel yesterday?" Maybe he'd gotten this all wrong. He'd assumed she'd been telling the truth, but if she'd only been playacting for Mrs. Vandenburg, where did that leave him?

Fern stared at the floor by her feet. "I didn't say anything untruthful, but I won't hold you to anything you said."

"I want you to." Knowing she truly cared about him set off a joyous chorus in his heart. "But I have some other confessions to make that might change your mind."

Although she stared at him with wary eyes, her response rang clear and true. "I prayed about this before I came in here. I told God I'd do His will no matter what. So please don't be afraid to tell me the truth. About anything."

"I did the same." If they'd both sought God's will, then he had to be honest. Gideon motioned to the nearby tables and waited until she sat facing him. "Yesterday, you mentioned several of my financial concerns, but I have others."

Fern nodded as if encouraging him to go on.

"My brother left behind some major debts, along with the Q & Z contract. With paying for that and the organic chickens, it may take three years or longer before I clear off all those bills."

"It's hard taking on someone else's debts."

Although Gideon appreciated her sympathy, she'd missed the main point. He'd come back to it after he explained about his other obligations. "To clear the debts, I put most of my savings into the expansion. I didn't count on the organic chicken fraud."

And taking on the stand rentals to help Fern and the others had depleted more of his savings, but he didn't intend to share his part in their lowered rentals. That was between him and God.

"But I have one huge expense I didn't mention yesterday. It's one of the main reasons I've avoided relationships." Once he told Fern this, she'd see a future together would be impossible.

Fern tensed, waiting for the bad news. Yesterday, he'd admitted he cared for her. Today, he planned to tell her he didn't want to court her. She prayed to take his news with grace.

With pain etched into every line in his face, Gideon drew in a breath. "After my brother died, I promised Nettie I'd always take care of her and the children. And I will. It's one of the reasons I never married."

Maybe Fern shouldn't admit she'd been eavesdropping on his conversation with his sister-in-law, but curiosity made her ask, "Is that the promise Nettie was talking about?"

Gideon looked off into the distance for a few moments before answering. "*Jah*. I meant I'd support her by paying the bills and keeping a roof over her head. From some of the things Nettie's said and done recently, I'm worried she may think I meant more."

Nettie had sounded upset that Gideon wouldn't be around for their evening routine. "You help her with the children at night?"

"And during the day whenever I'm home. It started the evening Thomas went into the hospital and Nettie stayed with him. The children missed their parents, so I took over putting the little ones to bed. Not too long after my brother"—Gideon swallowed hard—"passed away, Nettie moved into the house. She handles the girls at bedtime, and I take care of the boys."

"The boys seem very attached to you."

"They were so young when it happened, I guess they see me more as a father."

Did that mean Fern would have to accept his responsibilities to another family? Part of Fern rebelled at sharing Gideon with Nettie, but she couldn't deny fatherless children the chance to have Gideon's love.

"I see. So if you married, you'd have two families."

Gideon's creased brow smoothed. "I should have known you'd understand."

Although she understood, she'd find it hard. "Has Nettie ever thought of remarrying?"

"She's joked about it once or twice, but she says no man will want her because she has four children."

"That's not true. I know two widowers who've taken on large families."

"Nettie's pretty much clung to me since Thomas's death, so she hasn't looked around at others. I wish I'd been clearer when I offered to help."

Fern wished he had too, but she'd settle for whatever she could have of Gideon's time and attention. "You said this is one of the reasons. Are there others?" She'd face all the blows. She'd hoped Gideon would offer to date her, but so far, it seemed more like he wanted to explain why they couldn't be together.

Gideon squeezed his eyes shut and scrunched up his face as if in pain. When he spoke, his words came out hesitant and sad. "I don't know how much you know about Thomas and Nettie's story."

Fern stayed quiet. Other than rumors, she'd never heard the truth.

"They were only seventeen when—" Gideon lowered his eyes, and a deep crimson flush crept up his neck and splashed across his cheeks. "Well, when the church shunned them, and Thomas had to marry Nettie."

Fern shifted in her chair, almost as embarrassed as Gideon.

"I was only twelve, but Thomas warned me away from girls. I did have a budding interest in one special girl. But I cut that off. I didn't want to get shunned."

Twelve? She'd been eleven. Up until that year, she and Gideon had played together or spent time with each other. Then he stopped being friendly with her. He never came out of his family's stand to roam the aisles or share candy treats. He looked the other way when she came to buy chicken.

"I thought I'd done something to upset you," she admitted.

"*Ach*, no, Fern. I never meant to hurt you."

Had she been the special girl he'd mentioned? If she'd only known, she'd have saved herself years of heartache.

"I spent my teen years avoiding girls. And Thomas reinforced that the day he—he died." Gideon's words grew husky.

Fern wanted to reach out to smooth his wrinkled brow, to stroke away the tight lines around his eyes and mouth, to ease his anguish.

"Right before he—" Gideon's voice broke. "Thomas told me he was overwhelmed. They'd had one baby after the other, a year apart. He'd just learned they'd be having baby number five. He said he couldn't handle it."

"Five?" Nettie only had four children.

Gideon bowed his head. "Nettie lost that baby soon after Thomas—" Clenching his hands together in his lap, he continued, "She went into a depression. That's when she moved in with us. Mamm had gotten ill, so I cared for the children until Nettie recovered. Our evening bedtime routine began then."

"*Ach*, Gideon." He'd had so much to bear. "How did you handle all that and the business too?"

"You do what you need to do. Family and work kept me busy and away from the thoughts—*neh*, nightmares."

"Nightmares?" She hoped the gentleness in her tone would encourage him to confide in her, because from the misery on his face, those horrors weren't confined to sleep.

* * *

Gideon hadn't intended to share his inner torment. But Fern's caring expression and soft question uncorked the bottled-up guilt and shame. Once she heard the truth, would that light of admiration in her eyes die?

"What is it?" Fern asked.

"It's about my brother and . . . and how I failed . . ."

"Tell me."

At her soft command, Gideon began the story. "Thomas and I were repairing the barn roof when he told me about being overwhelmed."

Drifting back to that terrible day, Gideon relived the agony. He'd sensed his brother's unhappiness, but he'd been blindsided by Thomas's sudden admission of wrongdoing.

"I've done something terribly wrong," Thomas confessed, then stopped. *"Once you start down a path of sin, it's hard to go back."*

"That's what God's forgiveness is for," Gideon tried to reassure him. *"It won't be easy, but—"*

His words harsh, his brother cut him off. *"You don't understand. You didn't make a mistake as a teen. I was shunned, rushed into marriage, and now I'm stuck. We'll keep having babies year after year. Nettie's expecting again."*

"That's a good thing. God wants us to be fruitful and multiply."

"But you don't have to work two jobs to support them." Thomas's bitter tone echoed through Gideon's mind. *"I just can't do it anymore."*

"I'd never seen my brother that down, that guilt-ridden," Gideon told Fern. "Now I wonder if lying about the organic chicken bothered him. Plus he had all the children to support."

"That's a lot to handle."

"It was. And then—" Gideon clutched his suspenders so tightly his knuckles turned white. "Then he . . . his foot slipped . . ."

Fern sucked in a breath.

And Gideon plunged back into the nightmare that haunted him. Thomas sliding . . . sliding . . . sliding . . . in slow motion toward the edge of the roof.

Gideon dove for his brother. He smacked down on the roof with his arms outstretched. He tried to reach farther. Not far enough.

Thomas slipped over the edge, kicking and clawing the air.

His pinwheeling arms reached for the roof.

In a last-minute, desperate grab, one hand clutched the overhang. Just out of Gideon's reach.

"Hold on!" Gideon slithered on his belly to where his brother dangled.

He stretched his body. His arm. One more inch.

"I . . . can't do . . . it."

Thomas's fingers uncurled.

Gideon snatched for his brother's hand, but grabbed only air. "Noooo!"

Fern's worried "Gideon" drew him back to the room. Her brow creased in concern, she asked, "Are you all right?"

Gideon released the death grip he had on his suspenders and pressed his clenched fists on the table in front of him. "I tried to save him, but I didn't make it in time. I failed. If I'd been quicker, he'd still be alive."

"Oh, Gideon, no." Fern reached out and took his hands. "That's a terrible burden to bear."

"If only I'd been faster, crawled farther, stretched a few inches more."

"Don't blame yourself."

"I should have done more."

"You did what you could."

Gideon shook his head. "I let my brother die."

"That's not true. You tried to rescue him."

"But I didn't."

Terrifying memories closed over Gideon again, blocking out Fern's sympathetic face.

All the while Thomas lay in a coma, Gideon tried to pray, but his words seemed to bounce off the ceiling unheard. He begged the Lord for forgiveness, but guilt weighed him down.

All day long, questions haunted him. Had he been responsible for his brother's accident? Could he have prevented it? And he jolted awake, sweating, several times in the wee hours with the same nightmare. His fingers closing on empty air. He woke gasping for air, his arms outstretched, his muscles and his heart aching.

He still had the same nightmare. He clung to Fern's hands like a lifeline as he pulled himself up from the depths of despair.

Her eyes closed, her lips moving, she appeared to be praying. Gideon cleared his throat, and she jumped. Her lids flew up. "Can I do anything to help?"

"You already are." He motioned with his chin to her warm hands holding his. "Without that to anchor me, I'd be going to a much darker place." Not as dark as the place his brother had been before they started the roofing job. "I wish I'd known how upset Thomas was before—"

"Unless people confide their feelings, we can only guess."

Fern was right, but shouldn't he have noticed Thomas's troubles? His growing desperation? He'd asked himself that question every day for the past two years.

His mind filled with his *if onlys*. *If only I'd known Thomas's troubles sooner. If only I'd helped. If only I'd done the roofing job myself. If only I'd been quicker.*

"Gideon, are you blaming yourself?"

"Are you a mind reader?" He meant it as a joke to deflect her question, but she just studied him with her head tilted to one side. She seemed to sense people's unspoken feelings and needs, and she was right about his.

When he didn't answer, she didn't press him. Instead, she asked in a caring tone, "Do you want to talk more about it?"

If anyone else had asked that, he'd have changed the topic. But something about Fern made him want to spill out all the trauma he'd been hiding. Where did he start?

His mind combed over the past, searching for a thread to help her understand.

Thomas lingered in a coma for five days but never regained consciousness. Several times, when they were alone, Gideon took his brother's hand and prayed aloud. Once Thomas seemed to be murmuring along with him. Gideon opened his eyes, but other than a low guttural sound coming from his brother's lips, Thomas lay still and unmoving.

Gideon knelt by the bed. "Tell me. Did you do this on purpose? Or was it an accident?"

Although he got no answer, he pleaded with Thomas, "Forgive me. If I hadn't been so slow, I could have saved you."

The door creaked open, and Gideon stumbled to his feet before Nettie entered. Her face pale and drawn, she took her place beside the bed and held Thomas's hand.

Once she lifted tear-filled eyes to Gideon's. "What am I going to do?"

Gideon swallowed hard. "Whatever happens, I'll take care of you and the children." It was the least he could do. And maybe it would help to assuage his guilt.

Ever since, Gideon had honored that promise. He'd also kept Thomas's dark secrets hidden. From everyone, even Nettie.

Yet he longed to share everything with Fern. "It's a long story, and I've only mentioned bits and pieces."

"I'm happy to listen if it will help."

Grateful for her kindness, Gideon went back over the story, recounting every detail, sometimes repeating things several times, but Fern never appeared to grow tired or bored. Each time she commented, she made him see things in a different light.

Only once did her face pinch up. When he got to the part about his promise to Nettie.

"You can't break your promise to her."

She'd said as much earlier, but it seemed as if she were reinforcing her belief. Perhaps she'd hoped to hear a version that might free him from his obligation.

"I wouldn't go back on my word even if I could."

"I know. That's one thing I've always loved about you. You're trustworthy and honest."

Fern's smile—and her words—took his breath away. She'd said *love.* An emotion he'd tried so hard to avoid.

Except she'd said it about a characteristic of his rather than about him as a person.

"I can't believe you took on all that responsibility for your brother's family and the family business. It had to be overwhelming."

Overwhelming. That word again. Gideon pulled his hands from Fern's and then lowered his head into them and rubbed his forehead.

"Gideon, what's wrong?"

He groaned. "That's what Thomas said right before—"

"I'm so sorry. I didn't mean to remind you of that."

Although Gideon tried to block it out of his mind, that last conversation with Thomas still haunted him. He squeezed his eyes shut, but even that didn't block it out.

What had his brother been about to confess? Had being upset made Thomas careless? Or had his brother fallen on purpose?

Chapter Twenty-Nine

What could she do to lessen Gideon's pain? He'd spent so much time lost in the past. She'd encouraged him to tell her the whole story, hoping it might help. These memories weighed on him, and he blamed himself.

Saying the word *overwhelming* had sent him into a spiral of despair. He seemed to be unaware of her or anything around him.

"Gideon, can you share what's bothering you?"

He lifted his head, opened his eyes, and stared at her blankly for a few seconds. Then he blinked as if trying to focus. She sat quietly and waited.

"Fern?"

She leaned forward and gave him her full attention.

"I've never told anyone this. I've always wondered if Thomas fell accidentally or—"

"*Ach*, Gideon, no." He already felt guilty for not doing enough. He didn't need to add this worry, this burden.

"I failed to save my brother. Maybe if I'd paid more attention to his problems, noticed he needed help . . ."

"People often do careless things when they're distressed. I'm sure it was an accident."

"What if it wasn't?"

"You said he grabbed the edge of the roof. If he went over the edge on purpose, why would he try to stop his fall?"

Gideon stared at her. "I never thought of that. Do you think it's possible?"

"Why else would he do it?"

"But he said *I can't do it.*"

"And you thought he meant he couldn't keep going with his life? What if he meant he couldn't hold on?"

Gideon's eyes grew misty. "If that's true . . ."

"You can't know what your brother intended. Only God knows that. We have to accept it as His will." Fern waited while Gideon seemed to be processing this new way of looking at the tragedy.

Then she said, "What about in the hospital? You said Thomas made sounds. Maybe he was praying too."

"Do you think he was?"

"The only sounds he made were when you were praying, right?"

Gideon sat there dazed. "*Jah.* Maybe he was asking for forgiveness and getting his heart right with God."

Fern squeezed his hands. "I'm sure he must have been."

After Gideon spent a few minutes deep in thought, most of the lines on his face smoothed out. "I couldn't bear to tell my parents or Nettie what I suspected. Maybe now I have no need to."

"I'm glad you trusted me enough to tell me." She'd been privileged he'd opened up and shared his heartrending story.

Although she'd been hoping they'd discuss their relationship, talking about Gideon's pain had deepened their bonds. Fern still had no idea if Gideon planned to court her, yet she had a deep certainty God had planned this meeting.

Gideon struggled to revise his version of the story. Fern's suggestions made sense, and they fit more with the brother he'd played with, laughed with, and worked with over the years. Thomas had often complained, but he'd worked harder than anyone to fix problems and help others. Gideon had used his older brother as a role model.

"You know, I always looked up to Thomas. That's what made all this so hard to accept."

It also made his failure to save Thomas that much more devastating.

"I just wish I could have saved him."

"That must be so hard." Fern's sympathetic look touched Gideon. Then she added, "It's time to stop blaming yourself. Let it go."

"I'm not sure I can."

"Sometimes we hold on to guilt because we don't trust God to forgive us. And we can't forgive ourselves. Why not pray about it? Ask for God's help to let it go."

Once again, Fern had gone straight to his heart. Could he trust in God's forgiveness?

Father, forgive me for doubting You. Please help me to trust in Your power and grace.

Gideon had a Thomas-shaped hole inside, a spot no one else could fill. And he'd always miss his brother. Gideon had never imagined they wouldn't grow old together, but he needed to keep his focus on God, who had control of all circumstances, even the most painful ones.

Overhead, footsteps pounded along the hall, and keys jingled.

Fern jumped up. "We'd better go before Russell locks us in here."

"Or blames us for vandalizing."

She giggled, then sobered. "I guess that's not so funny, considering Aidan's his main suspect."

"I hope Mrs. Vandenburg's investigator finds out the truth."

"Me too."

Together, they rushed for the employee exit. Once they got outside, Gideon walked Fern to her buggy.

"I'd planned to have a different discussion with you tonight." After the emotional torrent he'd just poured out, he was drained. He had no energy for another serious talk. "Could we meet again tomorrow after the market closes?"

As she got into her buggy, Fern nodded, and Gideon breathed a sigh of relief. He hadn't totally scared her off. At least he hoped he hadn't. Maybe she was only being polite.

He wanted her to know he cared about her, but they had—or he had—too many issues keeping them apart. Years from now, he might be free to date, but he couldn't expect her to wait that long.

Fern left the market confused and uncertain. What had Gideon planned to tell her? From the way he'd started, it seemed he'd intended to warn her he had no plans to marry. He had heavy financial responsibilities, and she understood him not wanting to add more. But where did that leave her?

In love with an unavailable man.

She'd promised God to do His will, and maybe this was a sign she and Gideon didn't belong together. Her heart ached. She'd find it hard to work at the market if he pushed her away.

Perhaps she should look for another place to work. She could ask Daed to find someone to deliver the baked goods to Gideon while she rode with her cousins to the Maryland market. That might be the best solution.

At the supper table, Daed dipped his spoon into his chicken corn soup. "Mel lost one of his workers this week."

"Not again." Mamm blew on her spoonful. "He has a hard time keeping workers."

"It's not easy getting up long before dawn to travel to Maryland," Daed said. "Some of the *youngie* nowadays don't want to work as hard as we did."

"That's not true," Fern protested. "Plenty of *youngie* work hard at Valley Green."

"True." Daed scooped up another spoonful. "And look at you and Aaron. You both work hard."

"Speaking of Aaron," Mamm said, "we got another letter. The church that had been housing them needs the space for a nursery school, so the mission workers are moving to apartments until they can find new housing. He needs more money."

"Of course." Daed tipped his head in Fern's direction. "Sales are going well at the new bakery. We'll send him what he needs."

"He says it'll cost . . ." Mamm glanced at the letter beside her plate and read off a figure.

Daed spluttered, sending soup spraying onto the table.

Mamm jumped up to get a rag and wiped the table.

With a heavy heart, Fern volunteered, "If Onkel Mel needs a dependable worker, I could help him if we can find someone to deliver the baked goods to Gideon." She'd asked God for direction, and this seemed to be a sign.

Daed frowned. "That's a lot of work, *dochder*. You already spend long hours baking on your days off."

Fern couldn't go on the mission trip herself, but she could support it by sending more money to Aaron. She wished the money were helping people instead of paying for an apartment, but likely, those expenses would be temporary.

"If you think you can handle both jobs, I'll talk to Mel at church on Sunday."

She'd be supporting the mission, and staying busy might keep her mind off Gideon if he told her they couldn't be together.

Fern went to bed that night in low spirits, and when she woke the next morning, her mood hadn't improved. Not seeing Gideon again would be one of the hardest things she'd ever done. That, like giving up the mission trip, needed a lot of prayer.

She arrived at the market as Aidan hopped out of a van.

"Hey, Fern." He waved and headed toward her. "I can help you with that." He draped the striped apron in his hands around his neck, lifted some of her containers, and stacked them on the dolly.

"Thanks, Aidan. Is your dad coming in today?"

Aidan shrugged. "How should I know? It's not like he tells me his plans. He's barely civil to me."

The heavy cloud weighing Fern down grew darker. She hoped the morning wouldn't include family arguments or blowups.

Surprisingly, though, when Nick came in an hour later, he smiled at everyone. Everyone except his son. He tipped his head in Aidan's directions and said a gruff, "Good morning."

Aidan responded, "Hey," and stepped aside so Nick could don the candy-striped apron. "Um, I'll go help Gideon." Aidan scooted away and stayed near the barbecued chicken counter for most of the morning.

A group of teen girls gathered nearby, staring longingly at the candy. Then they turned disappointed gazes on Nick.

"Aidan," Nick bellowed, "you have some customers."

"Huh?" Aidan returned to the candy counter, and Nick stepped aside.

As soon as he did, the girls swarmed around the display case. They giggled and flirted and bought bag after bag of candy.

Nick drifted closer to Fern. "Would ya look at that? My son's a babe magnet." He sounded almost proud. Then his shoulders slumped. "Guess I should turn the business over to him. He's gotten more customers in ten minutes than I had in two hours."

"I'm sure customers appreciate having both of you. In fact, here comes someone who's been asking about you." Fern bobbed her head toward Mrs. Vandenburg, who was limping toward them.

While Aidan gave the last two girls their change, Nick headed over to greet her. Aidan ducked out of his dad's way and started to scoot off.

"Wait, Aidan," Mrs. Vandenburg called. "I want to talk to you."

Nick's face fell, and he stepped back.

"You too, Nicholas Green," she said, stopping him from retreating. "I have news that will interest both of you." She raised her voice. "Yoo-hoo, Gideon, you'll want to hear this." She beckoned for Gideon to join them.

He stood beside Fern, near enough that she could hear his slow, steady breaths, so unlike her own shallow, forced breaths.

As everybody leaned closer, two police officers burst through the back doors.

Aidan cowered behind his dad. "I didn't do anything wrong. You'll tell them that, Mrs. V, won't you?"

"Stop sniveling," Nick barked. "We'll fight this. I'm not letting you go to jail."

"Calm down." Leaning against the glass display case, Mrs. Vandenburg tapped the tip of her cane on the counter. "Russell's going to be shocked when these officers arrest the real culprit."

"It's not me." Aidan looked sick as the officers approached the counter, but they marched past the barbecued chicken stand and headed for the main staircase.

"Looks like they're going up to talk to Russell," Gideon said, so close to Fern her nerves jangled.

Struggling to breathe normally, she asked, "Are you sure they found out who did it?"

"I know they have, and I'm sure Russell will be down shortly. Then you'll all find out who vandalized the market. And they know it's not you, Aidan, so stop your shaking. Russell owes you a major apology."

A short while later, boots clattered down the stairs. Russell's protests could be heard. "You've made a terrible mistake. It was that juvie, I tell you."

When they appeared, the burly policemen flanked Russell, one on each side. And his hands were cuffed behind his back.

"What?" Aidan shouted.

As he passed them, Russell tossed his head frantically in Aidan's direction. "That's the real criminal. That kid right there."

"Come along, Mr. Evans," one officer said.

"You have no evidence," Russell insisted.

Mrs. Vandenburg hobbled into their path. "I'm afraid they do, Russell. Lots of evidence."

Russell's face was livid. "You betrayed me?"

"No, you betrayed yourself."

The officers nodded to Mrs. Vandenburg, then dragged Russell around her.

Everyone in the stand stared after Russell, their mouths open. Customers stayed frozen in place until the officers escorted Russell out the door. Then buzzing started all around the market. Customers who had been waiting in line for candy and baked goods circled Mrs. Vandenburg to hear her explanation.

"Don't look so surprised," she said. "Russell is the logical suspect."

"I don't understand." Fern wrinkled her brow. "Why would Russell vandalize a brand-new market stand?"

"A while back we talked about the only language Russell speaks—money. He collected insurance money for the vandalism, and he faked the robbery. Forty thousand dollars' worth of goods? He was lucky if he had several thousand in that office."

"But how did you find out?" Gideon asked.

"Most of what the investigator discovered needs to stay confidential until the trial." Mrs. Vandenburg's secretive smile left everyone curious.

"Can't you tell us anything?" Nick asked.

"The newspapers have already tracked some of this down, so it won't hurt to share. I suggested the investigator start by finding the spray paint purchases. I'm afraid Russell wasn't a canny criminal. He charged his purchase. Only one of many clues."

Gideon shifted behind Fern. "But why did he target Bo? That doesn't make sense."

"A few reasons, I suspect. That's the newest, most expensive part of the store, so he'd get more money for damages. Russell also had talked Bo into getting insurance. From a different company, of course. Russell must have hoped both of them would get paid by their insurance companies, but Bo would pay for repairs. And, most important, Russell wanted to blame someone who'd have a motive to hurt Bo."

"He set me up?" Aidan slammed his fist onto the counter, making the glass jars of candy rattle. "That dirty, lowdown . . ."

"Weasel?" Mrs. Vandenburg suggested.

Nick chuckled, and everyone turned to stare. His whole body shook with deep belly laughs. "You have to admit"—he sniggered—"seeing Russell strong-armed outta here in handcuffs . . ."

Aidan snickered. "Yeah, that was the best."

Nick held up his hand, and Aidan high-fived him.

The two of them had bonded over Russell's arrest. Although Fern wasn't sure a shared enemy provided the best reason to connect or lasting power to cement them together, they'd had their first positive interaction. She whispered a prayer they'd find a way past their hurts and differences.

She also prayed she and Gideon could find a way past their problems.

Chapter Thirty

Gideon stood beside Fern as she bowed her head and closed her eyes. Most likely, she was praying for Nick and Aidan. Gideon did the same.

When he lifted his head, Mrs. Vandenburg bobbed hers. "Glad to see the two of them will be surrounded by prayer." She kept her tone low. "They'll need it."

A huge grin on his face, Aidan slipped past Gideon and Fern to help Caroline, who had a long line.

Mrs. Vandenburg watched Aidan with an indulgent smile. "He looks more like the little boy I used to know." Then she turned to Gideon. "I know this isn't the best time for you to leave the stand, but someone needs to get Russell's keys to lock up the market tonight."

Gideon hadn't thought about that.

"I can't climb all those steps. Would you go up and get them?"

"I don't feel right going into his office. What about the police?"

"You don't need to go inside. If I remember correctly, he hangs them on a hook on the right as you enter."

Gideon vaguely recalled seeing a large key ring on the wall when he visited Russell's office.

"Don't worry. I'll call Mike to let him know I have the keys. And I'll wait for him over there." She pointed to one of the café tables nearby.

When Gideon hesitated, she said, "I am the main owner of this market."

"All right." He gave Fern, who'd been watching them, a sheepish half smile. "Didn't Bo say you should never say no to a lady?"

She laughed. "He'd be right, in Mrs. Vandenburg's case. She's quite an unusual lady, isn't she?"

"She certainly is." He waited to be sure Mrs. Vandenburg made it to a table before he headed upstairs. "I won't be gone long."

As Mrs. Vandenburg had said, the keys hung inside the doorway. Gideon didn't need to step over the threshold. He stretched his arm and snagged the keys from the hook.

Curiosity kept him in the doorway. Not much had changed. The big clunky computer on the desk had been replaced with a small laptop. A few desk drawers and their contents, mostly papers and files, lay scattered on the floor. He vaguely recalled a painting hanging on the large blank wall when Mike was here. An abstract filled with splashes of eye-popping color. A large bare spot, brighter than the rest of the wall, marked where it had been.

He'd wasted too much time. Caroline and Aidan needed him during their busiest time. Gideon hurried down the stairs to find Mrs. Vandenburg on the phone. He set the keys in front of her.

She motioned for him to wait. "He's here now. I'll check with him." She pulled the phone away from her mouth.

"Mike's not feeling well. Would you be able to lock up for him tonight? He's happy to pay you for your time."

"No need to pay me. I'll do it." Except he'd planned to talk to Fern.

"Mike? Gideon agreed to lock up. We both know he's dependable, so no worries about that." She listened a minute. "Yes, that is worrisome. I'll be praying."

Caroline frowned over at him and beckoned for help with the large lunchtime crowds.

"My sister needs me. Will you be all right here? Is your daughter with you?"

"I'll be fine. Go do your work." She shooed him off.

As he passed Fern, she was staring at a customer in shock. He wanted to stop to see what was wrong, but Caroline called to him. He'd stop back as soon as he could.

Fern had greeted Payton with a happy smile. Fern hadn't seen this regular customer since the move to Hartzler's.

"I can't believe it." Payton glanced around at the stand. "I'm gone for a few weeks, and when I get back, I don't even recognize the market. I thought you'd gone out of business."

"*Neh*, I moved here."

"I can see that. I'd never have known if I hadn't asked that dreamy man who took your place. He's so polite." She giggled. "Good thing I'm happily married, or I might have succumbed to his outrageous flirting."

Fern could only imagine. "What can I get you?"

"The usual, please, and a dozen cupcakes." As Fern reached for boxes, Payton dropped her bombshell.

"I saw your younger brother last week when we visited South Carolina."

"Aaron?" Payton had been in the area being rebuilt after the flood?

"I remember when he worked here. Now he's a big star."

What? Her brother was on a mission trip. She must have mistaken someone else for him.

"He's an amazing actor, although I suppose the comedy routine he's doing comes naturally." Payton dug through her purse. "I'm sure I saved the program in here somewhere."

Actor? Payton definitely hadn't seen her brother.

Payton pulled out a slightly wrinkled booklet and smoothed it. "I even had him autograph it. He was very reluctant. I know you Amish have a thing for being humble." She flipped through the pages. "Here it is. Aaron Blauch."

Fern's stomach clenched. Her brother's face stared up at her. Aaron? In a picture? Even the handwriting looked like his. She skimmed the small paragraph beside the photo.

Aaron Blauch grew up among the Lancaster County Amish, so his accent and actions are realistic. He has appeared in three previous productions . . .

The words blurred before Fern's eyes. This couldn't be right. Aaron was on a mission trip. Yet, this brochure proved otherwise.

"I didn't mean to upset you." Payton patted Fern's hand. "You must really miss him. You two were so close."

"I do miss him," Fern choked out. More than that, she missed the brother she once knew. They'd always been close, and he'd confided in her. Until he'd grown rebellious two years ago. Had he lied about the mission trip?

Neh. She'd been the one who'd wanted to go. She'd

researched it, brought home the brochure, helped Aaron fill out the application.

They'd dropped him off at the Mennonite Central Committee office with the other volunteers. Like Aaron, all the teens carried backpacks and sleeping bags. He'd definitely left for South Carolina with the group on the bus. But why would he leave the mission and not tell them?

Seeing her brother's face inside that program rattled Fern. Questions and worries skittered through her mind, but she pasted on a smile and pretended to pay attention to the customers.

The woman behind Payton refused the bag Fern handed her. "I asked for sugar cookies, not chocolate chip."

"I'm sorry." Fern switched the order.

Did Aaron get an extra job to pay the higher expenses he wrote about? If so, why did he choose a theater?

"A half dozen cupcakes, dear," a customer said as Fern absentmindedly pulled out a tray of pastries.

"Oh, right." Fern folded a cupcake box automatically and set each cupcake into the box as the woman chose them.

Comedy? Is Aaron making fun of being Amish? The program made it sound that way. How can I tell Mamm and Daed?

When the next man in line requested a cake, Fern managed to box it up without making a mistake. She took his payment and handed him his change.

"How can I help?" she asked the next customer.

The man, who'd been walking away, balanced the cake against his body with one arm to put the dollar bills back in his wallet. "Hey!" Holding a fistful of bills, he charged through the crowd. "You cheated me!"

He elbowed the other customers aside and waved the change in her face. "I gave you a twenty."

"Are you sure?" Fern had been distracted, but she distinctly recalled sliding his payment into the tens slot of the cash drawer.

Gideon and Nick both dashed over.

"Fern would never cheat."

The man's face purpled. "You people want to pretend you're all holy because you wear those old-fashioned getups, but you're worse than kids like that." He pointed at Aidan's nose ring and tattoos.

"What are you implying about my son?" Nick shouted.

Gideon held up a hand. "Calm down, Nick."

"But he insulted Aidan."

If Fern's mind hadn't been so fuzzy because of her brother, the irony of Nick defending Aidan's nose ring and tattoos might have struck her as funny. Especially after Nick had railed about his son's appearance almost every day.

"Fern and I can take care of this."

Nick growled once in the man's direction and stomped off.

"Hey, Dad, thanks for defending me," Aidan called.

"Don't think that means I agree with your lifestyle and friends," Nick muttered. "I just won't let anyone slur my kid."

Aidan grinned from behind his dad's back. *I think he loves me*, he mouthed to Fern.

She returned a weak smile and pulled out the cash drawer while Gideon defended her innocence. Even though she was certain she'd given him the correct change, she'd give him an extra ten. No sense in letting one irate customer scare off everyone else.

Ach! Fern fingered the bill in the tens slot. A twenty.

Flustered, she pulled it out and held it up. "You did give me a twenty. I placed it in the wrong slot."

Gideon stared at her.

"I owe you a ten." She handed him a ten-dollar bill. "I'm so sorry."

"I bet you are." He snatched the bill from her hand. "Watch this lady," he yelled to the crowd. "Be sure to count your change. She tries to cheat."

Fern blinked back tears. This, on top of the news about Aaron. What if she made more mistakes? She'd already made plenty.

Gideon studied her drawn face. "What's wrong?"

"I—I can't talk about it right now."

Of course she couldn't. She had a line of customers but seemed to be in no shape to deal with them.

"Nettie?" Gideon waved her over. "Can you wait on people for a while?"

His sister-in-law had looked up with a glowing face at his call, but as soon as she saw him standing with Fern, her expression fell. She came, but slowly and reluctantly.

"Nettie will be right with you," Gideon told the waiting customers. Then he took Fern's arm and gently steered her toward Mrs. Vandenburg's table. "You need a break."

He wished he could stay with her, but Caroline and Aidan were busy. Without Nettie, they'd have trouble keeping up.

Fern collapsed onto a chair across from Mrs. Vandenburg, worry lines etched into her face. "*Danke,*" she said to him. "Please tell Nettie I'll be back soon."

"Take as much time as you need. I have to wait on customers. We can talk later." Had she received bad news?

He'd leave her in Mrs. Vandenburg's excellent care. Gideon had no doubt the elderly woman would draw Fern out and give her advice. If only he could be the one to do that.

After he returned to the stand, he struggled to keep his mind on his work. His attention kept straying to Fern, who appeared close to tears, and to Mrs. Vandenburg reaching across the table to take Fern's hands and offer comfort.

Gideon wanted to take Mrs. Vandenburg's place and hold Fern's hands the way she'd held his last night. He'd been so overwrought he'd barely noticed her touch except as a gentle pressure that kept him grounded. But once he'd gotten home, the memory of her soft hands filled him with longing. All night long, he dreamed of holding her small, warm hand, their fingers entwined.

He jerked himself back to reality. Not holding her hands might be for the best. If he did, he'd never want to let go.

When Mrs. Vandenburg reached for her hands, Fern's tears almost overflowed. She took a breath and squeezed her eyes shut, hoping to trap the teardrops.

"Nothing wrong with crying."

Mrs. Vandenburg's brisk, no-nonsense tone helped Fern mop up most of the escaping moisture. Only one lone teardrop slid down her cheek.

"Do you want to talk about it?"

Fern shook her head. How could she describe the betrayal? Especially to an *Englischer*? Gideon would understand. Her gaze strayed in his direction to find him watching her with a concerned expression.

Mrs. Vandenburg's eyes twinkled as she checked to see where Fern had been staring. "Often it's easier to tell your problems to a stranger."

Fern doubted that, but knowing Mrs. Vandenburg, she'd prod and pry until she learned the whole story. It might be easier to spill the truth.

In halting words, Fern began by explaining her desire to go on a mission trip, only to have her brother take her place. Then she went on to describe the brochure and her fears about Aaron.

"You don't know any of that's true," Mrs. Vandenburg said when Fern had finished.

Mrs. Vandenburg was right. Fern didn't have any proof. All she had were conjectures and suspicions.

"You know what I'd do?" Mrs. Vandenburg didn't wait for an answer. "I'd go to South Carolina and find out the truth."

Although Fern's first impulse on seeing that brochure had been to rush to the mission and confront Aaron, she'd already marshaled all the reasons why she couldn't. She listed them for Mrs. Vandenburg. "First of all, it's much too expensive. I'd have to hire a car and find a place to stay. My parents would never agree to me going alone. And I can't leave Gideon."

Mrs. Vandenburg chuckled. "That's obvious. You've hardly taken your eyes off him since you sat down."

She hadn't been looking at him that often, had she? "I meant Gideon needs me—"

Before she could finish her sentence, Mrs. Vandenburg laughed. "I'll say he does."

Ducking her head to hide her burning cheeks, Fern finished her sentence. "Gideon needs me to take care of the bakery and make the baked goods. He's already short-handed."

"I noticed that. I'll suggest he hire someone else."

"He can't. He has all those bills and responsibilities."

Something Fern hadn't considered last night when she'd volunteered to work for her *onkel*. Gideon would have to pay someone to replace her.

"Hmm. That could be a problem."

Gideon could also use Fern's help right now. "I'd better get back." She stood. "Thank you for letting me talk. And for helping Aidan."

"It's been a pleasure. My days are lonely, so I enjoy doing some good in the world."

"You've done a lot."

Without Mrs. Vandenburg, Fern and Gideon would still be hiding their interest in each other. Mrs. Vandenburg had forced them to confront their true feelings, although a relationship seemed impossible.

Gideon tried to concentrate on his work, but each time he stood at the counter, he faced Fern. She sat at the table right behind his line of customers and drew his attention. Several times he had to ask people to repeat their orders.

Fern's serious expression worried him. He'd never seen her so upset. For all the years he'd known her, she'd weathered every crisis with a smile. He hoped their talk yesterday hadn't caused her preoccupation.

Then his eyes met hers, and she captivated him. Everything around him disappeared. Fern became the center of his universe. His feeling for her reminded him of a roller coaster he'd ridden at Hersheypark—chugging upward with awkward, uneven jerks, then whooshing down with stomach-dropping speed.

Caroline elbowed him. "We have a long line."

His heart still racing from the exhilarating emotional ride, Gideon plummeted back to reality with a thud.

Instead of teasing him, his sister furrowed her brow. "What's the matter with Fern?"

"I'm not sure." But he aimed to find out as soon as they closed.

After Fern returned to her bakery counter, Gideon relaxed. Perhaps talking to Mrs. Vandenburg had helped.

Mrs. Vandenburg pulled a notepad out of her purse and jotted on it as she made phone calls. Gideon marveled at her energy. About an hour later, a man entered, carrying a stack of black ledgers, and set them in front of her. For the next few hours, Mrs. Vandenburg pored through the books with pursed lips, stopping once in a while to make notes.

At four, Gideon asked the others to start the cleaning while he made the rounds to lock up. As he passed Fern, he stopped. "Would you be able to stay? I might be a little longer than I planned."

"Stay?" She appeared befuddled.

"We'd planned to talk after work, but I need to help Mrs. Vandenburg lock up."

"*Jah.* I guess I can wait."

Her lackluster answer made him fear he'd driven her off. That had been his intention. *Neh*, he'd only wanted to explain why they couldn't date. Perhaps this was for the best.

"I'm happy to stay here for as long as you need. It's just that . . . well, I'll explain later."

Maybe her sorrow had nothing to do with him. That possibility lightened Gideon's spirits, but concern for Fern stayed with him as he locked each door behind the departing customers.

When he returned to the stand, much of the cleaning had been completed. Nick, Aidan, and Fern had all pitched in to help.

"Nettie, I'll be staying late again tonight," Gideon said as he and Aidan slid the clean spits into place. "Can you let Mamm know?"

Nettie stared at Fern for a moment, then gazed at Gideon with sad eyes.

Nick caught her expression and moved closer to pat her on the shoulder. "Don't worry," he told her. "Your prince will come."

Nettie bit her lip, ducked her head, and hurried from the stand.

"Looks like you have women problems, Gid." Nick's voice boomed around the almost-empty market.

Gideon cringed. He needed to talk with Nettie tonight, but Nick's comment only added to the tension.

A guilty expression on her face, Fern watched Nettie rush for the employee exit.

With a helpless shrug, Caroline gestured toward Nettie's disappearing back. "It's not your fault, Fern. Nettie's had a hard time ever since—"

"I know." Fern's soft answer exuded sympathy.

Gideon's heart thumped in double time. He longed to enfold her in his arms. Except he had no right to do that. Too many debts and responsibilities stood in his way.

Several stand owners were still cleaning or closing their shops as Caroline left.

When Nick offered to drive Aidan home, his son stared at him. Nick added, "Only if you don't do any of that stupid vaping stuff or whatever."

Aidan's jaw set in stubborn lines, and he looked about to explode.

Fern stepped closer. "You know, Nick, I'm pretty sure you can trust Aidan to do the right thing."

Aidan shot her a grateful glance.

Then she leaned close to Aidan and whispered, "I'm sure you have an internal lecture for this."

The anger on his face cleared, and he made a face. "Ugh. Do I have to listen?"

"It might be wise." Fern smiled at him. "And I know you're wise."

"For twenty whole minutes though?"

"I'm sure you can talk about Russell in handcuffs for that long."

Aidan burst out laughing. "You're right." He turned to his dad. "Okay."

Nick looked from Aidan to Fern with a bemused expression. "Did you cast a spell on him?"

"I just reminded Aidan of his inner strength. He has plenty of it, if you choose to look for it, Nick." Then she directed her attention to Aidan. "You can do it."

He picked up on her cue. "Wasn't it awesome to see Russell squished between those cops?"

Nick roared with laughter. "That was the funniest thing I've ever seen."

Both of them headed for the exit, chuckling.

Gideon shook his head. Fern really was a miracle worker.

"Should I wait here while you talk to Mrs. Vandenburg?" Fern asked.

"I'm sure she'd be happy to have you join us." *And so would I.*

Despite his reassurance, Fern hung back until Mrs. Vandenburg beckoned her.

As soon as they sat at the table across from Mrs. Vandenburg, she asked Gideon, "Could you spare Fern if I found someone suitable to take her place?"

Gideon's mouth dropped open. What did Mrs. Vandenburg mean? Was she trying to get him to admit how much he'd miss her?

He stared at Mrs. Vandenburg, then turned to Fern and asked in a strangled voice, "You're leaving?"

At a booth nearby, Wilma Mast's eyebrows rose. The last thing he wanted was the market gossip to make up stories about Fern.

Too late. Wilma scurried in their direction. She slowed to an amble once she reached hearing distance.

"Fern will only be gone a short while," Mrs. Vandenburg answered.

Although Fern had every right to live her life, Gideon felt betrayed. "What will I do . . .?" He spotted Wilma moving closer and added hastily, "What will I do about baked goods?"

"You need a baker?" Wilma butted in. "My niece Sovilla will be staying with me. She's an excellent baker."

"I don't know." Gideon was still reeling from Fern's news. Had his talk last night driven her away?

"I just picked her up at the train station. She's been waiting in the car while I checked my stand to be sure nobody stole anything while I was gone. I'll bring her in to meet you. She'd be happy to work for you."

"Wait," Gideon said to empty air. Wilma had already scurried off.

He didn't want a replacement for Fern. People had come to depend on her baked goods. No one could bake cinnamon buns like hers. But that wasn't the main reason he didn't want to replace her. He never wanted to lose her. He couldn't live without her.

Chapter Thirty-One

Fern knitted her brows. What was Mrs. Vandenburg doing? Teasing Gideon?

Before she could protest that she had no intention of leaving, Mrs. Vandenburg said, "Fern probably hasn't had a chance to tell you about her brother. I'll let her do that later, but she needs to leave for South Carolina."

"I can't go to South Carolina." Fern thought she'd made that clear.

Gideon's eyes widened. "South Carolina? Did something happen to your brother?"

Fern shook her head, but he couldn't tell if she was answering his question or responding to Mrs. Vandenburg.

"I intend to leave for South Carolina early Monday morning," Mrs. Vandenburg said. "My foundation's considering donating to some mission work down there."

Fern stared at her. "The mission where my brother works? You're going to check on him?"

"How else will you find out the truth?" Mrs. Vandenburg rushed on. "I want to get this settled before that busybody returns. I'd like Fern to go along as my companion.

I can't travel all that way alone. We'll be gone until Wednesday, possibly longer."

"But, but—" Fern hadn't agreed to this. Everything seemed to be flying out of control. "My parents might not let me go."

"Don't worry about that." Mrs. Vandenburg brushed off her concerns. "I'm sure once I talk to them, they'll come around."

Fern didn't have Mrs. Vandenburg's confidence.

"We can talk later." Mrs. Vandenburg tilted her head toward the employee entrance. "Here comes Pickle Lady."

Fern met Gideon's eyes, and they both stifled a laugh.

"How do you know that nickname?"

"You'd be surprised at how much I know about this market. I always keep a close eye on my investments."

Wilma sailed toward the table, practically dragging a shy blond girl. To Fern's surprise, Wilma's niece wore the stiff-sided, pleated *kapp* of the Midwest. Yet Wilma had never worn a *kapp* or Plain clothing. Had Wilma once been Amish? If so, she'd left it all behind to adopt *Englisch* ways.

"This is my niece, Sovilla"—Wilma swelled with pride "the best baker in all of Holmes County, Ohio."

Sovilla, her cheeks flushed, ducked her head. "I'm not . . ." she mumbled.

Wilma sniffed. "Don't be ridiculous. Of course you are."

Out of Wilma's eyesight, Sovilla shook her head. She met Fern's gaze with a pleading look that conveyed a *please-don't-believe-that* message.

"So, Gideon," Wilma demanded, "give her a list of the baked goods you'll need."

"Fern would be better at that."

Gideon smiled at her, and Fern forgot all about the

conversation. Mrs. Vandenburg jarred her back to the business at hand by tearing a sheet from her notebook and sliding it across to Fern, along with a pen.

Reluctantly, Fern broke Gideon's gaze and tried to gather her thoughts enough to make a coherent list. She wouldn't expect Sovilla to make birthday cakes, even if she was the best baker in Holmes County. Fern limited her suggestions to the most popular items, and next to each, she noted the usual number sold.

When she handed the paper to Sovilla, Wilma sniffed. "I wouldn't stay away too long if I were you. Sovilla's so good, you might not have any customers left. They'll all flock to her stand when she opens."

Sovilla's violent headshakes contradicted her aunt's claims.

"Oh, really." Mrs. Vandenburg's icy tone showed Wilma's bragging left her unimpressed. "And where will this stand be?"

Wilma looked taken aback. "Sovilla will be taking over my stand to sell her world-class baking. She'll give Fern some competition. Or maybe not. Sovilla's in a class of her own."

Her eyes wide and shocked, Sovilla looked from her aunt to Fern. "*Neh*, I'm not. I'm sure Fern is an excellent baker." Sovilla spoke so quietly they could barely hear her.

Gideon couldn't take any more of Wilma's putdowns. He had to defend Fern. He'd never tasted any baked goods as delicious as hers. "Fern is the best—"

Wilma blew out an exasperated breath, cutting him off. "We don't have all evening. Now, about payment. Sovilla will need supply money up front."

Gideon pulled out his wallet and extracted his last two twenties. "This is all I have right now."

"That won't be anywhere near enough." Wilma reached out to snatch them anyway.

"Wait." Mrs. Vandenburg whipped her checkbook out of her purse. "I'll take care of it."

When he started to object, she silenced him with a wave. "You can pay me back after we return."

Gideon subsided but protested under his breath. He wouldn't contradict her in front of Wilma.

After scribbling in figures and signing the check, Mrs. Vandenburg handed it to Wilma. The Pickle Lady read the amount, and her eyes gleamed.

"I'll expect receipts, of course. And Hartzler's only does organic. Will that be a problem?"

Sovilla hesitated. "*Neh.*"

"That also includes pay for Sovilla to work all four days next week."

"But—" Fern tried to intervene.

Mrs. Vandenburg cut her off. "We don't know how long we'll be gone, and you may be tired after your trip."

Wilma leaned close, eagerness written in every line on her face. "Where are you going?"

"A mission trip, although it seems we could use one right here in this market." Mrs. Vandenburg's tart tone and pointed stare left no doubt whom she considered the target of her jab.

"Well." Wilma stuck her nose in the air. "I suppose that's a signal we should go. Come along, Sovilla."

Everyone at the table blew out a small breath of relief after the door shut behind Wilma.

"Now, we need to discuss repayment." Gideon kept his

voice firm. He did not intend to let Mrs. Vandenburg pay his bills.

"We can take care of it after Fern and I return, but I want to make one thing clear. I'm paying Sovilla's salary. It's the least I can do when I'm depriving you of Fern."

On the days the market stayed closed, Gideon missed being with Fern. He tried not to think of more than a week without her.

"Now that Pickle Lady's gone," Mrs. Vandenburg said, "let's get down to business. First, let's deal with the problem of Fern's brother."

"Wait a minute." Gideon held up a hand. "I didn't hear what happened."

Fern told him about Aaron's mission trip and ended with Payton's bombshell.

"You're sure it was your brother in the brochure?"

She squeezed her eyes shut for a moment before answering. "The page had his name and picture."

That must have been a shock. Gideon wanted to reach out and hold her hands the way she'd held his, but he folded them on the table to avoid temptation.

Mrs. Vandenburg reached for her pen. "Do you think Aaron is still working at the mission?"

"I hope so. He did say they needed to rent an apartment, which seemed odd. Why couldn't they just move to a different church?"

Mrs. Vandenburg frowned. "Most churches would be grateful the volunteers were rebuilding area homes and offer them space."

"Sometimes people open their homes," Gideon added. "Some of my friends stayed with local families when they went on mission trips."

"I know." Fern bit her lip. "When I planned to go on the

mission trip before my parents decided to send my brother instead, all my friends said the same thing."

The disappointment in her eyes revealed how important that trip must have been. "You really wanted to go, didn't you?"

She swallowed hard and then nodded.

"Might be something you consider in the future," Mrs. Vandenburg said so matter-of-factly Fern and Gideon both stared at her.

Fern's startled look quickly changed to thoughtfulness.

Neh, Gideon begged her silently. *Please don't leave me.* As much as he wanted her to fulfill her dreams, letting her go would be unbearable.

Mrs. Vandenburg jotted on her tablet. "I'll call the mission to check if Aaron's there. Do you have an address for him?"

"I can get it from Aaron's last letter."

In a few short minutes, Mrs. Vandenburg had upended Gideon's life. She ticked off a to-do list and made the necessary arrangements to take Fern to South Carolina and to install a shy, gawky, untried baker in Fern's place. But Mrs. Vandenburg wasn't done.

"Are you up for a challenge?" She examined Gideon.

As if she hadn't already given him enough to handle? Judging from her expression, this one might prove to be even worse. "Depends on what it is."

"I need someone to comb through Russell's records, identify his errors, and come up with a financial plan to make the market profitable. I'm willing to pay." She named a sum that took Gideon's breath away.

"Why me? Can't you ask your financial planner?"

"Anyone can analyze numbers. I want someone who cares about the people involved. Any accountant looking at Russell's plan to eliminate five low-paying stands to bring in Ridley's Organics would rubber-stamp it as a wise financial move. But you understood the human and historical toll. Mike had the accountant send these books because we believe you'd give us ideas that fit with our vision."

"I see." Her reasoning made sense. "Fine. I'll do it, but not for that price."

Her eyes widened. "You want more?"

"More? *Neh*, it's way too much. I'd be glad to help you for free." He suspected she might not accept that, so he added, "It's the least I can do after all you've done."

"I see we need to teach you how to be a cutthroat businessman."

"I'm not interested in learning that. I'd rather demonstrate godly values. I have a long way to go, but I'd prefer to be upright and honest and help others." He wasn't anywhere close to that ideal, but he wanted to please the Lord in everything he did.

Fern's heart swelled. What a wonderful example he'd be to his children! If only they had a future together. She'd be willing to wait for years until they could marry.

Mrs. Vandenburg's eyes twinkled. "I expected you'd say that." She reached into her purse and slid a check across the table.

Gideon shook his head. "I already said you don't have to pay me. Besides, I haven't done any work yet."

"This isn't for that work. I understand Russell told all five of the stand owners he wouldn't increase their rent the last two months." She looked at Fern for confirmation.

"That's right. None of us could afford to pay the tripled rates, and we all appreciated the extra two months."

Mrs. Vandenburg nodded. "Nick mentioned that." She patted one hand on the stack of black ledgers beside her. "I noticed a discrepancy in payments when I glanced over the books for those months." Mrs. Vandenburg pinned Gideon with a curious gaze. "Do you know anything about that?"

"It's all right." He shot a quick glance at Fern. "We worked out a deal."

"Not a fair one."

Fern looked from one to the other. Undercurrents flowed between Gideon and Mrs. Vandenburg. Gideon *rutsched* in his chair as if uncomfortable about Mrs. Vandenburg's accusation. Was she accusing Gideon of wrongdoing?

Mrs. Vandenburg's gnarled fingers pushed the check toward Gideon. "If Russell said the rent did not increase, then this is an overpayment."

"But I agreed to it."

"I didn't, and I'm in charge here."

This exchange puzzled Fern. "Did Russell raise your rent too?"

"*Jah.*" Gideon's face flamed.

Mrs. Vandenburg tapped her fingertips on the check Gideon hadn't taken. "This check has nothing to do with Gideon's stand rental. He paid—"

"Please don't tell her," he begged.

"Tell me what?" When Gideon refused to meet her eyes, she turned to Mrs. Vandenburg.

"If you intend to have a strong relationship, you have no business keeping secrets, Gideon. You should be the one to tell Fern."

Looking miserable, Gideon mumbled, "I paid Russell some extra."

"Some?" Mrs. Vandenburg's voice rose. "Quite a bit. Take a look at the check, Fern." Mrs. Vandenburg lifted her hand and waved toward the piece of paper in front of Gideon. "That's how much your future husband paid to prevent Russell from kicking all five of you out."

Gideon set a hand over the check, but not before Fern glimpsed the numbers. She gasped. "You paid Russell to keep us?"

"Nobody's supposed to know."

"Gideon Hartzler," Fern began in a harsh tone, "what were you thinking?"

"That it might give you—all of you—more time to get a new place. And maybe Bo would change his mind if he had to wait two months to get in. I guessed wrong."

"After all that, you invited us to work at your stand?" Fern couldn't believe it.

"I didn't want you to go out of business."

She'd always known Gideon to be caring, but this generosity took her breath away. Still, he shouldn't have done that when his own business was struggling. "But you can't pay your bills."

Gideon's blazing cheeks set off his dark brown eyes. "I could afford it. I didn't know about the chickens then."

"You could have used this to pay off your debt."

"He can now." Mrs. Vandenburg indicated the check. "Russell had no right raising the stand rates or taking that money."

Gideon appeared dazed. "I don't know what to say."

"*Dinky* or *Danky* or whatever you usually say is fine." Mrs. Vandenburg laughed. "Go on. Take it."

Gideon picked up the check. "*Danke.*"

Fern couldn't believe it. Gideon had cared enough to help all five businesses. If she'd known, she'd never have let him pay for her stand. But the thought that he had brought tears to her eyes.

"*Danke*, Lord," Gideon murmured. His heart overflowed with gratitude. This money would cover a sizable portion of the debt. If only he didn't have the Q & Z standing order, he might be able to consider dating.

Mrs. Vandenburg reached over and patted Fern's hand. "You've fallen for quite a man."

One more thing for him to be grateful for. The sweetest, kindest, prettiest woman he'd ever met cared for—loved?—him. The two of them might have a future after all.

"Oh, you need these." Mrs. Vandenburg pushed the ledgers toward him. "And I don't want to hear a word about the pay. You'll take what I give you. Unless you find you need to charge me more."

No way would he ask for anything else. In fact, he'd have to find a way to keep her from paying him at all. Although he had to admit having that money would allow him to pay off even more of Thomas's debts and court Fern much sooner.

Planting her cane on the floor and gripping the edge of the table, Mrs. Vandenburg wobbled to her feet. Gideon jumped up to assist her, but she brushed him away.

"Let's go, Fern," she said as she shuffled toward the exit. "We need to talk to your parents."

Behind Mrs. Vandenburg's back, Fern gave him an apologetic glance.

Gideon had been anticipating their time together, even

more so now that they'd be apart. He tamped down his disappointment. Fern's needs were more important.

"Don't forget to lock up," Mrs. Vandenburg called. "And please take care of that and look after the market next week while I'm gone."

What? She'd put him in charge of the whole market?

Still dazed, Gideon picked up the ledgers, did a quick sweep through both floors of the market to make sure everyone had left, and locked up as he left.

He arrived home as the family was gathering to eat.

"I thought you were going to be late." Nettie rushed to set another place.

"It didn't take as long as I expected."

"You don't look very happy." Nettie seemed to be glad about that. "Didn't it go well?"

What did he say to that? He didn't want her to get the impression anything went wrong between Fern and him.

He lifted the ledgers. "Mrs. Vandenburg had a lot of extra work for me." He passed her and went into his office to set them on the desk.

Nettie's reaction made it clear Gideon had to deal with this situation. Preferably tonight.

He kept up as best he could with the children's chatter, but when the meal ended, he remained at the table after the children hurried out to the living room to play a game. His parents joined them, leaving Nettie and Gideon alone in the kitchen.

He cleared his throat. "Nettie, when you're done with the dishes, we need to talk."

Her face brightened. "I won't be long."

"Let me help you dry." Keeping busy might make it easier for him to talk. He regretted his offer when Nettie beamed. He'd given her the wrong impression.

They worked in silence for several minutes while Gideon searched for a way to let Nettie down easily.

"Before you start, Gideon, I have something I'd like to say." Nettie swallowed hard. "The boys miss you when you aren't here at bedtime."

With Gideon's new market responsibilities next week, he needed to prepare the boys for possible changes to their routine. His parents would be willing to step in from time to time. Also, if he wanted to spend time with Fern, maybe he could ask her to join him sometimes for the nightly routine.

Nettie dipped a glass into the rinse water and then handed it to him.

Gideon had to take the plunge, get this over. "I've tried to be here for all of you."

"I'm grateful for that and for the way you tried so hard to rescue Thomas."

Gideon choked up. "But I failed. I wish I'd been faster, done more, and prevented it."

"I saw you on the roof, Gideon. You risked your life trying to save Thomas. You almost fell over too."

In Gideon's mind, he'd been too slow, too hesitant, not daring enough. "Don't make me out to be a hero. I'm not."

"You did your best." Nettie gazed at him with stars in her eyes. "I also appreciate you taking care of us since then." When Gideon didn't respond, she lowered her head and fidgeted with the glass in her hands. "I guess things are going to be different."

"That's what I wanted to discuss." Gideon took a deep breath. "First of all, I want you to know I'll always support you and the children. That will never change."

Nettie scrubbed so hard at the plate Gideon worried she'd break it.

He had to keep going and make things clear. "I'm not in a position to date anyone right now, but as soon as I am, I plan to ask—"

"Fern." The name dripped with bitterness. Her shoulders slumped, Nettie rinsed the plate and handed it to him. She mumbled something too low for Gideon to catch.

He didn't ask her to repeat it.

The past two years, he'd been racked with guilt over Thomas's death. And now, both Fern and Nettie had tried to absolve him of his blame. If only he could forgive himself and let it go. He'd never let his brother's memory fade, but he could ask God for forgiveness and peace.

Chapter Thirty-Two

Fern had no idea how Mrs. Vandenburg had persuaded her parents to let her go to South Carolina, but before daybreak on Monday morning, she and Mrs. Vandenburg sat in the back seat of a luxurious car gliding down the highway.

Mrs. Vandenburg pulled out a sheaf of papers. "My investigator has been busy. In addition to working on Russell's case and looking into the situation at Q & Z, he found time to track down your brother and see what he's been doing."

"Q & Z?" Fern didn't reach for the sheets Mrs. Vandenburg held out.

"Based on what we found, my lawyer's looking into a class action suit against them. They don't usually bring in much per person, but Gideon will be entitled to a small settlement."

"I don't think he'd like being named in a lawsuit."

"We've already set it in motion using Q & Z's client list."

Although it might bother Gideon, maybe he'd be freed from his monthly payments. "Will it end the contract?"

"We're asking for that as part of the deal." She thrust the papers in her hand toward Fern. "These contain information about your brother."

With dread, Fern accepted the stack. She didn't want to find out the truth.

The first sheet tracked Aaron's movements since arriving in South Carolina. He'd stayed at the mission the first two weeks, as he'd been scheduled. Then he stayed with a nearby family. An interview with the family indicated they'd recently kicked him out when they discovered he'd been acting in area theaters rather than working at the mission as he'd claimed. That had been the first date of Aaron's request for more money.

"Are you all right, dear?"

Mrs. Vandenburg's question penetrated the fog around Fern.

In a daze, she responded, "He only stayed two weeks. All this time we've been supporting him, he hasn't been at the mission. What did he do with all that money?"

She'd been working hard and stressing over making enough to pay his bills. Her parents had been so pleased he'd settled down. Instead, he'd been lying to them. Worst of all, she'd given up this mission trip so he could go in her place, and other than the first two weeks, he hadn't even done the work.

Mrs. Vandenburg patted Fern's hand. "Don't worry. We'll find him, and hopefully, we'll straighten him out."

Fern stared out the window as the landscape blurred by. Mrs. Vandenburg seemed able to manage people and situations, but she hadn't encountered Aaron at his most rebellious.

After several rest stops and breaks for meals, they made it to the hotel. While Mrs. Vandenburg settled in for a nap, she asked the driver to take Fern to the address Aaron had given in his letter.

Twenty minutes later, Fern, her stomach churning, stood outside the apartment building to gather her courage. What should she say and do?

Lord, please give me the right words. And give Aaron an open heart.

She entered the building, found apartment B, and tapped at the door.

A muffled *Coming* filtered through the metal. A few moments later, the door swung open.

"Fern?" Aaron stepped back, his face ashen.

He stared at her for a second. Then he slipped out of the apartment and slammed the door behind him, but not before Fern glimpsed dirty dishes, piles of laundry, and a blaring TV.

"Wh-what are you doing here?" he asked.

"I could ask you the same thing."

"I, um, well, remember I wrote about us needing to move to an apartment. I'm sharing this with a couple of the guys I work with."

"At the theater, you mean?"

From his wary look, she'd rattled him. His eyes moved rapidly as if he planned to come up with an excuse. "You know about that?" His defeated tone indicated he'd realized he couldn't lie.

"And that you stayed at the mission for only two weeks."

"That's how long mission trips are."

"We all expected you to come home after that. Mamm and Daed were thrilled when you sent a letter saying you were staying to continue working at the mission." She emphasized the last few words.

Aaron winced. "Do they know?"

"Not yet." Mrs. Vandenburg had suggested Fern wait until she'd talked with her brother and found out the truth. "I haven't told Mamm and Daed because it would break their hearts. They're proud of you working so hard to help others."

His tone defiant, Aaron said, "They sent me here because they were ashamed."

"They hoped you'd settle down and live like you should."

"I haven't joined the church yet."

"*Rumspringa* doesn't mean you should forget everything you've been taught. Is your heart right with God?"

Aaron hung his head. "Not really."

"Maybe it's time—"

A cell phone buzzed in his pocket. He pulled it out. "I have to go." Looking relieved, he headed for the apartment exit.

"Wait, we're not done talking."

"Sorry, but they need me." He pushed open the outside door and hurried out onto the porch.

"Aaron, if you don't talk to me, I won't send any more money."

That stopped him. "You can't mean it. It's expensive living in the city, and theater gigs don't pay much."

Fern couldn't believe he still expected to be supported. "If you're at the mission, we'll keep sending you money every month, but not otherwise."

"I can't talk now," he whined. "I need to go to work."

"Then I'll be back here tomorrow morning at nine."

"Nine? I work late. And we all sleep in." He rushed toward the parking lot.

Fern stared at him, shocked. "Nine," she called after him. "Or no money."

When she arrived back at the hotel, Mrs. Vandenburg

appeared refreshed. Then she caught sight of Fern's expression. "Oh, dear. Things didn't go well?"

Fern explained.

"We'll both meet him tomorrow. Then we can go and talk to the mission leaders. I hope we'll be able to take your brother with us."

Fern didn't contradict Mrs. Vandenburg, but she suspected Aaron might not cooperate.

The next morning, the driver pulled into the apartment parking lot five minutes before nine. To Fern's surprise, Aaron sat on the porch steps, dozing, his head against one of the pillars.

Mrs. Vandenburg hobbled over and poked him lightly with her cane. "Sleeping this time of morning?"

Aaron jumped to his feet. "No, ma'am, just resting my eyes."

"Sounds like you're turning into a Southern gentleman. You never *ma'am*ed me before."

He rubbed his eyes. "M-Mrs. Vandenburg?"

"That's better. I only hope they're teaching you to tell the truth." When Aaron shot a resentful glare at Fern, Mrs. Vandenburg brandished her cane. "You're not going to blame your fibs on your sister. You just told me one. Do you always snore when you rest your eyes?"

He lowered his eyes. "Sorry," he mumbled.

"For what?" she snapped back. "For snoring or for lying?"

"Both." He kept his gaze fixed on the ground.

"That's better. A real man takes responsibility for his words and deeds."

Aaron squirmed.

"Hop in the car, young man. We're taking you back to the mission."

Eyeing her cane, Aaron backed up a few steps. "I can't. I have work. This is the final week of the show."

"Aaron," Fern said, "I meant what I said about no more money. You need to go back to the mission or come home."

"Come on, Fern."

Aaron gave her the pleading look that had always caused her to give in when they were younger. She refused to let it sway her. For his good and for hers. "I'm not sending money when you're doing something Mamm and Daed would disapprove. And if you choose to stay here, you need to tell them."

"All right, all right. I'll go back to the mission. But I can't do it until next week after the show closes."

Fern hesitated. They couldn't stay that long to make sure he kept his promise.

"That sounds like a fair compromise," Mrs. Vandenburg said. "I'll ask the leader of the mission to keep us posted."

The sickly look on Aaron's face made it clear he hadn't intended to return.

"Come along, Fern. We're off to the mission."

Fern faced her brother. "I'll be praying that you choose to put God first in your life."

"Thanks," Aaron muttered, but he didn't sound grateful.

Her heart aching, Fern followed Mrs. Vandenburg to the car and prayed the whole way to the mission. By the time they arrived, everyone except the cook had gone out to repair a house.

"You're Aaron's sister?" The girl's eyes lit up. "I'm Bethany. Is he all right? I've been praying for him."

Fern explained about Aaron's Monday return.

"I'm so glad. I miss him." Her cheeks turned red. "I mean, we all do."

"Could I ask you a favor? Would you be willing to keep an eye on him and influence him in the right direction if you can?"

"Of course. I did talk him out of leaving before his two weeks ended. I can try to do that again."

Fern suspected Bethany could be quite persuasive. She might be just the one to keep Aaron out of trouble.

Mrs. Vandenburg let out a soft sigh. "I think you'll do, Bethany. Are you ready to go, Fern?"

"Already? I thought you wanted to talk to the leader?"

"I'm a bit tired. I can call him tomorrow. Besides, if we leave now, we'll get home late tonight, and you can have a day to rest before market."

Fern said a hasty goodbye and *danke* to Bethany before hurrying to the door.

Mrs. Vandenburg laughed. "I guess getting back to Gideon is a big incentive."

No doubt about that. Fern had missed being at market today, and it seemed forever since she'd seen Gideon. She also had a nagging worry. What if he preferred Sovilla's baking to hers?

To keep busy during Fern's absence, Gideon worked on the books for Mrs. Vandenburg and arranged for the food bank to buy the chicken for almost two-thirds of what he paid for it. With the check he'd received from Mrs. Vandenburg, he paid off a portion of the debt and cleared away some of the obstacles to dating Fern.

Although seeing Nettie's sorrowful eyes filled him with

guilt, he'd done what he needed to do. He cared about her as a sister and prayed she'd find happiness.

Gideon appreciated Sovilla baking and selling her goods while Fern was away, but every time he glanced at that end of the stand, he missed seeing Fern. He hoped they wouldn't be gone long.

During a lull, Sovilla brought him a cinnamon bun. Shyly, she said, "Caroline said these were your favorites."

"*Danke.*" The last thing Gideon wanted was a cinnamon bun Fern hadn't baked. He needed to be polite, though, so he choked it down with a forced smile.

What did Fern do to her buns that made them taste so much better? If he hadn't eaten Fern's, Sovilla's might have tasted delicious. But the two couldn't compare. In fact, no one could compare to Fern in anything.

Taking care of the market, answering other shop-keepers' questions, locking and unlocking the building, supervising the maintenance and janitorial crews, and coming up with creative ideas for making the market more profitable took a lot of Gideon's time and energy.

Caroline confronted him at the end of the day. "You've been so busy I haven't had a chance to spend time with Zach. For as much time as you spent in the stand today, I might as well be the owner."

"I'm sorry. I didn't realize doing all this for Mrs. Vanden-burg would be so time-consuming. It's only for this week. Go see Zach."

"What'll you do about the cleaning?"

"I'll do it after everyone leaves."

A quiet voice behind him said, "I'm happy to help."

"Oh, Sovilla, would you?" Caroline beamed at Wilma's niece.

Gideon would have preferred to do it alone so he could

concentrate on daydreams of Fern. Then he got called away over a maintenance problem. By the time he returned, Nettie, Sovilla, and Aidan had finished the cleaning. Although Gideon was grateful, he also felt guilty.

On Wednesday, he went in to check on the maintenance job and be sure it would be completed by Thursday. He had to admit he had a greater appreciation for Russell, and even more so for Russell's dad, Mike, who'd always remained cheerful.

Gideon went in early on Thursday. He made the rounds of the market before anyone arrived. The emptiness of the market resembled the void in his life without Fern. He'd give anything to see her.

And then he looked up, and there she was, heading his way. Impossible. But no, it really was Fern. He longed to race toward her and wrap his arms around her. He managed to restrain himself.

"I missed you," he said when she neared.

Her eyes shone. "I missed you too."

"Absence makes the heart grow fonder." Mrs. Vanderburg shuffled through the employee entrance.

Gideon's excitement deflated. He'd hoped for some time alone with Fern.

Mrs. Vandenburg glanced around the market. "Everything seems to be going well."

"We did need a few repairs." He pulled an invoice from his pocket detailing the maintenance he'd supervised yesterday.

While she studied the paper, Gideon soaked in Fern's beauty and her special smile. And when their eyes met, he was transported.

"Gideon?" Mrs. Vanderburg's voice broke their intense gaze. "Would you have time to go over the books?"

Gideon trudged over to the stand to get the books. If only Mrs. Vandenburg hadn't come in just then.

Between working with Mrs. Vandenburg and taking care of the market the rest of that week, he barely had any time to spend with Fern. She took his place helping Caroline and Nettie, while Sovilla handled the bakery. He'd be glad when Fern started making the cinnamon buns again. He missed her more delicate, airy rolls and pastries.

On Saturday, Gideon managed to whisper to Fern, asking if she could stay after work. He wanted to spend time alone with her. But Mrs. Vandenburg appeared just before closing and asked to speak to both of them. He bit back a sigh, but he did have to turn over the keys, and life would go back to normal next week.

Instead, Mrs. Vandenburg upended all of his expectations.

Chapter Thirty-Three

After everyone had cleared out of the market, Mrs. Vandenburg settled across from them with the stacks of ledgers in front of her. "Mike and I have been discussing what to do with the market now that Russell is headed to jail. Mike isn't well enough to handle things, and I'm getting up in years."

Gideon and Fern exchanged a secret smile. Most people her age would be resting at home rather than running a business, overseeing a charity, and helping others.

She patted the ledgers. "Mike and I both like your ideas for improving the business, Gideon." She took a check from her purse and slid it across the table.

"I told you I didn't want to be paid." He gulped at the figure on the check. Twice the amount she'd originally offered. He pushed it back across the table. "I can't take this."

"You can and you will. Mike and I checked into a business contractor, and this is the fee they'd have charged to give us the analysis you provided. You've earned every penny."

Accepting that check, which would cover more than a

third of his debt, was tempting. But he couldn't do it. "*Neh*, I did the business plan as a gift. You helped us with Aidan."

"And my brother," Fern added.

Gideon smiled at her. He appreciated her support. She must agree with his decision to return the check even though it would delay their courting. It pained him to put off a possible future together, but knowing they shared the same values made his spirits soar.

Mrs. Vandenburg sighed. "I was afraid you'd refuse. We need help with one more thing. We need someone trustworthy, dependable, honest, and caring to implement these ideas and oversee the market. Do you have any suggestions?" Rather than directing her suggestion to Gideon, she looked at Fern.

Fern glanced at Gideon.

Did Fern want his opinion, or was she indicating him as an answer to the question?

Mrs. Vandenburg's "I agree, Fern" seemed to indicate Fern had answered the question.

Before Gideon could protest, Mrs. Vandenburg lifted the cover of the top ledger to extract a pile of papers. "Mike and I want to sell the market, and because we want the owner to care about it as more than a business, he suggested you. Obviously, Fern and I both second that choice."

What? He couldn't handle the market and his stand. Besides, he had too many debts.

Mrs. Vandenburg handed the papers to Gideon. "Mike said you once told him you wanted to run the market."

He'd forgotten about that. As a youngster, he'd often trailed after Mike as the owner made his rounds and locked the doors. One day, Mike had asked Gideon, who was nine at the time, what he planned to do when he grew up, and he'd responded that he wanted to have a market just like Mike's.

That childhood dream had remained buried for years. But now was not the time to revive it.

He hated to disappoint Mrs. Vandenburg and Mike, but he couldn't take on anything more. "I'm honored, but I can't afford it." He had enough debt to clear away before he could ask Fern about dating. He had no intention of adding more.

"My accountant worked that out." She picked up the check. "Rather than cash up front, Mike and I will each take a percentage of monthly rental fees, leaving the rest for you to use for maintenance, expansion, and your own salary."

Gideon stared at her. "That wouldn't be fair to either of you." It would be decades or even centuries until he paid off that debt. Neither of them would live long enough to get their money back.

"You don't understand." Mrs. Vandenburg's face crumpled. "Mike and I are getting on in years. The market has become a burden for both of us. You'd be doing us a favor taking it off our hands."

"Why not sell it?"

With tears in her eyes, she waved a hand around. "Mike and I are both connected to this market, to its history. If we sold it, the new owner might come in and— Well, you saw what Russell did. We don't want that to happen here."

"That would be terrible." Fern turned to him. "You'd take care of the market, Gideon. You have to do it."

Mrs. Vandenburg added, "Mike and I don't care about money. We have more than enough. This is our legacy. The plans you submitted made both of us happy. Part of the agreement is that you'll implement those plans as you can afford it. Will you promise us that?"

How could Gideon say no? The job would be overwhelming. Trying to handle his own business and the market this week had shown him that, but he wanted to help.

"We've taken the liberty of hiring a property manager to oversee the day-to-day running of the business. Ron Johnson managed my apartment complexes for years. He wants a part-time job since he's almost ready to retire."

Was this God's answer to his prayer? Gideon met Fern's shining eyes.

"*Ach*, Gideon, you'd be wonderful at running the market."

Her belief in him validated his decision. "I'll do it."

"I'm so glad." Mrs. Vandenburg pushed the stack of ledgers across the table. "You can read the terms in those papers. We're open to negotiating if you want a higher percentage of the income."

Gideon had a feeling he'd want a smaller cut.

She picked up the check he'd refused. "This will go into the maintenance fund."

He'd never outgive Mrs. Vandenburg. All he could do was make sure this market lived up to her legacy.

Mrs. Vandenburg pulled herself to her feet. "Oh, dear, I almost forgot. Getting a bit older will do that to you sometimes." She leaned against the table and fumbled in her purse.

Gideon worried she'd topple over. He jumped to his feet to assist her, but she shook her head.

"I'll be fine." She pulled out a manila envelope. "I'll leave you two alone while you read this."

She looked so shaky, Gideon rounded the table and took her arm. "I'll help you out to the car."

"I appreciate that. It's been a busy week. I'm a little more tired than I expected."

Gideon struggled to put his gratitude into words as he helped her into the car.

She shushed him. "We're as grateful to you as you are to us. You've taken a burden from my shoulders. I no longer have to worry about the future of the market. It pleases me to think of it being passed down to your children and grandchildren."

Children and grandchildren? Gideon stared after the car as it pulled away. Mrs. Vandenburg had just made that a real possibility.

While Gideon escorted Mrs. Vandenburg out to the car, Fern sat dumbfounded. In less than an hour, Mrs. Vandenburg had changed Gideon's whole life. If anyone deserved this after all he'd done for others, he did.

"I can't believe this," Gideon said when he returned. He sat beside her and skimmed through the papers. "Look at this." He passed her the agreement.

Fern finished reading. As long as the stands stayed rented, Gideon would receive a large monthly income. Some of that would go toward his market expansion plans, but she hoped it might also free him financially. Maybe he'd consider a relationship.

Beside her, he'd opened the manila envelope and was shuffling through the pages. He groaned and lowered his head into his hands.

"What's wrong?"

He only shook his head and pushed the paperwork in front of her. "Read it," he said in a husky voice.

Fern took the sheaf of papers with a handwritten note on top.

Gideon,

My investigator looked into the situation at Q & 3. The allegations mentioned in the original newspaper article were dismissed a few months later. The company was cleared of all charges of fraud, but we found evidence of a kickback to government inspectors, who allowed Q & 3 to continue falsely labeling their chicken organic.

Fern made me aware that you might not want to be part of the class action suit we're bringing against Q & 3, so my lawyer negotiated a separate settlement for you the day we reported the kickbacks to the authorities. Everyone involved in the fraud has been arrested, and the remaining board members agreed to the repayment we requested.

I've attached the check and a letter from my lawyer. I hope this will remove any obstacles to courting the girl you love. In exchange, I only ask to be invited to the wedding.

All best,
Liesl D. Vandenburg

AN UNEXPECTED AMISH PROPOSAL   369

A check from Q & Z had been attached under the note. Fern sucked in a breath. "Why did they give you this much money?"

"The document from the lawyer explains it. It's for the difference between what Thomas and I paid and the real market value for nonorganic chicken."

"They overcharged by that much?"

"*Neh*, the lawyer also got them to pay for damages to my reputation. That's what most of it is for." He reached over and flipped to the last page. "There's more."

"They're letting you out of the contract? But that means . . ." Fern stopped. Just because the major obstacles had been eliminated didn't mean Gideon wanted to start a relationship. Maybe he'd have too much work with running the market.

"It means between this check and the canceled contract, I'll be debt-free. Much more than debt-free." He frowned. "There's only one problem."

Fern braced herself. Was he going to reveal another roadblock standing in the way of them being together?

Gideon had been so thrilled about his good fortune he'd failed to take one important thing into consideration. "What about the food bank? If my contract ends, they'll lose their chicken deliveries."

Fern let out a long, slow breath.

"I can donate money to cover their meat purchases every year. If that's all right with you?" Gideon looked at her for an answer.

"Me? You mean do I think it's a good idea? *Jah*, it's very kind."

Fern's confusion made him realize he'd jumped ahead.

In his mind, they'd become a team, running the stand and the market together, making joint decisions. But he hadn't even asked her out yet.

Being so close to his heart's desire brought up old anxieties. Thomas's warnings and threats. All the years of closing himself off to love. Would this be a foolish mistake?

Lord, all these blessings from You must be the sign I asked for. Please give me the courage to tell Fern what's in my heart.

The market wasn't the most romantic setting to ask a woman about courting, but in some ways, it was the most fitting. They'd met here, played together here, grown up here, first admitted their feelings here, and—he patted the papers in front of him—had their dreams fulfilled here. He'd asked God for direction in life, and the signs couldn't be clearer. The woman he wanted to marry sat beside him at this table.

"Fern?" He turned toward her. The eagerness in her expression encouraged him to continue. "This market is where our relationship first began so many years ago. I fell for you when you were six, and those feelings have grown ever since, no matter how much I tried to deny them."

A soft *ach* escaped her lips, and she gazed at him starry-eyed.

Blood thundered in his ears almost drowning out the words he'd planned to say. But he'd waited so long, he didn't want to delay another second. He reached for her hand.

Taking a deep breath, he formed the question that burned in his heart. "I never dreamed that one day I'd own this market, but more than anything, I love you and want you by my side as I start this new venture. Would you—?"

Without even letting him finish, Fern answered, "*Jah.*"

He laughed. "I've been worried you might not want to."

"Gideon, can I tell you a secret? From the first moment I met you, I adored you. Don't you remember how I followed you everywhere?"

"I liked that." He'd enjoyed being a year older and her protector. He still wanted to have that role in her life.

"I never outgrew that feeling." Fern stared at him with adoring eyes. "Over the years, it turned into a crush. My heart broke when you didn't want to spend time with me anymore."

"*Ach,* Fern. I'd give anything to go back and erase those years."

"Maybe your brother was right to warn you away. Maybe we'd have made a foolish mistake when we were younger, so God kept us apart until we were mature enough."

Gideon didn't feel mature right now. He wanted to run, jump, skip, and shout the way he had at age seven. But Fern had a point. He was grateful they'd waited. Young love may have fizzled. Caring for each other for all these years proved their attraction to each other was enduring.

"You were worth waiting for," she said.

Gideon wrapped his arms around her and cradled her head against his chest. "So were you."

Epilogue

Only three more days until their wedding. Gideon hummed as he hung the signs announcing the stand would be closed next Tuesday. They'd chosen Tuesday so they wouldn't have to close the stand for more than a day, and they'd have Wednesday off to help Fern's family clean up and repack the wedding wagon.

He could hardly believe the day had finally arrived. His heart leapt each time he glanced at the other end of the stand and met his beloved's eyes. God had blessed him with the most wonderful woman, and Gideon's whole being overflowed with gratitude.

A man stepped up to the counter. Gideon recognized him as Stephen Lapp, who'd rented a market stand several months ago.

Stephen looked around. "Where's Nettie?"

"She went home sick."

"I hope she feels better." He looked disappointed as he ordered.

Gideon smiled to himself as he slid a chicken half into the insulated bag. Maybe Nettie had an admirer. He'd like to see her happy.

After Gideon handed Stephen his change, Stephen stared up at the sign. "You'll be closed Tuesday?"

"Nettie will be back on Thursday."

Stephen flushed. "*Danke.*"

Gideon wasn't sure if Stephen was thanking him for the chicken or the information about Nettie.

Once Stephen had gone, Gideon said to Caroline, "I should leave now. I don't want to be late." He had to pick up a few pieces of furniture for their house before the shop closed.

"Sovilla will be here soon to help." His sister waited on the next customer.

"I'm going to see if Fern wants to go along."

Caroline laughed. "I figured you would. It's your last market day as an unmarried man. I'm not going to complain about the extra work you're leaving me with or try to make you feel guilty."

But she just had. Leave it to Caroline to jab him. Gideon's happiness overrode his desire to tease her back.

When he asked Fern, she beamed. Nick offered to handle her customers, and Sovilla arrived to help Aidan and Caroline.

"I'm sorry to leave you shorthanded," Fern told them.

"Not so sorry you'd skip going with my brother." Caroline softened her sarcastic remark with a smile.

"I can stay if you need me." Fern cast disappointed eyes in Gideon's direction.

"Don't be silly." His sister made shooing motions with her hands. "Go on. I was only kidding."

"Besides," Nick added, "I doubt you'd be much help if you're missing Gideon."

With everyone's good-natured laughter ringing in their

ears, Gideon took Fern's arm to escort her out to the farm wagon, which he'd brought to load the furniture.

Ron would lock up after everyone left, and he'd take care of opening and closing on Tuesday. Gideon had come to rely on the property manager in so many ways. And Ron would be doing him a big favor a few weeks from now.

They pulled in front of Bontrager's Woodworking Shop in town, and Gideon hopped out and hurried around to help Fern from the wagon. The softness of her hand in his and the special smile she gave him took his breath away. Three days seemed like an eternity.

He tied the horse to the hitching post, and then, fingers entwined, they headed into the store. Luke and several of his workers assisted Gideon in loading the wagon.

"*Ach*, Gideon." Fern ran a hand over the satiny smooth dresser. "This is beautiful."

He agreed. The Amish craftsmen who'd made their sturdy furniture had done a terrific job. Everything would last for generations.

At that thought, Gideon's heart swelled in his chest. Generations he and Fern would begin together.

After they loaded the last piece, Gideon started to climb in the wagon.

"Wait," Luke said. "There's one more."

Two of his employees came out carrying a huge ornate dish cupboard, the green one with painted flowers Fern had admired when they placed their order.

She gasped. "Gideon, you bought that?"

Neh, they'd decided it was much too fancy and much too expensive.

"It's a wedding gift." Luke helped rearrange the other furniture so the cupboard could fit in the back of the wagon. "An elderly lady—an *Englischer*—asked me for a suggestion. I mentioned you seemed interested in this. She took out cash and paid me."

Gideon only knew one elderly *Englischer* who might have done that.

"Mrs. Vandenburg," Fern said with tears in her eyes.

Gideon couldn't believe all she'd done for them. She'd volunteered to help him with another special surprise for Fern. And now this. They owed her so much. If it weren't for her, he and Fern would not be getting married.

"*Ach*, Gideon, it's so beautiful. Too beautiful for our house."

She was right. The house they'd built on the back acreage of his parents' farm and the *dawdihaus* they'd added for Fern's parents were plain and practical. But nothing was too beautiful or special for the woman he loved. He had another surprise for her today he hoped would thrill her even more.

Fern sat in stunned silence on the way home. She'd been drawn to that lovely cupboard as soon as they'd entered Bontrager's shop, but her parents had trained her to buy only necessities.

Gideon made good money running the market, but they'd decided their money should be put to better use than a fancy piece of furniture. Yet her spirits lifted each time she looked at the green cupboard. She'd enjoy getting dishes out every day when she made meals for her husband—she sneaked a glance at Gideon—and their children.

When they got to their house, several family members were waiting to help Gideon unload the furniture, including her brother.

"Aaron? What are you doing here?"

"Mrs. Vandenburg drove me and Bethany home for the wedding."

The girl they'd met at the mission smiled as she approached.

"By the way," Aaron said, "*danke* for not telling Mamm and Daed about the theater."

Fern had debated about it many times, but after Mrs. Vandenburg confirmed Aaron had returned to the mission and he'd stayed every week since then, she let it drop. She'd chosen not to tell because it would hurt her parents, but also because her motives weren't pure. Part of her wanted to get back at Aaron for taking her place at the mission.

She no longer held jealousy and bitterness toward her brother. Although a small part of her still ached inside when she thought about giving up her dreams about doing mission work, God had taken her life in a new and wonderful direction. And if she'd been at the mission when she'd originally planned, she and Gideon never would have gotten together.

Aaron cleared his throat. "Well, I confessed everything to Mamm and Daed, and they've forgiven me."

"Oh, Aaron, I'm so glad." Fern threw her arms around Aaron and hugged him.

"So am I. Living with guilt is rough."

Gideon came up behind her. When she stepped away from her brother's embrace, he leaned down to whisper in her ear, "I wish I could have one of those hugs."

"Soon," she promised. Waiting for the next three days would be torture.

"Let's go for a ride tonight after everyone's done eating." Out of everyone's sight, he squeezed her hand.

"I can't wait."

* * *

The full moon lit the night sky as they slipped away from the chattering crowd of family, who'd gathered to help arrange furniture, clean both houses, and picnic together. At last, they had time alone.

Running their business and the market kept them so busy, they rarely had uninterrupted time together. So Fern cherished every second they spent in each other's company. Gideon had arranged for Ron to supervise the market for the next five days. She could hardly believe they'd have all that time, although most of it would be spent in church and in preparing for the wedding.

They hadn't traveled far when Gideon pulled into a wooded cul-de-sac. He took her hand. "I can't wait until we can go home from work together every night."

Fern couldn't either. Separating at the end of the day and missing him all night long was difficult.

Gideon swallowed hard several times. "Admitting my love has been hard for me, but I want you to know I cherish you and will do everything I can to take care of you and make you happy."

"You already do make me happy." Just knowing he loved her enough to marry her had made her the happiest woman in the world.

Her response choked him up. "I'm so glad." He wanted to fulfill her every desire. "I made some arrangements I hope you'll like."

She stared up at him, her eyes wide and surprised and

maybe even a little hurt. So far, they'd made all their future plans together. But he wanted this to be a surprise.

Now that he was about to reveal this secret, he hoped he hadn't made a mistake. What if she no longer wanted to do this?

"I know how much you wanted to work at the mission, so I talked to the leader, and they have a two-week opening next month."

Fern's eyes filled with tears.

"You don't want to go?"

She turned her head away. "I've always dreamed of doing that, but not now."

He'd gotten it all wrong. He'd expected her to be overjoyed. Instead, he'd upset her.

Her voice quiet and shaky, she asked, "You're sending me away after we've only been married a month?"

"Sending you away? *Neh*, I'd never do that. I meant for us to go together."

Her head whipped around, and she gazed at him with a question in her eyes. "Together?"

"Of course. I'd never want to be separated. Not even for a day."

Fern released a slow, trembling breath. "I thought you were trying to get rid of me."

"Never."

Slowly, light dawned on her face. "We really are going to the mission? You're serious?"

"*Jah*, I am. We'll be in charge of a group of teens from my church—your church, too, now that you're moving to my family's farm."

She sat still for a moment. "I never imagined I'd ever

get to go on a mission trip. I—I can't believe it." Then her face glowed. "God is so good."

"He sure is." God had blessed them both in so many ways.

"*Ach*, Gideon." Laughing and crying at the same time, Fern flung her arms around him. "*Danke, danke, danke!*"

Having her in his arms was the most precious gift God could ever have given him. He gazed down into her eyes— her shining, adoring eyes—and he was lost. Bending his head, he reverently touched his lips to hers. His heart expanded with gratitude and love as he kissed Fern, the beautiful and beloved woman he'd spend his life with forever and ever.

Connect with 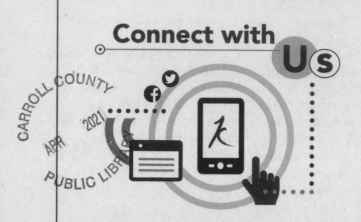 Us

Visit us online at
KensingtonBooks.com
to read more from your favorite authors, see books
by series, view reading group guides, and more.

 Join us on social media

for sneak peeks, chances to win books and prize packs,
and to share your thoughts with other readers.

facebook.com/kensingtonpublishing
twitter.com/kensingtonbooks

Tell us what you think!

To share your thoughts, submit a review,
or sign up for our eNewsletters, please visit:
KensingtonBooks.com/TellUs.